HOMEPLACE

Also by Anne Rivers Siddons

Fox's Earth

The House Next Door

Heartbreak Hotel

John Chancellor Makes Me Cry

Anne Rivers Siddons

HOMEPLACE

A NOVEL

HARPER & ROW, PUBLISHERS • New York

Cambridge, Philadelphia, San Francisco, Washington, London,

Mexico City, São Paulo, Singapore, Sydney

FIRST EDITION

Designer: Ruth Bornschlegel

Copyeditor: Mary Jane Alexander

Library of Congress Cataloging-in-Publication Data

Siddons, Anne Rivers.
  Homeplace.

  I. Title.
PS3569.I28H6   1987   813'.54   86–46099
ISBN 0–06–015758–5

87 88 89 90 91 RRD 10 9 8 7 6 5 4 3 2 1

For Larry Ashmead
First, last, and always

ONE

Even before she opened her eyes, the child was afraid.

Coming out of sleep, she was not sure where she was, only that it was wrong. She should not be in this place. He would be very angry. She was eight years old, and she had been afraid of him all of her life.

She lay still and listened, and heard the rain. The rain came riding on a vast gray wind, to pepper the flat tin roof and sing in the tops of the black-green pines in the woods across the road from the cabin. Over it, much nearer at hand, she heard the chink of the iron poker in the cooling fireplace, and the visceral, thumping wail of the Atlanta jigaboo station on the radio Rusky had given J.W. for Christmas.

Without opening her eyes, the child burrowed her head under the flaccid feather pillow and dragged the quilt closer around her. Her body was warm in the piled nest of quilts and blankets Rusky had heaped over her during the night, but her feet were icy and her nightgown must be up around her neck, because her legs were cold up to her thighs. She took a deep breath, inhaling musty bedclothes and the ashy, dark smell the cabin always had, made up of smoke from the fireplace and the smell of Rusky and J.W. themselves. It was not sweat, though that was part of it; it was more, was the fecund essence of the Cromies, who lived in the sagging cabin behind the big house on Pomeroy Street. It was a rich smell, deep and complicated, somehow very old, the essence of all Negroes Mike had ever known.

"Why do Nigras smell like ashes?" she had asked Rusky once.

" 'Cause dey spends so much time tendin' to white folkses' fires," Rusky said, thumping the iron down on the ironing board in the big, square, sweet-steamed kitchen. "And 'cause de Lord give 'em that smell, same as he give you a smell like a new li'l ol' puppy. Kindly of sweet and sour at the same time. It ain't polite to ax folks why they smells like they does, Mike. It hurts they feelings."

"Are your feelings hurt?"

"Naw, but I'm you' family. Don't you go axin' nobody outside yo' family why they smells like they does."

"Why are you my family if you're black and I'm white?"

"Go on, now, I got to finish this arnin' and get on to them beans, or ain't none of you gon' get any supper. You just axin' questions to hear yourself talk."

The child's name was Micah Winship. She did not want to open her eyes, to lose the cocoon of the bed and the covers. She drifted for a space of time, her legs and feet drawn up to her body, willing Rusky to remain silent, but she did not.

"Git up, Mike. Time to go over yonder an' start breakfast. You know you daddy don't know you over here."

"I don't want to get up."

"I don't care what you wants. You really be in a fix if he come back from his walk an' fin' you over here with me. I promise him the las' time I ain't gon' bring you home with me no more. He like to fire me if he catch you sleepin' over here with me, an' then what you all gon' do?"

"I don't care. I'm not going to get up."

"You promise me las' night after that nightmare an' all that hollerin' you doin' that you get up when I call you if I let you come home with me. Big girl like you, in the third grade, yellin' an' hollerin' like that. Git up, now. Move yo'self."

"I don't have to. You can't make me."

"Well, I know somebody what can make you, an' right quick, too. Come on, J.W. We gon' go tell Mr. John Mike over here in the baid an' we cain't git her out."

"Aw, Mama . . ." J.W. said from the shed room off the cabin's main room, where he slept winter and summer.

"I'm gon' out dis door, Mike, J.W.," Rusky said, and slammed it to emphasize her words.

"Wait!" Mike shrieked, jumping out of the cocoon of covers and rummaging blindly for her blue jeans and sweater. Fear leaped like brush fire. *"Wait for me, Rusky! I'm coming . . . don't tell him!"*

"Don't tell who what?" said Derek Blessing, and Mike awoke finally and abruptly, and sat up in the great bed in Derek's crow's nest of a bedroom atop the beach house on Potato Road, in Sagaponack, Long Island. Rain on a tin roof and the sough of the wind in the wet pines of Lytton, Georgia, became the residual spatter of the sullen, departing northeaster and the boom of the surf on the beach, and the acrid smell of Rusky Cromie's moribund fire became the first breath of the resurrected one in Derek's freestanding Swedish fireplace. J.W.'s radioed Little Richard became Bruce Springsteen. She looked around her. She was naked in the bed, with the ridiculous mink throw trailing across her and onto the floor, leaving her feet and legs bare to the cold air flooding in from the open sliding glass doors facing the heaving pewter sea. Her heart was still hammering with the now-familiar slow, dragging tattoo of the past two days, and her mouth tasted foul and metallic from the unaccustomed tranquilizer and the cognac they had drunk last night. The snifter still sat, half full, on the table beside her, and the sweet, cloying fumes sickened her slightly. She cleared her dry, edged throat and combed her hair back with cold fingers. She squinted up at Derek Blessing, who sat down on the bed with a proffered mug of coffee. It smelt only slightly better than the cognac, probably because of the cinnamon Derek ground into it, an affectation he had picked up somewhere on his latest promotional tour for *Broken Ties*.

"That must have been a world-class nightmare," he said, settling his bulk onto the low bed that was not really a bed at all, but a vast mattress resting bargelike on the pale wood of the floor. He wore blue velour sweat clothes and a piratical red sweatband around his head, and his wild cotton boll of coarse, curly gray hair was wet. Streams of water or sweat rolled down his neck, and the towel was wet.

"Have you been running?" Mike asked. Obviously he had, but she wanted diversion, not information.

"Six miles." He patted the pedometer attached to one trunklike leg. "Up a full mile in less than a week." He was between books and, admittedly, blocked in his attempts to start a new one. He was fiddling discontentedly with short articles and essays, which he disliked, and Mike knew that when he was in this state he became obsessed with exercise. His squat, muscular body had lost some of its soft blurring at belly and thigh, and he was not drinking as much as usual. "What were you, being chased by a rabid editor or something? You thrashed around like a water buffalo all night and talked to somebody half of it. I've never heard you talk in your sleep before."

"I don't remember," Mike said. She did, but found the dream profoundly disturbing, though on the face of it there was nothing about a dream of spending a long-ago night with Rusky in her little cabin that should have disturbed her. Annie Cochran had told her to pay particular attention to her dreams and to remember, even write down, as much as she could of them. But Mike did not want to write this one down. She did not even want to discuss it with Derek. She wanted instead to drink her coffee and slide back into the nest she had made under the throw and lie with Derek's arms around her for another hour or two, until the hammering in her chest had subsided and she could put her thoughts in order. It was Sunday morning, and she would have to get the one o'clock train back to Manhattan, otherwise she'd have to wait until seven, and that was too late to leave Rachel with the Perezes on Bleecker Street. That or take the jitney, and she hated the jitney . . .

She remembered then that her daughter was not waiting for her back in the city and would not be, and there was really no reason to get the one o'clock train or even the last one, at seven. There was no reason to go back to the city at all. There was no new assignment to begin. There was no one to call and check in with. There was not, now, a book in the offing, and soon there would not even be a place in the city to go back to.

The heart hammering accelerated until she could feel the pulse in her throat leaping with it and see it battering at the blue-white skin of her wrist like a frantic bird.

" 'Scuse," she said, and slipped out of bed and into the bathroom, where she had left her piled clothes and her handbag, and quickly gulped a Xanax. The alien reflex almost gagged her. She looked at her reflection in Derek's relentlessly floodlit, mirrored wall. Ribs and great fear-darkened gray eyes and wild, ashen, spindrift hair wet with sweat at the temples and matted into a sluttish tangle. White, flared nostrils. Bitten lips, puffed from the pressure of Derek's the night before, pressed so hard together that the muscles beside them stood out in the blaze of fluorescence. Greenish circles beneath the eyes and deeper shadows in the hollows beneath the sharp cheekbones. Mike smiled at herself, a ghastly rictus, and shut her eyes in pain.

I look like those photographs they made in the Nazi concentration camps, when they first went in and saw what was there, she thought. One of those living dead things grinning at its liberators. Welcome to Bergen-Belsen. My name is Micah Winship, and I'm your hostess for today.

She splashed water on the skeleton's face and turned Derek's shower on full force. The Hammacher-Schlemmer deluxe shower head was turned to massage, and she flinched under the assault of the pulsing needle spray. Her muscles were sore. Her very skin hurt to touch, as it does when you have a high fever.

"Hurry up," Derek shouted at her over the rush of the water and the driving bass of the music. "I'm going to make you eggs Benedict, and then I think I'll ask Alan and Chloe to come over for Bloodys. They've been in Sag Harbor for five days and I haven't seen them."

"You wouldn't consider just crawling back into bed for three or four years, would you?" Mike called back. The water masked the tremor in her voice quite effectively. "It's not a fit day for anything else."

"It's clearing in the west," he called back. "And I've got to talk to Alan about this *Rolling Stone* thing. I've got to get on it this afternoon and work all night, unless he can get me a few more days from that bastard. What's with you anyway? You've slept almost two straight days."

"San Francisco was a bitch, and you know I don't ever sleep much on assignment. I've got six weeks' catching up to do," Mike said, turning off the water. She leaned against the hand-painted tiles of the wall and closed her eyes, letting the smooth coolness seep into her flaming cheek. The downstairs shower had moss-slicked, bare lathing walls and a rough concrete floor and a drain, and no curtain. Photographers always gravitated to that shower, for some reason; it had appeared in almost as many glossy magazines as Derek's simian, punished face. But upstairs, where no photographers and few other people were ever permitted, Derek insisted on his creature comforts. He told her once that he had spent as much on his upstairs bedroom and bath as he had on the entire house when he'd bought it twenty years before. It did not particularly bother Mike that he posed and postured as he did, nor that the careful, rough-exterior–sensitive-interior image he presented to the world went only as deep as his K-Mart denims and Caterpillar billed caps and work boots. He had a soaring, eccentric talent, even if his critics were beginning to tear at his flanks like a pack of jackals now, and he was a tireless, inventive, and ardent lover. He demanded little of Mike, displayed little of his legendary temper, was generous with his time and attention, and was invariably delighted to see her when she came to the beach house for weekends, as she did a couple of times each month. Neither had ever spoken of love. He did not come into the city, and she did not press him to do so. They had been together for almost three years.

Rachel had not liked him.

"He's a phony baloney," she had said after she had met him at a large garden party in Southampton, where Mike had taken a rental house that first August. He and Mike had met at the home of his agent, Alan Peden, whom Mike knew and liked, and by the time Rachel had met him he had taken Mike to dinner three times and to bed once.

"He said he thought I was going to be a dynamite-looking broad when I grew up, just like you, and he wanted to get his name on the list early. But I could tell he didn't like little kids."

"How?" Mike had asked, half amused and half annoyed at both Rachel and Derek Blessing.

"Because nobody would say 'broad' to a little kid. It's embarrassing. He thought it was, you know, cute, but I don't like words like 'broad.' You always said tough talk was for boors. I think he's a boor."

"I do think it is, mostly, but there are also circumstances when it's okay. It's just his way. He's a very talented novelist, Rachel, one of the most noted ones in the country."

"He's a cocksman, too."

"I really do not like that kind of talk, my dear. Nine is a bit young for it. Where on earth did you hear that?"

"Georgette Peden told me he was, and she ought to know, she's almost twelve. Besides, I can read. He's been in *Us* and *People* and all sorts of places. They're always talking about all his women. I don't see why you want to go around with a cocksman. You're probably no more to him than a . . ."

"Rachel!"

"Well. I don't care. He's a phony just the same. He said he'd ridden all the way over here on his bicycle, but he wasn't even sweating. I bet he has a Lamborghini and a driver." Rachel was into exotic automobiles that year.

Mike had put the incident down to the natural animosity of a child of a single parent for an incipient rival. She knew Derek Blessing's reputation, and she also knew his talent. She had read his work and marveled at the surgical delicacy and unsentimental sensitivity with which he portrayed his female characters. Each one of them

6

fairly sang with life and reality, and their joys and sorrows were meticulously detailed and authentically and memorably moving. She liked them far more than she did the men in his fiction, who were, on the whole, as hard, bright, rigid, and identical as bullets. By the time they had become lovers in the accepted sense of the word, she was aware of the dichotomy between his simplistic, exaggeratedly male public persona and his sybaritic, self-absorbed private one, but it did not concern her unduly. More so than most people, she believed, Derek had layers and strata of reality; grasshopper and ant, ascetic and sensualist, could live happily together inside his pitted and leathery hide. No one who could so light a woman into life in his writing could be a poseur in any essential way. And she was honest enough to admit to herself that some secret core of her expanded like a flower in an April rain at the attention her role as Derek Blessing's longtime lover earned her.

"You don't need that kind of identity," Annie Cochran had said disapprovingly at one of their rare lunches. "You're as well-known in your profession as he is in his, or you will be. You need to watch that."

"It's not the journalist who likes sleeping with him, Annie," Mike had said. "It's the woman. He makes me feel like I look as good naked as I do when I'm all gotten up and out at a place like this." They were in the Bar Room of the Four Seasons—oddly, one of the only places in New York Annie Cochran could be persuaded to lunch. She was a few years older than Mike, black, sardonic, angry, amused and amusing. She was also a brilliant psychotherapist. They had been friends since the first year Mike and Richard came to New York.

"I should hope you know you're as attractive a woman as you are good a journalist," Annie said. "I should hope it doesn't take a *People* magazine centerfold to make you feel good about yourself."

"Oh, enough of the psychobabble," Mike said. Annie sometimes had a way of making her feel like she was pinioned and spread-eagled under glaring white lights. "You have to admit he's more interesting than Richard," she added.

"Not to mention the sportswriter before him, or the editor before that, or the minor-league anchorman before that. Or any of the others. I don't necessarily think you need to be married again, Mike, but I do think you need to be committed."

"In this day and age? It's a good thing you're not a call-in radio shrink, Annie. There aren't any women left on the East Coast who'd listen to you."

"You're not any woman," Annie Cochran had said, but that was all she did say. Later on, when Mike's alliance with Derek Blessing had become an accepted fact and then a continuum, she did not mention it again.

Mike wrapped Derek's thick terry-cloth robe around her and padded into the light-washed bedroom. The sky over the sea was lightening, and far out on the horizon a great sweep of sun lit the gunmetal into a startling milky aquamarine. She dropped the robe on the sheepskin rug in front of the fireplace and bent to step into her corduroys. Derek Blessing squinted at her through smoke from the custom-blended cigarette in his filter. He had ordered both from Dunhill.

"San Francisco must have been a bitch, indeed," he said. "You don't look so good, Mike. In fact, you look like you've been drowned and washed up on the beach for about six days. And your hands have been shaking ever since you got here, and you're talking in your sleep, and I've never seen you drink as much cognac as you did last night. You're on something, too; I can tell from your pupils. I never knew you to take so much as an aspirin before. You want to tell me about it, or what?"

"No." They never talked of personal problems, beyond the bare bones of information that had to be exchanged. Derek loathed what he called hormonal histrionics, and Mike had an almost British reluctance to fan out her pain. She was, she had told him on their first evening together, determined to anchor no relationship on pity.

This time, though, he surprised her.

"Come on," he said, pulling her toward him and down onto the bed. He drew the throw back up over them and settled her into the hollow of his shoulder. He smelled good, like cold, wet salt air and expensive tobacco and toothpaste.

"Spill," he said.

"You've got Alan and Chloe," she said, feeling terror stir and roil slowly in the bottom of the black pit within her, where the sea and the sleep and the drug had banished it. She did not know what would happen if she let it free . . . "You've got the *Rolling Stone* thing."

"Fuck Alan and Chloe. Fuck *Rolling Stone.* I've never seen you like this. I want to know what's happening with you."

"You know we agreed," Mike said. "No gut spilling. We drank to it at the Palm, that first night."

"That was a long time ago. Things change. You go deeper with me now than you did at first. You're tough and you're brave, Mike, but you're human like the rest of us, like it or not, and something's doing a fucking awful number on you. I'd be a real prick if I didn't want to know what it was. More than that, I need to know."

"Why?"

"Say you're under my hide. Stuck in my craw. I seem to hurt when you hurt."

"I . . . God, Derek, I don't know where to start. To make any sense at all I'd have to start so far back . . ."

"Start at the beginning. Start with 'I am born.' Surprisingly effective first sentence. I've always been intrigued with the notion of your past. Do you realize that I know virtually nothing about you before you left the South and came to New York? You look like a young Hepburn playing Scarlett O'Hara, but you act like you were born last Thursday in the Time-Life lobby."

"That's what Annie said."

"Annie?"

"Annie Cochran. You know, my shrink friend. You met her that first summer when she came out to Southampton."

"Ah, your black shrink friend. Mammy Courage. How like you to leave out the pivotal adjective."

"Black doesn't have anything to do with Annie."

"Give me a break. It has everything to do with her. It would have to. The fact that you left it out says something to me about your secret past. Except that I can't really believe you have one. I never knew a beautiful and successful woman so without history."

Mike knew that she was not beautiful, but was perhaps preternaturally vivid. It often seemed to have the same effect as beauty. Derek called it her white flame, and she accepted the carefully offhand compliment for both the elliptical truth in it and its purpose, which was, she knew, to make her feel better. It did, a little.

"Oh, I have a history," she said. "It just doesn't have anything to do with my present. Or I didn't think it did. But Annie says . . ."

"Have you been seeing Annie professionally?" He was alert; a soft motor seemed to start up somewhere within him.

"Oh, no. Or just once."

"When?"

"Friday. Friday night."

"Before you came here?"

"I . . . yes."

"So that's why you were late. What happened on Friday, Mike?"

"Oh, several things. Nothing that can't be handled. It was a bad day, but . . ."

"Mike."

"Goddamn it, Derek, I had an anxiety attack on the train and had to go back to town, and I thought Annie might be able to help, and she did. Period. End of crisis."

"No. Beginning of crisis, I think. And so Annie gave you whatever jolly stuff you're taking, and told you that something in your past was making you nuts. What else did she tell you?"

"That was the sum of it. And it wasn't nearly as dire as you make it sound. Haven't you ever had an anxiety attack?" Mike's voice was riding upward on the crest of the fear that was surging up from its pit despite the Xanax and had reached her wrists. They buzzed horridly, as they had on a few other occasions of great fatigue and tension in the past, when she had been near fainting.

"No. Not in living memory. And neither have you. You've been in tight spots all over the country for the past twenty years without turning a hair. Now I want you to tell me about this so-called anxiety attack in as much detail as you can, and take your time. It's not fair to me to keep it from me."

"Not fair . . . *what about me?* What if I don't want to tell you about it?"

"You have to. You finally have to tell me about your life, Mike." His voice had softened and deepened. She could feel it vibrating in his throat. "I can't fix anything for you if you don't. I can't help you."

"Are you going to fix things for me? Are you going to help me? Can you do that, Derek? I don't think you can."

"Well, I know I can. Goddamned right I can. I'm not going to leave you alone with whatever it is that makes you like this. I'm not going to just walk away from you."

Something seemed to break and flood its warmth out into Mike's cold, laboring chest. She felt an alien, treacherous prickling behind her eyes and in her nose. Her throat closed as if of its own volition.

I cannot be about to cry, she thought in alarm. I have not cried since . . . back then. Since that day.

She swallowed and sat up straight in the bed. Derek leaned back against the bookcase wall that served as a headboard and looked at her.

"Well?" he said.

"I really don't know if I can do this, Derek," she said. "I've never told anyone . . . all of it."

"It can't be any worse than some of the stuff I've already written." He grinned at her, the sudden and strangely sweet grin that was so at odds with his brutal Toltec face. "Tell you what. I'm going downstairs and call Alan and tell him to either get me some time on *Rolling Stone* or tell 'em to put it up their asses. And then I'm going to bring up not one but two bottles of Moët et Chandon, which I just happen to have on ice, and I'm going to build up the fire up here and put on that goddamned Vivaldi of yours and take the phone off the hook and swathe you in this here dead mink, and you are going to get a little drunk and tell about Mike Winship. Including how come you're called Mike Winship and not Sally Sue whatever. If it takes all day and into next week. Is that a deal?"

"Yes," said Mike faintly. "I guess it is, yes."

She lay still while he got up and went out of the room and down the circular wrought-iron staircase into the lower part of the house. She could hear his heavy padding in the kitchen, and the opening and closing of the refrigerator door, and an indistinguishable telephone conversation. Outside the sun stabbed in and out of the flying clouds over the ocean, a violent and apocalyptic seascape. It looked arctic, Siberian, though she knew that it probably was not. The chill that gripped her emanated from inside her, solid and heavy and cold, like a long-dead fetus. At the thought Mike jackknifed herself into a knot.

Derek Blessing came back up the stairs laden with bottles and glasses and set them on the floor beside the bed. He paused and looked at her, and then drew the mink throw up around her neck and added a goose-down comforter faintly redolent of spilt Wild Turkey.

"Just let me get the space heater out of the closet and hook it up," he said over his shoulder. "It's getting colder than a witch's teat out there. Don't be afraid, Mike. You can stop anytime it gets too tough. But you have to start. You have to do that, at least."

She said nothing. She moved closer in upon herself. By the time he had whisked the heater out of the closet and thumped it down on his side of the bed, she was curled in a ball on her side, facing away from him toward the cold sea, knees drawn up, arms crossed between them, fists knotted. Like a fetus. Again, the image of the fetus. Like the fetus she herself had been until she was born.

She lay perfectly still for a space of time, and when she finally spoke, it was in the frail, light voice of a tired child.

"Well, you know," Mike said, "the very first thing I did in my life was to kill my mother."

TWO

Forever after the summer night in Lytton, Georgia, that sent Mike Winship a world away from home, she spoke of her childhood—when she did speak of it—as normal.

"Absolutely average," she would say lightly at one party or another in those luminous, young, always-twilight first years in New York, when she was still going to a great many parties. "Textbook typical. Tadpoles and apple trees and bicycles and cutting your own Christmas tree from your grandparents' farm, and braces, and camp in the summer . . . the works."

"Were you in love with the boy next door?" someone was sure to ask, drawn, as were most people, by Mike's soft, rich alto laugh and accent, and the strange incandescence that sometimes played around her plain, sharp face.

"No. The boy up the street." She would smile, and they would invariably smile with her.

"But then you chucked it all and left the old plantation and the boy up the street and started writing for smartass magazines," more than one of Richard's intrigued Jewish liberal classmates had said, or words to that effect. "How'd a southern belle like you end up in New York with a smart-mouthed little Jewish mama's boy?"

"Oh," Mike would say, "I got tired of watching them flog the slaves and burn crosses on the Negroes' lawns."

"Did your family have a plantation really? Did your father grow cotton?" one stunningly witless blond nurse from Yonkers asked her once, and the entire party had groaned. It was a fund raiser for Shirley Chisholm, and all the young members of Richard's law firm were there.

"Oh, Lord, no." Mike smiled at the girl, for once not taking refuge in sarcasm. She knew that the nurse was a blind date, the daughter of one of her hapless date's mother's friends, and would not be asked again. Mike also knew that there would be general laughter after the couple had left, and several imitations. She felt sorry for her, and a small prick of kinship.

"I lived in a big old white elephant of a house in the middle of town, and my father was—is—a lawyer. I think my grandparents grew some cotton once, but I never saw it. The closest I ever got to a plantation was seeing *Gone With the Wind,* just like you. I really did have an extraordinarily ordinary childhood. It might have been in Connecticut or New Jersey or Yonkers, for that matter."

"But was it happy?" the girl pursued. It was as if the smooth white mind behind the equally pristine brow could not conceive of normality or content in such an exotic region as Georgia. Mike might have told her that she had grown up quietly and happily on Uranus.

"For God's sake, Elise," the nurse's date muttered.

"Yes, it was happy." Mike smiled again at the doomed Elise. "It was just a plain, garden-variety happy childhood."

"And that's true," she said to Richard, who challenged her on the way home. "It was, except for that last business, and that wasn't really part of my childhood. I can't think how all the other years could have been any more normal."

It is astonishing how the immutable slain child in all of us colludes with its murderers.

Claudia Searcy Winship, Mike's mother, died at age twenty-eight of an undiagnosed congenital heart malformation when her second daughter was born. In addition to the tiny, squalling female infant, who was to have been a boy and borne the name of the paternal grandfather, John Micah Winship, Claudia left behind her in the large old Victorian house on Pomeroy Street a five-year-old daughter who was a petite, blue-eyed, ebony-curled replica of herself and a tall, slender, ashen-haired Lowland Scot husband who turned, on the night of her death, from a proud and exuberant young man with the world by the tail into a remote holograph of himself.

For the remaining years that the new baby girl would live in the house that her father had bought his bride with his first year's savings as an associate in an Atlanta law firm, a great, formal emptiness reigned. Almost the only sounds that could be heard in that temple once dedicated to the sweet, orderly litanies of Family were the treble pipings of exquisite small DeeDee (named Daisy for her paternal grandmother), the fitful uproars of troublesome baby Mike herself, and the sonorous grumbling of loving black Rusky Cromie, who minded the Winship girls, kept the echoing house, and anchored the world within it.

In a large, dim study at the back of the first floor, outside the orbit of the house's life, John Worthy Winship dwelled in silence with his damaged and souring heart, immersed in papers from his briefcase. He looked up only to rest his eyes on the photograph of Claudia in her wedding dress that stood on the desk. It was a rolltop of great, smoky age and looked to be a family heirloom, but John had bought it from the estate of an impoverished farmer-scholar whose affairs the firm had handled; his own family had not been desk people. The only other ornament on its polished surface was a faded photo in a walnut frame of a plain white dogtrot farmhouse, leaning gently in on itself like a sturdy old woman settling into age, shaded by huge pecan trees. Behind the house were a few bleached outbuildings, and in the far distance fields stretched away into a streaked Kodak sky. Both the house and the photo had the look of age and weather and wear.

John Winship had always called the house the homeplace, as was the custom in that part of the red north Georgia hill country that owed so much of its provenance to the Scots and English who had trickled down from the Appalachian highlands. It had been in his family for five generations, being shored up and added to by each succeeding family of Winships, until it had attained a somewhat imposing bulk that was belied by the meagerness of its inner creature comforts and its furnishings. There was never more than just enough money to live on in the Winship clan, for this hundred-odd acres of corn, cotton, and oat land was farmed only by the current Winships in residence and two or three black sharecropping families, who occupied the precarious shanties along the creek bottom.

The earliest Winships had come to Georgia from Virginia, but before that they had dwelled in the wild, unnamed hills and secret coves of the Great Smoky Mountains, and before that, had followed the wrong young chieftain into battle at Culloden and had exited Scotland hard on his heels. Winships had, in essence, been backing the wrong horse ever since. In the years of drought, they planted oats. When they put in corn, the deluges came. When they sowed cotton, the boll weevil followed. The land was favorable for crops, but their luck did not seem to be. Nevertheless, after centuries of tending other men's holdings in Scotland, a fierce and silent passion had been born in them for these, their own few red acres across the western sea, and that passion had burned in their sallow breasts ever since, through good years and bad, like the subterranean fires that burned unseen for a hundred years in the mines of their own bleak north country. Both the land and the passion came down to John Worthy, the last male Winship to bear the name, who was also the first to leave the land since the original Great War (in which the Winships had, predictably, backed the losers), and the first to go away to school to learn to be other than a tender of the land.

"But I'm not thinking to leave it for good," John Winship told his bride-to-be, Claudia, when he took her home to meet wary, work-reddened John and Daisy Winship. They were plainly intimidated by this town-bred Dresden shepherdess that their incomprehensible lawyer son had brought home, perched on his arm like an exotic fowl from a strayed caravan.

"First I'm going to fix up the house in town, something you and our children will be proud of, and make Mama and Daddy comfortable for the rest of their lives," he elaborated, the dreams near to boiling in his gray eyes. "Then, one day, I'm going to make a real showplace of the homeplace, a real gentleman's farm. Get rid of the corn and cotton and put in a dairy herd. Mechanize the place, get some good help. Fix up the house from stem to stern, maybe add on some columns. Then we'll go back. My son is going to be the Winship of Winship Farms, and it's going to put everything else in this end of the county to shame."

Claudia, a celebrated beauty in the medium-sized town just to the east where she had grown up, a canny girl but no scholar and possessed of meager lineage and nonexistent dowry, as well as an abiding fear of cows, dimpled up at the tall young man with the dream-steeped gray eyes and held her tongue. Plenty of time yet to enjoy the Pomeroy Street house and her future status as a lawyer's wife before the time came to disabuse him of the notion that she would make a good farm wife, even on a gentleman's farm.

John Winship worshiped and sentimentalized his taciturn, hardworking parents, even though the flame of ambition warred in his breast with their credo of labor and sacrifice and the immutable sovereignty of the land. By the time they died of exhaustion and sheer boredom, as well as the virulent influenza that decimated Fulton County in the mean years of mid-Depression, they had become in his eyes wise and simple agrarian saints, and the scant and strictured childhood he had spent in the fields of the homeplace had been transmuted into a *McGuffey's Reader* boyhood. He mourned their passing long and passionately. Hardly a day went by that he did not capture small, squealing DeeDee after he returned home from work and drive the two miles down Highway 29 along the Atlanta and West Point tracks to where the old white house stood beside the road, its fallow fields sliding away into the fading sun. He kept the house roofed, painted, and squared. It was his fancy to keep fires laid in the whitewashed fireplaces, ready for the match. He paid the tenants, who stayed on working the only land they had ever known, to keep the hedges trimmed and the swept yard tidy, and he himself attended to the grape and scuppernong arbors and the field of daffodil bulbs that made a blazing yellow splendor beside the highway every spring.

John Winship worked hard and well at his profession, and he doted on small DeeDee, but it was Claudia who filled his whole heart, taking up the empty spaces where John and Daisy Winship had dwelled for so long. She was his life, his pretty, chiming wife; her Irish whimsy lit his dour Scot's temperament to frequent playfulness, and when she became pregnant with the baby who was to be John Micah Winship II and bear the name back into the homeplace, joy and fullness made his fair, freckled skin and the odd, light-struck gray eyes over the slanted cheekbones incandescent and arresting. He was, with his angles and sharpness, his ash-fair hair and brows and lashes, plain and almost sunless in repose. When joy or any other strong emotion took him, he drew the eye like wildfire. In those months of Claudia's second pregnancy, people often looked after him on the street, and looked away and back again, uncertain why their eyes kept returning to this unprepossessing man. At first glance, he appeared almost hookworm-wan. But in those days John Winship shimmered with his own fire. When Claudia died in the bleached November dawn, the fire went out, and the ashes lay on his face and his heart and home for the rest of his life.

At the grief-stricken old family doctor's suggestion, he engaged a wet nurse, a widow from nearby Lightning, who came with her own tiny son to keep the new white baby alive and stayed on to run the house and nurture tiny Micah . . . for he had not had the heart to call this child who had brought his wife to death by her name, and simply called her Micah, as they had planned to call the son she was supposed to have been. He did not bother with a middle name. Rusky Cromie loved pattering little DeeDee as quickly, if not as fully, as she did the new child, and cheerfully took her to her great, formless bosom along with baby Mike and her own infant. The latter she renamed J.W., out of a profound and not-at-all-awestruck admiration for John Winship, telling her compatriots in the Little Bethel African Methodist Church that any man who took on so after his dead wife so was most assuredly no tomcat, and moreover, that any man who worked such long, grueling hours both in nearby Atlanta and later in his own closed study to provide for his small, motherless daughters would be a good example for her son in his formative childhood years.

"Better than he own daddy, rest his soul, 'cause that man ain't never spent no more time than he could he'p at home with me. Fo' he died I reckon he knowed more about the inside of Gene Coggins's poolroom than he do his home or his church."

And so the three children, two small white girls and a huge-eyed, unsmiling black boy, grew from babyhood into childhood and beyond in that great, white shrine to a woman long dead.

THREE

By the time Micah Winship could reason, all three children in the house on Pomeroy Street knew without having been directly told at whose hands Claudia Winship had died. John Winship and Rusky Cromie would have dutifully denied her culpability at once had she mentioned it, but Mike never did. A greater truth than theirs prevailed. The terrible knowledge gradually sank like a lightless black stone into the depths of her unconscious, but the circles of its passing spread endlessly outward. Mike went from troubling infancy to difficult childhood.

John Winship continued to keep the homeplace mowed and swept and painted, but he dreamed no more grand dreams for it and could not have said why he did not sell or rent it, knowing only that he must not, that the land was not only his but was, in some indefinable way, him. He did not think to move there himself. All he would ever have of Claudia was moored in the Pomeroy Street house. If he thought at all, he thought that someday DeeDee and a shadow husband might live there. He did not consider that Mike would ever live in the homeplace. He did not consider Mike much at all. If he stayed in his study and kept the stout oak door shut, he could not hear her thin, starveling wails from the nursery and could forget for long stretches at a time that she was there. And somehow, when Mike was not there, Claudia was. To hear the baby's cries again after a long period of silence was to bear almost anew the terrible spear of his wife's death. John Winship's face gradually sank in upon itself like an effigy on a crusader's tomb.

Pixielike DeeDee, who grew more like her mother every day, was the only being in the house who could coax a ghost of the old magical animation back into her father's face. Despite Rusky's attempts to interest him in the new baby, an attenuated infant with his own long, light bones and narrow skull and lambent eyes, he could bring himself only to touch her silky skull with the tip of his finger occasionally, or let her tiny fist close over it. He could not and did not rock her and sing college songs and popular ballads to her, as he had to baby DeeDee. He grew more and more silent, rigid, withdrawn, canted within himself. Attitudes hardened into prejudices, ideas into obsessions. The law and the homeplace and the young wife frozen for all eternity into the silver frame on his desk were the bones of his life, the armature on which he hung his days. DeeDee could skip in and out of his tower at will. Mike hovered outside, staring in at him with his own luminous seawater eyes, and could not enter. But she never ceased in the battering.

She was, of course, a trying child from the beginning. She cried loudly and long, and could not be comforted except by Rusky, and then only after much rocking and crooning. DeeDee, busy with first grade at the Lytton Grammar School and her tea sets and coloring books and dolls, clearly had little use for this new doll that would not allow itself to be dressed and fondled, but only wailed its frail and inconsolable grief into the silent house. John Winship continued to close his study door against the importuning cries. Mike wept on alone except for the patient black woman and her tiny son, who slept tranquilly in a wash basket beside Mike's crib. After a while, as she grew, Mike stopped crying and began to do battle.

She balked and disputed on all sides the adults who attempted to manage her. Few even tried after a while, except Rusky, whose halfhearted admonitions never slid over into exasperation and whose arms were always outstretched for comfort instead of retribution. She fought with her small, flying fists the Lytton children who fell into her orbit. Not many did, until she entered first grade. Then she became the terror of her small society: slight, elfin, a slip of a child with thistledown hair and a quicksilver mind, curious about everything, contentious when the answers baffled her or failed to engage her intelligence, without physical fear, passionately devoted to the perceived underdogs around her. Her gruff goblin voice and belly laugh contrasted sharply with her spindrift appearance. Like her father, Mike in a passion drew eyes like a magnet. Notes and phone calls from her teachers streamed into the house at first, but John Winship dealt with them by not dealing with them, and eventually the stream dried to a trickle, then stopped. Mike's perverseness became as accepted a fact as her motherlessness.

By the time she was eight or nine, her companions were a phalanx of little black boys from Lightning and Rusky's sweet-tempered J.W., with whom she had grown up. With her band she roamed the deep woods behind the Winship house after school, swung from the dizzying heights of Indian Cave on a kudzu vine, caught crawfish in Turnipseed's Creek. When, at her puberty, John Winship intervened and forbade further association with the boys on the grounds that "it just won't do; it would break your mother's heart," Mike disappeared into the depths of the Lytton branch of the Carnegie Library in her free time, and only came out to eat and sleep. John Winship's quiet household bowled on into the 1960s.

As Mike grew, Rusky aged rapidly and her blood pressure and "the sugar" grew more virulent, and the fall Mike turned twelve Rusky settled with a sigh of relief into the tiny tenant house at the back of the Winship property, which had long stood vacant, and thereafter came to the big house only until midafternoon. J.W. faded away, too, into the shabby concrete-block Negro high school on the edge of Lightning, and pretty, feminine DeeDee became a fussy little mother to her rebellious, changeling younger sister and a ghastly miniature wife to John Winship. It pleased and involved her end-lessly to putter officiously with home economics and meals and little sugary treats for her father, and she never failed to lay out the least objectionable and most coordinated of Mike's outfits for her to wear to school each morning, clicking her tongue wearily like a woman three times her age when Mike refused to put them on. Rusky did the actual cooking, leaving a meal for DeeDee to heat up each eve-ning, and she did the heavy cleaning and washing and ironing, but John Winship was charmed and soothed with his fluttering surro-gate, and praised her ministrations with all the rusty animation left to him. He did not precisely ignore Mike; he took her, with DeeDee, to Sunday school and church each week, and asked her with remote courtesy at least once during each evening what she had done that day and what she had learned in school, but since she always an-swered, "Nothing," and since he knew that if fresh trouble broke over her duck-down head he would eventually learn of it from DeeDee, he did not try to peer beneath the smooth, closed surface of her angular little face. It would have seemed like prodding at a mirror.

DeeDee Winship could have had any young man she laid her blue eyes on, so Elizabeth Taylor–pretty was she, but from eighth grade on she had gone exclusively and inexplicably with Eugene Wingo, widely known as Duck, a handsome, hulking boy from Lytton's first and only trailer park on the outskirts of town. From the very beginning of their alliance Rusky had pronounced him "sorry" and the only time Mike ever saw the gleam of tears in John Winship's eyes was at DeeDee's wedding to him directly after their graduation from Lytton High. DeeDee dutifully settled into a new semi-wide with Duck and began classes at the nearby state teacher's college, and Duck took his bursting calves and biceps, his Robert Mitchum hooded eyes and sliding grin, and his reputation as the best Triple-A fullback in the state's recent history into sales. For that first year, he sold Ford pickups and John Deere tractors to every Lytton Blue Devils supporter in a fifty-mile radius. It was a job with a high gratification quotient, but certain limitations as to future. The dealership inevitably ended up with more pickups than the Blue Devils had supporters. Duck moved on into hardware.

DeeDee got her degree in elementary musical education six days before her first child was born. Duck got his fourth job, selling marine fixtures 350 miles inland, the day after the baby arrived. They named the child John Winship Wingo, and John Winship set up an ironclad trust for him and slipped DeeDee a thousand dollars so she could afford to stay home with him for a while. It was a good thing. By the time Duck lost the marine job and took one selling wholesale beauty supplies across six states from his Studebaker, the baby was old enough to bring to Rusky's laconic and short-lived successor, Pinky, at the Pomeroy Street house, and DeeDee was able to get her certificate and begin teaching music to the bovine, white-eyed children at the Lytton Grammar School. It was widely agreed among parents and faculty that DeeDee had a voice just like Yma Sumac's. Mike, closeted away in her upstairs room with copies of Look and Life and her hopeful columns for the Lytton High Blade, came to flinch as DeeDee warbled ersatz Andean arias to the baby when she came to pick him up after school.

A week after Mike's thirteenth birthday Rusky died in her sleep in the small house behind the privet hedge, and all the howling loneliness that her protective black bulk had held at bay crashed in on Mike. She was inconsolable. She wept behind her schoolbooks in her classes, she wept in her room in the afternoons, before her father came home from work, and try though she might, she could not keep the tears from sliding down her cheeks in the dreadful, silent dinner hours. John Winship finally lifted his head from his folded newspaper to say, "I think you'd better go stay with DeeDee until you can control yourself, Micah. She never carried on like this even when your mother died."

The thought of DeeDee's terrible miniature kingdom in the trailer, with Duck's endless television programs blaring out into the nighttime trailer park, made her swallow the tears, even though the cold salt lump sat stonelike in her throat for days and she could not eat. Dinner, which had been bad enough since DeeDee and Rusky had left the echoing house, became torturous to Mike and John Winship alike. Finally, to her vast relief, he gave up the charade and asked that she simply bring him his plate to his study, pleading the press of an unusually tedious and complicated tax case. He ate there in silence thereafter, and Mike retreated gratefully to the haven of her room with her own plate. After she had finished the meal—a sad affair compared to the ones that Rusky and even DeeDee had prepared—she fled to the library. And sometimes, without his knowledge and against his wishes, she slipped back through the privet hedge and spent the evenings with J.W.

The boy, grown now almost to man size, and so quiet in the presence of whites that it was nearly impossible to tell if he was possessed of a functioning intelligence, had simply stayed on in the little house after his mother's death. John Winship had not attended Rusky's splendid funeral at Little Bethel, and he had not allowed Mike to go, though she had pleaded and sobbed and stormed.

"It's not your place, Micah," he had said coldly and finally. "You'd make everyone there uncomfortable, and it would ruin things for everyone else who loved her. People want to be with their own kind at times like this." Mike had stayed closeted in her room for two days afterwards, until hunger had finally driven her out. John Winship did not speak of Rusky again to her for a long time.

But apparently he did to J.W., because from the weekend after Rusky's funeral on, J.W. appeared silently in the backyard to do yard work, and on most school afternoons he came for a couple of hours and did the heavy cleaning, vacuuming, and polishing that Rusky had always done. There was always a weekly sum of money left for him—an uncommonly generous one, for those times in the South—in the brass bowl that had been Daisy Winship's on the dining room table. He ate his supper at the home of a cousin in Lightning and seemed to have adequate money for schoolbooks, a few clothes, and most notably a used television set. He never went anywhere but school, church, across town to meals, and through the hedge to the Winship house to do his chores, and in the evenings afer he had walked back to the dim little cabin from the cousin's house, he did his homework and then switched on Jackie Gleason or Sid Caesar and Imogene Coca or Peter Gunn. At thirteen he might have been a resigned, not unhappy man of forty.

On the evenings that Mike joined him to sit on the edge of the swaybacked bed that had been Rusky's and stare at the blue-flickering old Dumont, they had as little to say to each other as they had in the days of crawfish and Indian Cave. But their silence was not strained. Mike never felt prickly or anxious with J.W., as she did with most other people, and he did not seem as eye-avertingly deferential with her as he did with other white people. It was as if there was a bond between them that was so deep that it did not need words, though aside from that bond there was no common ken at all in either. And it was true; the bond had been—and still was—their childhood in the shadow of the dead woman and the grieving, remote man in the Pomeroy Street house, and the constant benison of Rusky. Mike alone knew that J.W.'s closed, mulish face hid a sunny, unintimidated intelligence and a naive, biddable sweetness. He alone knew that she still sometimes wept for his mother. It was two or three months after Rusky's death before Mike learned that her father was paying for J.W.'s food, clothing, and incidental expenses. Priss Comfort told her.

"Then why wouldn't he let me go to her funeral?" Mike stormed. "It's hypocritical to support J.W. and look after him and not even go to her funeral, or let me go. It's worse than that. It's sneaky!"

"No, it's not," Priss Comfort said severely. "It's just his way. Your father may be a lot of things, but sneaky is not one of them. You don't begin to know what he's like. I'd advise you to leave off calling him names until you do."

Mike did.

FOUR

Priss Comfort was, besides Rusky, the only fixed star in Mike's firmament. Priss, from the odd-looking little stone cottage down by the high school athletic field, was stimulant, refuge, and friend to Mike from her babyhood on. A massive, chestnut-haired spinster with a precise, clarion voice who taught English at Lytton High and had been a childhood friend to John Winship, Priss had been the first person at the house after the doctor when Claudia died. Thereafter she was at the Winship house several times a week until Mike was in kindergarten, and then at least once each week.

When Mike was adjudged by Rusky old enough to cross the street, she spent a great deal of time in Priss's book-choked, cat-infested house, where Priss read aloud to her, answered her million restless questions, and talked reasonably with her on any subject one might pursue with a normally intelligent adult. In the savagely untidy little house Mike absorbed literature, liberal politics, art, music, Priss's own brand of fierce ethics, local history, and Lytton genealogy, along with elsewhere forbidden Coca-Colas and Nehis. Priss's own drinks were usually ruddy with bourbon, and sometimes she fell abruptly asleep on the sofa listening to Mike. This did not strike Mike as any odder than anything else about Priss, so she never thought to mention it at home. Priss filled an undefined but essential gap between Rusky and DeeDee, and she moved effortlessly into the space where John Winship might have been. She took Mike to buy clothes and have her fine, silky hair shaped and trimmed, and heard her homework and her deepest hopes, hurts, and confusions, as well as her frequent rages and frustration. As a result, Mike dressed as eccentrically as Priss did, with a severe style and flair that no one in Lytton recognized as such, and developed an acerbic, elliptical manner of thinking and speaking.

Priss did none of these things for DeeDee. DeeDee needed no advice on her frilled and starched clothes and curly hair, and John Winship never failed to listen gravely to her exemplary homework and her small, conventional indignities. She had no uncomfortable confusions of purpose, and no curiosity. Rusky shook her head darkly at Priss Comfort's fruity bourbon aura, but she said often, "I don't know what we do 'thout Miss Priss."

DeeDee called her Aunt Priss, but to Mike she was only, and always, Priss.

"I'm not your aunt," she had once said to DeeDee. "I'm not your father or mother's sister. Be precise, DeeDee. Call things what they are."

But DeeDee was not precise and could not remember.

"That's all right," Priss said to Mike later. "I ask the difficult, but not the impossible."

FIVE

When Mike was fourteen, Bayard Everett Sewell moved with his widowed mother into the old Parsons house three doors up, and her precariously spinning world settled into place around him like a kaleidoscope. Everything that had before seemed lonely, murky, or hostile seemed all at once crystalline and beautiful, sweet-fitting, anchored. Bay Sewell was wonderful; he was life and breath and noise and laughter; he was almost too good to be true. But he was true; he was real and solid, and from almost the precise instant that they met, in the Parsons house driveway where Mike had gone to gawk at the men unloading the scant Sewell furniture, he was *there.*

Bayard Sewell was dark-haired, blue-eyed, open-faced, and handsome; forthright, funny, and easygoing; bright, articulate, and even-tempered. He was as graceful as a cat; he could have been a consummate high school athlete, but he worked after school and on weekends to augment the slender earnings of his mother, who did custom baking and tailoring when her rheumatoid arthritis permitted it. Within the year he held every honor and office at Lytton High that did not demand after-school time, and he had the third highest grade average in the school's history. Within three years it was apparent that Bayard Sewell was what the educators of America meant when they spoke of "prime college material."

He had few prospects for college, but he did not complain, and matter-of-factly made plans to go to night school for his degree after he graduated from Lytton High and got a full-time job. By the time he was a senior, his mother's condition had progressed to the point that she no longer accepted work of any sort, and their genteel poverty was on the point of sliding over into the dirt-poor category.

Work after high school was simply a given. His mother's pension would keep only one.

"Don't you hate working all the time?" Mike asked him once, early on.

"Nope," he said. "I only hate two things."

"What are they?"

"Small towns," he said. "And being poor."

He was just Mike's age, and from that first moment in the driveway, they spoke a strange, identical language of the heart and were inseparable. He did not think her looks queer or her opinions outrageous or her actions objectionable. He thought her beautiful, brave, brilliant, and funny, and in the sun of his approval Mike stepped from her chrysalis and moved quite near those things. He also seemed to feel that she was in need of his immediate protection, and trounced with neat efficiency one meaty town boy who made fun of her. No one did again. Courted, defended, and cherished, Mike lost her sense of being a cuckoo's chick in an alien nest and her veins hummed with peace. This must be what DeeDee has always felt like, she marveled to herself. This is what my mother must have felt like. How awful to die and lose this.

And she felt anew the long-buried lance of guilt for the death of Claudia and a shamed yearning to make up to her father for his immeasurable loss at her hands. Out of her new happiness she sought for something to give him. As it happened, what she brought him was Bayard Sewell.

Bayard did not have many spare hours, but those he did he spent in her company. Usually they studied. After that, they necked. The boy was admiringly respectful to John Winship, and by the time he and Mike began their senior year in high school, John was spending many of his evenings with the two of them. He would come out of his study, rubbing his eyes and stretching, and put the coffeepot on in the kitchen and settle into the wing chair in the living room that had been his in the years when he and Claudia and baby DeeDee had gathered there in the evenings, and Bayard Sewell and a reluctant Mike would close their books and sit up straight on the couch, and John would engage Bayard and, peripherally, Mike in conversation.

Mostly, they talked about Negroes. Or John Winship did, and Mike and Bayard Sewell listened.

John Winship had become in his mid-forties one of those con-flicted and caricatured well-placed Southerners who professed to care for and understand individual blacks, but who feared and hated the race collectively. He had fed and supported Rusky and J.W. in his home, seen to their welfare, paid their medical bills, trusted his children with Rusky, paid her funeral costs, and was now supporting and educating her son. But he had no words but harsh and bitter ones for Negroes in the aggregate.

From the beginning, the burgeoning Civil Rights Movement had nearly maddened him.

"They're looking to take over everything. Our schools and churches, our daughters, our very land. We have to stop them here and now," he would intone, and Mike and Bayard Sewell would stare at him in the lamplight, seeing in the flush of animation on his ascetic face something of the magnetism that had first drawn Claudia Searcy to him. They listened attentively to his cant, but they paid little heed to his words. Somewhere in the long twilight of his isolation, John Winship had become a bigot, fearing and scorning, in addition to the Negroes, Jews, Republicans, and Northerners. The latter three were little more than the butt of his jokes, but the Negroes could move him to corrosive rage. Even though Mike and Bayard had heard these diatribes many times before, they always nodded, and Bayard usually would murmur something like, "Yes sir," or "I can see why you might say that." Mike knew that he did not share her father's sentiments, and she had, in the beginning, challenged his sincerity.

"Well, I like your daddy," he said. "He doesn't have anybody else to blow off steam to, and he's got a lot of sense about most other things. It doesn't hurt anything to listen to him."

And indeed, it did not. John Winship seemed, so far as he was able, to dote on Bayard Sewell.

"He's going to make his mark, that's for sure," he would say. "It's a shame there's no money for college, but I've spoken to Flora, and there isn't an extra cent. A boy like that shouldn't have to grub for a night-school education."

"You did, Daddy," Mike said.

He frowned. "But you always hope it'll be easier for the boy coming after you," he said.

"What about the girl?" Mike did not say.

To Bayard Sewell, she said, "You're the son I was supposed to be. You've made him happier than I ever could." She did not say it with bitterness, but gratitude and a sense of the fitness of things. She felt not the slightest curl of anger. Mike's anger had always radiated outward from the Pomeroy Street house, not in upon it. When she met Bayard, it had faded like smoke.

The whole town adored Bayard Sewell.

"You're a lucky girl," someone or other was always saying to Mike when it became clear that the friendship was more, was a flame, consumed everything, was destined to endure. And it was all those things. Mike was in love with every atom of her being. It was Bayard Sewell who was sensible and restrained in the long summer nights on the wisteria-hung side porch of the Pomeroy Street house, when they kissed until Mike was nearly mad with it.

"It'll be all that much better for waiting," he would say raggedly, pushing a blinded Mike away from him.

"But I don't want to wait," Mike raged to Priss Comfort on the day after one such episode. "What if I do get pregnant? We're going to get married anyway. We're going to have children anyway."

"Not, I hope, while you're still children yourselves," Priss said acidly.

"We're not children. He's not, anyway."

"You're right about that," Priss said. "There's nothing childish about Bayard."

"Then why wait?"

"Because not to wait is stupid, Mike. And you're not stupid. You'll be a mother, I hope, and a good one, but there's so much more you need to be first."

"Like what?"

"Like a person."

"I'm a person now."

"No. You're a promising cadet. Go on home, now. I'm tired and I want a bath and F. Scat Fitzgerald wants his supper."

By the time they were midway through their senior year, it was settled that they would be married the following August and John Winship would send them both through the Atlanta Division of the University of Georgia and Bayard could take an evening job if he liked, and they would live in the Pomeroy Street house until they graduated. There was more than ample room in that echoing temple to Claudia, and Flora Sewell was just up the street and could be kept under the watchful eye of her son. John Winship was as nearly jaunty as Mike had ever seen him, talking expansively, waving away their thanks. Bayard Sewell was incandescent with happiness and gratitude to John. Mike was stupid with joy. For the first time in her life, she felt her essential Winshipness, and sometimes she would look at her father, and he would catch the look and smile at her, or nearly, and she would think, I am Mike Winship. Micah *Winship.* I am him, and he is me. And she would know with an honesty far beyond her years that it did not matter in the least with what coin she had bought the belonging, nor how late. That only the belonging mattered. To belong. To be Mike Winship and to belong to John Winship and to Bayard Sewell. I have done well, she knew within herself.

Even DeeDee, worn with teaching, housework, and caring for the new baby, and thickening with Kraft Macaroni and Cheese Dinners, approved.

"Imagine my little scrawny chicken sister with a man like this," she said.

Priss Comfort alone did not seem entranced with the union.

"You just make sure you don't get pregnant before you finish high school and do some serious work," she snapped. "Do you know what to use?"

"Oh, Priss, of course. DeeDee told me . . ."

"DeeDee's a fine one to tell anybody about birth control," Priss growled, and took Mike to an Atlanta gynecologist to be fitted for a diaphragm.

"Aren't you glad for me?" Mike asked her once. "You don't seem to be."

"Let's just say the jury is still out," Priss said. More than once that winter, as spring approached, Mike found Priss frankly drunk on the sofa in the stone house. But she did not go there so often anymore, so it was hard to tell if Priss was drinking more than usual or not.

SIX

It was in Priss's senior English Literature class that Mike found another great piece of herself.

Priss had them reading *Othello,* and Mike had fallen under the rich, glinting spell of the tragic Moor. His complexity, grandeur, foolishness, pain—his sheer humanity—roared in her ears and filled her mind. She did not think she had ever encountered so complete and finished a human being. In this, she knew, she was alone.

The class was made up of Mike and a few other town students and a number of gangling, heavy-handed eighteen-and-nineteen-year-olds who dropped out each spring to plow and plant and each fall to harvest. Some were taking Priss's class for the second and third time, for unlike many other Lytton teachers, who sighed gratefully as soon as tenure was assured and automatically passed everyone who could write his name, she was adamant about her students earning at least their D's. And even Priss's D's came hard. Few of the farm and bus students liked Priss, but all were afraid of her. None of them liked Shakespeare. All of them hated *Othello.* It was well into the third week of January before Mike understood why.

"Well," Priss said on a gray morning of cold, tired rain, "we can see how external events conspired to set Othello up for his fall. But what about the internal things? What about the forces within the man himself? What single thing about Othello can you think of that, more than anything else, brought about his downfall? Yes, Wesley?"

Mike turned her head curiously. Wesley Cato was a lank, bull-necked giant from up around Red Oak, chiefly famed at Lytton High for the BB that had been lodged in his eyelid since he was a child and the fact that he had repeated the twelfth grade more often than any other student in the school's history. Mike had heard that this was his fourth go-round; she did not know how old Wesley must be by now. He was old enough to have fine, webbed lines in the thin, pouched skin around his prominent white-blue eyes, but that might have been from the sun. When Wesley was not working his father's fields, he was abroad on his Harley-Davidson. Mike had never heard him say a word in Priss's class.

"It's because he was a nigger," Wesley drawled adenoidally. "Everybody knows a nigger will screw up ever' time he gits a chance."

There was absolute silence. It rang in Mike's ears; it seemed to go on forever. She snapped her head around to look at Priss Comfort. As Priss opened her mouth to deliver doom, the class exploded in laughter, and whatever she had been going to say was drowned out. He's talking about J.W., Mike thought incredulously. He's talking about Rusky. She took a deep breath. She felt as if someone had struck her in the stomach and knocked the breath out of her. She felt as if she were watching them all from a distance of about fifty feet in the air. From this cold, remote blue height she watched herself rise from her seat and turn back to Wesley Cato, and she heard her voice say coldly, "That's not true. That's a rotten thing to say. Don't you ever say 'nigger' again in this class or in this school, you . . . trash. Othello is one of the saddest, best men I ever heard of; he's five hundred times a better man than you are."

And while she was saying it, Mike was perceiving it as a profound truth, as new and simple and world-consuming as the fact of her existence: the black people I know are fully as good as I am or anybody else, and we have been treating them dreadfully for hundreds of years. They are like me; they *are* me, and I am them. This is wrong, all of it is wrong. Why didn't I know this before? Why didn't somebody tell me this?

It was a moment out of time, unlike anything she had ever felt before, and she stood alone in the enormity of it, in Priss's stale, overheated classroom, for a long moment before Wesley Cato's furious drawl pierced it: "Well, it looks like Miss Mike Godamighty Winship is a nigger lover, don't it?"

A slow cold rage started in Mike, and a profound surprise. The thought formed in her mind and hung, perfect and heavy as fruit: How dare he call me that? How dare that white trash call me that? *I am Micah Winship.* She stared at him, anger coiling in her stomach.

"Sit down, Mike," Priss Comfort said into the silence that had fallen with Wesley's words. "Wesley, leave this class and take your things with you. Don't come back. I will not have that kind of talk in this classroom, and I will not have you in it either. I don't care if you graduate sometime in the year two thousand."

Wesley Cato stared at her insolently for a long moment, but he dug his books and letter jacket out of his desk and swaggered nonchalantly out of the room, slamming the door behind him. Mike sat down, her chest and forehead burning. She felt faint and light and cold with outrage and revelation. The rest of the class stared raptly into their Shakespeares, most of them for the first time since September. Priss went on with the lesson.

"That was quite an outburst," she said that afternoon, when Mike came by on her way to the library. "What on earth got into you?" She was looking at Mike very intently, as if trying to read her face for something outside Mike's ken.

"I don't know," Mike said, fidgeting a little, as she often did, under Priss's green stare. "It just seemed all of a sudden like . . . I can't explain it . . ."

"It's called an epiphany," Priss said. "Saul of Tarsus had something similar happen to him on the road to Damascus. Fair jerked him inside out, it did. Well. Now that you've had your epiphany, what are you going to do about it?"

"I don't know," Mike said. "I have to think about it some more. It does feel like something you have to do something about, though. Or I do. Only I can't think what. What do you think, Priss?"

"I think you'll know what you ought to do when the time comes," Priss said. "You might start with that essay. Go on to the library and see what's there about the Civil Rights Movement . . . though God knows, I doubt if anything much is, in Lytton . . . and put some facts behind this fine new passion of yours. That's a good place to start."

Mike thought, as she left, that she caught the nearest flicker of wetness in Priss's eyes, but only one lamp was on in the dark, crowded little living room, and she could not be sure. On reflection, she thought she must have been mistaken. Priss in tears was like the madonna in a fever of sexuality, simply beyond imagining.

"Good for you, for standing up to that jerk Cato," Bayard Sewell said, when she told him about the incident. "But you better hope your daddy doesn't hear about it. He'd have a fit."

Mike, who had been poised to tell him about the remarkable perception that had accompanied her words, did not. Somehow she had expected him to sense what she had felt, to understand, to share the fullness of it with her. She could not have said why she kept silent. He was, after all, dead right about her father. But there had been no thought in her mind of standing up to Wesley Cato; that had not been what her words were about. It was the first time their private lexicon had faltered. It disturbed her, and she did not mention it again.

As the slow spring came on, Mike devoted herself to her essay at the library while he worked evenings at Pembroke's Drugs, and when they met afterwards to talk of the day and the future and to hold one another and exchange their endless hungry caresses, the tremulous new truth in Mike's heart stayed there mute between them, as warm and living and secret as an embryo.

SEVEN

She was working on an essay for a contest sponsored by the Georgia Civil Liberties Union. The prize was a year's full scholarship, covering tuition, room and board, to the University of Georgia, and Mike yearned to present it triumphantly to her father, in the presence of Bayard Sewell, when the proper time came. She was aware that her new status as acknowledged daughter in the Winship house and her tentative favor in John Winship's eyes had been won by Bayard Sewell and by no innate qualities of her own, and though she was not resentful of this, still, the opportunity to make such a grand gesture shone in her mind like a lit white taper.

Neither Mike nor anyone else in Lytton with the exception of Priss Comfort, who was the administrator of the essay contest at Lytton High, would have known the Civil Liberties Union from the Supreme Court of the United States, and so Mike felt few qualms about pursuing the essay. Its subject, "The South on Fire: The Civil Rights Movement at the Crossroads," did give her a small, electric stab every now and then, especially when she imagined her father's reaction to her victory, but she dismissed it, seeing in her mind's eye his pride and awe when she presented him with the check for one thousand dollars. She went on with her research in the library, which was, as Priss had said, virginally innocent of materials on the Civil Rights Movement; but Priss supplied good source material, and Mike's own new convert's zeal carried her high and fast.

She talked of her work to no one except, and perhaps not surprisingly, J.W. Cromie. To Bayard Sewell and her father, she said only of her immersion in the library and her upstairs bedroom, "I want it all to be a surprise." And on the surface, this was true. Mike did not look any deeper than that. In the new momentum of her happiness, she had gratefully abandoned introspection. She might have spoken of her work to Priss, but Priss did not ask, and when Mike broached the subject, as she did once or twice at the beginning of the project, Priss had said, "We'll talk about it when the contest is over. I don't want to hear a word about it now. It's very important that everything you do be totally and completely yours, Mike."

But she talked to J.W. on many evenings, when she had finished working and Bayard had gone from his job at the drugstore straight into the Winship dining room to study at the huge, round oak table under the Searcy family chandelier. Later, around ten thirty, they would meet briefly for cocoa in the kitchen, and John Winship would join them, and after that he would retreat to his monastic bedroom with elaborate tact and leave the living room to them and their greedy and desperate hands and mouths. But the blank hour or so between she had come to fill again with the renewed visits to J.W. in the little house behind the hedge.

J.W. said little during these visits, as was his habit, but he listened. Mike told him what her reference books and newspapers and magazines said, and what she heard on the radio and television, as if he had no access to them himself, and most important, she told him what she thought about all of it. What she thought was quixotic and idealistic in the extreme at the beginning of her work, borne impossibly high on the updraft of her revelatory fire, but gradually a lean and reasoned shape began to emerge from her exhortations, something very near a whole and viable theory about the struggle for racial equality in the South, and what might be done about it, and what might not. Though she had virtually no experience of the world outside the South and no perspective to speak of on the phenomenon of the movement, Mike had the longtime native Southerner's almost subliminal knowledge of the day-to-day textures and realities of blacks living among whites. It lent her somewhat simplistic and passionate sentiments on the subject a convincing pragmatism.

And she had always had what Lytton would have called a way with words. She read her essay, in all its drafts and revisions, to J.W., and he said nothing, only nodded when she paused and looked at him, his face as solemn and apparently judicious as if it had not been, in effect, he she was talking about. Mike's long early years of feeling alone and exiled, of betrayal by her very birth, gave her words an urgency and homing precision that sometimes . . . very rarely . . .

brought a quick smile of recognition to his face; if she had seen the smiles, she would have known that she had in J.W. a more receptive audience than any of the judges in their offices in Atlanta, but she seldom looked up from her papers when she was reading aloud to him.

She might have seen something else, too; the small flame of a newborn pride and commitment. She had no way of knowing that in her words, on those spring evenings, J.W. Cromie was seeing dancing possibilities he had never known existed. Between the two of them, the essay was conceived, nurtured, and born. In mid-March she retyped it one last time and mailed it off.

In May she learned that she had won the competition.

Mike ran grinning and hugging herself from the Lytton post office to Priss Comfort's house. Priss looked at her a long moment, and then at the certified check for one thousand dollars, and smiled.

"Leave a copy of your piece for me when you go," she said. "Now I'll read it."

"It's a fine piece of work, Mike," she said the next day. "It tells me a lot about where you might take your life, if you work hard and have enough courage. That's the part I don't know about yet. Have you shown this to your father? Does he know about the prize?"

"No," Mike said. "I was going to wait and surprise him . . . oh, sometime later. You know, right when we're getting ready for the wedding and all, just say, 'Oh, by the way, you don't have to worry about school for me this year. This ought to cover it,' and sort of hand it to him casually."

Priss looked at her thoughtfully.

"What about Bayard?"

"I . . . well, no. He hasn't read the essay. And he doesn't know about this, yet. I just now got it, Priss; I came straight here . . ."

"I think you're right, Mike, even though you may not know why you want to wait. I think you ought to wait, maybe until you're married, if you're absolutely certain that that's what you want . . ."

"Oh Priss! Of course I'm certain; it's what I've always—"

"All right, okay." Priss held up a hand. "You can't blame me for trying, though. I can see so clearly from this essay how valuable you might come to be to the South; I'd always hoped you might want to be a journalist, and I think, with a lot of work and a lot of dedication and all the courage you've got, you might, in time, be one of the important young voices in the new South. If, God help us, we can throttle the old one."

"You can? You do? Well . . . gosh, Priss. Thanks. You never said . . . but why can't I do that anyway? What does being married have to do with it? Why can't I be both? I'd always planned to work; Bay always wanted me to do that . . ."

"I'll bet he did," Priss said. "I think you *could* be both, Mike. I just don't think you will. All the fire you'd need to go into your work is going right straight into that young man of yours," Priss said sadly. "You have the gift, and you have the fire, but I don't think you have enough of either to go around, and I think maybe you haven't built or found nearly enough courage yet."

"Why do you say that?" Mike was stung.

"Because you haven't shown that first-rate essay of yours to either your father or your fiancé, and you haven't told either one that you won the contest. Surprise, nothing. I don't know how that young man of yours feels about this race thing, but you and I both know how your father does."

"Well, if you think that, then I'll go home and show them both this check and this essay right this minute . . ."

"No. I think you're right. I don't think you should do that. I don't think they are ready for it, and I don't think you are, either. Wait until you're married. Wait until you're as good as enrolled in your classes at Georgia. Wait until *after* you are. It'll be much harder to change plans then."

"Why would plans change? You don't think that just because I wrote a silly little essay, Daddy would change his mind about our living with him, or paying our way . . . besides, I'm paying my own way. He'll be proud, Priss . . ."

Priss Comfort's face softened, and she put her arms around Mike's shoulder, a rare gesture. Priss was not much for touching.

"He certainly should be, Mike," she said. "He really should be. Congratulations. I told you way back that you needed to put your muscle where your mouth was, and you've made a good start on it. Now keep going, Micah Winship. They're going to hear that name outside Lytton one day, I'd bet on it."

"Micah Sewell." Mike smiled.

"Sewell," Priss corrected herself. She did not smile.

Mike took the check to the Lytton Bank and Trust and cashed

it, swearing Lavinia Calhoun, the middle-aged teller, to secrecy. She put the money in the silver duck bank that Priss Comfort had brought when she was born. She took it out and counted it so often that the crisp newness of the ten $100 bills began to soften and fade, and then she put them away for good, but she kept the duck polished bright, and looked often at it. It seemed tangible proof of her worth.

EIGHT

Graduation came and went, and the black-robed, candle-lit baccalaureate ceremonies. The capped and gowned, sweat-trickling graduation ceremonies in the stifling high school auditorium wheeled by in a blur. Mike watched and heard Bayard Sewell give the valedictory address through a sheen of tears and a high ringing of pride and love, and delivered her own salutatorian's briefer address faultlessly, to steady, if more modest, applause. Both of them graduated with honors, he with the highest, she with a still-respectable magna. John Winship hugged her glancingly and pumped Bayard's hand, and his mother mewled damply over both of them, and Priss gave her a long, hard, bourbon-fogged hug. DeeDee kissed her chastely and gave Bayard a giggling embrace. Her husband, Duck, gave Mike a rough, insinuating kiss on the mouth; Mike flinched in disgust at the wet lips and the seeking hardness of his groin as he ground it against her. He was always putting his hands on her, and calling her "little sis." DeeDee glared at him. He grinned hugely back and gave Bayard a resounding thump on the back and a savage and genial knuckling on the biceps.

John Winship's graduation present to them was a clean, seemly little two-year-old Ford coupe. He handed the keys to Bayard.

"Couldn't I keep it?" Mike entreated. "I wanted to go into Atlanta and see if the *Journal* or *Constitution* had any summer work. You'll be staying here at the drugstore, so I thought . . ."

"It's in Bayard's name, just to make things easier," John Winship said. "If you want to work for a newspaper, why don't you go see Carl Thigpen? He could use some help on the *Observer,* and you know he'd be glad to have you."

"Well, Daddy, you know, it's just a weekly," Mike said. She did not know why it stung her so, to have their joint gift put in

Bayard's name. In three months they would be a legal unit anyway. "I'd really like to get some experience on a daily. It would help me a lot after college, when I look for a full-time job."

"Maybe by that time you'll be starting a full-time family, and it won't amount to a hill of beans whether you worked for a daily or a weekly this summer," her father said. He almost twinkled it, a near-grotesque spasm.

She smiled. But often in those heat-jellied days of early summer, she remembered what Priss Comfort had said.

"Micah Winship. They're going to hear that name outside Lytton one day." And, "Put your muscle where your mouth is, Mike."

In the first week of that July 1964, the Student Nonviolent Coordinating Committee began a three-day sit-in at JoJo's Restaurant in downtown Atlanta, and on the second morning Mike astounded herself by recruiting a willing and nearly ebullient J.W. Cromie, catching the 9:40 A.M. Greyhound bus to Atlanta, and joining them.

She could not have said, at the time, why she chose to upset the frail equilibrium that her engagement to Bayard Sewell had achieved at the Pomeroy Street house. Priss Comfort could have said why, but did not get the chance; much later Annie Cochran could say why, and did. By that time, Mike did not care about her reasons. Or so she said. She had taken the action and walked the road on which it set her, and pronounced herself glad that she had done so.

"Because otherwise I'd have no life of my own, and no career," she told Annie.

"True enough," Annie Cochran said. "But don't give me that crap about being glad. You did it because you were forced to, not because you wanted to."

"Nobody forced me," Mike said.

"Everybody did," Annie replied.

Mike took it for granted that Bayard Sewell would support her; he always had. But she knew in the deepest, unsearched heart of herself, knew without allowing herself to know, that her father would be outraged and that the townspeople of Lytton would disapprove almost as heartily.

As for Lytton, Mike would have said that she did not care. She had largely washed her hands of it sometime in the long dawn of her awakening, in the transition from young teenager to woman. Her reading and her sessions with Priss had showed her a wider world of books and arts and ideas, of grace and beauty and stimulation, and her revelation in that winter classroom had limned for her another country entirely, and a kinder one. Moreover, her triumph with the essay had given her a heady taste of power, the tumescent flexing of unfolded wings.

To Bayard Sewell, but only to him and occasionally J.W. Cromie, Mike voiced her new scorn for the narrowness, the banality and triviality, the meanness of style and substance that she perceived everywhere in Lytton, now that the scales had fallen from her eyes. She disliked the church-and-gossip-dominated, time-stopped existence in the little town. Nothing, she said, ever happened in Lytton. Nothing worthwhile could flourish in such stony ground. No one of substance and vision would choose to dwell among such Philistines. They would tolerate no one and nothing in the slightest degree different from themselves. Mike was quite eloquent in these diatribes to Bayard and J.W., but with everyone else, even Priss, she held her tongue. Priss would have understood, she thought, but Mike feared that she would infer criticism where none was intended. Priss had, after all, opted to cast her lot here. Mike planned to lead her life with Bayard, once college was behind them, in a much larger and vastly more exotic arena than Lytton, Georgia. In this he agreed with her. Bayard Sewell was quietly, efficiently, and savagely ambitious.

"What do you want?" Mike would ask him often. "What do you want for the rest of our lives?"

"To be out of here," he said. "To be where things can happen. Then I'll see."

"Can they happen here?"

"No," he said. "Not ever here, and nowhere like here."

And she agreed.

So perhaps the flight to Atlanta to join the sit-in was the first step in that odyssey. Perhaps it was the first shot across John Winship's bow. And perhaps it was, as it seemed to her later, the first strong beat of a newly naked heart. In any event, Mike took it without conscious thought of the consequences. They were swift and final.

Inevitably, she and J.W. were arrested, along with most of the other protestors, and spent the night in the Fulton County Jail on Decatur Street in Atlanta. Just as inevitably, the press was there in full cry. It was pure bad luck that the television cameras found and dwelled on Mike as she was led away, struggling in honest surprise and indignation ("I am *Micah Winship!*") and in handcuffs. It was pure coincidence that the footage aired on the 6:00 P.M. local Atlanta newscast that almost every family in Lytton, including the Winships, watched at suppertime. It was the first time John Winship had seen Mike since breakfast that morning. He had thought nothing of her daylong absence; he had presumed her to be at Priss's, or the library, as she so often was.

He would not speak to her when she telephoned home, asking timidly to be bailed out. He hung up when he heard her voice. She finally reached DeeDee, who took her request and her own copious tears over to the Pomeroy Street house and laid them before John Winship. By that time a white-faced Bayard Sewell had joined Mike's father, but John would not allow him or DeeDee to speak with Mike, and forbade them to go and fetch her. He went to bed in silence, arose in silence the next morning, and closeted himself in silence at first light in his study. He would answer no knocks and calls from outside, and he would not open his door. In the end, it was Priss Comfort who went to Atlanta and bailed Mike and a bewildered J.W. out of jail and brought them home at dusk on that following day. Priss, who had been drinking steadily, was very nearly incoherent when she turned her car into the Winship driveway, but she parked it neatly. Even when she was drunk, Priss could always drive.

What she could not do was talk. And so she slumped into the wing chair that had been Claudia's and dropped her head into her hands, and said no word in Mike's defense when John Winship came into his twilit living room in the company of a red-eyed DeeDee and an ashen, drowned-looking Bayard Sewell, and looked at his youngest daughter and the drooping black boy behind her.

"I don't blame you, J.W.," he said finally to the terrified boy. "You're stupid, but you're not sorry. I know who made you go up there. But you, Micah . . . well. I guess we could start with whore, couldn't we? And after that we could add criminal, and race-mixer, and mother-killer . . ."

The words coiled out of him, snake-cold, thick, murderous, eighteen years of unspat phlegm.

"Daddy . . ." Mike whispered. She put out her hand and then dropped it onto the back of Priss's chair to steady herself. She thought that she would faint. There was a roaring in her ears, and her vision blurred whitely.

"I curse the day I earned that title," the terrible stranger's voice went on. "And I refuse to wear it any longer. You are not my daughter. I have only one daughter. The other one killed her mother and my wife, and then she died herself, in a jail full of nigger criminals."

A grotesque sort of snort, a gibbous snicker, came from J.W., and Mike saw with foolish incomprehension that he was crying. Opaque silver tears made snail's tracks down his black cheeks.

"I'm glad your mother is dead, J.W.," John Winship said in the frozen snake's voice. "Otherwise this day would have killed her for sure. Go on home now. As I said, no one can really blame you."

J.W. fled, snuffling. DeeDee burst into loud wails. John Winship and Bayard Sewell were silent.

Mike turned to the dark-haired boy, standing in the gloom of the unlighted living room. His face shone white. From outside, the scent of the wisteria along the side porch, in full summer flood, perfumed the air as if it were not alive with pain and awfulness.

"Bay," Mike whispered. "Help me. Tell him. I did the right thing; I tried . . . I wanted . . . tell him. And then let's go. Let's leave now."

She held out her hand. It felt impossibly heavy and tremulous, as if it balanced on the end of a thin wire yards long.

Bayard Sewell's face was a blanched mask in the dusk. He did not take her hand. He moved, one blind step, backwards and closer to John Winship. They stood together then, boy and man. He shook his head, back and forth, back and forth.

"I can't, Mike," he said. "I'm sorry. I can't."

She could scarcely hear him for the roaring in her ears. After a long moment that beat in the air like the concussion of thunder, she said mildly, "Well, that's all right, then."

She walked past the two of them, standing there on Claudia's cherished Bokhara rug. Past Priss Comfort, slumped in the wing chair, staring straight ahead of her. Upstairs to her room, and closed the door behind her. She did not lock it.

The next morning, before five, she took one suitcase full of clothes and the thousand dollars in the duck bank and caught the first morning bus to Atlanta. There were few people on it: workers on the early shift at the Ford assembly plant in Hapeville and one or two black women in maids' uniforms; no one she knew. She got a room at a Methodist Church home for bachelor girls near the art museum that she had seen before, and went the same day to register for her fall classes at the Atlanta Division of the University of Georgia. She paid her fees in cash. She did not contact anyone in Lytton, and she did not think they would come looking for her. She had moved outside the common kind. She did not think at all.

NINE

The morning after she registered for her fall classes, Mike took a city bus and went downtown to the main branch of the Carnegie Library. Walking into its somnolent green, cool dimness after the murderous white glare of the pavement was like slipping soundlessly into a cathedral, and she breathed fully and gratefully for the first time in two days and let herself sink, spinning slowly, into its cloistered hush. She went down the dingy stone steps to the basement, where the magazine and newspaper reference copies were kept, and ordered up everything she could find about the Civil Rights Movement in the years of its ascendancy. The Atlanta main library was a far richer trove than that in Lytton; it took Mike three full days to move from the movement's infancy to its fevered present. She read slowly, from midmorning until late afternoon, as absorbed as she had been in the distant, underwater summer when she had holed up on the side porch of the Pomeroy Street house and read *War and Peace* straight through, and when she was done with her day's reading and her spare Walgreen's supper, she went back to her cubicle in the church's home and stretched out on her single bed in the wash of the small fan she had bought and went immediately and dreamlessly to sleep.

When she reached the coverage of the previous week and the sit-in at JoJo's Restaurant, she read it with no more and no less detached interest and absorption than she had the rest of the material she had ordered. It seemed no more real than the slick paper of that week's *Time.*

On her way home from the library the last day, Mike took a shortcut through the basement of Kresge's Five and Ten Cent Store, and found herself drawn up in front of a display of billfolds. She was riveted to one, a lurid pink plastic item embossed in a snakeskin pattern, and all of a sudden wanted it as simply and totally as she wanted sleep and food. She opened and examined it. Its photo section had glossy, preening head shots of Rock Hudson and Doris Day and Anita Ekberg, and a group shot of the Cleaver family, with the Beaver twinkling impishly in front of his parents and brother Wally. She bought the billfold out of her day's allotment from the duck bank, which left her nothing for supper, but she was not hungry. She fidgeted impatiently on the bus until she reached her stop, and ran in the long, hot twilight across the street and into the church's home and up the diarrhea-brown stairs to her room, and dropped her purchase on the bed. Methodically, she switched the contents of her own wallet, a supple burgundy calfskin Priss had given her at Christmas, into the new flamingo-colored one, and threw the old wallet into the green tin trash can. She threw the photographs of her father and DeeDee and Bayard Sewell after it. In their places she put Rock and Doris and Anita and the Cleaver family.

The next morning, in the same five-and-dime store, she bought a money belt that fitted around her waist under her clothes, and after that she wore her eight-hundred-odd dollars against her sharpening ribs, even on the hottest days. They were as comforting there as the clasp of a parent or a lover.

After she had been in the church's home for a week, Mike had a dream. She dreamed that she stood on a wooden dock reaching out into a blue mountain lake, much like one she remembered from a trip she and DeeDee had made with John Winship up to Lake Burton in the north Georgia mountains, when she was very small. In a wooden rowboat tethered by a rope to a cleat in the dock were her father and sister, Bayard Sewell, Priss Comfort, Rusky, and a beautiful woman in dripping wet clothes whom she knew somehow to be her mother, Claudia. They smiled and beckoned to her, and she ran eagerly toward them at the edge of the dock. It did not strike her as odd that in the dream they were the ages they were in life, or would have been, while she was still a small child. Looking down, she could see the tiny, stubby white sandals on her feet and thin white socks with flowers embroidered on their cuffs that she remembered from a photograph of her fourth birthday. She skipped and capered with joy and held out her hands to meet their outstretched ones, in the gently bobbing boat.

But when she reached the edge of the dock and should have

stepped into the boat, she stooped instead to the cleat around which the rope was knotted and deftly unlooped it. In an instant, the boat and the people in it slid swiftly away from the dock and out into the lake, with the telescoping rapidity of dreams, and soon were mere specks in all the dancing, sun-struck blue. She could still see their arms waving to her long after their faces were too small to distinguish. In her dream she smiled and smiled, but when she awoke, sitting soaked with sweat and bolt upright in the pale light from the streetlight outside, there were tears running down her face and into the corner of her mouth. She wiped them away and got up and padded down the hall to the big communal bathroom, and splashed her face, and brushed her teeth, and went back to bed and to sleep.

She did not cry again for many years.

For the next week or so, she spent her mornings in the downtown library, and in the afternoon she read library books in her room, or went to a rare movie. Sometimes she went to nearby Piedmont Park and sat in a swing and looked out over the dirty little lake. She seemed to live on a peaceful plain, walled away by mountains of heat and distance and the simmering city from the barely remembered fear and pain of the last day in Lytton. She was careful with the money in the belt, eating in drugstores and cafeterias, for she knew that when it was gone she would have to find another way to finish her education. She cared about only that, and about leaving the South.

And she cared about the Civil Rights Movement. In those long, hot days it bloomed like a firestorm until it filled her entire consciousness, and she followed it obsessively in the newspapers and on the flickering black-and-white television set in the home's scanty parlor. In this she might have been invisible, a ghost, for the other girls in the home who gathered to watch television did not seem to notice the flying shadow images of marchers and crowds and sometimes dogs and firehoses, did not seem to hear the endless, ageless choruses of "We Shall Overcome" and the guttural flatulence of mob anger. Mostly, they waited for the news to be over so they could tune in *Gunsmoke.* Something in the pulsing images spoke to Mike of a feeling she had first had in the jail in Atlanta, after the sit-in and her arrest, a new and slyly pervasive emotion that seemed to be forged and born out of the fear and outrage and simple astonishment of that night: a ringing and clarion sense of fellowship, an almost martial camaraderie. Somewhere in those ghost dances on the church home's old GE console was, for Mike, a place of her own.

It was always the glamour of the movement, this demon charm of belonging, of kinship; the morality of the thing was self-evident and powerful, and the politics of it seductive, but it was the comrades-at-arms ties of danger and youth and violence, the sheer young animal strength of revolution, the frankly sexual excitement of riding a great hinge of history, that gave the Civil Rights Movement in the South its irresistible dark allure. When the Council of Federated Organizations sent the first busload of white college students rolling south into Mississippi that summer, Mike felt an abrupt, warm melting of the aspic that had held her immobile for weeks. She lifted her head and looked around her in the home's parlor. One girl, a thin, intense, homely redhead from New Jersey who lived down the hall from Mike, lifted her own head and met Mike's eyes. Mike got up off the Naugahyde sofa and sat down in a butterfly chair beside the girl. The next morning, they left Atlanta in the redhead's car and drove south and west, through Alabama toward Mississippi and Freedom Summer.

They caught up with the buses in Hattiesburg, where nothing much at all seemed to be happening. They encountered no guns, dogs, firehoses, angry mobs, Ku Klux Klansmen. What they did encounter was a wet, relentless, juggernaut heat, a vast and feral army of mosquitoes, and empty, sleepy, one-gas-pump towns where they alit stickily from the buses long after dark and trudged wearily into identical rural Negro shanties at the end of dirt roads in cotton fields and pastures, to sleep on pallets and quilts in the endless heat, wash at hand pumps, use privies, and eat greens and grits and pork gravy for days on end. To Mike, who had done the same thing on countless nights in Rusky and J.W.'s cabin back in Lytton—eaten the same food, smelled the same ashen smell—there was nothing remarkable at all about these thick, rank Mississippi nights, and she felt a small, flat itch to get on to the real business at hand, which she assumed to be the much-anticipated guns, dogs, and firehoses. But she stifled her impatience out of natural politeness and a desire not to spoil her compatriots' excitement. For they, most of them Northerners, were riding an incandescent crest of ebullience and nervy exhilaration, and she realized that to them, the miserable cabins of the silent, deferential Negroes were exotica of the highest order.

Oh, well, Mike thought, surely we'll get into it by Greenville.

And she sang with the others on the bus, "Yes, we are the Freedom Riders and we ride a long Greyhound, white or black, we know no difference, Lord, for we are glory bound," and she railed and howled with the others when the bodies of the three missing Summer Project workers were found buried in an earthen dam near Philadelphia, Mississippi, but still she saw, firsthand, none of the moral combat she had come seeking.

"Just wait till Greenville," the older heads on the bus counseled.

But she never made Greenville; never made even the edge of the vast, fecund, and dangerous Delta. For on her bus was a saturnine young man from Fairfax County, Connecticut, named Richard Singer, a young Jew of a certain melancholy beauty and mordant wit, between quarters at Harvard Law School. He was struck and held, as were many of the young Northerners on the bus, by the flame that seemed to dance around the slender, ash-gilt girl from the Deep South (for the great and electric sense of belonging and imminent peril and high resolve had lit in Mike the old, dead fire of her father, and she burned steadily in that dangerous air), and her conviction excited him as perversely as if she had been a spy against her own country, working deep behind enemy lines. Richard Singer was, in truth, a hopeless and untried romantic beneath the cultivated cynicism.

As for Mike, she found this lounging, sardonic Ivy Leaguer as unlike her father, or Bayard Sewell, or any other man that she had ever known, as an entirely new species. And in the hot, endless, identical nights, under the twin urgings of danger and proximity, she found that she wanted very much indeed to go to bed with him, and one evening outside Dooleyville, Mississippi, a scant fifty miles from the poisoned grail of the Delta, did just that, in a shed shared by a homemade tractor and a couple of roosting Dominecker hens, with a steaming, inexorable rain pounding dully on the corrugated tin roof.

To her vast surprise and pleasure, the earth did move, as it had for Robert Jordan and Maria, a circumstance that she had never imagined might occur with anyone other than Bayard Sewell. It was her first time, and she had thought it would hurt, would revolt her, until, as DeeDee had said, she had gotten used to it. When it did not, when it set her to moaning, and then thrashing, and then crying out in sweating release, she concluded that she was in love with Richard Singer. And although he would have died rather than admit to her or anyone else that it was his first time too, Richard Singer, out of relief and gratitude and infatuation and a certain goatish bravado, as well as a practical desire to make his first class of the fall quarter in Cambridge, asked her to marry him.

And she did, two days later in Winona, Mississippi, during the last week in August, with the redhead from New Jersey and a fat divinity student from Yale who kept saying, "Right on, man," as attendants. The stained, indifferent justice of the peace never introduced himself. A year later, neither Mike nor Richard could remember any of the names of the wedding party. Just before she said "I do," and became Mrs. Richard Isaac Singer III, Mike remembered the flicker of wetness in her father's eyes at DeeDee's wedding, and thought, I wish you could see me now, Daddy. You'd really have something to cry about. But never during the entire mumbled ceremony did she think of Bayard Sewell. When they went east and north the day after the wedding to meet Richard's parents in Connecticut and find lodgings in Cambridge, it was for good. Mike Winship did not go home again.

TEN

After that, her life swept like a locomotive down the track she had imagined for it, except that the man at her side was not Bayard Sewell. Mike was not unhappy. She was not recklessly, suffocatingly happy as she had been in the spring days in Lytton before the sit-in, but she was endlessly absorbed, engaged, interested. What pain she might have felt was driven deep under by the weight of sheer novelty. Every pore seemed opened to new stimuli, new information, new potential. Her horizons, laid down long ago in the microscopic universe of Lytton, sped away from her with the speed of light. Sometimes she felt herself to be a simple machine engaged solely in the receiving and processing of information. Her mind hummed with newness in the crispening fall days; in the nights, in the tiny apartment in Cambridge, after she and Richard had made love, her body thrummed with it. She did not stop to analyze all she was taking in, she only assimilated. Sometimes she did not even do that, only registered, filed away for future reference, raised her head for more. Somewhere at the barricaded rear of her mind, a small, stabbing voice that was not her voice said, "Do not stop. Do not look back. Do not think, not yet, not for a long time. Do not open doors."

Richard Singer's well-to-do parents were dismayed when their new daughter-in-law proved to be both a Gentile and a Southerner, and they mourned the lost wedding and country-club reception, but at least Mike was not pregnant and was presentable and reputedly of good enough family, and they were quick to realize that if they did not accept her, they would lose their lone princeling for good. There was a certain glamour and gallantry about Mike's circumstances, too, that appealed to their untested liberal sensibilities almost as strongly as they had to Richard's, who giddily believed that he had rescued with marriage a new kind of folk heroine. In his uncluttered mind, Mike was an aristocratic flower of a corrupt and dying old South who had rebelled against that decadent Arcadia's monstrous prejudices and been martyred for it. Had not her cruel and arrogant landed father cast her out without a penny to her name? Had he not deprived her of the family plantation that was her birthright? Had he not forbidden her her ancestral home for all time? Richard had been given *Uncle Tom's Cabin* at his Bar Mitzvah by a sentimental uncle who had spent several miserable years in Richmond, and it had had a profound influence on his life. Nothing he had seen in his short sojourn into Mississippi with the Freedom Riders had disabused him of the gothic impression he had garnered from the book.

Like many eastern liberals and self-proclaimed intellectuals of the time, the Singers and their son were unable to see the South and Southerners in more than one dimension. That the overbearing, patrician lawyer with his vast, sullied acreage was in truth a bitter, bereft, and frightened small-town attorney with a seared heart and stunted vision, one scrabbling generation away from a two-mule tenant farm, was beyond their ken. To her credit, Mike had never advanced this fiction, and was genuinely puzzled that she could not part her new family from it. Neither had she told them that John Winship had forbidden her to return home, for in truth, he had not. But she had not told them another and more stinging truth, either ... that his message to her when she called home to tell him she was married and living in Cambridge, delivered by a seemingly perennially tearful DeeDee, was, "Don't bring that Jew down here." At the words, a great lassitude took her, drowning for the moment the bubbling spring of her peripatetic energy. It seemed simpler to let the Singers believe what they pleased.

Mike did not speak of her family in Lytton after that phone call. Thinking the hurt of estrangement too deep for words, the Singers tactfully dropped the subject. The truth was that Mike had finally put the last shards of Lytton, and everyone in it, away in fatigue and lost interest. Dutiful letters from DeeDee and one or two subdued notes from Priss that mentioned nothing of the Winships or Bayard Sewell were her only links to the South. Somehow the newspaper accounts of riots and burning and beatings, of dogs and bombs and bullets, seemed to have to do with another country than the one she had left. The Civil Rights Movement boiled and eddied around Lytton, she knew, but the town stood silent and dreaming in Mike's mind, when she thought of it, like a sunstruck rock in a rapid. Mike thought of it seldom and then briefly.

It was in one of DeeDee's letters that she learned that Bayard Sewell had entered the University of Georgia in Athens, and that John Winship was paying his way through. She did not answer the letter, and she did not keep it.

As if in recompense for her suffering and deprivation, the Singers offered to pay Mike's tuition at Radcliffe until Richard graduated from Harvard Law, and she accepted simply and gratefully. After he graduated from Harvard, predictably with honors, Richard joined a struggling young firm in lower Manhattan specializing in legal aid cases, and they moved into a two-room apartment near Third Avenue, on 18th Street. Mike loved the grimy, throbbing city on sight, loved its energy and staggering variety and pragmatic meanness with a fierce and joyous answering affirmation. Most of all, she loved the sheer un-Southernness of it. It was one love affair that never faded.

She transferred to Columbia that summer, studying endlessly on the subway uptown and back, studying late into the blaring nights, when Richard was away at meetings and on difficult cases, as he often was. Sometimes in those headlong days and weeks they met only in the king-size bed that filled the whole of their tiny dark bedroom, so that the telephone sat underneath it and their clothes hung in a Sears cardboard armoire in the living room. She would raise her head from her arm, where it had fallen when the type in her textbooks had blurred and melted away like rain on a cold windowpane, and would hold out her arms to him, and they would make urgent and sweating love on the rumpled sheets that Mike would have forgotten to change for the third week on end. Often they did not speak, only moaned and gasped and cried out their climax and then fell into sleep with the overhead light still on, and sometimes, on weekends, they stayed in bed all of one and frequently both days, eating, sleeping, and copulating. Mike was on the pill, but still, she thought privately that it was a wonder she had not gotten pregnant almost instantaneously.

"All we ever do is eat and sleep and fuck like minks," she said to Richard once.

"What else is there?" he replied.

"What else, indeed," Mike said, and realized that for the moment it was true. Her studies never bored her, and neither did their lovemaking. If she never felt for him the helpless and liquid rush of wanting that had taken her almost every time she had looked at Bayard Sewell, she nevertheless responded quickly and ravenously whenever Richard entered her, and came explosively.

A mink is right, she thought, not without a certain self-satisfaction.

She graduated magna cum laude in journalism in 1968, and was hired almost immediately as a research assistant for a weekly newsmagazine, and by the time their daughter Rachel was born in 1974, when Mike was 28, she had had five years of relentless, single-minded work at her career as a free-lance journalist, and small plum assignments were beginning to come in.

Mike was slowly making a name as a chronicler of individuals caught in the mass shoals of contemporary conflicts . . . the faltering movement that had so drawn her, flailing and falling to earth by now like a wounded bird; the spiraling protests against the Vietnamese war on college campuses; the volatile political conventions; the groundswell of environmental concern. Her eye for searching out precisely the right face and voice to epitomize these issues was keen. But sometimes she would look at her own face in the mirror before a predawn taxi blared outside, or in the black glass of a jetport hung somewhere in an American night, and she would not recognize the pale, sharpened woman who looked back at her. And sometimes she would suddenly see Richard's face, frozen for a moment in conversation across a room at a client party, or intent on one of the glossy arts magazines he had taken to bringing home, and she would wonder when it had become so bursting, so suffused with sureness and self-congratulation, so beamishly ingratiating to all those people whose names she could not remember, to whose parties they were always going. Mike thought of them as the Other People. They had appeared about the time that Richard had left the small firm and joined a larger corporate law firm in midtown, a year or so before the baby came.

"Oh, yes, the writer," they said to Mike when they met in yet another Upper East Side twilight, over wine. They looked glossy, expensive, finished, nothing like the friends Mike and Richard had made in the 18th Street days, or the editors and photographers and fellow writers who inhabited her workday world. The Other People looked important. Richard, she realized in surprise, looked like them. Mike herself, even though she dressed each morning in good, if hastily chosen, clothes and left an apartment in the East Sixties much like those of the Other People, did not.

"Interesting," Richard said once, in the middle of the Other People's tenure, turning his head this way and that to regard her much as he did the postmodern paintings he was beginning to collect. He was trying to persuade her to buy some new clothes and go to Kenneth's.

"Intriguing," he went on judiciously. "Distinctive. But not distinguished. There's a difference. With a little effort you could be a memorable woman. Far better than pretty. But you don't do anything with yourself. You haven't changed your look since I met you."

"I thought you liked my look . . . whatever it is," Mike said.

"I liked it when you were a girl. You're a woman now."

"I don't have time for all that stuff, Richard," Mike said. But she pushed at her silky flyaway hair. It had long since grown out of its shag, and she had been tying it back in a ponytail with yarn. She had worn it that way on the bus in Mississippi, she remembered.

When the baby came, Richard hired a nurse and a housekeeper, both from an impeccable agency, and then Mike did have time. She had promised him she would stay home with Rachel for at least three years, and with no excuses left and few maternal or household duties, she did at least go shopping and have her hair done, and went to galleries and openings and lunches. And hated it.

In two years she was back at her assignments, with Richard's protests ringing in her ears and guilt eating at her heart, but small Rachel was thriving with her nanny and her play group, and soon Mike's momentum was snowballing again.

When Rachel was five and she was thirty-two, in 1979, she lifted her head from her typewriter to hear a perfectly tailored and not-quite-corpulent Richard announce that he was leaving and taking his library and records, his wardrobe and Porsche, his antique pillbox collection and his postmodern paintings, and moving in with a twenty-three-year-old MBA from Wharton named Tracy . . . one of the newest of the Other People . . . and his attorney would be in touch to talk about provisions for Rachel.

"I'm not going to try for custody, Micah," he said, "because I think she's too young to be uprooted. But you watch your step. I don't like your work or your hours or all your traveling or your housekeeping—or lack of it—and I don't like the lunatic fringe you run around with. You're a totally unfit wife and I could call you an unfit mother without stretching it too far, and you better believe I could make it stick. I'll be watching you. I won't have my daughter growing up to be some wild-haired international hippie who never bathes or shaves her legs. I won't have her making bombs or throwing them, or carrying signs in the streets about them. I won't have her screwing on mattresses in fucking communes in fucking Spanish Harlem."

"Would a chaise overlooking the park be better? With a little plastic Harvard MBA?" Mike retorted. "I won't have her growing up to be some . . . varnished little consuming machine in designer jeans." But she was frightened. Could he really take Rachel? Would he? She knew that he could, and would, if he chose. But he duly moved out and into a co-op on the park with the wellborn and cool-mouthed Tracy, and time passed, and he made no move to do so, and she gradually relaxed and felt control and assurance slip back.

For the next seven years she and Rachel lived existentially and at top speed and, Mike thought, happily, in the spacious, sunny, only slightly shabby apartment she found in the Village. Mike dismissed the nanny and the housekeeper, who wouldn't travel below Grand Central in any event, and found a neighborhood day-care cooperative for Rachel, put her in a public school, engaged a warm, sprawling Costa Rican widow in the building to stay over when she was away on assignment, organized a stimulating routine of museums, exhibits, and performances for Rachel's after-school and weekend hours (for she was adamant about her daughter's taking advantage of the city's incomparable resources), and plunged back into her throng of faces in crisis. Presently Richard shed his aging MBA and moved to Los Angeles to practice celebrity management and entertainment law and scatter Rachel with biweekly showers of stardust. Reserved and equable Rachel appeared to take them in stride, saving her sedate small passions for the eastern, urban largesse all around her; like Mike, and to her gratification, the spell of Manhattan held Rachel safely in thrall.

Mike found a pleasant and honorable succession of lovers with whom assorted beds, if not the earth, moved regularly, the last and most permanent, as well as spectacular, being Derek Blessing, and pursued her work with all the channeled velocity in her slender being. There was still little time for introspection, but Mike had jettisoned introspection when she left Lytton. She seldom looked back . . . not at Lytton, not at Bayard Sewell, not at Richard, never at John Winship. She juggled the shining balls of her life faultlessly. She invested no more of herself in her relationships than she could afford to lose. She rode her work intently, but lightly, and with skill and relish. She played all the skeins of her life with cool and expert hands.

And then came the lunatic week in May of her fortieth year, in which the glittering balls that Mike kept spinning so deftly spun into the sun and crashed to earth. A string of seven luminous, new green days in spring. One week—

It was like something out of a bad contemporary romance novel, the kind whose metallic, embossed mammarian covers irritated Mike in airports all over the country. Just home from a long assignment on a pioneer shelter and center for battered women in the Bay Area, Mike found a notice in her mailbox that the rent-controlled building in which she had lived for seven years was going co-op, and she had a month either to opt to buy or find another apartment. Buying was out; her income as a journalist had risen steadily with the increasing national assignments, but it was no match for the voracious maw that was life in New York. Checking in with the newsmagazine for which she had done most of her recent work, she learned to her shock and fury that the prized assignment that she would have undertaken that summer, a three-month stint in drought-stricken Africa with a legendary photographer, to be called "The Face of Famine," had gone to a very much younger, bitchier, and brilliantly gifted female journalist who had been sniffing obsequiously at Mike's heels for a couple of years. Her mentor, she had called Mike. Mike had contracted with a well-known publisher to expand the series into a book; it was an undisputed career maker, and she had long since spent the advance on summer camp and orthodontia for Rachel.

And then Rachel, whose capacity for conspicuous consumption

had risen dramatically along with the emergence of her budding breasts and elegantly lengthening legs, had calmly, even coldly, announced that she had decided to go and live with her father in Los Angeles.

Mike, reeling back in her mind over all the long years of her conscientious de-emphasis of the material, her careful attention to providing what she thought of as a "liberal humanist environment" for Rachel, could scarcely summon the breath to ask her daughter why. She knew, though, and damned Richard and his poisoned, shining letters.

"Because," said Rachel with stabbing betrayal, "I'm sick of living in a roach motel and never having anything decent to wear and going to school with half of Harlem and hanging around with all those stupid friends of yours with froozy hair and no makeup who pass out stuff about the stupid nuclear winter in stupid Washington Square."

It was an astonishing speech for normally sunny, unworldly Rachel, and Mike, looking at the belligerent changeling in the bright, spacious, maybe a *little* shabby breakfast room of the Bleecker Street apartment, felt emptiness open hissingly behind her eyes. To her vast surprise, she discovered that what she wanted more than anything in the world to do was smack the elaborate condescension off Rachel's face, screech her fury at her ex-husband, and crush her daughter in her sheltering arms for perhaps ten years. But she had always scrupulously honored Rachel's opinions and decisions, and so in the dizzying space of three days she had packed up Rachel's childhood ("Don't bother about my clothes; I'll be getting all new things from Dad") and put her on a United flight to Los Angeles, first class, of course, courtesy Richard. When she got home from the airport, Mike had methodically put Rachel's denuded room in antiseptic order, firmly closed the door on it, and gone out for the early *Times,* to begin the search for a new apartment. She did not eat much for the next day or so, she slept little, and she did not cry.

And then, on the seventh morning, a letter had come from her sister DeeDee, married and still living in Lytton, Georgia, saying that their father, who had lived alone since Mike left home in 1964, was suffering from prostate cancer and needed full-time attendance. DeeDee had been having him for lunch and dinner most days since his retirement, but now her own mother-in-law, an Alzheimer victim whose demeanor was only slightly more unpleasant than it had been before her illness, had come to live with her and her husband, Duck, and she simply could not stay with their father herself or have him in her home. And there was no money, at least in DeeDee's family, and their father stubbornly refused to tap or even discuss his own bank account. Could Mike send money for a live-in companion or, failing that, come herself?

"I know you have your career and have not seen Daddy for all these years—and I'm not blaming you, Mikie, it was terrible, all that name calling and refusing to see your husband and baby—but he is such an old man, and so sick, and he asked for you. He really did, Mikie, believe it or not. This would just be till we could decide what to do. It really can't be for long. Eugene has some good ideas. I don't want to sound whiny, but you know I've never asked you for anything, and it has been terribly hard on me for a long time . . ."

Well, that's exactly how you do sound, Mike thought, and then was stricken with exasperated guilt. Her head began to pound mightily. DeeDee's letters always seemed to stink sweetly of reproach, and she seldom answered them. For her father she felt nothing but a great, flat calm.

"Later for you," she said aloud, and swept the letter and the disastrous week out of her mind, and went straight to her closet for her weekend tote and dashed out to catch the 2:10 to Bridgehampton, where Derek Blessing had answered the telephone in his carefully Spartan, much photographed beach house in Sagaponack, and said yes, he was just getting into the piece for *Rolling Stone,* but he'd try to be at the station to meet her, and if not, just to get a cab and he'd pay for it.

And then the spiraling terror had struck on the train just out of Hampton Bays, and now Mike lay in the flying green ocean light of Derek's Sagaponack bedroom, on the other side of a great chasm in time.

ELEVEN

When she finally finished talking there was a long silence. In it she could hear the weary hiss of the moribund ashes settling in the Swedish fireplace and the sodden snap of the wind-savaged American flag on the lower deck, which Derek was forever forgetting to take down in bad weather. Under that was the grumble-hushhh of the surf. It was quieter, farther away. Mike turned her head. From the look of the pale-lemon sunlight on the deck outside the sliding doors, she judged it must be close to midafternoon. She had talked for at least three hours, then. She stretched in the great bed. Her limbs were stiff; she must not have moved much during the time she was talking. Her muscles must have been clenched. She rolled her head on her heavy neck and felt Derek's forearm beneath it. She felt clean, hollowed, weak, so light that she might float up to the ceiling, except for the weight of the fur throw.

"Holy shit," Derek Blessing said softly at last. "Jesus Christ."

"You wanted history," Mike said, in a scratched and used voice. "You got history."

He pulled her close to him, so that her face was pressed against his ribs. He smelled of sweat under the still-damp velour sweat shirt; the room was uncomfortably hot now. Without being able to see anything but velour, deck, and sky, Mike knew that spring was back outside. Her own breasts and legs and torso were damp with sweat, and the roots of her hair were wet. Her mouth tasted foully of the long-ago champagne, a bottle of which swam tepidly, unopened, in the ice bucket on Derek's side of the bed. Her head should, by all rights, be hurting now as it always did after she drank champagne, but it did not. The cold, nauseating snake of the anxiety was gone, too; was not even dormant, was not there at all. Gratefully, on a rush of pure affection, Mike stretched out her chin and took a small nibble of the fabric of Derek's shirt, and he swept the dandelion hair off her face with uncharacteristic gentleness. The word "cherished" sprang from nowhere and hung, whole and glowing, in Mike's mind.

"I asked for history and I got tragedy," he said. "Goddamn, Mike. Nothing in Russian literature beats it. Faulkner couldn't have invented it. Aeschylus might have. My God. No wonder you had an anxiety attack on the train. It was the letter that did it, of course. The fucking old bastard . . . he as good as mortally injured you and put you out on an ice floe to die."

"Well, I didn't die, did I?" Mike replied, sitting up. The throw fell to her waist. Her bare breasts were lightly sheened with perspiration. He looked at her silently, a measuring and abstracted look that she had seen only once or twice before, when he had been working well on a novel.

"Why are you staring at me like that?" she asked, reaching for her sweater and skinning it over her head. "Anna Karenina I'm not. I can handle this now. I was never in serious trouble. All of it coming at once threw me, but now that I've talked it out . . ."

"But you haven't," Derek Blessing said, reaching for one of his cigarettes. "You haven't in the least talked it out."

"There's not a single thing left to tell. I've told you everything that happened from the time I was born up to now . . ."

"Except how you feel about it." He drew smoke deep into his lungs and sat up abruptly, throwing the fur on the polished floor. He crossed his legs and rested his forearms on them and looked at her, his face alight with intensity. A pulse hammered in the side of his throat.

"Well, of course, I felt pretty awful about it when it happened, but that didn't last long, and after that I truly forgot . . . It doesn't matter now. It hasn't mattered for years." Mike was defensive. She did not know what he wanted from her. The snake of anxiety stirred slightly, far down; it had not gone, then.

"Bullshit, you forgot. Bullshit, it doesn't matter. It doesn't matter so much you went bonkers on the two ten to Bridgehampton. We're only half done here, Mike. Now I want you to tell me exactly how you felt about it . . . all of it. The pain, the fear, the grief, the rage . . . Christ, the rage must have been *enormous*. You must have enough rage in you to move a continent. I want it all . . . and then we'll decide what you're going to do."

"I . . . do? What do you mean, do? I'm not going to do anything; if you think I'm going back there to that house and that town and that . . . you're as crazy as Annie. I'm going to stay in New York and get on with my life, that's what I'm going to do. Derek, really, I'm talked out. I can't talk anymore. I haven't talked about this for years and years. There's simply nothing more to tell you."

"Yes. There's more. There are worlds more. And you're going to tell me. We'll have some supper first, if you like, or better still, a drink. But you're not going to leave here till you tell me how you feel about it. Feel, not think. Don't you see? It's a matter of resolution. You've got a great story but no resolution. You can't possibly get on with anything until you've resolved this godawful business with your father."

"Why do you care?" Mike asked simply.

"Because I care about you and I want you whole," he said, just as simply, looking at her with opaque, preternaturally focused eyes. They gave his eroded face a look of great, reined energy. Mike felt again the weak, warm stinging of tears in her throat and nose.

"Okay," she said. "All right. I'll do my best. But you're going to have to let me stretch first, and give me something to eat."

"Deal," he said. "Just let me take a piss here, and I'll whomp us up something. What do you feel like? Junk or elegant? Junk, I think. Nachos and beer. And maybe after we're done talking I'll take you to Bobby Van's for pizza."

He got up and walked toward the bathroom, peeling off the velour sweat suit.

"I can think of one resolution that sounds good," she called after him, her voice trembling a little with the effrontery of what she was about to ask. Her heart started its slow, sick thudding again.

"And that is?" he said, disappearing into the bathroom. She heard the splashing into the lavatory bowl.

"I . . . thought I might sort of keep you company this summer. Maybe put most of my stuff in storage and just bring a few things, and go in once or twice a week to get my mail and look at apartments. I could do some research for you; I know you hate that." She could hear her voice going on and on and hated it, but could not seem to stop it. If she stopped, she would have to hear what he would reply.

"I'll do de cookin', honey, I'll pay de rent," she added, and fell silent with the awfulness of it. In the silence, the thought formed and hung, perfect and terrible: I don't have anywhere else to go.

Water splashed into the basin, and then it stopped, and she heard the shower go on. Perhaps he had not heard her. Relief swept her; please God, don't let him have heard me, she prayed.

"Doesn't sound like a bad idea," he called back over the shower's luxurious thunder, and her heart leaped up again, from the cold floor of her stomach to her throat. Lightness flooded her once more. Not to be alone . . . just not to be alone right now . . . For the first time in more than twenty years she felt giddy with the need to be with someone, giddy with the relief of that tidal need met.

She sprang up out of bed, stumbling a little on pinprickling feet, and stepped into her slacks and slid her feet into her moccasins. She walked to the mirror over his bureau and looked at her face, which looked pale and luminous; her fire was back. She grinned at herself. Picking up the ivory-backed brush that he had gotten in Kenya last summer, she attacked her matted hair until it stood out around her head like a nimbus, and swept the rough bristles lightly over her cheeks, and watched the sepia freckles fade under the quick wash of color. She felt suddenly silly and capricious and very young, and did a small, quick dance step on the little square of Navaho rug he had laid down in front of the bureau.

The room was really very hot. Mike walked around to his side of the bed and leaned down to turn off the electric heater. Her foot struck something just beneath the edge of the bed and sent it spinning across the glassy floor, where it came to rest against a leather rhinoceros stool from Abercrombie and Fitch. It was a tape recorder, the old Panasonic he had had ever since she had known him. It gave a click and sighing whirr, and her own voice came bleating out into the room at full volume.

"You wanted history, you got history."

"I asked for history and I got tragedy," Derek squalled from the injured recorder, and Mike got up and went over to it and pressed the stop button. She sat back down on the side of the bed. She stared stupidly at the recorder.

She became aware presently that he was standing in the door of the bathroom, a towel around his waist, looking dispassionately at her. One eyebrow was cocked up.

She looked at him silently.

"I guess I can assume that the famous block is about to break and you'll be starting a new book soon so you won't be wanting company after all," she said finally. Her ears and head rang mightily. The hateful buzzing started in her wrists.

He reddened slightly and grimaced.

"Christ, I hope you don't think I'd use that," he said. "I just thought you ought to have it on tape, use it for a therapeutic tool, like Annie does."

She kept on looking at him steadily.

"Matter of fact, the dam does feel like it's breaking, a little," he went on. "You know how I am when I'm working, Mike. Sure, you can come stay with me if you want to, but I'm such a single-minded son of a bitch when I'm going good; well, you know that. It'd be no fun for you at all. Look, why don't you go on home, do like Annie says, mend your fences with the old man, see your sister and your friends, renew old ties and all, get some perspective on things? It's a great solution for the next two or three months, till you can find a new place and I can sort of get . . . a leg up on things. Then, when you come back, we'll have the whole fall . . ."

"You are a sorry son of a bitch, Derek," Mike said. "But you write good books about women. I always wondered how you did that. There must be quite a little stable of us around here some-where, all on our own little tapes. Or is it floppy disks now? Well. Sorry to leave before the literary fete ends, but you've undoubtedly got enough to go on from here. I'm sure just the right resolution will present itself, when the time comes."

"Jesus, I always knew there was probably a world-class bitch somewhere under all that southern ladyhood . . ."

"Fuck off, Derek," Mike said.

She left Manhattan three days later on a late morning Delta flight for Atlanta, and as the L-1011 circled back out over the sandy hook of Long Island and the glittering sea off the Hamptons and turned to the South, she thought with a small, cold smile that she had had to take the jitney in from Sagaponack after all.

TWELVE

"Isn't the new airport something?" DeeDee said gaily. "I bet there's nothing like it in New York."

"There certainly isn't. It beats even London and Paris and Rome," Mike said, with an enthusiasm that she did not feel. She ached with sleeplessness and the physical effort to control the anxiety, and her wrinkled linen skirt and silk shirt were rapidly drying into corrugated ridges in the arctic breath of the big Pontiac's air conditioner. The temperature when they had come out of the Atlanta terminal was ninety-one degrees at 1:00 P.M. and climbing steadily, and she had been wet through her underclothes to her skin when they had finally gained the car, prudently parked in the airport's faraway economy lot.

DeeDee's eyes disappeared into the folds of flesh surrounding them as she squinted at Mike, and her small scarlet mouth tightened. She said nothing, but her silence rang in the stale, chill air. Mike knew she had affronted DeeDee with her talk of foreign airports; she had meant to offer her sister the gift of incomparability for her hometown, but she knew she had sounded as if she were place dropping.

"Not that I've seen much of those," she added, and felt the newly familiar stab of annoyance at herself and her sister. She had been placating DeeDee since her arrival and was not quite sure why. She had never done so before.

She looked at DeeDee again, the glance hidden behind large, shielding sunglasses. It was hard not to look at her. DeeDee was immense. She still looked out of the beautiful blue, black-fringed eyes that Mike remembered, but the rest of her face was a travesty of the pretty, rose-flushed young woman she had been when Mike went away; was at once comic and pitiful, like a child's scrawl of stolen cosmetics on a melting snow woman. The pink flush was now round circles of magenta blusher on the apple-knobbed mounds of her cheeks, and her delicate, small flower mouth had all but disappeared in the folds that ran down from her pert nose. That nose, once Mike's despair and envy, was almost porcine now in all that lapping flesh, and the skin itself was the peculiar grayish blue-white of old snow.

The face rode atop an amorphous body that hove from side to side as DeeDee walked. She wore a powder blue polyester pantsuit and chalk white beads that flew up and down on her bosom, the astounding cleavage of which reached nearly to the last of her chins, even in the modestly cut polyester shell sweater. Sweat and talcum and a transmuted perfume rose steamily from between the great white pontoon breasts. Only the tiny pattering feet in elaborately strapped white high-heeled sandals spoke of the real long-ago DeeDee. Those, and the glossy pile of blue-black hair that helmeted her head in an intricate, lacquered hive of puffs and knobs. Mike felt her heart twist with pity, revulsion, and guilt. Beside her own sharpened thinness, her sister must look downright grotesque. She was glad that there was no family resemblance between them; gladder for DeeDee's sake than for her own. She did not care what the hot, jostling throngs of people passing them might think. But DeeDee had always cared.

Under Mike's fatigue there was a dead spot, as if a great balloon had deflated and collapsed, puddling to earth in an inert rubber pond. She realized that she had, on some subterranean level, been anticipating the comfort of her big sister's arms, waiting for the bossy but soothing, fluttering ministrations she had not even consciously remembered from her childhood, but that were, nevertheless, there, under the years of annoyance at DeeDee's nattering letters from Lytton. That comfort, those ministrations, were not going to be extended. Ever since their first formal little hug in the airport lounge, DeeDee had been sniping at her. Tiny, silvery barbs about Mike's accent, her career, her "New Yorky" clothes and "exciting jet-set life" swarmed like gnats over their first minutes together. True, she had thanked Mike profusely, over and over, for coming home to "lend a hand," and she was elaborately solicitous about Mike's divorce and the task of raising a child alone in a city like Manhattan, which her tone left hanging, depraved and Babylonesque, in the air between them. And she was even more vocally worried about Mike's all-too-apparent anxiety, which manifested itself in shaking hands and rapid, shallow breathing. But when Mike stopped at an airport water fountain to take another Xanax, the small, cold flare of triumph in DeeDee's eyes was unmistakable. And her allusions to Mike's love life, as she phrased it archly, were heavily treacled with insinuation. Mike, knowing that DeeDee could not possibly have heard of Derek Blessing or the others before him, nevertheless found herself bridling as mulishly as she always had when DeeDee had pressed her for information she did not want to give.

"My love life is about as unspectacular as my career at the moment." She smiled, hoping wearily to propitiate her sister into silence. She wanted some time to deal with the loss of the phantom filial support she had not known she hoped for. She wanted time to assimilate this fat, officious, discontented stranger. Where was pretty, breathless DeeDee, who had taken her part and restored the waters of family serenity after Mike's extravagant childhood outbursts; who wrote so faithfully, if nigglingly, during Mike's long years away from Lytton? Not in this ballooned and banal middle-aged woman.

"I really do appreciate you coming home, Mikie," DeeDee said again from the backseat, where she had slipped as if it were her proper place, leaving Mike to slide onto the scorching gold vinyl of the front seat beside Duck. "I know it wasn't easy for you to get away. You must work all the time; we really are proud of you, even if we don't tell you so. I bet I've got everything you've ever written in scrapbooks. I thought you might like to have them some day; I know how bad you used to be about keeping your things straight."

She patted Mike awkwardly on the shoulder, and the young DeeDee was back again, fleetingly, in the touch. Mike turned and smiled at her.

"It's not that much of an imposition, Dee," she said. "Rachel's with her father this summer, and things are going to be slow for me until fall. If I was ever going to come, this is as good a time as any. And I'm glad if it will give you a breather. To tell you the truth, I really came because I'm hungry for some of your cooking."

I am not going to tell her I came because there was nowhere else for me to go, she thought. I am not going to tell her about the awful, ridiculous week my life blew up. There's a core of DeeDee in this woman somewhere, but there's somebody else in there who likes the smell of my blood too much.

Her sister laughed, the pretty chime that had always so captivated their father.

"Well, you'll have some of that soon enough," she said. "I've left a hen and some dressing for you and Daddy to have tonight. It's about all he seems to want anymore, chicken and that cornbread dressing Rusky taught me to make. You eat every bit of it, too. I can see your ribs clear through that shirt."

"That's not all *I* can see," Duck said, and poked Mike's thigh with a large red finger. Mike's face and chest flamed. She knew that the damp cream silk of her shirt was glued like tissue paper to the sheer scrap of bra, and that her nipples were standing out in the freezing blast from the air conditioner like bas reliefs on a frieze. She crossed her arms over her chest and looked straight ahead, saying nothing. He had not changed appreciably since she had last seen him, those twenty-odd years ago, except to acquire blinding white ersatz Gucci loafers and belt and a great paunch. His hair was as thick and pompadoured and pomaded as ever, the same tawny-blond pelt, crawling down his bursting neck now in sideburns, and his hooded eyes still roamed like spiders or the eye stalks of crabs. They played over Mike's body and then slid up to her face, and he smiled his famous one-sided smile.

The silence from the backseat bit like adders. Mike was glad of the Xanax calm that hummed in her head and idled softly in her pulse. She called up a skill that she had acquired through the days of tumult and sometimes even mild danger over the years, the days in Los Angeles and Chicago and other cities where the cusp of crisis had called her; she shut him as cleanly out of her mind as if she had sheared him away. She turned her head and looked out of the blue-tinted window at the countryside flying by. She had never liked Duck, not from the very first. But she had been somewhat comforted in the beginning by DeeDee's obvious adoration of him. Now, though, DeeDee did not look at Duck adoringly whenever he spoke, or reach out to touch him for no reason at all. She looked at him little, Mike had noticed, and touched him even less.

Neither would I, Mike thought with a shudder. It would be like touching a dead frog.

Unlike Duck Wingo, the landscape had changed. Whenever Mike had thought of the country of home, which she seldom did, the images that sprang to her mind were old, softened, sliding ones: hills like the curves of a woman's body melting into one another, blurred by the inevitable black-green pine forests; wave upon wave of tawny broom sedge; fields starred with Jimsonweed and black-berry tangles; white frame and asbestos-siding farmhouses slumping into the tired, soft-red earth of swept yards, surrounded by gently sagging barbed-wire fences and tippled outbuildings; weather-silvered corpses of unpainted Negro shanties; blurred piles of orange-rusted automobile carcasses in rutted side yards and blind-gaping white refrigerators on front porches; Jesus Saves and palm readers' and Burma-Shave signs; herds of rough-coated cattle all facing the same way under pecan and walnut trees; great, virulent green shrouds and seas of kudzu surging across entire fields and rights-of-way, engulfing abandoned houses and telephone poles and stands of spiky trees, so that entire acres of the earth became demented green sculpture gardens.

But the land outside the Pontiac's window now was a sharp-edged quadrilinear suburbanscape. They flashed past a white concrete shopping mall gleaming like a city of tombs in the savage light. Arrows of fire glanced from the roofs of thousands of automobiles lapping at its fringes. Across the new four-lane access road on which they had turned from the Interstate, a support mall, panting treeless in the heat, offered a Big Star and a Treasury Drug, tax services and real estate offices, a discount video warehouse, a Catholic church incongruously occupying a commercial building, and a small village of fast-food outlets. Mike counted Burger King, Arby's, McDonald's, Del Taco, Kentucky Fried Chicken, and Long John Silver's all within a few feet of each other. All except the Del Taco were doing a thriving late-lunch business; AMCs and bestial big-tired torpedoes crawling with spoilers and pickups with bumpers boasting I ♥ THAT COUNTRY SOUND and SUPPORT YOUR NRA were bellied up in sun-stunned parking lots. It might have been anywhere in the country; they were whirling through vistas that Mike had driven through in rental cars from airports in a dozen different cities across the United States. The alien terrain was made even more unsettlingly anonymous by the cold, ghostly blue of the glass she was looking through. It was impossible to tell even whether it was winter or summer, except for the showering fullness of foliage and something inexorable in the slant of the light.

"Hasn't Tex-Mex caught on down here?" she asked idly.

"Tex-Mex?" DeeDee said, puzzled.

"There weren't any cars back at that taco place," Mike said, wishing she had not started the conversation. Her fatigue was nearly paralytic.

"Oh, the Spanish place in the mall. No, Spanish is real popular around here. There are two places at home, a Taco Bell and a Mr. Tortilla. People don't go to that particular one because the manager is a queer and all the help he hires is the same way. There's been a good bit of trouble there . . . fights and things, and we hear he was involved in some kind of child molesting back wherever it was he came from. Nobody from home goes there."

"The gentrification of Lytton," Mike murmured under her breath. They did not seem to hear her.

They were passing through a vast, treeless plain in what Mike knew had once been an area of farms and small communities of white frame general-merchandise stores and gas pumps and a few three- or four-room houses, but now was an endless diorama of small, seared, shrubless brick and wrought-iron subdivisions and condominium villages, scanty office parks, and raw new freeway construction. Atlanta, to the north and east, had sprawled out over its borders to engulf everything in its path, as the kudzu once had.

Duck leaned far back in the driver's seat and gestured expansively at the featureless plain.

"The whole area's on fire," he said. "We're not the sleepy ol' South anymore, we're the Sunbelt, and a man smart enough to see which side his bread's buttered on is gon' be a rich man. Watch out, New York. You'll be eatin' our dust before long."

He elbowed Mike genially, and his thick fingers grazed her breast quickly and lightly, a touch like a reptile's tongue. She turned as if to study the burgeoning Sunbelt.

"Would that I were eating it now," she said, but she did not say it aloud. How did DeeDee bear this troglodyte?

There was another space of silence, and then DeeDee cleared her throat as if she were preparing to chair a meeting.

"There's something we need to tell you before we get home," she said. She hesitated, as if to select her words, and then went on, her voice picking up cadence until it reached a chirruping canter.

"It's likely to be just a tempest in a teapot, but Daddy is real upset about it, and nobody can calm him down. The state Department of Transportation wants to build an access loop through the old homeplace property, and it will mean tearing down the house and outbuildings. Daddy says he'll see them all in hell before he'll sell it; he says the rest of the property will lie there like a ripe peach for anybody who wants it, and he won't accept the DOT's offer for the buildings and the little bit of land they'll need for the road. We're real worried about him. So is Dr. Gaddis."

"What would anybody want with the land?" Mike said, genuinely puzzled. It was comely land, she remembered, sweetly canted and deep forested, having gone back to the wild when her grandparents could no longer farm it, but it was isolated, untouched by an egress and ingress except the seldom traveled, pitted, two-lane U.S. 29 and a few double-rutted farm and wagon tracks. No water, sewer, or gas lines ran near it.

"Oh, he thinks somebody might want to develop it or put a subdivision on it, or something," DeeDee said dismissingly. "He's really hipped on it. He's even hired a lawyer, if you can call him that; some upstart white trash from Birmingham, of all places, who hasn't been in town but a little while; hasn't even got furniture in his office yet. Daddy's going to fight the DOT tooth and nail. We're afraid it's just going to kill him."

There was another silence, and Mike realized that they expected her to make some comment. She did not know what they wanted to hear.

"Is it a good offer?" she said finally.

"*Real* good," Duck said. "Real generous, for the government. Land prices down here are starting to take off. Hell, John could open up that land, once that old eyesore is down and a good road's in there, and make himself a killin'."

"I don't guess he needs another killing," Mike said acidly. She did not care about the homeplace and had never understood her father's reverence for the land of his forebears, but she recoiled at the easy presumptuousness, the sheer venality, that lay beneath Duck's words.

"No," DeeDee murmured. "I guess that's one thing he doesn't need. Poor Daddy, he loves that silly old house and land. It's a shame. The damned state government, just grabbing whatever it wants, and from a sick old man . . . it makes me want to upchuck. It's not worth what Daddy's putting himself through, though. I wish he'd just go on and sell it so he could get it off his mind, before it kills him. He'd have close to a hundred acres left. It's not like he'll ever live in that awful old house, and I sure won't . . ."

She stopped and skewed her eyes at Mike.

"I hope you aren't going to feel bad about it," she said, not quite meeting Mike's eyes, "but Daddy has left that land to me. He knew you wouldn't . . . that you were taken care of, and your life was somewhere else . . ."

Where? Mike thought. Where is my life? Not where I thought. I guess I have an extremely portable life. The anxiety spurted from under the edges of the drug's blanket.

Aloud she said, quickly, "Oh, Dee, of course. You should have it. You've taken care of him all these years; you've been the one who stayed. I wouldn't have it on a bet. You're right, my life *is* somewhere else. Will you keep it . . . you know, when it comes to you?" She did not want to say "when he dies." She could, and did, talk about John Winship's eventual death easily and without appreciable feeling in New York; at that remove in time and space, he seemed almost a figure of legend, without substance, someone in a story told long ago, without the claim of blood. But she could not do it here, not to her sister, not in this projectile hurtling her toward the moment when the legend became clothed in decaying kindred flesh. No more than she could call him "Daddy" or "Father."

"I don't even like to think about that," DeeDee said. "I'd rather have Daddy alive and well than all the land in Georgia. But yes, I mean to keep it in the family, for Claudia and little John, because that's what Daddy wants. For me to keep the land, I mean. But that old house is different. The upkeep on it is just bleeding him dry; he can't find anybody to stay on the place; not even a Negro wants to do that. And of course, Daddy can't go down there every day like he used to, to see about it, and it's gotten to be a real mess. We've been trying real gently to get him to change his mind about selling it. For his own sake. But he gets so upset we don't talk about it anymore. Maybe he'll listen to you. We really need you on our side. Mikie, will you try and help us make him see reason?"

"What makes you think he'll listen to me?" Mike said. "I'll bet he'll throw me out of the house again if he can. Oh, of course, Dee, sure, if I can. I see what you mean. That house is a white elephant for everybody, I guess."

"Good girl," Duck boomed, moving to pat her again. She shrugged away from his hand and he dropped it. He beamed at her, ferally.

"This time the Yankees are in the fight with us," he said. "We can't lose."

"Don't bet on it," Mike said. "Does he even know for sure that I'm coming?"

"Oh, yeah." Duck nodded vigorously. "You bet he does. Looking forward to it. He asked for you when he first had the stroke, several times."

Mike lifted her head and looked at him, and then at her sister in the backseat. DeeDee flushed dark red.

"Stroke?" Mike said.

"It's not such a bad one," DeeDee said placatingly, her words tumbling over themselves. "He's a whole lot better now. He can move everything just like he always could, except for his legs, a little. He can talk as well as he ever could, and there's nothing but a little kind of drag to his mouth. You wouldn't even know he'd had it, Mike, except that he uses a wheelchair some, but that's mainly because he's weak from the chemotherapy, you know. His mind is as good as it ever was. Nothing wrong with his mind. Even better, *I* think. He's really feisty now, really sharp and snappy, and before he just kind of sat there all day looking off into space and not saying anything. We're going to help you find a nice, strong Negro girl to come and stay during the day and until after dinner, to do the lifting and heavy stuff, so you won't have to do anything except sort of keep the house running along . . ." Her momentum faltered and the stream of words pattered to a stop. She looked down at her hands and then out of the window.

"Dr. Gaddis stops by all the time, too," Duck said, catching up the flag where DeeDee had dropped it. "He says John's doing just fine, getting better every day. Be up and around before you know it. You won't be there by yourself with him hardly any at all. That lawyer of his is in and out all the time, and Ba—"

"Dr. Gaddis said to tell you *specifically* that there was nothing to worry about," DeeDee chimed in again hastily. "There's nothing wrong with Daddy that a little time and not worrying so much about that darned old house won't cure."

"Nothing wrong but cancer, you mean," Mike said levelly, looking at Duck and her sister. "Cancer and now a stroke. Why didn't you tell me about the stroke, DeeDee?"

"I was afraid you wouldn't come," her sister said, reddening again. "I was afraid you'd think he'd be too much for you, with a stroke on top of the cancer. But he truly isn't a burden, Mike, and he's not even in any pain to speak of from the cancer yet. Dr. Gaddis says that sometimes they aren't, even up to the end, and he's a long way from that yet."

"Yeah, he might even beat it, tough as he is," put in Duck. "Why, you wouldn't even know he had the cancer, and like DeeDee said, except for the wheelchair—"

"Are you sure he asked for me?" Mike broke in. She looked at DeeDee.

"Yes," DeeDee said. "He did." Her face was turned away.

Duck drove for a space in the silence that had fallen within the Pontiac's cold blue interior and then switched on the radio. Crystal Gayle wailed forth. Mike flinched, and Duck glanced at her under his plushy, veined lids (Mike had thought of him immediately when she had studied nictitating reptilian eyelids in high school biology, she remembered) and turned the volume down. They were silent again.

"Are you mad at us?" DeeDee asked presently. Her voice fluted like a child's, fearful of reprimand.

"No," Mike said. "But you should have told me about the stroke."

"We should have, you're right," DeeDee said sweetly. "I'm glad you're not mad. You used to have an awful temper. I just didn't feel like I could go through one of your spells right now."

"I haven't had a spell, as you put it, since I left here," Mike said waspishly. "I can't afford temperament in my work. You can take that off your list of burdens, Dee."

"Well, you don't need to snap," Dee said tightly. It was a tone that reverberated with porcelain clarity in Mike's mind. So did her own. DeeDee's persimmony sufferance rang through their child-hood, as did her own irritable response to it. She could not remember snapping at anyone in all of her adulthood. Even during the worst of the battles with Richard, even during crises with temperamental cameramen and stupidly obstinate minor officials, even in those last charring moments of betrayal with Derek Blessing, Mike had not niggled or carped. She had either retreated into icy calm or, far more rarely, shouted. She prized her professionalism second only to Rachel. Her reputation for calm and absence of temperament were near legendary in a field ripe with swollen, glistening egos.

I sound like a bratty thirteen-year-old, she thought. I'll be damned if I'll turn into one just because I'm back at home.

"No snapping," she said. "Truce. I'll treat you like an adult if you'll treat me like one."

DeeDee smiled, mollified. Mike thought, unkindly, that in her vast petal blue and white, with the small, curly smile wreathing her stretched shiny pink face, her sister looked like something in Macy's Thanksgiving Day parade.

They turned off the access road and onto old Highway 29, the doughty, potholed old blacktop paralleling the Atlanta and West Point Rail Road tracks that had been the only link with the world beyond Lytton when Mike had left. Immediately the countryside sprang back into another South, one of fierce, eroded red-clay banks and sharp green second-growth pines; asbestos-shingled drive-ins selling Dr. Pepper and filling stations advertising red wigglers and tackle; sun-baked automobile lots running heavily to pickups and Kubota tractors. Mike knew it was the road to Lytton, but she could not place where they were on it. No familiar landmark loomed. They might have been in Alabama, Mississippi, North or South Carolina, Louisiana. They could not, however, have been anywhere but the Deep South. Mike could not explain this sharp particularity of place, but knew it to be true. Her journalist's mind began to worry the concept and then dropped it, seeming to lose the sense of it in a dense, soundless blanket of fog. She realized that she could not think clearly. She realized also that she could not seem to feel.

I must be feeling something, she thought. If ever a situation was ripe for feeling, this has to be it. Coming back to all this, after all this time, after all that happened . . . My mind ought to be like some kind of chemical experiment with a cap on it, smoke and vapors roiling around like mad in there. But nothing seems to register. How *do* I feel?

She made a heroic effort to peer into herself, past the Xanax.

Anger? Surely, there must be anger in there. Long-festered anger at her father, anger at Priss Comfort; fresh anger at her editor, her landlord, at Richard, at Rachel; anger at Derek Blessing . . . Annie Cochran had said when she wrote the prescription for the Xanax pills that they were for short-term help only, that Mike needed to face her anger. Derek had said that there must be enough anger in her to power a continent. A normal person, then, would be feeling anger now. But she could detect nothing in herself except a rather perfunctory annoyance at DeeDee and Duck and a profound wish to be asleep, unconscious. Could you be angry, really angry, and truly not feel it?

Fear crawled again, and she rubbed wet palms together. Was that what it was about, then, this crippling fear that had dogged her for the past several days? Anger? Was she afraid on some deep level that this homecoming, this meeting with her father, would activate a savage, long-denied rage that would boil free and . . . what? Cause her to shriek? Weep? Do violence? The very notion of these was too absurd even to entertain. Mike Winship did none of these things, had not, in memory, done them. She could not imagine ever doing them.

Pain, perhaps, then. Fear of those near-mortal, long-ago losses finally welling up from their ice crypt and overwhelming her; fear of coming home to this place that had dealt her so much anguish? Fear of what this terrible, sunlit world might do to her again?

Mike was not accustomed to looking into herself. She had, instead, fine-tuned her ability to read other faces, other minds and hearts. She had always taken a workmanlike pride in the detachment and perceptivity that this skill demanded. Now, in herself, she met nothing but the stale, faintly nauseous calm of the drug and beneath it, far beneath it, the leaping, impersonal viper tongues of the fear.

She closed her eyes and rubbed them hard with her forefingers, concentrating on the wheeling aurora borealis of dull red and flaring white against the blackness. She wished she could take another tranquilizer. She would do so the minute they got home . . .

"Well, here we are," DeeDee said. "Welcome home, prodigal daughter," Duck Wingo said. Mike opened her eyes and looked at Lytton.

At first glance it did not seem to have changed, sleeping in the spell of the early June sun. The stark, shadowless play of light on the red-brick store facades might have lanced out of another sky, a decades-old sky. The twin brick freight depots beside the railroad tracks, the phallic white thrust of the World War I monument, the beetling, lopsided old cedar with the wounded gap where the power lines went through, which had served through her childhood as a municipal Christmas tree, stood wavering with heat beside the highway that became, for the space of three blocks, Lytton's main street. Taller buildings and new, alien shapes registered dimly in her sight then, and she got an impression of many more cars; of unremembered bustle and density on the sidewalks; of glass and plastic and neon and smart wrought iron where once there had been only dingy red or cream brick and tin awnings. But the essential Lyttonness of it was the first thing that struck her. In some indefinable way it had not changed; would not change, perhaps could not change. She would have known where she was if she and the town had been set down, unwarned, in the middle of Ohio or Kuala Lumpur. Duck slowed the Pontiac to a crawl, grinning broadly at her, and Mike stared at Lytton sliding by.

"Well, what do you think of it?" DeeDee caroled, leaning on the front seat. "You wouldn't even know it was the same place, would you? How does it feel, Mikie, after all these years?"

"It feels like I've always known about it but never seen it," Mike said. "It feels like I've heard stories about it all my life, but never visited it before now. Or like something in an old children's book. Somehow it doesn't seem real."

"Well, it may not be Paris or Rome or London, but we like it and it sure is real." DeeDee sniffed, choosing to be offended. "I sure hope home is a little realer to you, because it's right over there behind the church and the post office. If you remember those."

"I remember," Mike said.

Passing the old gray stone Methodist church where they had always gone on Sundays and sometimes on Wednesday nights, DeeDee said, "By the way, Mikie, what does Rachel look like?"

"Rachel?" Mike was startled out of her reverie. Aside from a perfunctory tongue-clicking at Rachel's fatherlessness and urbanized state when they first met at the airport, DeeDee had shown little interest in her niece and had said only, when Mike had asked about her son John and her daughter, both now grown, or nearly: "Oh, they're just grand. I'll fill you in about them later, when we can sit down and have a regular old heart-to-heart."

"Rachel," DeeDee said again now with elaborate patience. "Daddy keeps asking."

"Daddy asks about Rachel? What she looks like?" Mike realized she sounded stupid. The question was totally unexpected; John Winship had announced at her daughter's birth, and DeeDee had relayed the proclamation, that Mike was to bring no little Jew child or big Jew husband home to Lytton while he lived. Mike had buried the comment deep, in the ice crypt with the rest of that time; she had not thought of it until now. The fact that Rachel was John Winship's granddaughter had not occurred to her since the day of the child's birth.

"Several times," DeeDee said. "Right after I told him you were coming, and again just last night. I had to tell him I didn't know; you haven't sent any pictures in years and years, you know. Anybody'd think you were ashamed of her."

Mike did feel anger, then; a smoking curl of it, but it was not directed at her father. She felt a sudden, bright rage at DeeDee, at the utter banality and ordinariness of the unmistakable barb. DeeDee sounded like any affronted aunt whose beloved niece has been somehow withheld willfully from the benison of her attention and affection. The old irritation leaped and bloomed.

"Rachel looks like any little New York Jew, which is just what she is," she said to her sister. "She has kinky hair and a nose just like Barbara Streisand. We hope she's going to make us all rich doing impersonations."

"Mikie! You don't mean that! The idea!" gasped DeeDee, truly shocked.

"Oh, yes, I do," Mike said silkily. "And you can tell him so for me. Too bad if he had his heart set on Brooke Shields."

I'm sorry, Rachel, she said silently to her daughter, who did, in fact, look unsettlingly like Brooke Shields. And then she shoved Rachel away, deeply, back into that ice crypt inside her, where the pain of her image did not threaten to blow her apart.

"You all stow that stuff, now," Duck said. "We're here."

Mike turned her head and looked through the blue glass and the endless years at the house on Pomeroy Street where she had been born.

THIRTEEN

When Mike was almost six and began Lytton Elementary School, she first heard the house on Pomeroy Street in which she lived called the Winship Mansion. This extraordinary appellation was offered to her by Fletcher Grubbs, ten years old, fat with the rubbery toughness of a squid, mean as a junkyard dog, and the undisputed dean of Miss Tommie Golightly's first grade.

The name was proffered with no more intent to flatter than that of "Princess Chickenhead," which was also the handiwork of Fletcher Grubbs, and seemed entirely appropriate for the downy-blond, wizened youngest inhabitant of that house. The jeering ring of seasoned elementary schoolers who had assembled to torment Mike cheered and laughed mightily at Fletcher's creativity, and Mike sailed without hesitation into the first fistfight of her educational career. She did not know what a mansion was, but she did comprehend chickenhead, and with an embattled wisdom far beyond her tender years determined that they were going to earn dearly their continued right to call her and her home by the new names. The same wisdom told her that she could not win the fights, and she was right, but she could and did give her tormentors a run for their money. Mike remained Princess Chickenhead until a palsied child from Valdosta moved to town and provided new fodder for nicknaming. The Pomeroy Street house remained the Winship Mansion to an entire generation of Lytton children.

The house was not a mansion, was not even particularly large, but it was possessed of a number of fanciful turrets and gables and ells and a great quantity of gingerbread, in the Victorian manner, and it sat far back in a dappled cave of overarching water oak trees. Great twin hydrangea bushes flanked the front porch, and the latticed side porches were hung with venerable, shaggy old wisteria vines, giving them in the late spring an incandescent lavender nimbus, a sort of enchanted purple milieu. All these embellishments, plus the trimness of the lawn and shrubbery . . . the handiwork of tyrannical, shuffling old John, from Lightning . . . made the house seem far more imposing than it was; gave it presence, a kind of charisma.

There were not many Victorian structures in Lytton, not even many two-story residences. The town had not the distinction of being a real suburb of Atlanta, being too far away, and so there were few of the large homes one sees in all suburbs, and none of the really grand ones evident in some of them. Conversely, Lytton did not lie in deep agricultural country, either, so there were few vast gentlemen's farms and no surviving antebellum plantations. General Sherman had attended to what antebellum edifices there were around the little town, but in any case there had never been anything on the order of Tara or Twelve Oaks. One-story shotgun, or dogtrot, houses were the rule, painted white or sided in gray or pastel green asbestos shingles. The only two other genuinely Victorian structures in Mike's childhood were a shabby old behemoth in the center of town with, always, a yard full of mournful automobiles and a blue neon sign that said TOURISTS but that harbored only roomers, and the Reverend Ike Steed's funeral home. This latter was shingled in funereal gray and sported black shutters like grief-closed eyelids; it was born to be, and said to be, haunted.

So by default, the Winship house had become Lytton's unofficial "great house," and though Fletcher Grubbs and his followers had meant only to wound Mike with their taunts of "Winship Mansion," she secretly relished the name, and felt, sailing into each defensive fistfight, that she was protecting the escutcheon of a grand and honored family seat. Privately, she came to love being Princess Chickenhead of the Winship Mansion. It gave her the only distinction she knew for a long time, until Bayard Sewell arrived and bestowed upon her the status of his girl and, indirectly, John Winship's daughter.

The house did not look grand now. It looked, flattened under the hammer of the midafternoon sun, totally unremarkable and, simply, small. The vast green lawn had somehow, in these ensuing years, shrunk to ordinary proportions, and the great hydrangeas were pruned stumps now, so that the pitted brick and lattice foundation of the house showed through on either side of the steps. All the shrubbery had been cut back to nearly ground level, in fact, and the lawn, though freshly cut, was the whitened green of summer-scorched Bermuda grass. The old oaks still spread protective arms over the gabled and mansarded roof, and the side porches were again purple with wisteria, but the concrete front walk was cracked in several places and the sun had burnt the smart whiteness out of the paint, so that the house seemed to bleed into the milky no-color of the blinding sky. Doors and windows were closed, and several upstairs and one downstairs window had laboring air conditioners churning in them. Mike could hear them through the closed windows of the Pontiac, and the stuttering drone of a power mower somewhere out of sight.

Duck Wingo got out of the car and came around to her side, and simultaneously J.W. Cromie came around the side of the house, pushing the power mower, and stopped, mower still running, and stood still, looking at her.

Mike felt a powerful jolt somewhere in the core of her, a jolt, then a stopping, and then a forward lurching, as if some interior motor had stalled and then regained itself. For a moment she felt very dizzy. Impressions flooded her; not memories, nothing so concrete, but visual images and a kaleidoscope of sensations, none of which she could seem to sort out or name. She sat on the edge of the car's front seat, one foot on the curb beside the old, softly hollowed carriage block that had always stood there, and looked back at J.W. She had had no idea he was still in Lytton. Priss Comfort had written her, soon after she had married Richard Singer and begun college at Radcliffe, that J.W. had moved to Atlanta and started a little lawn service business. Mike had been glad to hear the news, had felt, somehow, faintly vindicated.

She got out of the car stiffly, very conscious of her thinness, her pallor, the oversized black sunglasses and huge, battered Gucci tote that had been everywhere with her during the past ten years of assignments, her soft, slender Italian shoes. All spoke of citiness; seemed suddenly effete, alien. In the shadowless light J.W. seemed to have been untouched by the years. His yellowish, Indian-cast face was unmarked and his tall body lounged over the mower with a deceptive indolence that came sharply back to her. His mouth still had its sweet, adenoidal looseness, which sometimes had made him appear simpleminded to people who did not know him. His eyes were not the same, though. Once they had been deep, liquid with a kind of extra light, rich like wet black winter leaves. They were flat and opaque now, like dried river pebbles. He stood beside the stilled mower and looked at them, not moving forward. Mike felt a smile of involuntary pleasure curving her mouth. She started toward him, arms outstretched.

He stepped back slightly from her arms.

"Hey, Miss Mike," he said.

She faltered and stared. "Good God, J.W., what's this Miss business? This is me. I'm glad to see you; I didn't know you were in Lytton. You look good. You look fine, J.W., just like you always did. Tell me what's been happening with you . . ."

Aware that she was chattering, she stopped.

"Nothin' much be happenin' in Lytton, look like," J.W. said, looking thoughtfully at something in the distance, and then up at the sun. He squinted.

"You lookin' good too, Miss Mike. We hears about you down here . . ."

DeeDee cut in brightly, "J.W. helps us and Daddy in the yard and around the house, and drives for Daddy sometimes, and I don't know what on earth we'd do without him. He works down at the cemetery in the mornings, too. Come on, you all can catch up later. It's almost time for Daddy's nap, and he gets sort of confused if he misses it."

She took Mike's arm and steered her up the crazed front walk. J.W. touched the bill of his Atlanta Braves baseball cap and turned away. He did not smile, and had not, and something akin to sullenness washed his mustardy face. Mike knew that J.W. had had no sullenness in him. She felt like an actor in a play for which she had no script. What was the sense of that Negro dialect? She had not heard it from a black in years, only from the sort of whites she refused to know. J.W. had always spoken fairly precisely. Rusky, who had not, had insisted that he do so. She stopped on the walkway and pulled her arm out of DeeDee's grasp.

"How long has J.W. been doing yard work for you and Daddy?" she asked.

"Oh, ever since right after you left," DeeDee said. "Priss set him up in a little lawn business here, but nothing would do but Atlanta, so he went up there to make his fortune. It lasted about six months. What does J.W. know about running a business? He came dragging back here, but nobody in Lytton would hire him after . . . well, you know. Daddy took him in and gave him that room over the garage free and paid him a little something to keep the place up, and he's been here ever since. He has a hot plate and a shower, and Daddy gave him some old furniture and a bed, and he has the job at the cemetery. Daddy got him that, too. He gets by real nicely. He's real comfortable."

Mike's face burned. John Winship had obviously felt obligated to help the badly used J.W. back onto the path from which she had so disastrously led him, and in doing so had cast around J.W. bars as real as those in the Fulton County Jail. For a moment she felt hot anger at both of them. Why on earth had J.W. accepted such an ignominious patronage? Surely there were other towns, other jobs.

She looked over her shoulder at J.W., who was retreating around the side of the house, the mower grumbling once again. He wore what might have been the same faded overalls and work shirt that he had worn the day the two of them took the bus to Atlanta to join the protesters at JoJo's. It struck Mike that they would be considered chic now in the circles in which she moved in New York. Derek Blessing sometimes affected the identical costume, especially if photographers were going to be present.

"Come on," DeeDee said again, and Mike took a deep breath that whistled a little in her dry nostrils, and went into the house to meet her father.

At first she could see nothing, the gloom in the foyer was so intense, and the sunlight she had just left so bright. The Xanax calm cracked and broke. She felt the sudden panic of the blind person confronted by danger, but unable to see it. Her heart began the frantic, caged-bird struggling in her throat, and the buzzing fear ran up her arms. She thought she might faint, there in that same shadowy foyer that she had left in such pain so long ago, and for a moment the thought held great and simple charm and succor. Just not to be here, not to be . . .

There was a movement in the gloom, and a wheelchair slid forward into the dusty sunlight filtering through the front door, and she saw him. Or saw, at least, a skeleton, a corpse, a cadaver, peering up at her from the sterile armature of the aluminum chair. She thought, suddenly and wildly, of a movie she had seen when she was ten or eleven that had frightened her so intensely that she sometimes still had nightmares about it, a movie called *I Walked with a Zombie,* in which a ghastly, enormously tall, impossibly gaunt Negro zombie stumbled blindly and inexorably after assorted shrieking young women on a dark beach in Haiti, the only sounds the huge, misshapen feet dragging in the sand and the eerie crooning of the warm night wind. The figure in the chair, the parchment face that looked up at her, wrecked and frozen, reminded her of the Negro zombie. But it was not black, and it was not dead; it only seemed so. It was the waxen yellow-white of the supermarket menorah candles Richard's family had used, and it was her father's. It must be. Was this not her father's house?

There was nothing in this creature of the man whose lean face she had last seen frozen in anger on this spot more than twenty years before. This man's face was set in its own wreckage. This man was completely bald, the skull the decayed mottle of a long-rotted egg. This man was unspeakably frail, almost luminous, and bowed in the chair, and the gray eyes did not move or blink as he peered up at her. There was a sheen of tears in them, the easy tears of weakness, illness, age; they had nothing to do with greeting or memory. Even in the long moment of ringing shock, Mike knew that. One corner of the mouth and an eyebrow were drawn down into a permanent grimace. A transparent yellow hand plucked mechanically at the thermal blanket tucked around him. His breathing was light and shallow and audible, but he made no other sound.

Something in Mike unclenched, relaxed so suddenly that it left her limp and hollow-feeling, scooped out. Her head rang with lightness and her knees and elbows felt unjointed. She thought again that she might collapse onto the foyer rug. There was nothing here of the tall, remote presence that had shadowed her childhood. This husk was not her father. There was not, in this house, anything left that could hurt her now.

Mike moved forward a little, but did not speak. A kind of deliverance leaped in her. The beginnings of safety sang in her head.

"Well," John Winship said. His voice was thin and querulous, high and fretful as a child's. No one's voice that she knew. Not, certainly, a voice that could flay one alive. Gone, that voice. Gone.

"So here you are."

"Here I am," Mike said. She tried a smile. It stretched her dry mouth, a polite, social rictus.

"You by yourself?" he said, after a space of silence in which his breathing came and went like a flaccid August tide.

"You mean did I bring my Jew husband and Jew child?" Mike said, with something mimicking amusement. "No."

He appeared not to have registered that.

"Did they tell you I couldn't take care of myself?" he said, and his voice seemed to pick up life and strength with use. "You think you had to come all the way down here from New York or wherever it is and look after me?"

"Daddy!" DeeDee bleated breathlessly. "You *know* we talked about this! You know you said you thought it would be a good idea if Mikie came; you know I've got Mama Wingo at my house now and I just can't . . ."

The desiccated figure held up one hand. It was as spotted and brittle as a November leaf; light came through it, outlining clean old bones.

"Daddy . . ." DeeDee began again.

"Be quiet, Daisy," John Winship said irritably. "I know what I said. I just wanted to see if Micah knew what she was getting into. Wanted to see if you all had told her the real score. Did they tell you about the diapers, Micah? Did they tell you they have to hand-feed me like a little bird, bite by bite? Tell you about havin' to hold my pecker so the piss won't go all over the—"

"Daddy!" DeeDee squalled. Her chins quivered. "That's not the truth! You know you can eat and . . . everything else . . . as well as you ever could! What on earth has gotten into you, lying to Mike like that? You know you're the one that asked for her in the first place!"

A cracked, keening sound came from the old man's mouth, or from half of it, and Mike thought for a second that he was crying, but then she realized that the sound was laughter, and that the tears that runneled from the staring eyes were those of glee. Revulsion and relief, polar twins, leaped in her. She smiled around them.

"Just wanted to see if Micah had any of the common touch left, a high-falutin' big writer like her, down here to spread joy amongst us peasants," John Winship said. "Just wanted to see if you had any life in you still, Daisy. Gettin' boring in your middle age, you are."

DeeDee sniffed and laid her hand none too gently on her father's shoulder.

"Let's move you out on the sun porch where it's lighter, Daddy," she said. "You and Mikie can chat a little, and then it's time for your nap. Sounds like you need it today."

He shrugged off her hand as if it were a biting insect and peered up at Mike again.

"Just a minute," he said. "Stay where you are, Micah. Want you to meet somebody. Daisy, go get us some iced coffee. There's some still left in the pot from breakfast. Take Duck with you."

"Daddy, you'll never get to sleep if you have iced coffee now, and you need your nap . . ." DeeDee started in.

"Better make it buttermilk, Pop. Good for what ails you." Duck Wingo beamed ferociously.

"DeeDee, I want that coffee *now,*" the wrecked man in the chair said in a soft, dangerous slide of voice, fully a register lower than the cracked chime that he had been using, and for a terrifying eyeblink Mike was a child standing in disgrace before a man whom her viscera remembered better than her mind. Then the impression was gone. DeeDee turned silently and made for the kitchen, vast and blue. Duck padded behind her, heavy-haunched in straining polyester plaid. John Winship made a motion with his autumnal hand and a man came out of the dark-shuttered living room behind him.

"Sam, this is Micah Winship," John Winship said over his shoulder. He did not say "my daughter." "Micah Singer, I believe she is now. A famous lady writer, or so they tell me. Come all the way back here to clean up my slops. Micah, this is Sam Canaday. My lawyer. Excuse me, Sam, my attorney of record."

He grinned, a feral, death's-head grin. The man at his side grinned back and then looked at Mike and put out his hand.

"Evenin', Miz Winship," he said. "Or Singer. It's a real pleasure to meet Lytton's most famous native daughter. Though a pity it had to be under these circumstances. But a real honor just the same. I've read your work often, of course."

"Thank you," Mike said. "I'm happy to know you, Mr. Canaday."

His hand was hard and dry and callused, and felt warm to her icy fingers.

"Call me Sam," he said affably. "Everybody does. One big happy family we've got here in Lytton, yessir."

"Sam," Mike amended. She withdrew her hand.

She disliked him on sight. He spoke like the kind of professional Southerner who drew arrows of scorn in her circle in New York. His white smile was vivid and flirted with insolence. He was massively built, almost square, deeply tanned, and dressed in faded blue jeans and dusty cowboy boots with turned-up toes. Thick, straight blond hair, lighter than his skin, looped down over one eyebrow, and he had what looked suspiciously like a wad of tobacco in his pale-stubbled jaw. His eyes were a startling amber green, and deeply circled. Wolf's eyes, Mike thought. Cold, missing nothing. He wore round, wire-framed glasses. His voice was mild, deep and flat, and he had a slow drawl. He looked . . . she searched for it. Unblinking. Implacable. Planted, somehow, in earth.

He went on grinning amiably at her, while John Winship looked from one to the other with the interest of a spectator at a tennis match. Neither Mike nor the lawyer said anything else, but something seemed to satisfy the old man, because he gave another eldritch cackle and jerked his hand again at Sam Canaday.

"Wheel this thing out on the sun porch, Sam," he said. "Tired of sitting in the dark like a goddamned bullfrog. Micah, go in the kitchen and tell Daisy and that idiot to forget the coffee. Sam's gon' get us a real drink. Bourbon's on the tray by the secretary, Sam."

"I know where it is, Colonel," said Sam Canaday. "I brought it to you. 'Scuse us a minute, Miz Singer."

"Call her Mike," John Winship said. "I don't know any Singer."

"By all means, do call me Mike," she said sarcastically, but Sam Canaday was already wheeling her father out onto the bright sun porch off the foyer, and she said it to his broad back.

"Mike, then," floated back in his wake.

Mike went into the kitchen as if by rote. Nothing seemed to have changed in the big, square white room. Duck Wingo was wrenching at the ice trays in the yellowed old refrigerator, and DeeDee was putting tall glasses on a tray. Mike remembered the tray, an old, lacquered Chinese one of her mother's, with white rings on it where wet glasses had been carelessly set. The glasses in

DeeDee's hands, scattered with white and yellow daisies, she did not know.

"He says to forget the coffee," she said. "He's going to have bourbon instead. I guess those glasses will do; why don't you just bring them?"

"Bourbon! He is *not!*" DeeDee snorted indignantly. "He knows darned well he's not supposed to *touch* alcohol. Dr. Gaddis was *explicit* about that. It could kill him. It's that shyster lawyer of his, that Sam whatsisname . . ."

"Canaday," Mike said.

"Canaday. He knows as well as we do Daddy can't drink, but he keeps right on bringing it in the house, and when you call him on it, he just smiles that . . . I-don't-know-*what*-kind-of smile . . ."

"Shiteatin'," Duck put in.

". . . and says he hasn't noticed that Daddy's senile yet, and seems to him he's capable of making up his own mind what kills him. I know he gives Daddy all he wants when he's here by himself with him."

"Is he, very often?" Mike asked.

"Oh, yes, *every* afternoon after work, practically, and sometimes he stays for supper . . . cooks it himself, if he doesn't like what I've left. Lord knows it's a wonder he hasn't poisoned Daddy . . . and then either stays on and plays cards or chess with him, or comes back around ten for another drink. I think he'd move in here if he could. And the way Daddy dotes on him, that'll probably be next. He's wormed his way into Daddy's confidence, and he's not going to let go of him until he gets all he can out of him. He's encouraging Daddy to make a spectacle of himself over that old house, telling him he can fight the DOT, telling him he thinks they can win. He's nothing but a social-climbing opportunist!"

DeeDee's great shelf of bosom was heaving like a barge on a storm-tossed sea, and there were circles of dull red under the vermilion rouge on her cheeks. Her chest and neck flushed in the same way that Mike's own did when she was angry or embarrassed. Mike had wondered, when she was a child, if their mother's fair skin had done the same thing.

"What on earth has he got to gain socially in Lytton by latching onto Daddy?" she asked. The name slid out naturally here in this resonating kitchen, but its aftertaste was alien. She licked her lips as if to dislodge it.

"Daddy's somebody in this town," her sister spat. "The Winships always have been somebody in Lytton; you know that. Or you would if you'd bothered to stay here and find out. He's got plenty to gain. He's probably after Daddy's money, too. And on top of it all, he's ignorant, and arrogant, and downright common!"

Mike thought of the man she had just met. DeeDee was wrong. Arrogant Sam Canaday certainly was. Common, probably. Ignorant, no.

"Daisy!" John Winship's voice called from the sun porch, surprisingly robust.

"Coming, Daddy," her sister trilled back. To Mike, she said, "Come on and see if you can talk some sense into him about the bourbon. If not, you're at least somebody fresh for him to yell at."

Fatigue suddenly flooded Mike like dirty water. Sensation and nuance weighted and numbed her. Her entire body sagged with it. The kitchen spun slowly out of focus and then swam back in.

"Please make my excuses, Dee," she said. "I just can't hold myself up much longer. I've got to lie down for a little while. I think I'll go on up; where do you want me to put my things?"

"I've made up your old room," DeeDee said. "But you might at least make an effort, Mike. We're all tired, you know. And I'm paying Estelle extra to stay with Mama Wingo; we can't stay here all afternoon and night waiting for you to take a nap."

"Never mind, Miss Daisy," said Sam Canaday, coming into the kitchen in amazing silence, considering the taps on the cowboy boots. "You and Duck go right on home. Let Miz Singer go on up and get some rest; she looks worn out. It's a long way back home in more than miles, I guess. I'll sit with the Colonel, and I'll be glad to fix us all some supper later, if she doesn't feel like it."

He smiled at Mike, his white teeth vulpine in the ocher face. She could not read in his strange green eyes whether or not he had heard what DeeDee had said about him. Somehow she did not think he would care if he had.

"Thank you," she said. "I'm no good to anybody right now."

"I couldn't dream of letting you do that, Mr. Canaday," DeeDee said, puckered with disapproval.

"No trouble at all," he said. "You know I get supper for the Colonel and me about half the time."

"Come on, DeeDee," Duck Wingo said. "I got to see Curtis Pike about the Turnipseed place before supper. Let Mr. Canaday take over the housekeeping and so on, since he's so good at it."

It was obvious that he meant the words to be insulting, but Sam Canaday just broadened the white grin to include Duck and settled himself comfortably against the scarred counter. He looked completely at home in the kitchen.

Mike did not wait to see the tiny drama out. Suddenly they all wearied her nearly mortally.

"I'll see you all later," she said, walking out of the kitchen and up the hall stairs into the dark, still interior of the Winship house. She felt as if her legs were a hundred feet long and made of wire. The only thought in her mind was getting to her bed before her knees buckled. She found the door to her old room, moved blindly across the stale-smelling carpeting, and turned on the window air-conditioning unit to high. She dropped her satchel and stepped out of her shoes and was asleep before her face hit the piled pillows on the high, narrow white bed with the pineapple finials that had always, in her lifetime, stood in this room. She did not move in her sleep, and she did not dream.

Sometime later—how much later she could not tell, for the blinds were shut tight and the room's chill darkness might have been that of early night or early morning—she woke. She knew instantly where she was, and the fear that had stirred sluggishly all during that long day under the mantle of the drug made as if to uncoil swiftly and engulf her before she could clench herself against it. She was out of bed and reaching in her purse for the Xanax, scrambling frantically among the flotsam of tissues and cosmetics and ball-point pens, when she heard sounds from the kitchen directly below her. She paused and listened, remembering that she had listened like this many times before, when she had wakened from a nightmare-troubled sleep, and heard the comforting sound of Rusky's big bulk moving slowly about the kitchen. She heard, now, the same slow movement of bulk, the same practiced handling of pots and chink of dishes, the same soft rumblings of conversation and laughter. Only this time it was not Rusky talking to J.W., but Sam Canaday saying something to her father. She recognized the laconic voice.

"Oh, Rusky," Mike said aloud, and felt such a great stab of pure, howling aloneness that she felt flattened, pulverized, obliterated. And then, like a benediction, a blessing, came the slow, unmistakable, and inexorable draining away of the fear. In its place there was a great, level languor, an endless, simple, and final white peace. Stumbling with the weariness of a child, Mike went into the bulbous white bathroom and dropped the Xanax pills, one by one, into the toilet, and flushed it. Then she went back to the bed and crawled underneath the covers and pulled them over her head and slid deeply and finally toward oblivion.

The last thing she heard was Sam Canaday's faraway voice saying, "That can wait until the morning. Let her sleep."

Mike did.

FOURTEEN

The new languor was there when she woke the next morning. She lay still, unable to tell what time it was from the slant of the light through the old-fashioned wooden venetian blinds, only that the sun was shining. When she lifted her arm to look at her watch, she felt as if she had slept a long time in one position, or was recovering from influenza. Her arm was infinitely heavy, and there was a deep, sweet ache in it. The same ache pervaded her entire body. She stretched her legs as far as they would go, and then her arms, and flexed her fingers and toes, and still the not-unpleasant ache persisted. She blinked her eyes hard several times, until the watch's deceptively simple face swam into focus. It was a square Cartier quartz tank watch that Derek Blessing had given her the first Christmas they were together, and it had, for the first time in her memory, stopped.

It did not bother Mike at all that she did not know what time it was. The white languor around her held her as completely and airlessly as a bell jar, a hermetic dome. She knew precisely where she was and why she was there; she knew that when she got out of bed and went downstairs it would be to confront, not only her father, but the entire first half of her life, a life that she had put neatly away years before and not thought to take out again. She knew that waiting there for her at the bottom of the scarred oak stairs, seared into the very walls, soaked into the carpet, was the most she had ever known of pain. She did not care. She knew, too, knew to the tips of her nerveless fingers and toes and without knowing how she knew, that the great, drowning surge of fear and agony and the avalanche of memory that she had dreaded would not materialize. The bell jar, she sensed, was impenetrable; would hold.

She lay for a time listening to the deep-sea hum of the air

conditioner and her own tranquil blood, pouring sweetly through her veins. The window unit shut out all other sound in the big, dark room. She would have known where she was if she had waked out of a ten-year coma, though. The smell of years-old lemon polish and dust from the worn blue carpet that had been laid down in her thirteenth year was as familiar in her nostrils as the acrid demon's breath of New York. The feel of the thin-worn, silky old percale pillowcases against her cheek was the same as she remembered, though they smelt powerfully of mothballs, as they had not then. She could almost trace in her mind the design of scallop shells along their hems, so powerful was the effect of rote memory. All her senses seemed sharper with it, heightened to near-painful awareness, a pleasant contrast to her languorous, weighted limbs. The effect was one of luxurious physical indolence. Mike could feel every inch of her skin.

Presently she crawled out from under the covers and padded over to the windows, raking her fingers through her hair. She switched off the air conditioner and pulled up the blinds. Sunlight so white that it blinded her flooded the room, dust motes dancing crazily in its strata. Eyes squeezed shut, she jerked at the paint-sealed old window frame until finally, with a despairing squeal and a shower of ivory paint flakes, it flew up. Heat and the great, fragrant ocean of wisteria scent and the buzz of early cicadas swam into the room. Mike opened her eyes and took a great, deep draft of home.

She took a bath in the bulbous old bathtub, the porcelain worn to grittiness on her buttocks. There had never been a shower in the Winship house, and so she squirmed around in the tub and lay on her back, knees in the air, and washed her hair under the scanty stream from the faucet, with the new bar of Ivory soap in the wire soap dish. She remembered that when she had lived here, she had used a snakelike tube that attached to the faucet and ended in a sprinkler that was given to escaping and whipping around the bathroom, spraying everything. She could still hear Rusky grumbling about it. Sometimes she had washed her hair downstairs at the kitchen sink, where there was a rudimentary dish sprayer and Rusky to guide it and rinse her fine, silken hair twice in water, once in vinegar for shine, and once again in water. The vinegar, Rusky said, brought out the highlights in Mike's hair and made it shine white-gold in the sun. For DeeDee, she used strong tea, to enhance the satiny darkness. Mike had stopped washing her hair in the kitchen when Duck Wingo had once come to pick up DeeDee unexpectedly early and caught Mike at the sink with dripping hair and her hated cotton undershirt clinging, sopping, to her barrel-stave ribs and pussy-willow breasts, and called her a banty pullet. His eyes had been on her breasts, though. She had stopped using vinegar as a rinse the first time Bayard Sewell had put his face to her thistledown hair and said that she smelled like chowchow, and had gone up to the drugstore and bought a great pink bottle of Tame.

She got out of the bathtub and scrubbed her body with the thin, grainy old towel, and wrapped her wet hair in another, and stepped into bikini pants and bra from her suitcase. She rummaged for slacks, and then, on impulse, went to the great old mahogany bureau against the far wall of the bedroom and opened the drawers. The various mothballed years of her life lay there, neatly folded by some hand other than hers. Who could have put them there? Rusky was years dead when she had left this house, DeeDee married and gone, John Winship unthinkable. In the bottom drawer she found and put on a faded-to-milk-white pair of blue jeans she must have had when she was a preteen, because they still bore the name tag that Rusky had sewn into her clothes when she went away to Camp Greystone, and that had been when she was eleven. The blue jeans fit; were, in fact, a little loose in the waist. She grimaced at her thinness. In another drawer she found T-shirts and put on one that had the face of Mickey Mouse on it. Like the blue jeans, it was clean and faded and smelled of mothballs and fit loosely. Mike remembered her joy at joining the Mickey Mouse Club, the new and warming sense of belonging that flooded her when she became a Mouseketeer. In the bureau's wavery, bluish mirror, her face looked back at her as if up through water, and her eyes, large and light and slightly puffed from sleep, could have been the eyes that first gleamed silver with joy at being one of Mickey's children. She anchored the towel into a damp turban with an old leopard-printed scarf and padded, barefoot, down the stairs and through the foyer into the kitchen.

Her father was there, sitting, not in the wheelchair, but in one of the blue and white chrome chairs that matched a hideous dinette set she had not seen before. A small Sony TV set on the counter next to a new microwave oven brayed out a game show; captive in it, a fat girl and a chinless young man jumped up and down in slack-mouthed excitement. Her father was staring expressionlessly at the set while a cup of coffee cooled in front of him. A barely touched plate of toast and scrambled eggs sat on the table in front of him, and a jar of strawberry preserves with a spoon in it. While she watched, he reached over and dug a heaping spoonful of the viscous red substance out of the jar and put it into his mouth, not taking his eyes off the Sony. Some of the preserves missed his mouth on the side that curved downward into his neck, and clung there on his chin, glistening. He did not seem to notice. A soapy clink sounded from across the room then, and Mike looked in the direction of the sound. Sam Canaday stood at the sink, his back just as broad in an improbable cotton-knit burgundy this morning, his arms disappearing up to the elbows in dishwater. The round clock over the stove said quarter past eleven.

"Is it possible to get some of that coffee?" Mike said over the idiot babbling of the game-show host, who was visibly flinching away from the embrace of the fat girl. She had obviously won something of great value to her.

John Winship's eyes swung away from the set and fastened on her blankly for a moment, as if he did not know who she was. She saw recognition come into them then, and a kind of narrow life, as if he had focused them on her with the intent to memorize her. Sam Canaday turned from the sink, his lifted hands dripping. He wore, this morning, appalling plaid polyester beltless slacks of the kind called Sansabelt, in shades of burgundy, pink, white, and yellow, and his burgundy polo shirt had an alligator on it. On his feet he wore, instead of the cowboy boots, white bucks of a blinding cleanliness. The effect was that of a voyager on a cut-rate cruise ship plying between Miami and San Juan. The tan of his face and the tow-yellow of his hair, more apparent in the light-flooded kitchen, heightened the door-prize–cruise effect. He grinned the wolf's-head grin.

"Morning, Miz Singer," he said. "Trust we didn't wake you carousing over brunch down here. Have a seat, there's fresh coffee perking, and some cheese Danish in the oven."

"Just coffee, thank you," Mike said primly. The sight of him, pastel and bustling in this familiar kitchen, irritated her with its easy presumption of belonging; she almost felt as though she were the

97

visitor to this house, and not he. But she was glad, on the whole, that she would not be alone with John Winship just yet. She glanced at him. He was staring at her as though in disapproval, but that might have been the newly canted scowl the stroke had painted on his mouth and eyebrow.

"Good morning," she said to him, rather formally. She still had trouble with "Daddy," and she had never said "Father." "I hope you had a good night. I certainly did. I don't think I turned over once."

"Well, you've got another think coming," John Winship cackled at her. "You rolled and wallowed like a forty-dollar mule with the colic. Hollered out once, too. Could hear you all the way downstairs. Thought at first you were having a fit."

Abruptly one side of his mouth flew up, and she realized he was smiling with the same glee he had shown when tormenting DeeDee the day before.

"Sam, get her some milk and pablum," he said. "Can't give coffee to a baby. This here's a baby, all dressed up in mouse clothes and a big bow on her head. Thought we had us a big-shot writer from New York down here, but this isn't anything but a baby."

Outside of the bell jar, Mike saw anger. It swam up to the edge of the glass globe that enclosed her and bumped against it like a shark in an aquarium, looking in, but it did not penetrate. She studied the gaunt man in the chair, thinking again, as she had the previous day, that there was nothing of her father left in him. The difference seemed to go even deeper today; this man seemed not changed from the man she had left in the twilit foyer twenty-two years before, but another man entirely. This man seemed never to have been different from the way he was now. The shape of feature, play of muscle, cant of mind, pattern of speech, manner of thinking and speaking . . . all were the property of this wrecked man, coarse and simplified into caricature. That other man . . . slim, austere, fine-bladed, wounding . . . was gone from this house.

"Well, this baby has fallen into some bad habits and needs her coffee," she said.

"Coming up," said Sam Canaday. "Mind your mouth, Colonel. Miz Singer would be within her rights if she booted you in the bee-hind. Besides, I think she looks cute as a bug in those britches and that T-shirt. Vintage Mickey Mouse Club, if I'm not mistaken."

"You're not," Mike said crisply. The "bee-hind" and "bug"

grated on her ear as if he had scraped his fingernails down a chalk-board.

"Were you one of us?" she asked acidly. She could not imagine this man's feral white smile over a Mickey Mouse T-shirt.

"Charter member," he said. "First Mouseketeer in Birmingham. Almost the last, too. The only thing they knew to do with mice in the part of town I grew up in was to shoot 'em or squash 'em with a baseball bat. Rats, rather. They were native fauna in Elyton Village."

Mike wondered detachedly how this crude, square man from the smoldering, sunless slums of Birmingham, Alabama, had won the right to be called attorney, practice law; had found his way to Lytton, Georgia, and into this house. She thought dispassionately that he might well be the charlatan DeeDee pronounced him to be, and that the association might be disastrous for her father. Her imagination played around the edges of Sam Canaday, nibbled desultorily at the potential drama of the situation. But the new peace was too seamless to permit much mental effort, and too attractive to risk it. She concluded, after a brief scan of the possibilities, that her father was, after all, an attorney himself, and a good one, and should surely know the difference between one of his kind and an outright inept. Also, the association had to it the patina of long wear and comfortable use, and surely must have been formed well before John Winship's illness. Mike let the opening gambit about Sam Canaday's background lie where he had tossed it and drank the coffee that he set before her. It was good, fresh and strong; perked, not instant. She was surprised to find that she was hungry.

She finished the warm cheese Danish in silence and had another cup of coffee. Sam Canaday dried and put away the dishes they had used, ignoring the dishwasher that squatted now under the counter beside the sink. Looking around the kitchen, Mike saw other labor-saving devices that had not been there when she had left: a disposal switch, a food processor, a gleaming mixer stand bristling with attachments, the microwave she had noticed before. DeeDee may have spent her days laboring in her father's kitchen, but she had had, to be sure, a space-age arena for her labors. It occurred to Mike to wonder who had paid for the appliances. Not, she would have bet, Duck Wingo.

She flexed her bare foot idly in a shaft of sunlight, watching the fine bones play beneath the bluish-white skin. The same sun, not yet savage with noon, was warm between her shoulder blades, and Sam Canaday had switched off the television set and turned on the radio. A little Haydn quartet purred into the room, like water pouring over crystal, and he did not move to change the station, but hummed along with the radio under his breath as he moved about the kitchen, occasionally conducting with a soapy forefinger. Her father dozed in the chair, his chin nodding to his chest and jerking upward, then nodding again. He had said nothing further. Mike supposed that he must sleep or doze much of the time, and was grateful. It would spare conversation. She felt lulled and mindless, as floated on the pure ontology of the moment as an animal with a full belly in the sun. It was not content; more nonbeing. She could not remember a moment in her life like it, no eyeblink of time in which she did not yearn toward something, was not focused upon something.

The Haydn spilled to an end and an announcer's lugubrious voice said, "This is WABE, the Voice of the Arts in Atlanta. That concludes our Second Cup Concert for this morning. Stay tuned—" and Sam Canaday clicked it off and sat down at the table opposite Mike, scraping his chair loudly and thumping down a half-full cup of coffee. John Winship jerked and slid dull old eyes toward the two of them from under half-lowered turtle's lids.

"We need to talk a little business, Miz Singer, and then I'll get on down to the office and let you and the Colonel get acquainted," he said. "I'd have made myself scarce this morning, but I thought you could use some sleep." His voice was different, somehow, quicker, deeper. The thick-flowing banter was gone out of it.

"By all means, let's do," Mike said. "And call me Mike, for God's sake, or Micah, or anything but Miz Singer. I'm not Mrs. Singer anymore, and I never used it anyway."

"I know," he said. "As I said, I've seen your by-line every now and then. Micah Winship. For the longest time I thought you were a man."

"Sorry to disappoint you," Mike said, flicked through the bell jar by the tiniest refraction of irritation. Why did that all-too-understandable assumption suddenly rankle? "You were saying about business?" she went on.

"Yeah. Well, I think you need to understand the basis you'll be operating the house on, where the money stands, what's outstanding, and so on. It's not complicated, but it's a little unusual . . ."

"I don't need to know all that, and I don't want to," Mike said. "I'm really not going to be here that long. You must know that DeeDee will be finding me some live-in help for . . . my father . . . and as soon as that's done and she and I are satisfied that things are running smoothly, I'll be going back . . ."

"Back to New York?"

"Yes, of course New York. Where did you think?"

"Just making conversation. Well, I'm sorry to hear that, and I'm sure the Colonel is, too. We'd hoped you'd be able to stay awhile, get reacquainted with your folks and the town, all that. Everybody's mighty curious about you, anxious to meet you. You're our only claim to fame, you know."

He spoke of Lytton as though it had been his town since birth, and Mike felt the faint smoke-curl of irritation again.

"I'll just bet they are," she said. "But Lytton's in pretty bad shape if I'm the only thing between it and obscurity. No, of course I'll be here for a while . . . two or three weeks; I'm not going to run off and leave DeeDee with everything on her hands. I just want to know what sort of household account I have to draw from, and where . . . he does his banking now, and what I have to do to get power of attorney. I guess you can handle that for me."

"As a matter of fact, I have power of attorney," Sam Canaday said. He did not say anything else. Across the table, John Winship raised his head and looked straight at Mike. He grinned openly and unmistakably, an evil old goat's grin.

"You have power of attorney?" Mike parroted. She felt simple incredulity. Why would this poor-white upstart have power of attorney over John Winship's assets? Why not DeeDee, if her father was incapable of managing his money, which she did not think that he was. Was her sister right, after all?

"That's right. The Colonel thought it would be less worry for Miz Wingo . . . for DeeDee . . . if she had a set amount of cash to work with every week and didn't have to worry about paying bills and tending to everything else. I just gave it to her every Monday morning . . . and it's a right generous piece of change, too, if I may say so . . . and I handle everything else, pay the bills, all the other expenses. It's worked out right well. Of course, if you want to change the arrangement . . ."

He looked, not at her, but at John Winship. The old man blinked slowly, like a desiccated snapping turtle on a sunny rock, and then gave one of the surprising bleats of cracked laughter.

"Don't see any reason to change things if Micah's only going to be here a little while," he said. "Don't reckon she needs to bother with it. Of course, if she needs some spending money, we can fatten up that envelope some. Don't guess she does, though. She must be rich by now."

"I've got money," Mike said tersely. She did, but it was dwindling fast. The plane fare to Atlanta and the storage bill for her furniture had eaten drastically into her checking account, and the savings account had always been slender. She did not want to think of the publisher's advance that must now be repaid, or what a new apartment would cost her, in the event that she was able to find one. And there was no way, now, to know what Rachel's needs would be . . . She willed the thoughts beyond the confines of the bell jar, and they slunk there.

"All right, then," Sam Canaday said, and stood and fished a fat white business envelope out of his back pocket and handed it to her. She took it, feeling slimily like a child or a servant, or a whore.

"The arrangement is that I bring this over every Monday morning," he said. "Of course, if you run short, just holler. All other household bills come to me, and any repairs. You can use the Colonel's charge cards, but bring me the receipts. I know you need some help in the house, and that's already taken care of. J.W.'s found a woman over in Lightning, a widow with a practical nursing license, who'll come every morning at nine and stay until three, when her son gets out of school. She doesn't do housework, but the Colonel keeps all but these two rooms and his bedroom downstairs closed off, and only your room upstairs is open, so there's not that much to do, and we can get somebody in once a week to clean if you like. Mrs. Lester . . . Lavinia . . . will leave supper for the two of you to warm up before she goes home, so you're free to come and go as you please until about three. J.W.'s here afternoons, too, and does what lawn work needs doing, and sometimes he takes the Colonel out for a drive when he wakes up from his nap. He always sleeps from two to about four. J.W.'s not underfoot; he never comes to the house unless somebody calls him . . . I put a phone out there when the Colonel got sick . . . but he's generally around. I've been taking him his supper, and Mrs. Lester says she'll do that, too. He eats at his place or goes out for breakfast and lunch. I think it's a good setup. You won't be burdened any at all, just need to keep a light hand on the tiller, and you can go around and see folks, or do some writing, or just rest if you want to. I've been to see Mrs. Lester and I think she's sound as a bell, but you'll be the one to approve her, of course. Here's her number. She's expecting you to call."

"Don't want a strange nigger in here," John Winship snapped petulantly, but Sam Canaday ignored him as though the objection were merely rote. Mike suspected he had heard it many times, remembering her father's virulent bigotry. He handed a slip of paper across the table to Mike, and she took it and then put it down on the table. The level calm was slumping again, incredibly, into fatigue.

"I'm sure she's fine," she said. "Anybody J.W. picks is all right with me. What does DeeDee think of her?"

"Haven't asked her," Sam said briefly. "This is your decision, not Miz Wingo's."

"Thinks she's an uppity nigger, too prissy and put on for her own good," droned John Winship. "Got a degree from some junior college. Calls herself Miz Lester. Daisy says she isn't gon' have her in this house."

"Well, then, it's lucky DeeDee isn't going to be around much, because I think she sounds perfect," Mike said evenly. "Will you call her for me, Sam, since you've already talked to her? Whenever she wants to come is fine."

John Winship cackled again, and Sam Canaday took the slip of paper back. "I'll call her when I get to the office," he said. "She can probably come in Monday morning. She needs the money. Well, I better be shoving off. I've got to go into Atlanta and take a deposition from one Mr. Bob Carithers at three."

"Goddamned son of a bitch . . ." The words exploded from John Winship. They were as unlike his other grumblings and protests as a dagger was a child's plastic scissors. Mike jerked her head around to look at him. Fury burned the pale, whitish eyes to fire and his palsied mouth trembled.

"He's just the surveyor, Colonel," Sam Canaday said matter-of-factly, but she saw that he was watching her father closely. "He was just doing his job. I'm not going to be talking directly to the high-up DOT weasels. I'll talk to their lawyers. That's down the road a piece, anyway. We're just beginning. You're going to have to calm down, or we're not going to get to first base."

John Winship lowered his head and clasped his mottled hands on the table in front of him. Mike sent the scene spinning to beyond the glass wall of the dome. She said nothing, asked no questions. She had no intention of getting involved in this business, wanted to know as little as possible about it. Her father raised his head, and there were hectic red spots on his sharp cheekbones, and the weak tears were back in his eyes. At first she thought he was looking at her, but then realized that he was looking beyond her at nothing that she could see.

"My daddy told me time and time again that his heart's blood was in that land," he said, and his voice was faraway, an echo of another man's in another time. "He gave his very blood for it. And on the day he died, I went out to the lily pond in the side yard, where he always sat in the evenings when it was fair, and I took my pocketknife that he gave me when I was twelve years old, and I cut my hand and left my own blood right there in the earth, with his. And now those goddamned hyenas from Atlanta think they're just going to take it away from me. Build a goddamned road through it so the jungle bunnies can swarm in there and build nests all over everywhere. Tear down that house that my folks built with blood and sweat and muscle. Well, by God, they've got another think coming, eh, Sam?"

The look he gave Sam Canaday, though filtered through tears, was that of a molting old eagle.

"We'll make 'em think hard, at least, Colonel," Sam Canaday said. He smiled, an easy, defusing smile, and John Winship's face relaxed and slid back into its strictured calm.

"Goddamn right," he said.

From her sphere of distance, Mike heard herself say, "Daddy, the way you're carrying on is going to make you sick again," and was astonished, both at the epithet, untasted all those years, and at the exasperation she felt at Sam Canaday for egging her father on.

"Thought you were a fighter, Miz Singer-Winship," Sam Canaday drawled, grinning the doggy white grin. "Understood you were a pretty tough lady, a real champion of the underdog."

"And what makes you think that?" Mike snapped. She really did dislike this insinuating man.

"Oh, I read you sometimes, like I said. When I'm not reading *Car and Driver* or *Penthouse.* Seems like I saw something you did just recently in *People.*"

"I don't write for *People.*"

"Well, then, it must have been the *New Republic* or the *Nation.* And then the Colonel's told me a lot about you."

Mike looked at her father, who had picked up a cast-off piece of toast and was chewing it wetly. He did not raise his eyes from his plate. Behind his diminished figure she seemed suddenly to see another man sitting at another table in this same spot, in this same kitchen: a young man, fine-faced, erect, remote, contained. It was the first sense of John Winship as the man she had once known that she had had. The gray eyes of both men, real and spectral, were veiled with lashes, and did not look up. Then the shadow figure vanished and only the old man chewing toast was left.

Sam Canaday walked to the door of the kitchen just as J.W. Cromie came up onto the back porch.

"Good, here's J.W.," he said. "He'll wheel the Colonel back to his room for a little nap, and you won't need to worry about his lunch till midafternoon, since we had breakfast so late. Why don't you take the car and get out a little while? Drive around, go see Priss Comfort, maybe? She's real eager to see you."

The thought was like sunlight pouring down onto dark water. Mike smiled with pure pleasure.

"Oh, yes, Priss. Oh, that's a good idea, I will. How *is* Priss? Does she still live in that funny little stone house down by the ball field? Does she still knock back the bourbon in her iced tea? Do you know her well?"

"She still lives there," Sam Canaday said, smiling at her tumble of words. "And no, I don't think she's had a drink in years. And yes, I do know her right well. I was by there after I left here last night, in fact. Priss is one of the main reasons I stay in Lytton. Her and the Colonel here."

"Oh, maybe we can have her to dinner one night soon," Mike said. "I'd like to show her that I really can cook. She used to say I was going to starve by the time I was twenty-five."

"Priss Comfort hasn't set foot in this house in more than twenty years," John Winship spat from the chair where he had been chewing and nodding. "Not since the day you slunk out of here, Micah. So you want to do any cooking for her, you best plan on doing it in that rathole of hers."

Mike went still-faced with the venom in the words. Anger crawled again at the glass. She stared at her father, who raised his head and gave her back the look.

"Then that's just what I'll do," she said. "That's a fine idea. Thanks for filling me in, Sam."

"You're real welcome, Miz Singer-Winship." She felt, rather than saw, his amusement as she went smartly up the stairs to change her clothes. A moment later she heard the screen door bang softly behind him and knew he was gone.

FIFTEEN

Priss Comfort had not so much changed in twenty-two years as she had, simply, expanded. Before, she had had the look of petrified redwood, all massive, columnar height and rich, Renaissance coloring. Now her body was as formless as DeeDee's, but it was androgynous, not DeeDee's melted and sprawling femaleness, and she carried its bulk as lightly as she ever had. Her stride, as she moved through the familiar dim clutter of the little house's living room to greet Mike, was as free and impatient as ever, and the eyes that glowed from the serene, unlined face were as raw a green. Priss's face was like a great harvest moon, smooth and high-colored and magnetizing to the eye. Her shining coil of chestnut hair was still vivid, even with strands of vigorous iron gray woven through it here and there. Her arms around Mike were as solid as chestnut wood. Only the smell of her was different. Where once Priss Comfort had breathed forth warm gusts of bourbon and Lavoris, now she smelt powerfully of Calgon Bouquet and the arid, inoffensive sweat of age.

She held Mike hard against her for a long time, saying nothing, breathing audibly, and then held her off with both strong hands and looked at her. Priss's smile had not changed, either; it was even more Buddha-like in the large, untroubled face. The fierce hawk's eyes, unclouded and unprompted by lenses, searched Mike's face like electronic scanners.

" 'For lo, the winter is past, the rain is over and gone; the flowers appear on the earth; the time of the singing of birds is come, and the voice of the turtle is heard in our land,' " she intoned, in the powerful clarion voice that might have rung in Mike's ears only this morning. Mike felt a surge of lightness and what might pass for joy.

"I've missed you," she said, smiling at Priss. "I didn't know how much until I saw you. Priss, you're uncanny; you look years younger than you did when I left. And you still sound like Brünnhilde riding into battle. What on earth have you done, found the fountain of youth?"

"Laid off the sauce," Priss said in her beautiful contralto, leading Mike across the room to where the deep old sofa and Priss's shapeless leather Morris chair still sat. "When I stopped drinking I started eating, and all the wrinkles and crannies filled in. I'm not younger, I'm just stretched like a balloon. If I lost any weight I'd look like the picture of Dorian Gray."

She stepped deftly over the objects strewing the faded old Navaho rug that had always lain in the middle of the floor, and Mike picked her way behind her. Shoes, a pile of books and magazines, an unopened sack of birdseed, and one rubber Wellington boot cluttered the path to the sofa. One anonymous heap uncoiled from the floor and scurried away under the coffee table, and Mike remembered Priss's omnipresent cats. Time seemed to have passed the tiny house by entirely.

Priss sagged into the Morris chair and gestured at the pitcher of iced tea on the table. A plate of store-bought chocolate chip cookies sat beside it. Mike shook her head, and Priss raised one coppery eyebrow.

"I started eating and you stopped, apparently," she said. "Are you anorexic, or is this what the best skeletons in the naked city are wearing these days?"

"I know, I know . . . I look like a gay young thing of a hundred and ten," Mike said. "You don't have to rub it in. I've just gotten in off a long assignment. I'll make it up in a week."

"You don't look a hundred and ten, you look fourteen," Priss Comfort said, frowning at her. "An Ethiopian fourteen. How old are you now, Mike? I forget exactly . . . thirty-seven? Thirty-eight?"

"I'll be forty in November." Mike grimaced. "You ought to remember, Priss. You saw me before anybody else in the world did, except the doctor and Rusky."

Priss smiled. "So I did," she said. "A ridiculous, squalling little scrap with a cotton boll on your head and the face of John Winship on you before you were an hour old. And that hasn't changed, Mike. You look so much like your father when he was your age that it's almost laughable. I'd know you were his daughter if I were meeting you for the first time today. Even more now, somehow. It's the eyes, I think . . ."

"I've never really seen that," Mike said.

"No," Priss said. "I guess you wouldn't."

The cat came warily out from under the coffee table and wafted up onto Priss's polyester lap and settled himself into its cushiony vastness. Like DeeDee, Priss wore a pantsuit, hers green with a mammoth floral top to complement the shiny trousers. The cat was white, with a large bullet head and thick neck and slanted, mad blue eyes. It stared steadily at Mike, purring like a Mixmaster and kneading its big front paws on Priss's knee.

"This is Walker Pussy," Priss said. "So named because of his startling resemblance to—"

"Don't tell me," Mike said, laughing. "He really does, doesn't he? Can he write?"

"I suspect he can, and quite well," Priss said, rubbing the big, blunt head. "But he's been blocked ever since I had him. Found him last winter up that chinaberry tree out back, where Cooper's brute of a Doberman had chased him. He was so traumatized that he hasn't written a word yet. But I think it may break any day now. I hope so. People are going to forget who he is; you know how fickle the reading public is. He's only as good as his last book."

"You ought to be writing literature, not teaching it," Mike said. "You're wasted on ninety nine percent of the little wretches in your classes."

"What classes?" Priss Comfort said. "I've been retired for more than twenty years. I do absolutely nothing I don't have to do now, except read, work doublecrostics, and take care of this failed poet here. And eat, of course."

"Why did you quit?" Mike asked in genuine bewilderment. "I can't imagine you not teaching English literature. It's like the ocean without tides."

"Mike, I'm exactly your father's age. They'd have had to put me out to pasture eventually, even if I hadn't wanted to retire. Which I did."

Mike looked at Priss, huge and vital in the dimness of the room. That she could be the same age as the embittered and embattled cadaver back in the Pomeroy Street house was nearly incomprehensible. Yet she knew that it was true. Priss and her father had gone all the way through grammar and high school together.

"You seem about a century younger than he does," she said.

"Four months and five days, to be exact," Priss said. "The only difference is that I don't have cancer and I haven't had a stroke."

"No," Mike said. "That's not the only difference." But she did not pursue it, and Priss let the statement lie. They sat in peaceful silence for a space of time, memories and impressions from the nearly two decades of afternoons and evenings she had spent in this room rolling over Mike like a warm sea.

Presently Priss said, "Tell me what's happened in your life since you left here. I don't mean the divorce and all that . . . DeeDee's kept me filled in on the mechanics. I mean what's really been happening with you. I can't tell from your writing. There's nothing of you in it."

"There's not supposed to be," Mike said, a bit testily. "A journalist isn't supposed to intrude herself into her work. I've always tried to let my subjects speak for themselves . . ."

"I wasn't criticizing your work," Priss said, holding up one large hand and smiling. "I'm very proud of your work. You've made a good start on what you can do. But you're by no means there yet. And I think you're wrong. The best journalists . . . the very top two or three . . . aren't afraid to let themselves show under and through their work. They don't hide behind it. It's what makes them the best; a kind of pentimento. You're still hiding, no matter what you think. What *has* happened to you, Mike?"

Without meaning to at all, Mike found herself telling Priss. She talked and talked, about the early days of her marriage and her career, about the growing estrangement between her and Richard, and the divorce; about Rachel and her troubling transmutation and abrupt, agonizing defection; about the job and the apartment and all the other events of that bizarre and devastating week in May just past; about DeeDee's importuning letter, and her own decision to come home and help her sister with their father. She said nothing of the terrible, killing fear that had struck her on the train to Bridgehampton, or of the flight to Derek Blessing and his betrayal; nor of the Xanax trance that had ended only the night before, in her old bedroom upstairs in the Pomeroy Street house, or of the bell jar that had since slid down over her. She simply and meticulously offered the bare, neatened bones of her life for Priss, aware as she talked of the brisk, neutral northeastern timbre of her voice in her own ears, of what DeeDee had called the "New Yorkiness" of her speech.

When she was through, Priss grinned at her.

"So the whole shooting match just fell in on you, did it?" she said. "And now here you are, back where you started out. Well, good for you, Mike, though I don't for a minute suppose you came for the reasons you say you did. Since when did you give a tinker's damn about helping DeeDee, or did she need help, for that matter? Duck's sorry slob of a sister could take on that old harpy as well as he and DeeDee. She didn't have to call you home. Whatever the reasons, though, I'm glad you're here. It's time you came home."

"I'm not here to stay," Mike said hastily. "I didn't really come home to stay, Priss. Please don't think that. This is just for a while . . ."

"Where will you go, then? When you do go."

"Back to New York, I guess. Or almost anywhere my work takes me. On. I'll go on. I always meant to do that. You know as well as I do that you can't go home again," Mike said.

"Sometimes you have to go home before you *can* go on," Priss said. "Almost all of us do, Mike, some time or other."

They were silent again, and then Mike said, "Is he really dying?"

"Yes," Priss Comfort said. "He really is."

"Does he know it?"

"I don't know," Priss said. "I haven't talked to your father since the day you left that house. Seen or talked to him. I'm sure DeeDee has told you that, or John himself. It's certainly no secret in Lytton."

"Oh, Priss . . . why?" Mike cried softly. The old pain deep under Priss's words, not the words themselves, hurt her in turn.

"Because," said Priss Comfort, "I can't forgive either one of us. Him or me."

"Priss . . ." Mike began, but the older woman held her hand up again, a white blur in the hot red dimness of the room.

"No, Mike, I'm not going to talk about it with you, now or ever," she said. "I was drunk and I let you down, and I will never forgive myself for it, and I stopped drinking that day . . . stopped teaching, too . . . but that's neither here nor there. And I will not forgive your father for what he said to you that day, in that house, and I will not go into that house again while he lives in it. And if you persist in talking to me about it, I'm going to ask you to go home."

"Priss, I can't bear you punishing yourself for something that doesn't matter," Mike said urgently. "Believe me, I never . . ."

"Mike!"

"All right," Mike said, a prickle of salt in her eyes and throat. "Then we won't talk about it. Tell me about this business with the . . . what is it? The DOT? Tell me about the homeplace."

Priss looked at her with the mulish, oblique look she remembered from her high school days, when Mike had stopped short of grasping some point Priss had been trying to make to her, or from arriving at some conclusion. There was no help in that look.

"Do you really care about the homeplace, Mike? Or any of this business with the Department of Transportation? I don't think you do," she said.

"No," Mike said, relieved that once again Priss had read her thoughts, and that, in this house, at least, she did not have to pretend. "I don't especially care, except that it's obvious I'm going to be hearing it night and day while I'm here. It seems to upset him . . . my father . . . a great deal, and that's obviously not good for someone who's already had one stroke. I couldn't care less what happens to that broken down old farmhouse—Dee's probably right; he'd be far better off without the worry of it hanging over him, and after all, he *would* still have the land—but I can tell already that he's not about to drop the suit, or whatever it is he and that Canaday person have going. I just thought it might be good for me to know a little of what's been going on."

"You really ought to ask Sam Canaday, then," Priss said. "I'm hazy on the details and timing. All I know is that the whole thing boiled up about six months ago; I heard at the Food Giant that the state wanted to build an access road from all that new development over to the west of us, around Carrollton and all, to I-85 over east yonder, and that it would come right smack through the old Winship homeplace. I can't imagine why they want to do it; there's another access road not five miles down toward Shelbyville. It's not going to save anybody but about two minutes. Well, the next thing I knew, your daddy had hired Sam Canaday to fight it, and that's really the gist and sum of it. You ask Sam. You're right; you really ought to know what's going on if you're in the house with it, whether or not you give a flip about the old place. Tell you the truth, it *has* gotten to be an eyesore since your daddy hasn't been able to keep it up."

"I don't want to ask Sam Canaday anything," Mike said. "He's a boor and a bore and a professional Southerner, which is even worse, and I'm already tired of having him shamble around the house being all folksy and warm and cotton-mouthed. I don't plan to have anything more to do with him than I have to. It'll be easy enough to stay out of his way. How in God's name did my father find him in the first place?"

"As a matter of fact, I sent him over there about four months ago," Priss said enigmatically, feeding bits of chocolate chip cookies to the mad-eyed white cat, who gobbled them indelicately. "I knew John wasn't up to going up to East Point every day to see that McDonough fellow up there, and there hasn't been another lawyer in Lytton since your father retired. Sam Canaday came to town about a year ago and set up an office over the hardware store, in that space old Dr. Gaddis used to have . . . not much more than a slum now . . . and I had a little law business over a piece of property needing doing, and I didn't want to drive to East Point to do it. So I went to see him, and he did a real good job for me and didn't charge me an arm and a leg, so I told him to go on over there and see John Winship about this DOT thing, and he did, and the rest, as they say, is history."

"I didn't know reputable lawyers went around soliciting business door-to-door," Mike said. "Though I haven't seen anything yet to make me think he's reputable."

"Oh, he's reputable," Priss said. "He hasn't had time to be disreputable yet. Only got his law degree a couple of years ago. Put himself through Oglethorpe University law school at night, I think. Came straight on down here from Atlanta and hung out his shingle. I think I was his first client, and John is probably his second and only one so far. Like to be his last, too. Folks down here don't like him much."

"I can see why," Mike said.

"No, you can't," Priss said tartly. "The reason they don't is that he got up in Sunday school class one morning right after he got here and as much as told that pompous old fool Horace Tait that he didn't know his Old Testament, and then proceeded to make a speech about integration."

"God, really?"

"Really. You know—or I guess you don't know—Horace Tait thinks he's the greatest expert on Bible history since the Dead Sea scrolls, and he was blowing up like a puff adder, and then when Sam made his little speech on the ancient and modern prophets and the Civil Rights Movement, you could have heard a pin drop. Melvin and Carrie Sue Hinds got up and walked out. I knew he'd just cooked his goose in Lytton, of course, so I asked him over here for Sunday dinner and he came, and we've been friends ever since."

"I bet you have." Mike smiled at her, interested in spite of herself. "What on earth did he say?"

"Well, Horace was holding forth about Ezra in the court of the high priest, and how the high priest told him to go on back south, that he was nothing but a tender of sycamore trees. And Sam got up and said that wasn't Ezra, it was Amos. He was right, of course; Horace is getting as senile as a goat. And while he was sputtering, Sam went on and said that Amos had always reminded him of the 'outside agitators' in the Civil Rights Movement, the ones who came in from up north and kicked up such a fuss and made such trouble and almost got run out of town by the very liberal white Southerners who were trying to do the same things that the agitators were. Well, you could cut the quiet with a knife, and I got tickled and interested, so I said that I thought they *were* too strident for their own good, whatever they were trying to do; the northern agitators, I meant. And he said yes, but, like Amos and the others, it was the strident outside saints, the troublesome loudmouths, that got the changes made, not those of us down here who had all the experience and tools and sensitivities and understanding that our long association with the blacks gave us to work with. And so then I asked why he thought that was, and he said because the blacks are us, a part of us, whether we like it or not, and that working for their real liberation would be like self-mutilation. That's when Melvin and Carrie Sue got up and left, when he said they were us. Didn't have any more idea than a pair of donkeys what he was talking about. And then he went on to say that the real prophets were more than just liberal humanists; they were mystics as well as social activists; and that their social activism sprang from a strong inner life, a sharp sense of vocation and a single-minded obsession, a real mystical vision. Like Gandhi, he said, or Martin Luther King. I knew then he wasn't going to get any more clients in Lytton, so that's when I asked him home to dinner, and I was right. He hasn't had another one."

"I'm surprised anybody's still speaking to you," Mike said, amused.

"Oh, everybody's used to me," Priss said comfortably. "Everybody knows that the Comforts were always wild-eyed and smart-mouthed, and half-cracked to boot. They grew up with me. Sam made the mistake of spouting off way too early in the game."

"Well, it really was pretty stupid," Mike said. "Especially if he'd just gotten his law degree at age . . . what? He must be my age or older. I wonder why he bothered to get a degree if he was going to blow it the first time he opened his mouth? He must have known what this town was like. What has he done for the rest of his life, anyway? Sold Chevrolets?"

"You'll have to ask him that," Priss said. "I never bothered. Doesn't matter a happy rat's fanny to me what he did. He's a good lawyer and he makes me laugh, and that's enough for me."

"Well, he may be smarter than I thought, but I still don't like him," Mike said. "He's ruder and cruder than he has to be if he does indeed know better, as you say he does, and he's in and out of that house far too much. He calls Daddy 'Colonel,' did you know that? It makes me want to throw up."

She was aware that she had said "Daddy" freely and naturally, and for some reason felt heat rising from her chest and neck into her face.

"What does it matter to you what he calls your father, if you're not going to be around him and don't care about the whole DOT thing? The point is that John likes and trusts him, and he doesn't anybody else, much. You ought to be glad he's got some company and won't be on your neck. How *do* you and John get along, anyway?" Priss Comfort said. She looked keenly at Mike.

"We get along as well as we need to," Mike said. "He's changed so much that it's like being around a stranger. He's cranky and mean-mouthed, but I don't care about that. Like I said, I don't plan to be around him that much. We've got a competent woman coming in on Monday, and Sam is there at night, and J.W. is around, of course. Daddy doesn't have to see much of me, either, and I think that suits him as well as it does me. We can certainly be polite to each other, or at least I can be to him, and I really don't care what he says to me. He hasn't any power to hurt me. What he thinks of me hasn't mattered to me for a very long time, Priss."

"My poor Mike," Priss Comfort said softly, and Mike stared at her as if she had not heard her correctly. Priss was gazing out the window of the living room where the burning light of afternoon was slowly fading into the still-hot mauve of early evening. She did not say anything else.

"DeeDee thinks Sam Canaday is after my father's money," Mike said into the silence, more to get Priss back than anything else.

"DeeDee has got a fixation about money," Priss said. "She hasn't had any for so long that she thinks it's the reason anybody anywhere does anything. Your father hasn't got any money to speak of, Mike; he never did have, except for what he set aside for your college . . ." She faltered and looked at Mike. Mike looked back impassively.

"Anyway, all he's really got is that old farm," Priss went on, "and with the price of land down here in this end of the county lying there like a dead dog in a ditch, it's not worth much either. I think the price the DOT offered him is probably more than fair. Thing is, he doesn't need the money; he'll be dead long before he could spend it. It's that land he needs."

"What on earth for?" Mike said. "If he's going to be dead so soon, why does he need the stupid land? He sounds like Gerald O'Hara: 'The land is all that matters, Katie Scarlett. Look to the land.' Does he think it's going to make the family fortune? I certainly don't want it; DeeDee's going to get it, anyway; he knows it's going to stay in the family . . ."

"I don't know why he needs the stupid land so much, as you say," Priss said severely. "I just know that he does; it's probably kept him alive up to now, through a year of cancer and two months of stroke. It's always had a powerful hold on him; I've always thought that next to your mama, he cared more about the land than anything else on earth. I'd watch my mouth if I were you, Mike. It's not up to you to legislate what a man loves."

"I thought you weren't ever going to forgive him," Mike said, and the words sounded sullen in her own ears. But Priss's words had chastened her as they always had, and she disliked the ensuing feelings of childish petulance.

"I'm not, for what he did to you," Priss said evenly. "But that doesn't mean I'm blind to what hurts him, or hard enough not to care just a little. Which is more than I can say for his younger daughter."

"Why should I?" Mike said, looking straight at Priss in the gathering twilight. "He doesn't about me. And I don't care that he doesn't. He and I are two adults, and at least we know where we stand with each other . . ."

"I wonder," Priss Comfort said, but then she was silent.

"DeeDee is in bad shape, then," Mike said presently. She knew that she ought to get back to the house on Pomeroy Street, that her father would be waking from his nap and find himself unattended. But despite the small, stinging exchange between them, she did not want to leave the warm stasis of Priss's little house.

"Well, you saw her," Priss said. "She looks awful, and I can't think her health is any too good with all that extra weight she's carrying, and it must be agony for her to look like that, as pretty as she always was, and as proud of it. And then those two children have turned out real badly; the boy left here about a year ago after some funny business at the Genuine Parts place up in Red Oak where he worked . . . never had held a steady job, just like his pa . . . and the girl married soon as she turned sixteen and went off somewhere with her no-good husband on a motorcycle. Heard she's divorced and working in some kind of health spa thing down around Panama City. She's not but nineteen now, and little John, as DeeDee still calls him, is twenty-three. They've been a terrible disappointment to her, though she never will admit it, and talks about them as though they'd graduated summa cum laude from the best Ivy League schools in the country."

"Ah, poor Dee," Mike said. "I thought Daddy had set up some kind of trust for little John, something to get him through college."

"He did, yes," Priss said. "That much I do know. But that boy couldn't have gotten through freshman year at the Georgia College of Bartending. Just like his father. Duck's still too sorry to live. Always was. He's got DeeDee stuck in some godawful little shotgun house out from town next to the old trailer park he grew up in, and now he's moved that demented old slut of a mother of his in there for DeeDee to take care of, so she can't even go back to teaching and make a little extra money if she wanted to."

"I thought Duck was burning up the woods in real estate,"

Mike said. "He told me on the way home all about how South Fulton was riding the crest of a real boom . . ."

"South Fulton County may be on the edge of a boom, but Duck Wingo isn't on the edge of anything except bankruptcy, and never will be," Priss said. "He can't hold a job; I don't know how many he must have had over the years. The only real estate he knows about is the crumbs he gets . . ." She fell silent, abruptly. "Anyway," she went on presently, "your daddy is about all that DeeDee has left, him and being a Winship, which is no bad thing, of course, but not what it used to be. Half of Lytton is new people now, and they don't even know who DeeDee is, or who your father is, for that matter. DeeDee won't admit that, of course; it's the life raft she's holding onto. In her mind she's still pretty, pampered little DeeDee Winship, the apple of her daddy's eye and the heir to his name and the old family plantation. No wonder she thinks Sam Canaday is after John's money. I think it's gall and wormwood to her that John seems to like having Sam around more than he does her, now."

"Well," Mike said, "she *is* pretty hard to take sometimes, Priss. She hasn't had the needle out of me since I got here."

"I don't wonder," Priss said. "Think how you must look to her. Elegant, citified, even famous by her lights, without the ties of a no-good husband and kids, plenty of money, a smart daughter . . ."

"Oh, God, poor Dee," Mike said again, smiling unwillingly. "If she only knew! Anyway, it was she who begged me to come down here . . ."

"But he asked for you, first," Priss said. "Don't forget that. He's all she has, and now she has to share him with you and Sam Canaday. I don't like to be around her either, so I'm not, but I can understand why she's the way she is."

"Well, so can I, of course, now that you've told me how it is with her," Mike said. "Who told you Daddy asked for me, anyway?"

"Sam did," Priss said.

"It strikes me that Sam Canaday knows entirely too god-damned much about all the Winships, including me," Mike snapped, rising to leave. "I'll come see you again tomorrow, if I may."

She was nearly to the door of the little house when Priss Comfort said, "Mike, wait. There's one more thing I think you ought to know."

Mike paused and turned to look at her. Priss's green eyes gleamed in the dusk.

"What?" she said.

"Bayard Sewell is around that house a lot, too," Priss said. Her voice was neutral, pleasant, but Mike caught something in it, a carefulness, a kind of delicate groping.

"Bayard Sewell?" Mike echoed. "Bay?"

"Yes," Priss said. "He usually comes by about four, leaves his office early, and has a drink and a chat with your dad. He's been doing it ever since he got home from college; he's crazy about John, and has been awfully good to him, especially since the cancer. He's . . . away now, on business, I think . . . but he'll be back in a few days, and I didn't want him to catch you by surprise. He says he's looking forward to seeing you, but I didn't know how you'd feel about seeing him. I didn't even know if you knew he was still in Lytton . . ."

Priss's voice trailed off. Mike said nothing. The bell jar snugged close around her, and through it the interior of the little room and the heat-hazed trees and shrubbery outside the windows shimmered as though through crystal. Inside the bell, Mike felt nothing at all.

"I didn't know, as a matter of fact," she said easily. "And I'm glad you told me. It will be good to see Bay; I'm glad he's still fond of Daddy, and seeing a lot of him. Daddy was always crazy about Bay; you remember. How is he? What is he doing, still in Lytton? I thought surely he'd end up somewhere in a city . . ."

"He's doing as well as you'd expect," Priss said. "Wonderfully well, as a matter of fact. He came back here after he finished the university; you know, of course, that John sent him through, and he's always saying how grateful he is to John, and how much he owes him. And well he should. Your daddy set him up in his real estate business, and gave him thirty acres of the homeplace property to get started with, and introduced him to a few of the right people in Atlanta, from his old firm, and Bayard hasn't stopped since. He's one of the most successful real estate men in the area now, and has held about every office and honor there is in this end of the county . . . he was mayor for almost ten years . . . and he's just recently been elected to the state legislature. Just as popular there as he is here, too; I hear that there's beginning to be some talk about grooming him for governor in a few years. So he's right; he owes your daddy a lot. And to give him his due, he's as crazy about your father as John is about him, or seems to be. He's taken on Duck in his firm; God knows how he keeps him from wrecking it, and he spends more time with him and DeeDee than you'd think a sane man could stand. I understand he's the only reason their boy isn't in jail now. And like I said, he's over at your dad's every day, even if it's just for a minute. Couldn't be any closer to him than if he was a son."

"He always was fond of Daddy," Mike said conversationally. "I'm glad to hear he's done so well. I never doubted that he would. What about his family? He must have one . . ."

"Oh, yes, a family, and a beautiful house just up the street and around the corner from yours. He built it back awhile when he bought that old rooming house where he and his mother used to live when you all were growing up. Made it into big lots and put up really nice houses on it, and moved into the biggest one himself. Has a pool and all. Yes, he married Sally Chambers when he got out of college . . . remember her, that little blond cheerleader from up around College Park? . . . and has two fine children. Really outstanding boys; just everything in high school, like he was, and are in real good schools . . . They're at camp this summer, I think, in North Carolina. Their oldest, Win . . . they named him Winship, after your father . . . drowned in the pool when he was just five, long time ago. I don't suppose Bay ever really got over it, and I know Sally didn't. She's . . . delicate. He's had a pretty bad time with her, over the years. Loves her and those two boys to death, though. Never leaves her alone. They're in church every Sunday morning without fail, except when she's in the hospital . . ."

"Does she have some sort of disease or condition?" Mike asked civilly. She might have been hearing news of a pleasant, long-ago acquaintance.

"Well, like I said, she's frail," Priss said. "She's been in and out of several psychiatric facilities."

"I *am* sorry," Mike said. "That must be hard on Bay, too."

"You'd never know it," Priss said. "He doesn't complain."

"No. Well, thank you for telling me," Mike said. "I wonder why Daddy hasn't said anything about him being around?"

"Sam made him promise not to, unless I'd talked to you and found out how you felt about things," Priss said. "We weren't sure you'd want to see him. It's just coincidence that he's away now."

"Well, how should I feel?" Mike asked. "I'm happy for Bay and Daddy both that the association is so pleasant, and I'm glad to hear about his success, and I'm sorry to hear about his wife and his son. That's all. Really, Priss, it was all so long ago; I never think of it. I hardly ever did, after I left."

She was silent a moment, and then she said, "Does Sam Canaday know about . . . Bay and me, then?"

"Yes," Priss said. "He knows about that, and about that business with your father . . . all of it."

Anger flared again, faintly, through the bell jar.

"I'm surprised Daddy told him about that," she said. "I'd have thought he'd want to forget it. I thought he *had* forgotten it, or put it out of his mind. He certainly managed to do that with me. I don't like that . . . shyster lawyer . . . knowing everything about me . . ."

"It wasn't your father," Priss said mildly. "I told him."

"Why? Why did you have to drag all that up to a perfect stranger, a nobody?" The thought of that lank-haired, slow-smiling man looking at her with his wolf's grin and knowing the old intimacies of her pain made Mike cringe as if he had laid too familiar hands on her body.

"I thought he ought to know," Priss Comfort said.

Abruptly, the heat went out of Mike, and she shrugged. Yesterday's fatigue came crawling back on sucking hands and feet.

"Oh, well, it doesn't matter," she said. "Somebody would have told him sooner or later. It must have been the biggest thing that happened in Lytton since the boll weevil."

"You'd be surprised," Priss said.

Getting out of the big old Cadillac in the driveway of the Pomeroy Street house, Mike found a small, dusty Toyota parked just ahead of her, with an Oglethorpe College decal on its bumper, and knew that Sam Canaday had come back to see her father. She planned to go straight up to her room and lie down and see if she could outwait him before getting herself some supper. She knew that he would see that her father ate, and she was not hungry now. The heat was still heavy and oppressive, and killed appetite along with energy.

J.W. Cromie came around the side of the garage dragging a hose as she started for the front door.

"Evenin', Miss Mike," he said, touching the baseball cap again, not stopping.

She sighed. "Good evening, J.W.," she said, picking up his cue. "Doing a little watering?"

"Yessum," he said over his shoulder. "Ain't had no rain since the end of April, practically, and the grass done burnt right up. Look like we gon' have a long dry spell."

"You can say that again," Mike said, turning her back on his tall figure and walking across the wide, echoing old boards of the porch. But she said it softly, so that he could not hear.

SIXTEEN

Often during those first days in Lytton, especially when she passed one of the old cloudy, speckled mirrors in her father's house, Mike had the feeling that just behind her fluttered the incorporeal figure of a young girl with flyaway hair and light-drowned gray eyes. The girl was not distinct, and her image became no sharper behind Mike's own reflection, but she was unsettling and oddly heartbreaking. The swimming glimpse of her . . . or impression, rather, for Mike never actually saw her plain . . . sometimes brought a salt swelling to her throat.

The girl was herself, of course; Mike knew that, and knew that her appearance was not at all strange in this house of submerged memories and waiting death. Indeed, the absence of any such phenomenon would be stranger than its materialization. Nevertheless, she caught herself looking quickly sideways whenever she passed a mirror, and soon abandoned looking into them entirely except to brush her hair and dab on lipstick in the mornings. She did not want to meet her long-dead self in any mirrors or on any stairs; wanted no intercourse with that vulnerable apparition in the hot, thick nights. She was afraid that despite the bell jar, that wounded ghost would creep back to haunt the woman who had sealed her, brick by brick, into the crypt of her own pain. She was afraid that in the face of her father's diminishment and obsession, staring daily at the death that stood behind him, she would revert to childhood as John Winship himself was doing. Priss Comfort's words about pentimento went with her through the first weekend in the Pomeroy Street house.

Lavinia Lester proved to be a godsend. She came the Monday morning after Mike's visit to Priss Comfort, arriving at the front door promptly at eight o'clock, before John Winship was awake and while Mike was still mooching around the kitchen in her housecoat and bare feet, drinking coffee. She answered the door bell with teeth bared jocosely, prepared, she realized later, to find a pillowy, beaming Rusky or a contemporary facsimile thereof, and finding instead a tall, angular, impassive black woman with designer Polaroid glasses on her generous nose. The woman wore a white nylon pantsuit and white nurse's oxfords and carried an enormous clear plastic tote in which Mike could see a pair of rubber flipflops, a yellow bouclé cardigan, a neatly rolled *USA Today,* a plastic thermos, a white McDonald's sack, and a startling auburn pageboy wig. Mike had unconsciously prepared a warm, gracious, and girlish little speech of welcome that included fulsome praise for Lavinia Lester's promptness, an avowal of intention to "stay out of Lavinia's kitchen and out from underfoot," and winsome gratitude at the woman's agreeing to accept their employment. "You are mighty sweet to take us on like this at such short notice," was hovering on her lips, but the phrase died, fortunately and naturally, under the appraising stare from the green Polaroid lenses. It was the sort of phrase that people had once used unconsciously with the Rusky-women of the South; the sort of words that had not passed her lips since she had left, and Mike cringed, appalled at her recidivism. She held out her hand and said, "I am Micah Winship. I'm glad you could come."

"I'm Mrs. Lester," the woman said. She was an inch or so taller than Mike, and almost as thin, but she gave no impression of gauntness. She carried herself very erectly and held her small head high and straight on its long neck. Her shapely head was cropped into a skull-fitting cap, and there was no hint of age or loosening along her jawline. She was by no means a beautiful woman, but she was an arresting one, and Mike thought that she must be the kind of nurse who healed her patients through sheer presence and authority rather than warm, sprawling lovingkindness. Her voice was neutral and clear, and though it was impossible to tell her age, you knew immediately that she was no longer young. That sort of self-possession did not spring from the country of youth.

"Please come in," Mike said. "I'll show you where to put your things, and then I'll take you over the house before Daddy gets up. I've opened the little bedroom next to my father's for you, in case you'd like to have a place to change and rest when he's asleep or watching TV; there's a bath that connects with his room that you're welcome to use."

"I know this house," Lavinia Lester said. "And I know Mr. Winship. I've been here several times when he was practicing. He handled my husband's will and estate for me, and helped me set up a trust for my son."

"Oh," Mike said, profoundly surprised. This was a formidable woman, but . . . black? A black client in this house? "Well, then, come and have a cup of coffee while I get him up. I've just made fresh."

"I brought my own thermos, thank you," the dark woman said, but she sounded only composed, not forbidding. "I brought my lunch, too. I will do that every day, so you won't need to bother keeping food for me. I'll be happy to get Mr. Winship's breakfast and lunch, and leave something for the two of you for supper, like Mr. Canaday said, but it suits me better to bring my own and eat it after Mr. Winship has had his. I eat later than most people."

"Well . . . if you're sure," Mike said. She supposed she should have demurred, protested that the extra groceries would be no trouble, but she sensed that this dignified personage meant just what she said, and would not in any case have relished dining with John Winship any more than he would have enjoyed sharing his meal with her. Business was one thing, the intimacy of meals quite another. Mike breathed an inward sigh of relief. She had been afraid that something about the woman would provoke her father to one of his easily aroused, weak, abusive rages, but she could see nothing, no snags or roughness, on this flawless surface that might catch his temper.

"I ought to warn you that my father is probably not like you remember him," she said. "I'm afraid his state of mind and temper aren't too good these days."

"Most people who've had strokes undergo personality changes," Mrs. Lester said. "And cancer almost always causes depression. Don't worry, Miss Winship. I'm used to both of them."

"Call me Mike," Mike said. "I won't know who you're talking to if you call me Miss Winship."

"Mike," said Lavinia Lester with a small, formal smile. But she did not ask Mike to call her Lavinia, and so Mike didn't. She left the kitchen feeling oddly bested in some contest in which she had not known she was engaged, but also relieved that no contrived jocularity or kitchen-sink camaraderie was going to be required of her. She knew as if she could see into the future that Lavinia Lester would be efficient, dependable, quiet, competent, and unobtrusive, and that she would go out from the Pomeroy Street house when she was no longer needed as much an enigma as she had come into it this morning.

"Good," Mike said to herself, going to wake her father while Mrs. Lester began, as smoothly as if oiled, to prepare his breakfast. "I'll have all the time in the world to myself, and I won't have to watch *Wheel of Fortune* with her. She probably watches *MacNeil-Lehrer*, anyway. And she sure as hell won't tote."

Her father's bedroom was the same one that he had used all during Mike's childhood and adolescence. It was a large square room with a high ceiling and crown moldings at the back of the first floor, directly across the long hall from his study. A rudimentary bathroom joined it and the smaller room behind the large living room that Mike had opened and put in order for Lavinia Lester. Her own childhood room was as far away from it as it was possible to be in the house; she did not know if this was by his long-ago design or simple expediency. Hers was at the top of the house and looked out over the front yard and Pomeroy Street, above the dining room. DeeDee had had the room opposite hers, above the living room and on the same side as her father's. Now it and the other rooms upstairs, except Mike's, were closed and, Mike found when she tried a knob, locked. She was not particularly curious as to why.

She rapped softly on her father's closed door and, getting no reply, opened the door and went a cautious step or two into the room. It was curtained and dark, and the old air conditioner made a weary cave sound in the high-ceilinged room, as hers did upstairs. She looked around hesitantly. She could have counted on both hands the times in her entire life that she had been in this room. Not even DeeDee had frequented it, though she had come in and out more often than Mike had. Somehow, in childhood, it had been unthinkable to disturb John Winship in the room where he slept and dressed and undressed and kept his clothes. What if she should see him naked? She would, she had thought, be blinded if she did. Mike did not like entering the room now; she moved, unconsciously, on tiptoe, and when she called him, she did so in a whisper. He was not in his bed.

"What do you want?" he replied in the thin, peevish voice of the new-old man, and she started, and turned toward the sound. He was sitting in his wheelchair in the corner of the room, fully dressed, in the dimness . . . not reading, not looking out of the window into the back garden, not drowsing. Simply sitting there, looking straight ahead at her as she came into his field of vision.

"Well, look at you," Mike said heartily, as if to a child. "You're all dressed and everything. I didn't know you could do that by yourself. How long have you been up?"

"Since five o'clock, like I always am," he snapped. "Of course I can get myself dressed. Did you think I had to have somebody come in here and dress me like a baby? Did you think you were going to have to do that, too? Wonder you came down here at all."

Mike bit back a curt reply and walked over to the window behind him. She drew aside the curtains and light flooded in. In it, she saw that where once there had been near-monastic spareness and linear order, a dismal jumble of clothes and shoes and piled magazines and newspapers and books now prevailed. Among them sat empty plates and cups and glasses, and bottles and medicine vials covered nearly every flat surface in the room. It was as bad as Priss's house, except that Priss's clutter had the richness and resonance of a vital, living personality about it. This was simply mess, old and stale and dying, or dead. She could not suppress an involuntary gasp, and her father grabbed the cord to the drapes from her hands and jerked them savagely together again.

"If I'd wanted light, I'd have opened the goddamned curtains myself," he spat. "Leave my room alone, Micah. You and that high-falutin' nigger in there can scrub the rest of this house till your knuckles bleed, but leave this room alone."

"I wouldn't touch it with a ten-foot pole," Mike said distantly, and put her hands on the back of his chair to wheel him into the kitchen. From the good smells that crept into the room, Mrs. Lester had his breakfast ready. Let her have him, and all the joy of him.

"And I can get around by myself," he added.

"Fine," Mike said peacefully and turned to leave the room. She was not about to risk the ringing purity of the bell jar on this petulant old man. She intended, from then on, to leave him as completely and politely alone as occupancy under this roof allowed.

"Wait a minute," he said. "What's she calling herself these days . . . that nigger you've got in there to ride herd on me?"

"Mrs. Lester is what she's calling herself," Mike said equably. "And if you call her a nigger in her hearing, she'll probably hand you your head. On her way out the door. And then you *will* be in the soup, because I'll get you somebody so much worse than her that you'll rue the day you opened your mouth. And while I'm at it, I'll get somebody deaf, so you can't run them off. Now. Are you ready to go out, or shall I tell Mrs. Lester that you'll be staying in here until lunchtime?"

There was a long silence, and then he laughed, the sound of powdering old eggshells that she remembered from the day before.

"Tell her I'll be out terreckly," he said. "And that I want the crusts cut off my toast *before* she puts it in the toaster. Goddamned crumbs all over the place if you cut 'em off after. And tell her I'm obliged to her for coming. She's not so bad for a nigger. Pretty smart. I did a little work for her a while back, and she seemed to understand what I told her, and paid me right off. First time I can remember that a nigger ever did either one."

Mike ignored the apology implicit in the little speech and went out of the room, her mouth stiff with distaste. She knew that it was useless to challenge her father's obscenely prejudicial speech, or even to protest it, but she did not intend to listen to it. As she shut the door, just barely refraining from slamming it, she heard the eggshell cackle again.

She dressed in white pants and the striped fisherman's jersey from L. L. Bean that Rachel had given her for her last birthday ("*Oh, Rachel!*") and went out of the still-cool house into the June sun. She had pocketed the keys to the clifflike old Cadillac, and thought to drive around a bit before the morning shoppers appeared in the streets. Her spirits shrank restlessly from the thought of confinement in the house with her father, and the day loomed emptily ahead of her. Walking seemed suddenly unthinkable; she did not feel, yet, like meeting and talking to anyone she might have known before.

Mike was certain that the whole town knew by now that John Winship's prodigal daughter, the New York writer, the defiant child, was home again after her long exile . . . home in that house on which she had brought such shame, and without her Jewish husband and child, or any visible means of support. She remembered how she had felt about Lytton in those last days of her senior year, when she was so eager to leave it in its sucking insularity and smugness and get on with her life . . . hers and Bayard Sewell's. All those people, the ones whose parochialism and stricture of vision had roused her to such a passion of impatience, whose meager hands and minds had made as if to hold her . . . all of them, she thought, would be waiting avidly for some new explosion in the Winship house, some new Winship drama for their delectation. Mike knew she could not avoid them, but, as with her father, she did not intend to seek confrontation. She would, she thought, looking at her watch, be safe. It was not yet nine o'clock. If she recalled correctly, no one and nothing stirred on the streets of Lytton until after ten.

She met J.W. Cromie coming down the stairs from his apartment over the garage, dressed in green coveralls. They were starched to glassiness, and he smelled powerfully of Old Spice. He nodded at her, not breaking his stride.

"Good morning, J.W.," she said, implacably cheerful and noncommittal. "I thought I'd take the car out for a little while, if you don't mind. I'm anxious to get a look at town. I promise I won't run it into a tree or a parking meter, and I'll have it back before lunchtime."

"It your car, Miss Mike," he said. "Yours and Mr. John's. I don't be drivin' it except when Mr. John want to go for a ride, or need somethin' from the sto'."

"Well . . . thank you," Mike said. She did not move, and he paused and looked at her, waiting for her to finish what she had to say. But it was obvious to her that he was not going to speak of his own accord, and so she said again, "Thank you," and went into the garage.

"You welcome," J.W. said, and disappeared into the sunlight.

Mike slid the big old car silently down Pomeroy Street and turned onto Main, which ran, fittingly enough, through the center of town. The powerful V-8 engine purred with cleanliness and care. The interior leather shone softly and even the worn floor mats were spotless. The car was bigger than anything she had driven in recent years; she had never owned a car in Manhattan, but opted for subcompacts whenever she needed a rental on assignment, which was often. She felt now as if she were sliding along in a great, silent, ornate Pharaoh's barge on an equally silent river. It was a cloistered, invulnerable, and almost invisible feeling. Mike felt protected from the eyes of Lytton.

She was wrong about the people. The streets were full of them. People in cars and trucks, queuing up at the three new stoplights in the middle of town; people walking briskly in and out of stores whose facades and names she did not know; people going in and out of the two large shopping centers at either end of Lytton's business district. Mike drifted the Cadillac up one street and down another, recognizing all of them but feeling no stirring of familiarity, no pull of particularity to crack the hemisphere of the bell jar. Sealed within it and borne along in the great bronze coffin of the automobile, she drove the streets of Lytton and saw no face that she knew. In the drugstores, the bank, the hardware and insurance and real estate offices, the tax service office, the barber and beauty shops, the florist and the laundromat and the service stations and the appliance store and the cafés and fast-food outlets and the post office and library, in the new medical mall and the Ford, Chevrolet, and GM lots, in the parking lots of the condominiums and apartment complexes that had not been there when she left, and the churches and funeral homes that had, there were people: men, women, and children, as prosperous and banal and anonymous as starlings, and Mike knew none of them. The only blacks she saw were in small knots at the bus stops; riding, as she was, in cars; or going in and out of the supermarkets.

Later that afternoon, she stopped in to see Priss Comfort.

"How did you find Lytton?" Priss asked, over coffee and strawberry Pop Tarts. "Changed much?"

"Not at all, except that I don't know anybody anymore," Mike said. "Oh, there are some new stores, and a few more traffic lights, but it looks just as quaint and adorable and Brigadoony as it did in 1964. The Lyttons of the world don't change. Especially for the blacks. I've been all over town, and I could swear integration hasn't gotten here yet. Nobody's gotten the word. The only black faces you see are in the supermarkets or somebody's kitchen or backyard, like J.W. and Lavinia Lester. I didn't see a single black face in a single restaurant, or at the library or the bank or city hall . . . not even the car wash. Not even the *laundromat,* that great leveler of men. They don't even call them blacks; it's still Negroes in Lytton. Or worse. Much worse, at my house. And J.W. God, he's about to 'yassum' me to death. What's the matter with J.W., Priss? Why didn't he get out of here while he had the chance? He must hate it here. He's in virtual bondage to my father. Why does he go along with this yard-boy shit?"

Priss Comfort regarded Mike in silence for a while and then sighed.

"This is his home, Mike," she said. "This town is his; it's all he knows. It's him. How can he hate it? He goes along because he has to *get* along. You're looking just at surfaces, just at the bad side of us; you haven't had time to see the good yet, even if you're able. And it's here. There's great good in Lytton; there always was, no matter what you thought . . . and think. Of course, there's plenty of not so good, too. Lord, sometimes I think . . . we've known the best and the worst of the South, you and I. One day maybe the worst will be just a . . . sliver, like a waning moon. Each generation that comes along moves us further from our darker side. Sometimes I'm afraid we'll move too far and lose the sweetness and bite of the South, along with the rot. But move we must. Don't hate Lytton, Mike. It's you, just like it's J.W. Cromie."

"I wish you'd take to drink again," Mike said. "This metaphysical wisdom is more than I can stand. I will not be swayed."

"Oh, you will be." Priss grinned evilly at her. "I have only just begun to work on you."

They sat in silence for a while, and the white cat came stretching his bulk out from Priss's bedroom and jumped up into Mike's lap. He butted his large head against her hand until, laughing, she petted him, and he settled down comfortably in her lap and began a rusty, rumbling purr. Priss beamed at them like a fond parent with a precocious child.

"Are things any better with you and John?" she said presently.

"I guess they're as good as they're going to be," Mike said. "He's doing his dead-level best to provoke me, and I'm not letting him do it. He'll probably stop if I just don't respond, which I don't. You know, Priss, we've done a complete switch. He never paid half this much attention to me when I was little; I'd almost have welcomed this then. It would have been better than what he gave me. But now, it's like he's trying his best to drive me away. I could understand it after that last business, when I left home; he did say he never wanted to see me again, after all. And that suited me just fine. But now everybody's saying that he's the one who asked for me to come back. So here I am. And as far as I can tell, he doesn't feel one shred of sentiment of any kind for me. Or anything else, for that matter. Except that old house, of course."

Priss frowned. "People think old people are sentimental, but they're not," she said. "We're ruthless, most of us. We've had to say good-bye to too many things to afford sentiment. At best we're ruthlessly selective. No matter what your father might feel for you, he can't show it, not even to himself. He's lost you once."

"And whose fault was that?"

"I know," Priss said. "Old people aren't rational, either. Mainly it bores us. Too many years of trying to make rationalization work like it's supposed to. Finally we just stop trying to make sense. The point is, John stands to maybe lose that house now, and he knows he's going to lose his life sooner rather than later. He's not a fool. So I think he figures to see if he can run you off again before you go on your own. And you will, you know. You said so yourself."

"Well, this was never meant to be permanent, Priss. I've made that plain to everybody. As soon as we see how Mrs. Lester is going to work out . . ."

"I know, I know," Press said impatiently. "You're off after the brass ring again. Only it strikes me that maybe it's not what or where you thought it was."

"What do you mean?" Mike said. Uneasiness swam past the glass around her like a young barracuda, distant but potentially harmful.

"Oh, nothing really. I just had some idea that sooner or later, if you stayed long enough, you might come to write something about Lytton and the people here," Priss said. "Just to pass the time, keep your hand in and all, since you've more or less got to be here anyway. It would be interesting to see what you had to say about your own folks."

"A, they're not my own folks, Priss, present company and a few others excepted, and B, I don't have anything at all to say about them. What on earth would there be for me to write about in Lytton? There's no pivotal crisis here, no contemporary drama going on. You know that's what I do. It's how I've made my name. What on earth has anybody around here *done* that I would want to write about them?"

"I'm not interested in what they've done . . . though it's a damned sight more than you seem to think. I'm interested in what you *think* about them. How you feel about them. How it feels to come home again at just this time and place in history; what resonances you feel now, what speaks to you out of your time here before. It could make a pretty interesting book, you know, and from what you said, you need a book."

"Except that it's already been written," Mike said. "By Thomas Wolfe. And look where it got him."

"Yes," Priss said, and she was not smiling. "Look."

"Oh, come on, Priss," Mike said. "I don't want to commit Literature with a capital L. I don't even think I could. I'm simply too . . . detached, too journalistic, if you will . . . to handle that kind of point of view."

"Too scared, you mean," Priss said. "Because it would mean opening yourself up to everything . . . what's past, what's happening right now, what's likely to happen. It would mean going through it, experiencing it, feeling it. I guess you're right at that, Mike. I guess you really can't do that."

"Well, I told you that two days ago, didn't I?" Mike said, irritated and oddly hurt by Priss's words. "I'm just not interested in spill-your-guts prose. It's . . . unseemly, somehow. It offends me."

"Just a thought," Priss said. "Hand me that sorry cat and get on out of here, now. Your Mrs. Lester is going to want to go home; it's past three. Mrs. Lester. Hmm. I can remember when she was Lavinia Parrott, a skinny little thing without enough to eat, helping her mother take in wash and carry it back to folks. Smart as a whip even then. I always wished I could have gotten hold of her in my class."

Mike handed the limp, purring Walker Pussy to Priss and left. Priss's talk of a book about Lytton left her feeling inadequate, chastened, slightly foolish and recalcitrant, exactly as if she had negligently done far less than her best at some assignment in class to which Priss had set her. She remembered the feeling well. Priss would never settle for mere competence from Mike. When she had protested, rightly, that not nearly so much was demanded of the other students in Priss's classes, Priss had said only, "It's relative, Mike."

"What the hell does she expect from me?" Mike said aloud,

getting out of the Cadillac into the whitened heat of the Winship backyard. "I do what I do better than anybody in New York. What does Priss know, anyhow?"

"Knows an awful lot for a maiden lady from little ol' Lytton, Georgia, seems to me," Sam Canaday said, materializing at her elbow and taking it showily to help her from the car. "But she sure doesn't let on that she does. A virtuous woman. She openeth her mouth with wisdom; and in her tongue is the law of kindness. Her price is far above rubies."

"Do you always sneak up behind people?" Mike snapped, the hot, treacherous color flooding up her neck from her chest. "Every time I look up, there you are, lurking. Don't you ever work?"

"Not if I can help it," he said, grinning. "Sorry if I startled you. I was looking for J.W. No, I think there's altogether too much toil and labor in the world. Look at you Yankees; skin and bones and stress headaches and all such; like to jump right out of your skins. You should consider the lilies of the field. They toil not, neither do they spin . . ."

"And what is it with you and the Bible?" Mike asked. "Priss tells me nobody in town is speaking to you because you shot your mouth off about the Old Testament in church. Do you really think it impresses us Yankees, as you're fond of calling us when you're in your Jeeter Lester mode . . . which is most of the time?"

"Why, Miz Singer-Winship." He beamed, hand still under Mike's elbow. "I didn't mean *you* were a Yankee. Cross my heart. Southern girl like you ought to know that all us southern boys know our Good Book, even if we don't learn anything else. It makes us good lawyers."

"It sounds more like you're on the back of a flatbed truck speaking in tongues," Mike said.

"Oh, I've done that, too," Sam Canaday said comfortably.

"And handled snakes, I presume."

"Something like that."

He laughed, gave her elbow a squeeze, and ran up the outside garage stairs toward J.W.'s aerie, taking the creaking wooden steps two at a time. Mike looked after him in open dislike. In the merciless sunlight, she could see that the dark blue polo shirt that he wore today strained across his back, and that it was not fat that tautened it, but packed, sliding muscle. His biceps seemed to burst with muscle, too, as did his forearms, and the open hand that gripped the weathered railing was webbed with playing muscle. It was callused and scarred too; Mike saw the glisten of tight-pulled scar tissue, as if he had been scalded or burnt, on the back of his hand and on two of his fingers. Primitive hands, powerful and broken. Not a lawyer's hands.

Her eyes traveled up his arm to his chest and neck, and then further, and she saw that he had stopped on the small porch outside J.W.'s door and was looking down at her. Her face flamed anew, and she turned and hurried through the heat haze over the driveway into the house. At every step she could feel his eyes on her back.

Later that evening, after she had warmed up the excellent chicken pot pie that Lavinia Lester had left for her and her father and they had eaten it in silence, staring at the kitchen television set, DeeDee came by for a quick visit. She and Mike sat in the still-hot lavender seclusion of the wisteria bower while *Let's Make a Deal* brayed from the kitchen, DeeDee fanning herself mightily and greedily attacking the peach cobbler that neither Mike nor her father had wanted. She had come to invite Mike to dinner at her house the following evening and would not take Mike's halfhearted no for an answer.

"Don't be silly. You need to get out, and you haven't ever seen my house," she said, when Mike had protested that the little dinner party would be too much effort, with Duck's mother needing so much attention.

"I'll just sweeten up her five o'clock medicine a tad," DeeDee said, dabbing at her sweat-bedewed upper lip with the tail of her astounding coral T-shirt. "I think it's got belladonna or something in it. She nods right off, usually. You think I'm going to let my little sister sit over here in this heat eating in front of the television set when my house is all air-conditioned and my famous Coca-Cola ham is already in the oven?"

"Well, that's sweet of you, and I'd love to come," Mike lied. The thought of DeeDee's great, fat-glistening ham, basted liberally with Coca-Cola, that she had been much praised for in high school home economics, was about as appetizing as eating boiled, rice-stuffed dog, Chinese-style.

"Oh, I'm glad," DeeDee bubbled, and Mike thought that she did sound glad; sounded almost excited.

"I hope you're not going to work yourself to death," she said. "It's just plain too hot to eat much, let alone cook all day."

"Oh, shoot, I need a little festivity as much as anybody," DeeDee said. "I don't ever go anywhere or do anything but church, and I don't even do that since Mama Wingo came. This will be a real treat for me. Duck, too. You come on, hear?"

"I will, then."

"And Mikie, put on something besides pants, why don't you? Something pretty." DeeDee said it archly, but she was looking at Mike closely, and something in her gaze reminded Mike of Sam Canaday's eyes as they had followed her into the house that afternoon.

Why does everybody keep *looking* at me? she wondered fretfully.

"What's wrong with pants?" she said to DeeDee.

"Oh, nothing," her sister said, smiling placatingly. "You just look like a skinny little boy in them, that's all. And you could be so pretty. It sort of hurts me to see you looking so . . . thin and unfeminine. Not that you look *bad,* you understand, just . . ."

"I know." Mike smiled at her discomfort. "Thin and unfeminine."

She remembered what Priss had said about DeeDee, about how she must seem to her sister: slender and alien and severely chic in her narrow pants and shirts and expensive shoes.

"Okay, Dee," she said. "I promise. The ruffledy-est thing I've got. Scarlett O'Hara wouldn't be caught dead in it."

"Good," DeeDee said, waddling heavily across the parched grass to where her battered little Volkswagen beetle squatted under one of the great water oaks. It had a huge orange daisy fastened to the end of its radio antenna.

"You'll be glad you did," she called back over her shoulder.

"Sure I will," Mike called back. "And Mama Wingo will be enchanted."

"She won't be the only one," DeeDee caroled gaily, and got into the beetle and closed the door tinnily.

Mike went back into the house and shut the front door against the exhausted evening air. At a quarter of eight, the thermometer beside the front door read ninety-four degrees.

SEVENTEEN

The first thing she thought when she saw him was that she should have known from DeeDee's behavior the previous night that he would be here. The second was that he had become the only kind of man possible to him: that he had been genetically programmed at birth to look like this in his fortieth year.

"Hello," she said. Her voice sounded faraway and fragile in her own ears. "I might have known I'd find you here."

And then, because it sounded so rude and abrupt, she flushed violently, and was so embarrassed by the flood of heat on her neck and face that she reddened a second time.

"Hello," said Bayard Sewell. "I *did* know I'd find you here."

He rose from the La-Z-Boy recliner in the Wingos' stunted, pine-paneled den and walked across the orange shag carpet toward her, hand outstretched, as she had last seen him in the foyer of her father's house on a summer night two decades before. He moved as lightly as always, like a hip-hung jungle cat, and as deliberately, and Mike thought that she might have watched him walk toward her in just that way only hours before, instead of years. She put out her hand, and he covered it with his.

"Cat got your tongue?" He smiled, his teeth flashing white in the sun-dark of his face. He had said it to her many times, she remembered, when anger or some other strong emotion had silenced her temporarily. He bent and kissed her cheek, and Mike made the ridiculous, automatic air-kissing motion that she had learned long ago in Manhattan beside his ear. He smelled of starched cotton and gin and something indefinable that had always been Bayard. Had she been long blinded, Mike would have known that it was Bayard Sewell who kissed her by the smell of him.

"It's good to see you, Bay," she said. "Priss told me you were

137

still here. I was a little surprised. You look . . . just like you always did."

What in God's name is the matter with me? she thought detachedly, still smiling her cool social smile at him, her hand still in his. My brain has turned to syrup. He doesn't look in the least like he always did. He is the best-looking man I have ever seen.

He was not, of course, but he was undoubtedly an arresting man. Heads would and undoubtedly did turn after him frequently in public places. He had the sort of visual impact that certain celebrities have, and heads of state; something indefinable that stopped the eye and breath without any debt to conventional handsomeness. On a trip to Washington with her sophomore class, Mike had seen President John Kennedy rise to throw out the first ball at a Senators' game, and had felt the same leaping wildfire force about his sheer physical presence. Bayard Sewell was as apparently unaware of his aura as the young president had been.

He was lean to thinness, and his thick, dark hair was frosted now with gray, and there were deep creases in his narrow face, the kind that pain leaves, and webs of fine wrinkles beside his eyes that stood out like white crosshatching. He wore sharply creased khakis and a blue oxford shirt open at the throat, sleeves rolled up to expose his forearms. His feet were thrust sockless into age-softened Topsiders. It was the uniform of her time and caste, as familiar to her as any other accoutrement of her world in the East, but it seemed on Bayard Sewell as if some cosmic tailor had fitted him alone in the twentieth century to wear it. His hand over hers was warm, almost hot, and a small pulse leaped in the hollow of his throat. Otherwise, he might have been carved of ebony and blue ice and some sort of golden wood.

"You don't," Bayard Sewell said, leading her across the hideous carpet to the pine-and-leather sofa between the twin recliners, at the end of the room. "You look better than you ever did, and just as good as I thought you would. I like you in ruffles. You never used to wear them."

"I never used to dare," Mike said lightly, hating the ruffled skirt and embroidered blouse that she had bought on some long-forgotten impulse in Puerto Vallarta and seldom worn since. Derek Blessing had told her once that she looked like a plucked duckling in a doily in the clothes, and she had regretted the lapse from androgynous simplicity and not repeated it. She felt mild rage at DeeDee for tricking her into furbelows for Bayard Sewell's sake, and disgust at herself for allowing the manipulation.

They sat down on the sofa, and he leaned back and crossed one bare ankle over the other knee and laced his fingers behind his dark head.

"You were probably lured over here under distinctly false pretenses, and I should feel badly about it, but I don't," he said. "I'm gladder to see you than I can say, and I was afraid you wouldn't want to see me. I put DeeDee up to this, so you can spare her your considerable wrath."

"Why on earth did you think I wouldn't want to see you?" Mike asked. Inside the bell jar there was a curious shortness to her breath, as if she could not lift her words out on it.

"After my performance the last time I saw you, you'd have every right to turn around and walk out of here," he said simply, and all at once things were all right again, uncomplicatedly and ordinarily all right and okay.

"I haven't thought of that in years." She smiled, a free and natural smile now, feeling nothing so much as pure, unremarkable comfort.

"I have," he said, but he smiled too. The smile deepened the creases beside his mouth and wrapped their last searing meeting in light and tossed it forever away.

The swinging door at the opposite end of the den opened, and DeeDee came sweeping into the room with a tray, propelled by a powerful gust of Krystle. She wore a vast peony-printed caftan that was caught under her huge breasts by a velvet drawstring, leaving bat-wing sleeves to fall free from her great white arms. The sleeves were so amply cut that Mike could see her sister's fiercely boned and cantilevered brassiere, cutting so deeply into the bleached flesh that it lapped and surged over the stout nylon and buried it. DeeDee's cleavage was beyond reaction tonight; the deep V of the caftan must have been chosen to showcase it. Pink crystal beads slid hopelessly into it, and matching crystal chandeliers swung at DeeDee's shapely little ears. Her heavy black hair was loose down her back tonight, and gave her the look of an immense and terrifyingly arch witch. Her eyelids were the pure flat blue of a bluejay's wing, and stark black rimmed her eyes and arched her brows. On her little feet were high-heeled gold mules. Mike wanted to avert her eyes and felt the heat rising again on her neck, but Bayard Sewell gave DeeDee an easy smile.

"The matchmaker cometh," he said, and there was affection in his voice as well as amusement.

"Well, you two, are you getting reacquainted after all these years?" DeeDee piped, putting the tray down on the raw yellow pine coffee table in front of the sofa. The table was shaped, vaguely, like a kidney. On the tray were little frankfurters wrapped in bacon on toothpicks, and a bowl of something colored a primary purple.

She gave Mike a hostessy red smile and patted Bayard Sewell proprietarily on the shoulder and lowered her flowered bulk into the recliner nearest him. Her short legs flew a little into the air, and the gilt mules flashed up at Mike. The soles were so new that they bore no scratches, and as DeeDee pulled herself upright by the arms of the recliner, Mike caught a glimpse of a dangling price tag under one bat-winged arm. Her heart twisted suddenly with pity for the pretty, petite good girl buried somewhere deep in the hopeless flesh of this mountainous woman. DeeDee's flushed cheeks and sparkling eyes, as well as the new finery and the Krystle, spoke of the rarity of this small party. Mike resolved to take DeeDee into Atlanta soon and often for shopping and movies and lunches and such other treats as she would accept.

"What's to catch up on?" Bayard Sewell said. "I know everything about Mike; I've read everything she's ever written, and you've kept me posted on the rest of it. She's left us all in the dust, and I've been applauding her trajectory for years. And God knows there's precious little to know about me, and what there is I'm sure you told her before her feet hit the ground at the airport."

His smile took the heat out of his words, and DeeDee made a grotesquely coy grimace.

"I never did, Mr. Smartypants, so there." She dimpled at him. "I didn't say and she didn't ask. If she knows anything about you, she found out from somebody besides me. Conceited thing."

"I know about all the honors and the career and the legislature and being mayor and everything because Priss told me," Mike said. "None of it surprised me. I was only surprised because he was still in Lytton. I thought he'd at least be president by now."

She smiled at her sister and Bayard Sewell in turn, who gave her an exaggerated leer of mock modesty.

"What's wrong with Lytton?" DeeDee cried. "Who'd appreciate him more than we do in Lytton? And *pooh* about being president; did Priss tell you he was Mr. South Fulton County last year? Nobody from Lytton has ever been that before. He got a plaque and a silver cup and there was an *enormous* banquet for him."

"All that was missing was the white smoke coming out the chimney," Bayard Sewell said. "But everybody *did* get to kiss my ring."

"Kiss your ring? Nobody kissed your ring, you silly—" began DeeDee.

"Congratulations, your Holiness," Mike said quickly. "Everybody must be awfully proud of you. Why aren't you at Castel Gondolfo in this heat?"

"Bay's just back from Tennessee," DeeDee said.

"Just as good." Mike twinkled at him. A secret glee seemed to bubble somewhere deep within her; a small part of her wanted to giggle and laugh and hold her sides. The rest of her stood far back and smiled with indulgent amusement at the silly-child part. It had not shown itself in many years.

"Were you waltzing with your darling?" the silly-child part said brightly.

"Well, not exactly," he said "But I did bring her home."

Mike remembered Priss Comfort's words about Bayard Sewell's wife and her illness, and flinched. He caught the movement, slight though it was.

"It's all right," he said. "I know Priss probably told you Sally wasn't well. She's been in the hospital in Nashville, and she's much better. I'm glad to have her home. But she wasn't quite up to tonight, so I came by myself. Dee and Duck are family enough so I felt like I could."

"Bay!" Duck Wingo's voice bellowed from behind the swinging door. "Get off your scrawny ass and help me with these martinis. Anybody that drinks these goddamn things in my house got to make 'em himself."

Mike frowned involuntarily at the bludgeoning familiarity of the voice and words, but Bayard winked at them and got up lazily from the sofa and padded toward the kitchen. In the dreadful, over-crowded, and bibeloted little den he looked more than ever like an attenuated great cat in a western doll's house.

"Excuse me while I save the holy elixir from the infidel," he said, and disappeared behind the swinging door. He moved with the ease born of long familiarity, but Mike found it nearly impossible to imagine that he had spent much time in this house. He might have been the spawn of an entirely different planet than DeeDee and Duck Wingo.

DeeDee beamed after him and then turned conspiratorially to Mike.

"He's a saint, just a saint," she said in a loud whisper. "Not well, my foot. She was drying out again; everybody knows that. Sally Sewell has been a drunk for years. She's dying by inches with her liver, and none too soon, *I* say. She's mortified him in public a million times. Everything from drunk driving to public drunkenness, and the *men!* She's been in and out of all the motels around here so often they don't even make her sign the register anymore. Just wait till the man leaves and then call Bay, and he goes and gets her and takes her home. Just a rabbit. But he's never been anything with her but gentle and patient. It would break your heart to see them to-gether. He hired her old nurse to come and stay full time with her, and he built her a great big house not long before the oldest little boy died. I guess Priss told you about that, didn't she? They'd named him Win, after Daddy, and he drowned in the swimming pool. Nobody comes right out and says so, but everybody knows she was drinking when it happened. He's never really gotten over it. She wasn't fit to raise the other two children—and they're outstanding, Mike, just like him—so he and old Opal did that. He's trying to get the Department of Transportation to back off Daddy's old house; he's got lots of influence in the legislature, even though he's so new. But I'm afraid he's putting his career in jeopardy. There's a powerful lobby for the DOT there."

"I'm sorry," Mike murmured, feeling the silly-child part of her vanish as if by magic outside the shell of the bell jar. "I'm sorry he's had such a bad time. I'm sorry she has. Priss didn't tell me that."

But there was a tiny part of her, tiny and ratlike and biting, that was not sorry at all for the ruin and shame of Sally Chambers Sewell.

Duck came blustering into the den then, carrying a bottle of bourbon and two glasses, and Bayard came behind him with a stemmed glass, whisper-pale and frosted, in each hand. He handed one to Mike and lifted the other.

"To us, one and all," he said. "And to Mike in particular. Home is really home again now."

Mike nodded, suddenly shy, and they all lifted glasses, Duck slopping a little of his bourbon over his wrist and DeeDee taking a great gulp and squeezing her eyes fiercely shut in an effort not to cough.

"How's yours?" Bayard said to Mike. "I didn't even ask you if you drank martinis. Hardly anybody does, anymore."

"I do," Mike said. "I always did."

The evening that might have been such a strain wasn't. That it was not, she saw later, was a triumph over the sheer awfulness of DeeDee and Duck's mean little tinderbox house; tricked out in savagely yellow, shellacked Colorado pine furniture and ersatz varnished western artifacts, it reminded her of a plastic toy bunkhouse and stunted all feeling and nuance out of the air and the evening. It was simply not possible to sense subtleties, currents and eddies of resonance after an hour or so in DeeDee Wingo's home. But in spite of the oppressive weight of the house, Mike realized gratefully and obscurely that what she felt at her sister's dinner table was comfort. Looking around the round wagon-wheel table, she realized that DeeDee and Duck felt at ease, too, and under the ease there bubbled in each of them a sort of conspiratorial glee, the feverish excitement of sly children. DeeDee was even more arch and proprietary than usual, Duck even more gelatinously expansive. Bayard Sewell, on her right, was as loosely and dryly ironic with her as he was with DeeDee and Duck, as he had always been, and Mike knew that it was from him that the warm, fluid flow of the evening emanated. He generated good feeling like a fountain.

He spoke of Mike's work with a real and obvious respect and admiration, untainted by the sliding envy that she was accustomed to encountering among certain acquaintances who had known her for many years. For a few minutes, warmed at the fire of his interest, her work became real again to her, as it had not been since the first tongue of fear seared her on the train to Bridgehampton, and she could feel the cool, preternaturally focused wash of pure energy that she always felt in the midst of an actual story or during an interview.

Her fingertips could, for a moment, actually feel the light, silky surge of the word processor keyboard under them; her eyes could see the liquid spill of the green letters and words across the black screen. Her whole being felt poised and concentrated again, as it did when a piece was going well.

"Sometimes," he said, "reading some of your stuff, I get the feeling that you're not so much the writer as a kind of . . ."

". . . magnifying glass," Mike finished the sentence for him, catching the thought from out of the air as she had done so often all those years ago. She stopped and stared at him, startled, and then flushed.

"You always could do that." He smiled at her. It was, as was everything else about him, a natural and spontaneous smile.

Nothing else of their shared past was mentioned. They did not speak of John Winship or the DOT action, or of his life or her homecoming. He led the conversation like a dolphin leaping through warm seas, and DeeDee and Duck followed him with more grace and agility than they actually possessed, speaking and responding outside and above themselves. They talked of national and local politics, of the gossip of Lytton and the progress of Atlanta, of the rococo excesses and arabesques in the state legislature; his fund of anecdotes about his companions in the statehouse was extensive and bordered on the scurrilous, but he included himself in the dry japery and shared the laughter that he drew down on his own head, along with those of his fellow lawmakers. Mike said little, but laughed as heartily as the rest of them at his foolishness, and with the same honest savor. He was a genuinely funny man, and over the course of the evening, as DeeDee and Duck shone with a light brighter than either possessed under the sun of his wit, she began to sense the power of him.

He's wasted here, she thought. He'd be sensational in New York or Washington. Why in God's name does he put up with DeeDee and Duck? He's light-years out of their class.

For toward the end of the evening, after the Coca-Cola ham had been reduced to glistening scraps of clotted fat on the platter and a second and third bottle of Lancer's had been produced and drunk, they began to behave embarrassingly badly. DeeDee's proprietary manner toward him slid over into the grotesque; she was as offensively bossy and familiar as if he had been a gifted, precocious younger brother, or a brilliant young monarch and she a privileged peasant retainer, and she twitted him continuously and with obvious strutting pride about the hours he worked and the state of his health and his tendency to let his fellow legislators, and indeed, according to DeeDee, most of the human race, take advantage of his good nature and kind heart. Duck, heavy-lidded and bursting-faced with wine and pleasure in himself, dropped incident after incident from their apparent long association into the conversation, each time cutting his eyes at Mike to gauge her reaction to his intimacy with this golden lion who was a willing captive in his house. Mike grew more and more annoyed with them and more and more mystified by Bayard Sewell's tolerance, and when DeeDee leaned over him from behind to drop a loud kiss on the top of his black head, her great breasts swallowing his ears on either side of his head and bobbling against his cheeks, and shrilled bibulously, "I could just spank him most of the time, he's so bad, but I can make him mind," Mike's entire chest and face burned with embarrassment and irritation.

DeeDee and Duck rose to clear the table and sent Mike and Bayard back into the living room to "take your shoes off and get comfortable; it's just the shank of the evening, and there's some Amaretto and cream coming." They obeyed. Mike dropped wearily into one of the La-Z-Boys, and Bayard sat on the end of the sofa nearest her and rolled his eyes goodhumoredly at DeeDee's vast, retreating back.

"It's like being hugged by a 1947 Studebaker bumper," he said, but there was no spite in his words. "She's a little much sometimes, and he is pretty much all the time. But she's been as faithful as a good dog to John—to your dad—and she hasn't had a great life. I think of John as family, and so DeeDee and Duck are family, too."

Mike nodded, ashamed of her embarrassment over her sister. The comfort she felt in his presence expanded to include simple, one-celled gratitude. Even though she was bone-tired, marrow-tired, with the new, all-pervasive weariness that had come with the cessation of the great fear and the dropping down of the bell jar, and though she detested Amaretto among all liqueurs within her experience, she was content to let the night bowl on, humming along to whatever conclusion it might take.

For a small space of time, they sat silently, and then he reached over and switched on a small, Stetson-shaped plastic radio. He fiddled with the dial until Barbara Streisand swam smokily into the room, and then leaned back and put his feet up on the coffee table and closed his eyes. Mike saw that there were transparent bluish shadows under them.

"I want to hear everything about you," he said, eyes still closed. "What you think and eat and wear and laugh at, and what your daughter is like, and how you live. But right now I just want to sit here in this room with you and listen to that lady sing. There'll be plenty of time for the other. At least, I hope there will be."

"I expect there will," Mike said. "Don't feel that you have to chat. You look tired."

"It's been a godawful week," he said. He did not open his eyes. It was the only time he came near to speaking of his life in Lytton.

An avian caw from some out-of-sight room pierced the taut, satiny voice from the radio, and Duck and DeeDee came back into the den.

"It's your turn," DeeDee said to her husband. "I did her before dinner." Duck Wingo swore under his breath and went toward the sound, and Bayard Sewell rose, saying that he had to get home and let Opal get some sleep. Surprisingly, DeeDee did not press him to stay, but walked with him to the back door. Following them, Mike thought that he had probably long since stopped using the front one.

At the door, he stopped and looked at them with the first hesitation and uncertainty Mike had seen on his face during the entire evening, or, for that matter, ever.

"Do you think the three of you might come have a little supper with us toward the end of the week?" he said. "Maybe on Friday?"

DeeDee's face leaped immediately into lines of exaggerated concern.

"Are you sure, Bay?" she asked solicitously. "You know, *really* sure?" Her lash-veiled look at him was avid with import.

"Oh, yes," he said. "Sally's much better this time, really. She can handle a quiet dinner; Opal and I will come up with something. Kill the fatted calf for you, Mike."

"If you're sure," Mike said doubtfully. "I don't want to cause a fuss."

He looked at her intently for a moment, and then said, "My wife has an alcohol problem, Mike. I'm sure you've heard. She's a pretty high-strung girl, and she never really got over our son, the one

146

—who died. But she's brave and a fighter, and she's been going like gangbusters since she came home this time. I'm proud of her. I want to show her off. And she wants to meet you. She's kept up with you, like we all have. She's one of your greatest fans."

He dropped his eyes and studied the meager shag beneath his feet with absorption, and then looked back at her.

"I'd be truly grateful if you'd come," he said. "It would be a real favor."

"Of course, Bay," Mike said warmly. "Of course I'll come. I think it sounds lovely."

EIGHTEEN

On the second Friday evening that she was in Lytton, Mike walked in the twilight around the corner from her father's house and up the street to where Bayard Sewell lived with Sally Chambers Sewell.

There had been a fierce, brief thunderstorm earlier, and the heat and humidity had retreated momentarily, leaving Lytton washed and cool and fragrant. Leaves sparkled, and gutters foamed with muddy torrents, and earthworms wiggled in ecstasy on sidewalks, and the sweet, grassy earth breathed and sucked loudly as it drank in wetness and deliverance. Birds shouted and the wisteria and mimosa were near to heartbreaking. Mike slipped off her sandals and rolled up the cuffs of her linen pants and waded in the puddles, feeling light-headed and on the verge of something huge and wonderful, just out of sight. She remembered the feeling from childhood. She had had it ever since DeeDee's dinner party, but had refused to examine it.

She had not been up this street in the week she had been home. She had not even looked in this direction from her bathroom window. She remembered that she had once been able to see the roof of the Parsons house from there, but now the chinaberry tree that had been young then was grown and full and shielding, and in any case she had not looked. Now she saw that the Parsons house and the three other old houses on the street were gone, and that the entire block was taken up with low, rambling colonials in soft, rosy brick, set on spacious green lawns and shaded by great old trees. These trees, apparently, had been undisturbed when the development was built. It was not an old development; from the look of the plantings, it might have been ten years old at the most, but it had about it the gentle, graceful patina of mellowness and maturity. On an old-brick gatepost at the beginning of the block, a simple bronze plate read, LYTTONWOOD. A SEWELL COMMUNITY. Mike walked past the post and three of the houses to Bayard Sewell's house. It was, he had said, the last one on the block.

It was larger than the others, but not much, and like them, it sat far back on a velvet lawn under a canopy of gnarled, mossy old oaks. It, too, was of rose-flushed old brick, long and low, with black shutters and wrought-iron trim on the low pillars that supported the deep roof overhang, and a pierced-brick serpentine wall extended from each end of the house and back toward the denser trees at the rear of the deep lot. Perfectly pruned glossy rhododendrons softened the angularity of the wall, and in front of them, symmetrical hillocks of azaleas in a lighter, rain-washed green drooped wet, heavy foliage over to meet the lush grass. It was not the burnt white of the grass at the Pomeroy Street house, but the shimmering blue-green of good emeralds. Incandescent white clematis glowed from the wrought-iron mailbox that said only 142 CHURCH STREET, and a double row of huge, vivid pink-and-green caladiums spread shining, ruffled leaves along the curving brick path to the front veranda. Mike stopped at the bottom of the path and looked at Bayard Sewell's house, swinging her shoes in her hand.

It might and should have looked too perfect, too suburban-symmetrical, too groomed and tended and clipped and carved. But somehow it didn't. Closer scrutiny revealed an untidy, sprawling rock garden against the end of the brick wall, where delicate, old-fashioned flowers rioted in the last of the sun . . . thrift, candytuft, ragged robins, dwarf iris, the trailing white fountains of spirea. High on one of a small stand of pines a basketball hoop was fastened, and some small bird had fashioned a nest in it, abandoned now. Midway up the sweep of lawn, centering a low semicircle of junipers at the base of a huge, showering old willow, a brightly painted antique carousel horse pranced and snorted and tossed his gilded mane. Mike smiled at the horse and walked up the path and rang the bell.

It was answered presently by a massive old black woman in a print rayon dress and laced-up nurse's oxfords. Mike knew that this was Opal, Sally Chambers Sewell's childhood nurse and present tender, and she extended her hand and said, "I'm Mike Winship from around the corner. I think I'm expected."

The old woman stared impassively at Mike and made no move to take her hand; Mike remembered that, of course, you did not shake servants' hands. That the woman wore no uniform was not unusual; no one's maid ever had, in Lytton. She stood still while the old woman took her in, bare feet and all, and when she said briefly, "They 'round back by the pool" and walked away, Mike followed her, pausing to slip back into her sandals.

The inside of the house was like the outside: symmetrical, perfectly ordered, polished, substantially but not spectacularly appointed. There were the expected deep, glowing Orientals, the softly shining Chippendale and Hepplewhite, the Waterford and Rose Medallion and florals and landscapes in ornate gold frames that you would think to find in the affluent suburban home of a successful man. But like the outside, there were the grace notes, too, the artfully artless surprises: a joyously primitive Haitian seascape over a credenza in the foyer, a blazing Navaho rug thrown down in front of a fireplace, a silk banner in the Bhutanese manner in a small sitting room, a grouping of what looked at a glance to be Picasso sketches in a hall, a great bobbling scarlet mobile that might have been a Calder.

Somehow, Mike thought, walking through the rich-smelling dimness behind the taciturn maid, Bay fits this house perfectly. He and it both are . . . what? Refined? Stylized? No . . . cultivated is the word I want. Everything about them both is well and thoughtfully cultivated.

They came out into the blaze of late sun by the blue pool, and the maid slipped back into the shadows, leaving Mike face to face with Bay Sewell. He took her hand as he had a few evenings before, at DeeDee's, and leaned over and kissed her cheek, and she caught the same smell of fresh cotton and gin and Bayard Sewell.

"I'm glad you could come," he said, smiling at her, and she smiled back at him and then laughed aloud. He was wearing, with his white duck trousers and blue summer-weight blazer, an ascot, tucked into the throat of his open blue oxford-cloth shirt. He looked in it theatrically and impossibly handsome, like an actor hired to lounge by a blue pool in a glossy, expensive, witless magazine.

"I know." He grimaced. "Is it awful, or is it awful? Sal brought it to me from Nashville, and even she agrees that it makes me look like Richard Gere in *American Gigolo.* But I'm not about to take it off.

Come on, say hello. She's been waiting with bated breath to meet the author."

That's it, Mike thought. That's his power. There are no accidents about him, or if there are, he turns them to his use. But there are surprises. Like that silly ascot.

She smiled around him at the woman who stood just at his elbow, both hands outstretched.

"I can't tell you what an honor this is," Sally Chambers Sewell said, a small bubble of something . . . laughter or nervousness . . . in her light voice. "Bay has talked of nothing and nobody for twenty years but you. We're all so proud of you in Lytton; nobody else from here has ever had their name in a magazine, you know. Not a national one, anyway."

"It's really no recommendation." Mike smiled at her. "Some of the worst people I know have their names in magazines with astounding regularity."

"But not as the person who wrote the story," Sally Sewell said. "That's something else. Writers are really special."

She was a very small woman, no taller than a twelve-year-old child; she came only to Mike's chin, and hardly to Bayard's shoulder. She had a little snub nose peeling from the sun, and a soft, formless mouth innocent of lipstick, and her white-blond hair was tied back in a ponytail. Mike thought that the platinum color must have come from sun and chlorine and artful tinting, because her skin was the deep, coarse-grained mahogany of overtanned middle-aged skin, lusterless and opaque, but somehow it did not make Sally Sewell look middle-aged. She had the frail bones, small, stubby hands and feet, and shyly ducked chin of a child, and she was thin, thin to near emaciation, the sexless thinness of a prepubescent girl. She wore a bright-flowered sundress with spaghetti straps, and her shoulder blades and collarbones stood out as sharply as Mike's own. One of the collarbones was knobbed and oddly dented, as if it had been broken and badly reset, and there were fading saffron bruises on her brown shins and ankles. Great, round black sunglasses shielded her eyes, but did not lend her mystery or maturity; in them, she looked like a child masquerading in its mother's sunglasses. She smelled of old-fashioned toilet water and sun oil and something else: there was about her the musty, sweet smell of fresh yeast. Mike had smelled it before, on certain doomed, talented, and wasted newspeople and photographers and one or two of Derek Blessing's friends: it was the smell of chronic alcoholism.

Sally Sewell took off the sunglasses and looked up at Mike. Her eyes were large and blue and puffed beneath, and haunted. But her unguarded face was snub-pretty and friendly, and empty of everything except pleasure at Mike's presence and a tinge of honest awe. She smiled again and widened her eyes, and Mike thought of a thin, undaunted mongrel puppy.

"Lord, you're skinny," Sally Sewell said. "You're almost as skinny as me. And pretty; well, Bay said you were that, but he didn't say how skinny you were. It makes me feel a lot better. I thought you were going to look like Joan Crawford or Meryl Streep or Gloria Steinem, or one of those tough, important women with the noses and shoulder pads. I'm so *relieved.*"

Mike grinned, and Sally Sewell clapped her hands over her mouth. "Oh, Lord, that was an awful thing to say; Bay will kill me. But you look just so . . . nice, or something. Not like you'd been in riots and gone on marches and all that. Not at all tough. You know, I wanted to march once, back during the Selma thing; a girlfriend and I almost went. We really did want to. But . . . you'll think this is silly, but it's true . . . we finally didn't, because we didn't know what to wear."

Mike burst into laughter, liking her, and Bayard Sewell, from behind her, said, "Well, now you know Sal. What you see is what you get."

He ruffled his wife's ponytail and turned toward the pool apron where DeeDee and Duck sat stiffly in wicker chairs, and his wife looked after him with her entire heart in her haunted eyes.

As voluble and garrulous as they had been two nights before, DeeDee and Duck Wingo were stilted and stifled now. DeeDee wore a gigantic tent of rose-printed polyester and the high-heeled gold mules she had worn the other evening, and was sweating in the late sun, her short upper lip and temples and neck dewed with large drops. She crossed her legs mincingly and looked around brightly at Mike. Duck was in plaid golf pants and black T-shirt, with a white belt and loafers and a liberal dose of pomade on his thick pelt and sideburns. Brut smote the air around him. He, too, was sweating copiously, and in his huge hand he held a candy-pink concoction of shaved ice and fruit with a gardenia in it. An identical drink sat next to DeeDee on a low glass-and-wicker table. They smiled at Mike when she came in, DeeDee primly and Duck in what looked to be relief, and DeeDee gave a strange little chipmunk chirk of artificial laughter.

"There you are in those awful pants again, Mikie," she said. "I really don't know why you do that to yourself. Didn't she look pretty in her ruffles the other night, Bay?"

"I like the pants," Bayard said over his shoulder. "I think Mike looks terrific in pants. Suits her." He bent over a gas grill in a corner of the pool terrace, and a jet whooshed into life.

"They really do." Sally Sewell smiled at Mike. "You look great. So smart. I'd wear pants all the time, but Bay says I look ridiculous in them, too thin. You don't though. Maybe if I got some linen ones like that . . ." She looked at her husband, but he was bent over the grill and didn't hear her.

"Oh, well," she said, with a resigned little gesture and the sweet, swift smile.

"That's an awfully cute sundress," DeeDee said, speaking carefully as to a small child. "Did Bay pick it out for you?"

"No," Sally said. "I got this . . . on my trip."

"Oh, yes," Dee said, and smirked. She looked significantly at Mike. Mike did not look back.

"Oh, my manners!" Sally cried. "Letting you stand here without a drink. You just sit down anywhere that's comfortable and I'll be right back. I'm making strawberry daiquiris, with real strawberries, in the blender. They're super."

"I think Mike might like to have a martini, Sal," Bayard Sewell said mildly, materializing at her elbow. "Why don't you let me do the honors? You've been working like a slave. Sit down and talk to your guests for a while."

"Oh, Bay, please!" The blue eyes pleaded with his. "I've got the strawberries all cut up and everything. Aren't they good? Don't you think they're good, Mrs. Wingo? Mr. Wingo?" She looked importuningly from DeeDee to Duck.

"Simply delicious," DeeDee said, dimpling prissily and taking a butterfly sip from her daiquiri.

"Real tasty," Duck said. He did not sip.

"I'd really rather have one of Sally's daiquiris, Bay," Mike said, smiling at the eager girl-woman, and Sally Sewell clapped her stubby little hands together and trotted off toward the kitchen.

"Isn't this a gorgeous house, Mike?" DeeDee said, gesturing broadly with a great, braceleted arm. "And the pool and everything, just so perfect . . . Bay picked it all out, I happen to know. Every little vase and pillow and chair. Just cream de cream. Duck and I have talked about putting in a pool, you know, but we've just never gotten around to it, and I blister so . . ."

Bayard Sewell gave Mike a tiny, conspiratorial smile. DeeDee in a swimming pool behind the miniature hacienda on the edge of the trailer park hung elephantine and sun-reddened in the air between them.

"Every bit of this is Sal's doing," he said. "I take credit for none of it; you've got your signals twisted, Dee. The walls and floors and ceilings are my department. What goes inside them is hers."

"That's not what a little bird told me," DeeDee said archly.

Sally Sewell came back onto the terrace with a tray of daiquiris, walking very slowly and carefully, her tongue between her teeth in an effort not to spill. Mike took her drink and sipped it. It was savage and fiery with rum.

"Good," she said, her eyes watering.

"I'm glad," Sally Sewell said. "I'm sticking to orange juice. The doctor said I had to drink lots of it. My potassium level is down and my . . . electrodes . . . are out of whack. Thank God I like orange juice."

She drank deeply from an oversized white-frosted glass full of juice. Bayard Sewell rolled his eyes at her, smiling again.

"Your electrolytes, you mean," he said. "Though with you it could well be electrodes. You're really wired tonight, Sal. Good drinks, by the way."

She beamed at him.

A small white dog pattered out onto the terrace, bell tinkling from its collar, and jumped into Sally's lap. She kissed its silky head and fondled the thin hair over the ears. The little dog squirmed and showed its teeth foolishly.

"This is Snicker," she said. "Bay gave him to me when Stuart . . . our youngest . . . went away to school last year. I swear, the house was just so awfully empty, and I missed them so much . . . I cried all the time; it was awful. But Snicker is my bootiful baby, my lovums, isn't he?" She buried her face in the dog's fur and looked up at DeeDee.

"You know how it is, don't you, Mrs. Wingo?" she said. "Didn't Bay say your children were out of the nest and gone? I know you must miss them awfully."

"Oh, yes, awfully," DeeDee said lugubriously. "But they're doing so well I really can't complain. Claudia is an exercise therapist and counselor at a big physiological complex in Florida, and Johnny has a new business interest in Dallas."

"Oh, that's wonderful," Sally Sewell said with unfeigned delight. "What sort of business interest?"

"I think he said oil." DeeDee simpered. "Lots of that in Big D, you know."

"I'm going to put the lamb on now, okay, Sal?" Bayard Sewell said. He did not look at DeeDee or Duck or Mike. She remembered what Priss had said about the trouble DeeDee's son had been in at his filling station job, and how Bayard had somehow straightened it out for him. Her heart lurched with pain for her sister. Outclassed, DeeDee still flew her gallant, pretentious flags.

The twilight deepened and the underwater pool lights came on. The oval pool shone like a jewel in the dusk, dreamlike, unreal. Mike did not like to look at it. She kept seeing, on its empty satin surface, the small, utterly limp shape of a child bobbing, face down, turning slowly and slowly around. But the pool held no ghosts for anyone else; DeeDee continued to simper and preen, and Duck to posture, and Sally Sewell to chatter artlessly. She kept the icy daiquiris coming nicely, all the while sipping obediently at her orange juice, and by the time Bay pronounced the butterflied lamb grilled to perfection, the last of the light had gone out of the evening sky and it was after nine o'clock.

Dinner, Mike thought, was wonderful: elegant and simple, with just the pink-grilled lamb and steamed, fresh tiny vegetables and feathery hot rolls drenched in sweet butter. The rolls, Sally said, were courtesy Opal, but she had done the vegetables herself; had gone that day to the state farmers' market up near the airport and picked out each one, and had washed and trimmed and steamed them with herbs instead of simmering them in bacon grease.

"Just for you, Mike," she said. "I know Yankees can't stand the way we cook vegetables down here."

"I was a Southerner before I got to be a Yankee," Mike said. "But I never tasted vegetables this good, north or south."

Sally Sewell beamed. "Let me get you some more," she said. "We need more wine, too. And I think there's one more pan of rolls in the oven." She rose from her chair and started for the kitchen.

Old black Opal was there as if by magic.

"I do it, Miss Sally," she said firmly. "You set back down an' enjoy yo' comp'ny."

"Oh, Opal, let me do it! Bay, I want to do it; make her let me. I've been away so long, and you all hardly ever let me do anything . . . let me at least serve my own dinner to my guests," she pleaded, looking from glowering Opal to Bayard Sewell at the head of the table.

"Let's let her, Opal," Bayard said. "I know she's supposed to rest, but it's just tonight, and she's doing wonderfully well."

The old woman looked at him with utter ferocity for a moment and then stalked out of the dining room. Sally Sewell slipped out of her chair with a triumphant smile and hurried into the kitchen. The swinging door shut behind her. There was a little silence.

"Opal thinks Sally is still five years old and her own child," Bay said into it. "Sometimes I have to sit on her a little, and she doesn't like it worth a damn. She's a proper old tyrant, but she's been wonderful with Sally, and we couldn't do without her. I'll smooth her down later."

Sally Sewell came back into the dining room with wine, orange juice, and second helpings of everything, and the evening eddied and swirled and flowed on. They nibbled and talked for perhaps another hour; or at least Mike and Bayard Sewell talked. DeeDee and Duck and Sally mostly listened, laughing occasionally at the free-ranging banter. It was good talk; comfortable, easy.

Bayard Sewell had just said, "I heard a rumor that there was fresh peach cobbler for dessert," when Sally folded her hands carefully into her lap, nodded as if in prayer, and slid sideways out of her chair onto the floor.

"Shit," she said.

For a moment they sat in simple disbelief, staring at her as she rose heavily, holding onto the table, and settled herself awkwardly back into her chair. Her face was, suddenly, flushed and loose, and her eyes were glittering and unfocused. Mike saw with incredulity that she was very drunk. The orange juice . . .?

Bayard Sewell got out of his chair and started around the table, but Sally held up her hand, and he stopped. She looked at Mike, focusing her eyes with an effort. She smiled, a sly, confiding smile, with nothing in it of her earlier open, ingenuous sunniness.

"You're my punishment, did you know that?" she said to Mike, with dreadful precision. "My husband threatens me with you. He's always telling me how he'll put me in Parkwood for good, and divorce me, and set you up in my house if I don't shape up. And I didn't, and here you are. I used to hope you'd just die on one of those famous assignments of yours, and I wouldn't have to hear about you anymore. But it's too late for that; you can bet your skinny New York ass it's back to the funny farm for me, in two shakes of a sheep's tail. C'est la guerre, Mike. I hope you both fry in hell."

Her chin slipped out of her supporting hand, and she followed it over and onto the floor again, and this time she lay still on the beautiful muted Kerwin.

DeeDee and Duck sat, stone-still and openmouthed, and Mike was frozen with cold horror, though her face was hot and stiff with pain. Her ears rang shrilly. Bayard Sewell did not look at any of them.

"Excuse me," he said briefly, and went around the table and knelt beside his wife. "Here we go, Sal," he said, and scooped her into his arms, and carried her easily out of the dining room. The blond ponytail bobbed gaily over his arm as they went. The three left at the table did not look at one another, did not speak, hardly seemed to breath. Outside the bell jar, the world roared, but inside, Mike felt only emptied out and drugged once more, content to study the uneaten food on her plate.

In a long moment he was back. His face was very white, and ridges of muscle stood out on either side of his mouth, but he was composed and his voice was even.

"I'm most terribly sorry," he said formally. "She'll sleep till morning, and then she'll be okay, except for a roaring headache and an awful conscience. Of course, she didn't mean anything she said. She's been full of this terrible anger ever since Win—and sometimes she just can't stand the weight of it any longer, and she drinks until it stops hurting. Then the anger comes out at other people. But it's usually me. I don't know where she got the booze tonight; she must have had it stashed out in the kitchen. It's my fault. I should have seen she was still too fragile for a dinner party. I should have paid closer attention to her. She'll call you all tomorrow and apologize if she remembers, but she usually doesn't, and I don't like to remind her . . ."

"Don't think of it," Mike said. "I hope she'll just forget it. I hope you both will. It doesn't make a bit of difference." Her heart pounded with hurt, his and her own, and her ears still rang. She wanted desperately to be gone.

"It makes a terrible lot of difference," he said. "But I can't think how to make it up to you."

"Do you think you'll have to take her back to the . . . you know?" Dee said in an apocalyptic whisper.

"No," he said. "I just can't put her through that again. She hates it so much she doesn't get any benefit from it any longer. And she simply won't talk to shrinks anymore. Opal and I can look after her just as well here. Poor Sal. I really thought this time . . . she was so excited about having dinner guests. It's been such a long time."

As DeeDee and Duck took themselves reluctantly out the door and into the fragrant night, Mike said, "I'll just walk on home, Dee. It's not half a block."

DeeDee started to protest, and Bayard Sewell said, "I'll walk her, DeeDee. I need the air." DeeDee Wingo looked from one of them to the other, but she said nothing further. She and Duck left with promises to call in the morning. Mike knew that her sister would, before the sun was full up.

They walked in silence until they reached the bottom of the front walk to Mike's house. The dissonant song of the cicadas in the dark mass of the trees and their own twin footsteps, slow and regular, were the only sounds in the night. Mike did not think it was late. The little wind that had followed the rain had died down again, and the incredible sweetness of the mimosa and wisteria and the cascading, old-fashioned sweetheart roses beside the fence between the Winship house and its neighbor were almost palpable on their faces. There was no moon, but the stars were very clear.

"Don't bother to come any further," Mike said. "You need to get back, I know. I can find my way blindfolded, and there's a light at the top of the stairs. Daddy may even still be up. It's a real treat for me to be out at night; I never get to do it much in New York. Too easy to get mugged. But who on earth would mug you in Lytton, especially on a night like this? That mimosa . . ."

She knew that she was chattering, but she could not seem to stop her words. She did not know what waited for her in silence, only that something enormous and immutable did.

"It's no bother to walk you to the door," he said. His voice sounded ordinary, almost casual. "I'd like to do that, at least. Opal's with Sally, and this air feels wonderful. Did you realize that you called your father 'Daddy'? I haven't heard you do that since you've been home."

"No," Mike said. "I didn't. I guess old habits really don't die, do they?"

"No," Bayard Sewell said. "They don't die."

Mike looked up at him, standing silently in the shadow of the old water oaks in front of the house on Pomeroy Street, and saw that he was crying.

She did not know when her fingers reached up to touch his face and came away wet. Later, she could not have said how or when they moved silently together to the old striped canvas glider in the shelter of the wisteria bower on the side porch, or precisely how she came into his arms, came to be lying beneath him on the plunging glider, her hands frantic on his half-naked body, her breath coming fast and ragged in her nostrils, her eyes blinded, both their cheeks wet with each other's tears. She did not know when sensation became pain and went beyond, when urgency exploded into unendurable pleasure and became irrevocability, when she cried aloud and he stopped her cries with his hand and then half-choked on his own. But even before he entered her, and thrust and thrust, and burst with the unleashed force of twenty barren and blasted years, all within her that was Micah Winship . . . pain and pleasure, passion and denial, fear and joy and misery; the irreducible essence of her . . . surged out through her very pores and fingertips and mouth and eyes and into the flesh of him, and she was home.

And so it began again.

NINETEEN

All that summer, in the late afternoons, a pair of redbirds came to the misshapen old magnolia tree outside the window of Mike's room, and forever after, when she heard their joyous, "Pretty-pretty-pretty-pretty-cheer-cheer-cheer," she felt again the sweet, heavy weight of satiation. It was an odd time of day for the birds; the wrong time. The other cardinals in her father's yard fed and sang in the cool dawns and late twilights.

"They approve," she told Bayard Sewell. "It's the official seal of approval. You don't have to feel guilty."

"I don't," he said, raising himself on one elbow to look at her, flung out naked and boneless with completion in the tumble of the pineapple bed. "I wouldn't feel guilty if every jaybird in South Fulton County was out there threatening to go tell the devil."

They met two or three afternoons each week in Mike's upstairs room in the Pomeroy Street house. He came at three o'clock, instead of his customary four, and John Winship would have been asleep for an hour. Mike would be waiting for him in the darkened room, naked after the first two or three tentative meetings, and often he would have shed his coat and tie and belt by the time he rapped softly on her closed door. Lavinia Lester would have gone, John Winship was not due to waken for another hour and seldom did, and the house was hushed and somnolent in the heat. Bayard would be downstairs having coffee with Mike when her father woke, and Sam Canaday never came until after six. It was not ideal; was, they knew, risky, but it was the best they could devise, and Mike would have coldly and placidly killed anyone who tried to curtail the meetings.

After the first night, they had met again a couple of times on the porch, on the old glider, but their couplings were too frantic and the porch too exposed to continue. The few days' abstinence until they decided on her room in the afternoons was almost past enduring. Mike wanted to howl aloud, to pull him down when he came into the house to visit her father and have him on the kitchen table or the living room rug. She was, she thought ruefully to herself, frankly and rankly in heat, crying aloud her need and pleasure and fruition; there was nothing in their union of maturity or judiciousness. His touch plummeted her back into childhood—not the shadowed child she had been in this house, but a naked pagan child, obsessive and insatiable, like a starveling with periodic unsupervised access to a candy store, who came alive only when alone with the confections. Mike shimmered when she was with Bayard Sewell. The rest of her time she spent trembling under the sheer weight of appetite. None of her past physical relationships had so drowned and burned her.

The room had been his idea; he had chosen it swiftly and practically.

"I've told them at the office and at home that I'm on a new project that takes me out of the office a few times a week in the afternoon," he said on the first time there, after he had taken her so silently and savagely and quickly that she had not had time to disentangle herself from the silk robe she had put on, nervously, for the occasion. It was crumpled and stained with the fury and substance of him. His own clothes were thrown anyhow over the booming air conditioner.

"It's the best way, I think. Everybody's used to seeing me come in and out of here anyway, and even if your father should wake, he can't leave his room. Christ, I hate the craftiness of it. I'd like to yell it from the housetops: 'I'm fucking Mike Winship like I was always meant to do, and anybody who doesn't like it can lump it.' But we've got to be awfully careful. I don't give much of a damn about my so-called position in this town, or even in the legislature, but I'm not going to hurt Sally or your father. Those are the two things I just can't do. He's crazy about Sally; did anyone ever tell you that it was he who introduced us? Her father was a client of his, and John practically took me by the scruff of the neck and presented me to her. I thought he was going to propose for me. He *did* pay for the engagement ring, and he's never let me pay him back."

"She must have seemed as opposite of me as he could find," Mike said. The thought did not trouble her in the slightest; it seemed to have formed beyond the bell jar.

"Maybe so, at the time," Bay said. "But she's long since been a person in her own right to him. He calls her Miss Sally. She calls him Papa John. He may be the only man in Lytton who doesn't know what she's turned into. I hope he never finds out."

"Neither of them has to know about this," Mike said. "I don't really see how they could find out. But of course, I'll be more careful than I've ever been in my life. I think it's a great idea, your just walking into this house and strolling upstairs to my room and screwing the daylights out of me. It has the virtue of utter simplicity. I'd never have thought of it."

"Well, I'm an expert in guile after dealing with Sally," he said, laughing. She laughed, too. There was nothing, no fiber or sinew or molecule, within her that tasted guilt or compunction.

Never during that summer did Mike examine the morality of the affair, or even look ahead to its conclusion. She thought no further than the next time they would meet. He filled every fold and fissure of the emptiness within her that the recent howling losses and the new vulnerability had left. If she thought at all, she thought of herself and Bayard Sewell as casualties of some private catastrophe, clinging together for their very survival. His hands on her body were justification enough. Each afternoon together meant they could exist another day.

It can't hurt anyone, she thought. Sally will never find out, and I would never ask Bay to leave her. Daddy won't know. Who can it hurt?

It was the first time in her adult life that she had been dependent on another person for her entire emotional existence, and instead of reacting with her customary cool wariness, she abandoned herself to it entirely and voluptuously. This is what love is, then, she would think as she felt him swell inside her until he filled the world. Yes. How could I not have known?

On that first afternoon, he said, "I've never forgotten you, not for one minute of one day, after all this time. That last day—that was the worst day of my life, except the next one, when we knew you'd gone. I'd give anything I've got to be able to go back and undo that day. I should have gone with you, I should have looked for you until

I found you—but I didn't. I thought you would come home when school started. I waited and waited. I was so sure you would. And then we heard you were married. I thought I was going to die. I don't even remember that fall and winter. And now I want you so much I think I'm going to die again, and I'm . . . locked in. I can't leave. You do know that, don't you, Mike? I can't leave . . ."

"I don't want you to leave," she said, burying her face in the musky wetness where his arm joined his chest. "I will never ask you to leave. I only want this, now, right now at this minute. That's all; that's enough. I can't really regret the way things happened, Bay. I can't even say that my marriage was a mistake. Without it, I never would have had Rachel. I never would have had any sort of career . . ."

"Is it so important, then? Your career? Is it enough?" he looked at her searchingly in the dim amber light from behind the venetian blinds.

"It has been," she said slowly. "It always has been. But now . . . I don't know. I don't feel like a journalist. I don't feel like a mother. I don't feel like anything but . . . a body with a huge hole in it. Which you are about to plug with extreme gusto, aren't you? Right here? And then . . . oh, God, here . . ."

Afterwards, his breath laboring in his throat, he touched the warm wetness between her legs.

"I'd like to kill anybody who's ever touched you here," he said. "Your famous Richard, or anybody else. I don't ever want to know about the others who have. But . . . oh, Christ, Mike, were there many others?"

"Yes," Mike said, in pain. "There were . . . a good many others. I've been looking for something . . . somebody . . . all my life who could . . . fill me up, I guess I mean. Stop that dull, awful, constant, itching ache in there. Nobody did, nobody could, but I sure gave it a good try. And I regret every one of them, Bay. It was just so obviously you that I wanted. All over me. And in me and through me and behind and in front of me . . . always you. You don't need to hear about the men. You don't need to know anything about how I've lived before now. It doesn't matter. What comes next is not going to matter. I don't want to think about it. I don't want to talk about it . . . not yesterday, not tomorrow. And I won't talk about it. I don't give a damn about anything but now."

"Then now it is, and now it will be," he said. "You're home now. I'm here now."

Yes, Mike thought. I *am* home. Home is where Bay is.

She was adamant about it. She would not discuss her life before she came home to Lytton. She would not discuss her father. She would not talk about the action that Sam Canaday was bringing against the Department of Transportation on his behalf. One afternoon, early on in their relationship, Bayard Sewell pushed her gently to tell him about the status of the action, and she demurred impatiently.

"We've only got an hour," she said fretfully. "I don't want to waste it talking about that damned case. I don't *know* anything about it. I don't want to know."

"I'm only concerned because I want so badly to help John," Bayard Sewell said. "And I feel so helpless. Canaday is playing it goddamned closemouthed, and your dad seems . . . vague, uncertain . . . when I try to talk to him. I'm awfully afraid that know-nothing shyster is riding him for a bad fall. I wish he'd leave your dad the hell alone. I wish he wasn't in the house with you."

"Oh, God, Bay, I don't even *see* him," she said impatiently. "I make it a point not to go near him when he's here. I'm bored sick with Sam Canaday and I'm bored with talking about him."

She shook her hair back off her damp face as if tossing aside a biting insect. Even unseen, Sam Canaday was as all-pervasive and pungent as a powerful odor.

"I only care about it because I don't want it to touch you. I don't want whatever's hurting your father to hurt you, and I don't want *him* to hurt you," he said, smoothing the wild, silken mop away from her flushed face.

"He can't," Mike said. "Nothing can, now."

Bayard Sewell spoke no more of Sam Canaday and the action against the Department of Transportation.

Nearly two weeks went by before Mike went again to Priss Comfort's little stone house by the ball field. She had not consciously stayed away, but the blazing reality of the few afternoon hours in her dim, enclosing cave of a room had dwarfed and distanced everything else around her in Lytton, and most of the time that she was not actually in the room and joined with Bayard Sewell, pumping with all her body and soul to turn herself inside out and

164

into the very flesh of him, she was remembering just how it had been the last time, or waiting in pure flame for it to happen again. Mike was an abstracted automaton with quivering nerve endings on every inch of her skin. When she found occasion to do so, she mentioned Bayard Sewell to whoever was present, just to taste the roundness of his name on her tongue as she would, later that day, taste the hot, damp flesh of him. She did a few dreamlike errands in town, cooked a few perfunctory meals, slept in long, deadened drifts of time, ate little, nodded dreamily to Sam Canaday the few times she could not avoid seeing him in the house, and took a great many baths. Somehow, in the tepid water of the grainy old tub, the fires inside her cooled and softened a little. She found a box of her old childhood books in the back of the closet in her room, and after that, late into the cicada-humming nights, her lamp spilled down over the yellowed and crumbling pages of *Black Beauty* and *The Wind in the Willows* and the old Arthur Rackham edition of *The Water Babies.* The loved, half-remembered small worlds of the books were as real to her, in those first hot nights, as the one around her.

"Well, I thought you'd left us for good," Priss grumbled as Mike ambled into the little house one hot morning, eating the first of the local peaches. "Holed up in your room and starved yourself to death, or something. Sit down there and let me get you something with more heft to it than that peach. You look like Mahatma Gandhi. I feel very honored that you'd leave the inner sanctum for the likes of me."

"Oh, don't be cross." Mike grinned at her. "Who told you I was holed up in my room, as you put it?" Her words were casual, but she felt sharpened and alerted. No one must know about the afternoons in that room . . .

"DeeDee said that Lavinia Lester told her you spent a lot of time up there," Priss said. "DeeDee made a special trip last week to see if I'd heard about the charming little dinner party at the Sewells' house. Said she thought sure you'd have told me about it, and when I said no, you hadn't been by, she said Lavinia had said you'd taken to your bed. Proper full of it, Dee was. Absolutely sure you were stricken to the vapors with embarrassment and God knows what else. I told her most likely you were stricken with a powerful urge to avoid her. I think I may have made her mad. She turned right red."

"Oh, lord, Dee drives me crazy," Mike snapped. "I'm not

stricken with embarrassment, and I haven't been hiding in my room. I'm just catching up on my sleep, like I always do when I let down after a long assignment. I told you I would. As for the dinner party, it was pretty awful, but nothing Bay couldn't and didn't handle. I guess he's an old hand at it by now. It was terrible, though, Priss. I'm truly sorry for her; she's an appealing little thing, and she obviously adores him, and he does her. But why in God's name, if she does, can't she control herself on the one night when he's got an old friend back in town and wants to show his wife off? He was wonderful about the whole thing, but you could tell he was just in agony over her. It was such a godawful, ghastly shock."

"I don't know why it should be," Priss said coldly. Mike looked at her in surprise. Priss's serene face was stony.

"I don't know what he thought would happen to her, just a few days out of a sanitarium and meeting the woman her husband almost married for the first time. I don't know what he thought she'd do. Booze flowing like water, and her trying to be a hostess, and please him, and make a good impression on you, and deal with Duck and DeeDee, which would turn many a stronger soul to the bottle for good . . . I don't know what in God's name he expected. Maybe just what he got."

"Priss!" Mike was shrill with surprise and outrage.

Priss looked at her, a long, measuring look, and then the ice-green eyes softened, and dropped.

"Oh, God, Mike," she said. "Don't mind me. You just seemed so like the eight-year-old I remember for a minute . . . forget it, please. I never could talk to you about Bayard Sewell."

After that, Mike spoke no more of him, to Priss or anyone else, but he roared inside her like the sea.

TWENTY

"Don't tell me, let me guess . . . Gidget goes to cooking school?" Sam Canaday said, coming into the kitchen on a thundery morning that June. Mike looked up from the kitchen counter, where she was stirring butter and cocoa. Her hair was tied back into a ponytail with blue yarn, and she wore cutoff blue jeans and a soft old shirt of Richard's. Her feet were bare.

"And who're you this morning, Tab Hunter on date night?" She took in his blue blazer, gray slacks, and red-striped tie. She had never seen him in a coat and tie. He looked totally different; thinner, finer-featured, somehow younger. His blond hair was dark-damp, comb tracks showing clearly under the fluorescent overhead light. The high ridges of his cheekbones looked newly touched by sun.

"Touché. You do look about fourteen, though. And I'd say you'd either gotten an A on your algebra final or broken up with your boyfriend. Is that fudge for celebration or consolation?"

"It's for an orgy. I'm going to eat the whole panful by myself in front of the television set this afternoon. Have a piece of that other; you'd better move fast, before it's gone."

He reached for a piece of glossy fudge cooling on the old yellow Fiestaware platter that Mike had pulled out of a bottom cupboard.

"Mmmm," he said. "From the looks of your chin, I'd say you've been hitting the fudge fairly steadily. Better watch out, or you'll come up with a crop of zits. Not to mention a real behind. Is that the beginning of a hip I see there?"

He leered at her tight denim shorts.

"I'm afraid so," Mike said. "They were baggy not two weeks ago. God knows what I'll have to wear if I don't stop eating and get some exercise."

"Well, it looks good," he said appraisingly. "Like you've finally gotten enough sleep. All the corners are gone. You've gotten a little sun, too. It's not hard to see that you were the cutest girl at the prom."

"I never went to the prom," she said. "But thanks for them kind words. I didn't know you noticed things like hips and suntans."

"Good God, woman, and me a true son of the old South? I didn't spend four years in the horniest high school in America for nothing. Of course I notice hips."

He was as good as his word. His gaze followed her as she moved around the kitchen, pouring the fudge onto a second buttered platter, washing the mixing bowl, putting it away. She could feel his eyes on her body and legs; she began to be almost uncomfortable in the short shorts and the soft-clinging shirt. She wore no bra beneath it, and she was suddenly very conscious of her nipples pushing against the thin-worn oxford cloth.

She did, she knew, look almost like a teenager. It was by design. Bayard Sewell had told her, hand deep in the tangle of her ashen hair, that he had always loved the ponytail she had worn during high school, and she had tied it back that same evening and left it that way. When he had mentioned how pale and gaunt her body looked, remembering the summers when she was lithe and golden from the constant swimming, she began lying out on the grass behind the house in the mornings, till she ran with sweat and could bear it no longer. He had an insatiable sweet tooth that he had not had when they had been together before for bland, cloying, nurserylike concoctions, and so she made it her custom to take a sweet treat up to the bedroom each afternoon that he came, and they demolished the candy and cakes and cookies as ravenously as they fed on each other's bodies, and Mike soon began to lose the sharp edges and angles that had made her avert her head when she passed a mirror. He liked the change in her; liked the greedy, sated, knowing child she had become. With him she was a wanton prepubescent in whom appetite and impulse held sway as they never had in her actual child's years in this house, and in whom she moved like a swimmer fathoms deep in a warm sea.

"You're almost like you used to be, but about a hundred thousand times sexier," he said. "A little girl who knows a fancy whore's tricks. It's an incredible combination."

She wondered, though, what sort of child it was he really met in her; somehow she thought perhaps it was that forlorn child of this place that he saw.

Mike knew that the others saw a change, too, and knew that they studied her when they thought she was not aware of it. More than once she had caught long, measuring looks from Priss and Sam Canaday, and veiled ones from Dee. Her father alone of the people around her did not seem to notice a difference. There was less tension, less revived animosity, between them, but then, she saw him even less now that Lavinia Lester had established herself in the house during the days, and in her newly obsessive state, the contacts that she did have with him nettled her less. The upshot was that Mike was kinder to her father, and he, in turn, had drawn in his horns somewhat.

"Looks like you're settling in pretty good," he said to her once, as she sang to herself putting away the supper dishes. "Looking less like a plucked canary that lit on a live wire."

"I take it that's a compliment," Mike said.

Her father made the cracked sound that might mean mirth or annoyance, and commented no more on her manner or appearance. But she knew that she had, somehow, pleased him a trifle.

Well, she thought, why not? Nothing wrong with a little of this whatever it is spilling over on him. It's certainly not like he was going to get attached to me. And I can't just pretend nothing has changed. It has. I think I may actually be happy.

She was, or as near it as she could remember being. She sang in the honeysuckle-freighted mornings and laughed at DeeDee's scandalized face when her free breasts under the soft T-shirts and blouses drew stares in the A&P, that last bastion of Lycra and underwiring in Lytton. Since resuming her affair with Bayard Sewell, she had given up wearing underwear entirely, loving the feeling of her clothing rubbing her sensitized skin, imagining, with slightly caught breath, how the places that they brushed would feel when his hands touched them again. She did not care who noticed that she was naked under her clothes.

Mike had observed early on that there was a strict social striation in the grocery shopping habits of Lytton. The industrious mornings were the province of pantsuited, boned, stockinged, and permanented middle-aged women with four-door family sedans and proper lists, while in the hot, indolent afternoons battalions of younger women in shorts and slacks and rubber flipflops and plastic curlers boiled into the stores, towing shoals of piping, grasping children. Nighttime was when the blacks came. She saw few people she had known before. Once the phenomenon would have engaged her journalist's sensibilities like an anthropological study. Now it merely amused her, especially when she noticed that several of the morning women seemed to be whispering together about her as she passed with DeeDee.

"This is where old panty girdles and dress shields go to die," she teased her sister. "Relax, Dee. I could go into purdah and it wouldn't change anything; they're going to talk about me anyway. Better my underwear—or lack thereof—today than my wild indiscretion of yesteryear. I think I'll ask that lady with the face like a boiled egg where they keep the condoms. They'll think I'm getting it on with J.W. and that should keep them happy all summer."

"That sorry business back then has almost died down now," DeeDee snapped. "Why on earth you have to parade half-naked all over town and stir it up again I don't know."

"Lytton has other things to do besides talk about you, Mike," Priss Comfort told her when Mike recounted the morning at the A&P with glee. "Half the town is newcomers these days, or kids too young to remember you. They don't see Mike Winship, free spirit, up to her old tricks. They see a skinny middle-aged lady with hair like a gone-to-seed dandelion in the grocery store, with her tits bouncing. Sorry to disappoint you. And it's not as if you needed a bra, anyhow. Couple of Band-Aids would do just as well."

"I love you, Priss," Mike gasped through helpless laughter. "You never once let me get away with anything, not even when I was eight years old."

"Which is exactly how you're acting now," Priss said. "For God's sake, put on some underwear so poor DeeDee can hold her head up in the produce department."

In the morning kitchen, now, she looked at Sam Canaday with sharpened attention.

"What are you doing here in the middle of the day?" she said. "I've hardly ever seen you in the daylight."

"I'm going to take your dad to the doctor in East Point," he said. "Didn't Lavinia tell you?"

"I haven't seen Lavinia this morning. She'd left for an appointment at her son's school when I got downstairs. What's the matter with my father?"

"He's been having some pain, Mrs. Lester says. Keeping him up nights. I've been wondering when it would start. His doctor said he might get lucky and miss the pain, but that's bullshit; did you ever know a cancer that didn't hurt sooner or later? It's probably been hurting him a good bit longer than he'll admit, and God knows how bad it really is. His regular doctor's appointment is next week anyway, so I thought this time I'd take him and talk to the doctor myself. J.W. usually drives him, and the doctor won't tell him anything."

"Why on earth didn't he tell *me* if he needed to go to the doctor?" Mike said. "Or why didn't Mrs. Lester? It's my place to take him; it's one of the reasons I came down here. I can't let it take your time like this . . ."

"No problem," Sam Canaday said easily. "He wouldn't let Lavinia tell you, so don't jump on her about it. He said he didn't want to disturb you. He says you're doing some writing in your room, and he doesn't want to bother the genius at work. I take that to mean that he's very proud of you. I didn't know you were working on anything; that's good news."

"I . . . well, just fiddling around a little," Mike mumbled, embarrassed and annoyed at her father, Lavinia Lester, and Sam Canaday. She did not like lying and did it poorly. "Who on earth told him that, anyway?"

"I gather Sewell did, or intimated as much. I didn't hear him. I rarely have the pleasure of Mr. South Fulton's company these days; he's out and gone like a scalded tomcat by the time I get here in the evenings. One would almost think he was avoiding me if one didn't know better. Or that the Colonel was trying to keep us apart. I used to run into him some, but he's apparently changed his visiting hours."

Mike glared at him. "I doubt if he cares a tinker's damn whether he sees you or not," she said. "He's got a new project going, and he's had to change his routine a little. But he still sees Daddy when he can. He's been very faithful."

"He has that," Sam said. "Faithful is just the word for Bayard

Everett Sewell. Well, if he has what it takes to get you writing again, more power to him. Let him come at noon and stay till dinnertime. May one ask what it is you're working on?"

"One may not," Mike said, feeling the traitorous heat rising in her chest and neck. "It's absolutely nothing; and it probably won't ever turn into anything. Bay shouldn't have . . . mentioned it."

"Maybe not." He looked at her keenly. "Well, I won't press you about it. I'm real glad to hear it, though, Mike. I mean that. And your dad is truly proud, even though you must know he'll never tell you so. I'll be eager to read the finished product."

"Mmmm," Mike said uncomfortably. She felt, for some reason, small and very guilty, for the first time in this house. Under the guilt she felt a crawling unease. She had been very careless; she had not known that her father was not feeling well, and she had not known that someone came into the house at least once a month to take him to the doctor. She should have made it her business to know those things.

"Will you be coming straight back after his appointment?" she asked briskly.

"I don't know," he said. "It depends on how he feels. He wants to go down and take a look at the homeplace, and I see no reason not to take him, if he seems up to it. We can't keep him away from it forever."

"You know that's just going to stir him up all over again," Mike objected.

"For God's sake, Mike, it's his house," Sam Canaday said. "Who has more right to go and see it when he wants to? Besides, what do *you* care? You said right off you didn't care what we did about it as long as you didn't have to hear about it. I don't imagine you've changed your mind."

"You're right, I haven't," she said, turning to leave the kitchen in irritation. There had been real warmth and approval in his voice and eyes when he was talking about her writing, but apparently warmth and approval were two things he could not long sustain, at least not with her. Now she would have to call Bayard Sewell at his office and stop him from coming to the house that afternoon; they could not risk an encounter with Sam Canaday. With her father out of the house, there was no reason for Bayard to be in it. She did not like calling his office, and he did not like her to do it. She was in her room with the door closed when she heard them leave the house, and shortly after that she heard the Toyota start up. She waited five more minutes and then called and left a message with Bayard Sewell's secretary that Mr. Winship was not feeling well and could not have visitors that day. It was the emergency signal they had agreed upon.

"Never ask for me unless it's a dire necessity," he had cautioned her. "Old Dorothy Blair is the self-appointed stringer for all three major news networks."

"Oh, that's too bad, honey," the redoubtable Miss Blair said to Mike when she phoned. "You tell your daddy we all hope he feels better real soon. And you come to see us, hear? I hear you've turned into a mighty pretty girl, but it looks like I'll never get the chance to see for myself."

"I will, thanks, Miss Blair," Mike said, making a hideous grimace at the old woman over the telephone. "And I'll tell Daddy you asked after him."

"Old trout," she said under her breath, sitting on the edge of her bed and staring out at the thick gray day. Then she shook her head. There had, after all, been nothing in Dorothy Blair's voice but interest and kindness. The air was as sullen and freighted with unshed rain as a swollen cow's udder, and the dropping barometric pressure combined with disappointment at not seeing Bayard Sewell that afternoon and unaccustomed shame at the lie she had told Sam Canaday about her writing to make her feel nervy and prowling with undischarged emotion. Why in God's name had Bayard had to say she was writing? He could have said anything else; he could, preferably, have said nothing at all.

J.W. Cromie's tall figure appeared around the corner of the garage, dragging the rotating lawn sprinkler, and on impulse Mike got up and went downstairs and wrapped the plate of fudge in plastic wrap and took it back to the back fence, where J.W. was setting up the sprinkler. She had paid as little notice to him as to anyone else except Bayard Sewell in the past weeks; could not, in fact, remember the last conversation she had had with him. The indignation she had felt at J.W.'s apparent espousal of, or at least collusion in, his own indenture to John Winship had, somehow, ceased to prickle at her. She supposed it was a part of the same overall gentling of her attitude toward Lytton and everything connected with it that the affair had precipitated. He turned at the sound of her footsteps, and she smiled and held out the platter.

"I made some fudge, and I can't eat it all," she said. "I thought I remembered you had an incorrigible sweet tooth."

"Yes'm, sure do," he said, and took the platter, looking not quite into her face. "Appreciate it, sure do. I'll have me a piece after I get this here sprinkler to going."

He did not bend to set up the sprinkler, but did not say anything else, and she realized that he was waiting for her to end the encounter and go back to the house. She stood there with him in the hot, thick day, not sure what it was that she waited for, and then she took a deep breath and said, "I think I owe you an apology, J.W. That business with the sit-ins . . . it got you in a lot of trouble here, didn't it? I never meant to do that."

He sighed and put the platter down in the shade. Finally, he looked directly at her.

"No'm," he said. "I knows that. You done right by your lights. You meant to do good by me. Look like I just ain't cut out for no liberation. Mama told me I ain't."

"But still—you made a start. J.W., you took the first step, you made a change in things. Why on earth did you just give up when things got a little tough in Atlanta and come back here? This is nowhere."

"This here what I knows. This here really all I does know, Miss Mike. This suit me all right, I reckon."

"You're no more free right now than you were in 1964," Mike said. "J.W., you could be *really* free by now; you could have . . ."

His head came up, and there was a brief flare of something savage in his opaque eyes.

"You ain't ever thought what we s'pose to do after we free, is you? Yes'm, now I can order me anything I wants in any restaurant in the world. I just cain't pay for it."

"You have to *earn* it," Mike cried. "You have to go somewhere else and *earn* it! My God, J.W. I did it. Look at . . . look at Charlayne Hunter Gault; she's just our age; she got out; she earned herself a place . . ."

"I looks at Charlayne Hunter Gault a lot," J.W. said fiercely and evenly. It was a tone she had never heard in his voice, not even before she had left home, twenty years before. "She had the whole movement behind her."

"Well, it would have been behind you, too. That was the whole point of it."

"No'm. Difference is, the movement be behind her an' I be behind the movement. It a big difference, Miss Mike."

"Oh, for God's sake," Mike exploded. "Stop with the Miss Mike crap. I'm from this town just like you; the same folks were mad at me as were mad at you. And I don't go around in sackcloth and ashes with my eyes on the ground, thanking them for the scraps from their tables. I give it right back to them."

J.W. smiled. It was not a cheerful smile. It was feral, contemptuous. When he spoke, the slow, thick blackness was gone from his speech.

"Yeah, you from Lytton too. Just like me. Except you left it when it got hot, Mike. Ran right on out of here and married you a rich Yankee. Most of us, we had to stay. This was the only brier patch we had. And you don't spray the brier patch with Agent Orange if you need it to hide in. What do you know about staying?"

She was silent. The unfairness of it smote her. She had had no choice—had she? Did he really think she had *chosen* to run? Then she said, "But why on earth did you come back to this house? To him? He was furious with you; don't you see that this indentured servitude he's put you in is his way of punishing you?"

He looked up at the big house, then back at her.

"He was good to Mama," he said slowly. "To Mama and me both, when I was little. He's still good to me lots of ways you don't know about. I'm not going to forget that. Nothing that happened later can change that. This job he gave me, this place to stay . . . you call it punishment. Looks more like . . . atonement to me. You can slap down a man's punishment, and you should, but it's a real sin to refuse his atonement. Looks to me like you doin' a lot of slapping, Mike."

He turned and walked away toward the house, carrying the platter. At the foot of the garage stairs, he turned and smiled at her again. The remembered sweetness struck her heart anew. "You make fudge nearly 'bout as good as a nigger, Mike," he called.

Mike grinned back, finally. The grin had to work its way around a cold salty tightness in her chest, but by the time it reached her mouth it tasted as strong and free as the smile of a young girl she had known twenty years before.

"Sucks to you, J.W. Cromie," she yelled after his retreating figure.

"Same to you," floated back on the still, empty air.

Sam brought her father back an hour later, just as the thunderstorm that had been growling and muttering in the west broke over Lytton. The air inside the house went suddenly dark and strange, and the wind blew silver sheets of rain past the windows and against the front and side porches. The smell of warm, soaking earth mingled with the acrid, hellfire smell of ozone as a bolt shot home somewhere near, and Mike flew, barefoot and exhilarated, out into the wisteria bower to bring in the cushions. She had just unbound her hair and was toweling it dry when they burst into the kitchen from the garage.

"Come in before you drown," she said, holding the door while her father wheeled himself up the ramp into the room. He was not wet, but Sam Canaday, following with a disreputable dripping umbrella, was streaked and spotted with rain.

"Like a cow pissing on a flat rock," John Winship said. "Do the homeplace good. Lawns and scuppernong vines were looking pretty bad."

His face was startlingly white in the dark room, paler than Mike had ever seen it, and there was a yellow pinch to his mouth that spoke of pain and the effort to control it, and the death that was spinning toward him like a star. But there were hectic splotches of color on his sunken cheeks, and his eyes had a knife-edge glitter. He carried his narrow death's head high on the thin stalk of a neck, and a feverish ebullience shimmered in the air around him like an aura. From one of Priss's long-ago English classes the image of Death as a reveler at a masquerade ball snapped into Mike's mind. She recognized it: Poe's "The Masque of the Red Death." To waltz with her father at this moment, in his strange excitement, would be to dance with death. She shivered and flicked on the overhead light, and the room sprang into fluorescent whiteness, livid against the storm outside.

"Did you have a good trip?" Mike said. "What did the doctor say?"

"Said just what I thought he'd say, the old fool," John Winship said, and his voice was stronger than she had heard it for weeks.

"Said that little twinge last night was more than likely gas and I'm not a bit worse than I was a month ago. Not much better, but no worse, either. Waste of time. Told Sam so. But I finally got to see what needs doing down at the homeplace, and I'm gon' get J.W. right on that, and I got to thinking: 'stead of lying around looking at the goddamn TV every morning and evening, I think I'm gon' start me a letter-writing campaign. Bury every newspaper and TV and radio station in a hundred-mile radius so deep in paper that they'll have to pay attention eventually. Tell 'em how it feels to have a bunch of government sons of bitches just come and take your property, show 'em what a real Southerner does when some jackass tries to steal his land . . ."

"You know the DOT isn't breaking any laws, Colonel," Sam Canaday said mildly, his eyes on her father's face.

"Then we'll get the goddamned laws changed," John Winship exclaimed. "I'll write letters to every man jack in the goddamned legislature, too. Sooner or later, they'll have to do something about it just to shut me up."

He turned to Mike, his eyes and cheeks burning. "Want to help out in the crusade, Micah?" he said, using her full name for only the second time she could remember since the night she left this house, twenty-two years before. "You can put some of that fancy journalism of yours to good use, for a change. Or you can just lick stamps, if you want to."

"I . . . Daddy, do you really think you ought to . . ." Mike began. She wanted no part of the skewed, futile campaign, did not even want to hear about it. It could accomplish nothing; was as foolish and quixotic as the original windmill tilt. But he had not asked anything at all from her in the time she had been back, not even for a glass of water or an assist in the wheelchair. And though his effort to suppress the interest in his voice and eyes was visible, it was there.

"We better let Mike get on with her own writing, Colonel," Sam said smoothly, before she could go on. "She's got a living to make and bills to pay in New York, and she'll have to hit the typewriter if we want to keep her around. Who knows, there might be a great American novel going on up there behind that closed door. Don't want to distract her just when she's going good."

She shot him a look over her father's head, mingled gratitude and annoyance. He had delivered her from a sticky situation with her father, but he was digging her deeper and deeper into the fiction of writing in the afternoons. Her unease at the charade was mushrooming. He caught the look and grinned blandly. John Winship nodded.

"Yeah, better let the genius perk along," he said, apparently satisfied with Sam's words. "Don't need her, anyhow. Sam's going to get me one of those little transistor tape recorders, Mike, and I'm going to dictate, and he's going to get it transcribed and sent off for me."

"Well . . . good," Mike said, looking again at Sam Canaday over her father's mottled head. "Only what's he going to do for help?" She knew that he did not have a secretary yet, and suspected that he could not afford one. "Why don't you let Bay's office do them for you?" she suggested, turning back to her father. "He's got other help besides Miss Blair, and a whole mailroom, and you know he'd be more than glad . . ."

Her father dropped his eyes to his hands, folded in his lap. "Sam knows what's going on with the DOT," he said. "Don't want Bay to have to mess with it." There was something muted and mulish on his face. He did not look at either of them.

"It's no problem," Sam said. "Ouida Quigley at the post office is going to take the tapes home with her at night, and the Colonel is going to pay her a little something to type and mail them. She's thrilled to get the money."

"Well, then," Mike said, looking from one to the other in the little strangeness. "I guess if the doctor says it's okay, it is. He *did* say it was, didn't he?"

"Oh, hell yes," John Winship said loudly. "Said anything I feel like doing is okay with him."

"Did he give you anything for the pain?" Mike asked.

"Don't need anything," her father said. "I told you it was just gas. Probably won't come back. It was gone by this morning, anyway."

Sam Canaday shook his head over the wheelchair. His mouth was grim. But his voice was even when he said, "Come on, Colonel. You know you promised you'd go straight to bed if I took you down to the homeplace. You don't need to tire yourself out right off the bat if you're going to take on the DOT single-handed. A deal's a deal."

"Okay. But I want you to come back here tonight after supper. We've got a lot of planning to do."

"I'll be here," Sam said, and wheeled the old man out of the room.

He was back in a few minutes.

"He isn't all right, is he?" Mike asked.

"No," Sam said. "He isn't all right at all. He's in pain and he's been in pain for some time, and it's going to get worse before it's over. He's just too frail from the stroke to stand any more chemotherapy and surgery's out of the question. The doctor gave him something stronger for the pain, and said he thought it would handle it for some little time . . . things could rock on like this for quite a while, apparently . . . but sooner or later it's going to get bad."

Mike's throat felt dry, and her voice was scratched and stiff. "How bad?"

"Hard to tell. Maybe no worse than a moderate amount of painkiller can handle. That's what we have to hope for. That we don't have to dope him into a coma and let him just lie there until he dies. That we can keep the pain manageable until it's time for him to go."

"How long . . . will that be?" Mike felt as though she were talking about something that was happening behind a thick pane of glass. The bell jar, which had been as dense with thoughts of Bayard Sewell and nothing else as a paperweight snowstorm, cleared enough to show her a distant, blurred landscape of mortality and smells and disorder and pain. "I . . . really didn't know it was going to be like this."

"What did you think it was going to be like? A segment on the six o'clock news? I don't know how long it's going to be. The doctor doesn't know. A month. A year. How long isn't the point. How well he can live *until* is."

She was suddenly angry. "Then why in God's name are you letting him screw up whatever time he has left with this stupidity about the DOT? Why do you even think of encouraging him to start this poor, useless letter campaign? You know it's not going to make any difference; you know he can't win. Why do you keep putting off the day he finds that out? It's cruel, it's terrible. I'm going to tell him it's no use. Somebody needs to spare him at least this. He's going to look like an awful fool to all those people . . ."

He moved so quickly across the linoleum that she hardly saw the motion. He leaned over her, his face pulled to the bone, his green eyes no longer sleepy, but leaping with fire.

"You fool," he said, in a shaking near-whisper. "Don't you see that this foolishness, as you call it, is the only thing keeping him alive?"

"Alive till what?" She hissed back. "Alive for *what?*"

"Alive until he doesn't want to be anymore!" Sam Canaday looked as if he wanted to grasp her shoulders and shake her, and she stepped back a pace. "Alive till he wants to die, alive until he feels like he's given this whole thing his best shot. Alive till *he* decides not to be. Goddamn it, Mike, it's his land and it's keeping him here on this earth, and you stay the hell out of it or you'll truly have me to answer to!"

"I don't want him to hurt!" Mike all but shouted.

"Well, he's going to hurt! Telling him he hasn't got a snowball's chance in hell with the Department of Transportation isn't going to keep him from hurting." He turned and walked across the kitchen to the garage door and turned back to her. "I don't mean to be rough on you, Mike, but you don't seem to be in touch with what's going on with your father, and you haven't since you got here. He's dying of cancer and it's going to hurt him before he does. It isn't going to be fun to watch him do it. If you think you can't handle that without its puncturing that famous detachment of yours, maybe you ought to go on back home and leave it to me and DeeDee. She ain't much, but she knows what's real."

Mike started to flare at him, but instead leaned against the refrigerator. The scene in the kitchen, on top of the odd and disorienting interlude with J.W. that afternoon, had drained and somehow flattened her. It did not seem worth it to argue with Sam Canaday about the proper treatment of a dying father, and in any case, some small and surprised part of her far outside the bell jar suspected that he was right.

"Come on back about six and I'll give you some supper," she said in a smaller voice than she usually used with him.

"Thanks," he said. "I'd like that," and was gone into the last of the evening rain.

TWENTY-ONE

"Have you ever had a married man before?" Bayard Sewell asked her, his words blurred with the rasp of his breathing and the guttural sulk of thunder behind the drone of the air conditioner. The storm that had broken the heat earlier in the week had repeated itself every day since, but it was not until the third afternoon of rain and tumult that he had finally been able to come to her. The pent force of the wait had all but blown Mike apart at the moment of her climax, and Bayard, who was normally silent, had shouted hoarsely when his moment came. They lay now, wet and panting in the rain-swimming room. Mike felt as though the center of her body was missing, cold and hollow and ebbing and light. It occurred to her that it might feel this way to die.

"Of course not," she said, profoundly surprised, almost shocked, at the question. "I wouldn't do that. I don't believe in that."

And then she laughed, because, of course, she was doing it, and intended to continue. He laughed, too.

"Why do you ask? Is it bothering you?" she said, turning over to look at him.

"No. I just wondered if you had, and if it was as good with him as it is with me," he said, yawning hugely. "Do I look like it's bothering me?"

He didn't. He looked wonderful. He looked rested and loosened and ten years younger, like an indolent big cat in the first year of its prime. The deep, dry lines of pain in his face had somehow softened and faded, and there was a new fullness to his cheeks and the skin under his neck, as if they had been plumped slightly with air.

"No," Mike said. "I don't think it's bothering you in the least."

"I think it is you, a little, though. You look beat," he said, sitting up and reaching for the sheet, to draw it over their sweat-slick bodies. The sound-muffling air conditioner was invariably cold after their sex. She noticed that he had the small, purselike beginning of a pot to his belly; it had been flat to gauntness before. She smiled indulgently at the soft little bag of flesh. It seemed a totem of content.

"No. Not at all. I'm just sort of worried about my father, to tell you the truth. He's been having a lot of pain, and the doctor says it's going to get worse. I guess just sitting around waiting for him to start hurting is getting to me."

He sat up straighter, all languor gone.

"Tell me," he said. She did, about the visit to the doctor, and the pain, and the fervent letter-writing campaign on which her father had embarked. He was silent for a little space after she stopped talking, whistling very softly through his teeth and staring into middle distance.

"When is he going to . . . leave us?" he said, finally. "Soon? Did the doctor say?"

"No. He really couldn't tell. Maybe not for a long time. Bay, I want to ask you something," Mike said.

"Shoot."

"Well, when I suggested that he ask you to let some of your people help him with his silly letters, he . . . I don't know. Kind of blew me off. Muttered something about not wanting to bother you. Wouldn't look at me. And he doesn't talk about you, or even talk much to you, when you're with him. I know you've noticed. It isn't like him. Do you think . . . he suspects about us?"

"No," he said. "No. I'm sure he doesn't. He doesn't even seem to know I'm here half the time."

"He knows," Mike said. "He always remembers when you've been here. And he sure does know I come up here every afternoon and shut the door. He's known that from the start. Bay, why on earth did you tell him I was writing?"

"Why not?" he said. "It covers our tracks perfectly. I thought it was a small inspiration, myself."

"I don't like to lie," she said. "I don't think you had to tell him anything. I don't think it would have come up."

"Maybe not yet, but sooner or later he might have begun to wonder, and now there's the perfect answer for him," Bay Sewell said. "Relax, Mike. I don't like to lie, either, unless I have to, but I sure will, for us. It seems a little . . . picky to screw a married man every afternoon and then balk at a little lie."

Mike's face burned.

"Is that how you think of this?" she said.

"No. I just don't like to be jumped on," he said briefly. There was the barest hint of remoteness in his voice.

"I wasn't jumping on you. I just hate to see him . . . shut you out, after you've been so close all these years. I was afraid it was this."

"Well, put your mind at rest. Canaday's behind it, if anybody is. It's obvious he doesn't want me to know what he's up to with your dad. I haven't brought it up again, Mike, because it seemed to upset you so much the only time I did . . . but I really need you to be my eyes and ears with John. I want to look after his interests, and the only way I have of knowing what's going on with the DOT is you. Will you tell me? I want to keep a finger on this."

"I truly do not know what's going on," Mike said. She did not know why she was so reluctant to talk with him about her father and Sam Canaday and the action involving the homeplace. "I've told them both I didn't want to know."

"Well, I want you to find out. And I want you to tell me. I'm serious, Mike. If he's getting worse, if the pain is getting bad and they're increasing his medication, the day might come when he can't look out for himself. Somebody else besides Canaday needs to know what's what."

"Oh . . . all right. I'll ask Sam and let you know."

"When?"

"Oh, *Bay* . . . soon. When I get a chance. When the time seems right. Okay?"

"Okay," Bayard Sewell said. "Okay."

John Winship's pain returned the following night.

Sam Canaday had come by after supper with copies of the first few letters that Ouida Quigley had typed for him, and the old man had been fiercely jubilant at seeing his words in print. He had read them off to Sam and Mike in a thin, savage old falcon's shriek, and Mike, unable to leave the kitchen without seeming intolerably rude, had busied herself at the sink so that he could not see her face. The words were puerile and clotted with weak rage, and the abuse was that of a breath-holding child in a tantrum. The thought of anyone in the news media seeing the letters made her teeth clench with embarrassment. She could not imagine that any responsible editor would respond. Sam Canaday nodded occasionally, his face sober and thoughtful, and once or twice said, "Good point, Colonel." Mike wondered if he could see the contempt that stiffened her shoulders and back.

Midway through one of the letters her father drew a sharp, shallow breath and broke off his words. Mike waited for the droning diatribe to continue, but it did not, and when she turned to the pair of them it was to see her father rigid in his chair, his face turned the color of tallow, his eyes rolled nearly back into the sunken sockets. There were stark white lines around his tight-clamped lips, and his nostrils whitened as she stared at him. A thin, mewling, almost electronic sound, a keening hum, swelled gradually in the kitchen, and she started to look about for it until she realized, stupidly, that it was coming from between his clenched teeth. Sweat sheeted his sunken face.

She stood still, rooted to the rug in front of the sink, staring. There was nothing at all in her mind except the word "stroke," hanging as perfect and palpable in the thrumming air before her as if it had been on a dictionary page. The keening went on and on.

". . . the doctor, for God's sake, Mike, right *now!* MOVE!" Sam Canaday's voice cut through the dreadful whine and penetrated the thickness around her, and she saw that he was kneeling before her father with his fingers on his pulse.

"I . . . where's the book . . ."

The sound stopped as if a switch had been thrown, and John Winship took a great, rattling gulp of air, and his rigid body slowly relaxed and slumped low into the wheelchair. His terrible eyes focused on Sam Canaday, and he struggled to push words out on the laboring breath.

"No . . . doctor. Better now. No doctor."

"The hell you say, Colonel. Mike, look on the wall by the phone, the number's there . . ."

"No doctor!" The cry was so hoarse and guttural and strong that Mike actually dropped the telephone she was dialing. She turned wildly to her father, and then to Sam. He was looking keenly at her father, who stared back at him with a fiercely focused, milky glare.

A wash of color so faint that she could hardly be sure she saw it was creeping into John Winship's cheeks, and the cords and ridges of whitened flesh beside his mouth relaxed. Sam sat back on his heels.

"Okay. No doctor for right now," he said, in a normal voice. "What was it, Colonel? Pain?"

"A twinge," her father said, the momentary substance draining from his voice. "Just another goddamned gas twinge. You call the doctor every time I have one of those, and you'll be on the phone right much."

"It wasn't a gas pain, and you know it," Sam said. "You know what it was. You've known right along. And you know it's probably going to come back, maybe tonight, and that it's probably going to be worse next time. I'm going to make a deal with you. You're going to go to bed and take some of that medicine Dr. French gave you . . . and take *enough* of the goddamned stuff, and take it without saying a single word . . . and I won't call the doctor until I've seen how you are in the morning. But give me one *word* of crap and I'm getting on the phone that second. Take it or leave it."

"Screw you, Canaday," John Winship said, but he nodded his skull's head. His voice had faded almost to nothing, and his wasted hands and arms were limp in his lap. The cold, oily moisture still sheened his face. A slow paling of the mouth and nose skin told Mike that the pain was starting again.

She moved forward to push the chair into his bedroom, and without turning to look at her or opening the closed old dead fowl's eyes, he said, "Get away from me, Micah. I don't want you near me. Don't want you in my room. Don't even want you in the house with me. Wish you'd just suck on back to where you came from."

Mike drew in her breath as sharply as if he had struck her. Her face burned and ridiculous tears stung her nose. She wheeled and put her arms back into the cooling dishwater, fighting back the old rage and pain that she remembered as if she had felt them only the day before.

Sam Canaday said only, "Come on, Colonel. Let's roll."

When he came back into the kitchen, Mike was sitting at the table, her face stiff with hard-won control. She wanted desperately to be away from them, shut into the silence and sanctuary of her room, but she needed to know that her father was asleep or at least resting and unlikely to need attention again that evening before she felt free to flee to it. She thought no further than the refrain that echoed in her ringing head: I'm going to leave this house tomorrow. I'm not going to stay here one minute longer. Nobody and nothing can make me.

"He's asleep," Sam said, dropping into the chair opposite her and scrubbing at his eyes with his fist. "I gave him enough Demerol to stun a mule. I doubt if he'll wake till morning. But we're going to have to do something about this pain then. Get him stronger stuff, or have a nurse come in for injections, or something. Much more like that will kill him. I'll call French first thing tomorrow."

Mike said nothing.

"I'm sorry he popped off at you," Sam said. "He didn't mean it, of course. He didn't want you to see him in pain, is all. He can't handle your having to watch his weakness or tend to him when the pain and the mess get bad. So he strikes out. You're going to have to get used to that kind of thing from here on out."

"There's not going to be any here on out," Mike said. Her voice shook very slightly. "I'm not staying. He doesn't want me here; it's obvious he never did. DeeDee was lying to me. Good Christ, he acts like I *wanted* to come home, like he was doing me a big favor, letting me come. Some damn favor. When in hell has he ever done me a favor?"

He was silent for a while, and then he said, mildly, "How sharper than a serpent's tooth."

Her head went up. "Why should I be grateful to him? What did he ever do for me that he didn't absolutely have to do? You don't know, you can't know . . . he never just *gave* me anything. Not ever. I remember when I was little, I wanted two things more than anything I've ever wanted in the world. Just two things, little things. I wanted a catcher's mitt and I wanted a live rabbit for Easter. I begged him for them. And he said I was too irresponsible for the rabbit and that girls didn't get catcher's mitts. He'd buy me things that somebody told him I *needed* . . . Priss or Rusky or Dee or my teachers . . . but he never just *gave* me anything in his life. You tell me one thing I ought to be grateful to him for."

"More than you may ever know," he said. "Why are you so cold and distant with him? I know what happened when you were a kid, about the sit-ins and all. It's too bad. But it was twenty-two years ago, and you've done very well for yourself. And he doesn't have much time left, and what he does have is going to be more and more like tonight. He needs to be close to his daughter now."

"He has DeeDee. She's all he ever wanted, except Mother and the homeplace."

"No," Sam said. "She's not all. He wants you. Why else would he call you home?"

"He didn't," Mike said. "A fool could see after tonight that he didn't."

"Don't kid yourself. He might never be able to say it, but he needs you now, in a lot of ways you don't even suspect."

"He has a funny way of showing it. He's the one who built the wall between us."

"But you built it up twice as high. Watch out, Mike," Sam Canaday said. "Something there is that doesn't love a wall."

"Not bad, a redneck quoting Frost."

"Oh, well, it's the one single thing I learned at college besides how to drink warm bourbon and Coke out of Dixie cups and make water balloons out of Trojans." He smiled at her, a worn, brief phantom grin.

"Why did you take this case?" Mike asked. Fatigue to match his was curling stealthily through her veins, and she did not think she could stand up to leave the kitchen. "Why are you spending so much time on it? He can't be paying you that much; he doesn't have anything but that damned old house and that little bit of land."

"I don't have all that much business, either," he said. "The stench of coal smoke and steel mills lingers about me; it offends Lytton's delicate nostrils. I guess I took the case because of the land. Because of what it means to him. Family, roots, identity. I never had any of that. Roots don't go very deep in Birmingham. The land, though . . . it's always seemed to me that the land is a person's place. Not just something he owns, but a context. It's where he belongs in the order of things. And consequently, it's who he is."

"My work is who I am," Mike said.

"No. That's what you've *done*. The land is who, where, and when you *are*. I guess it's why, too."

"You're the right person for this ridiculous case, then," Mike snapped. "You sound just like him."

"I happen to like your father," Sam Canaday said. "He's good for me. He's good for the South. The South is being gobbled up by asphalt and concrete just like it once was by kudzu. This Sunbelt shit is changing everything that matters to me. It's changing Southerners, too. We used to have men like your father, men who knew what was important and where they stood on things. Now we have men like your brother-in-law. And of course, your old friend Bayard Everett Sewell. Mr. South Fulton County."

Mike let it slide. She must not leap to defend Bay.

"You make my father sound like Robert E. Lee," she said. "But you must know what a bigot he is; you hear him every night."

"That's not important. That doesn't mean anything. It's not the blacks he's mad at, it's the loss. Your mother. The life he thought he was going to have. You. The homeplace. He has to be mad at somebody. It just isn't important. The point is, he knows what *is* important. And he knows it's worth a fight. He's not paying me one red cent, incidentally; this is a professional courtesy between attorneys. Lord, lord. He's still a burr under your saddle, isn't he?"

"I don't think much about it anymore."

"The hell you don't," he said.

She sat in silence for a while, wondering if she would ever be able to get up unaided from the chair in which she sat. Presently she said, slowly, "It's very strange. I'm not, right at this minute and in this house, anything in particular. Nothing I used to be. I don't feel like a writer or a mother or a wife, or much of a woman, even. I may be all those things again sometime, but right now I'm some kind of . . . emotional gelding."

"Well," he said companionably, "you *are* a daughter, you know."

Mike laughed harshly. "I haven't been that in more than twenty years."

"Then why do you stay on in this house, if his whole thrust, his impetus, the thing that's keeping him going, touches you so little? If you're not his daughter, why did you really come in the first place?"

In her fatigue and the ebbing of the alarm at her father's seizure, Mike came close to telling him about the lost assignment and book and apartment, and about Rachel's and Derek Blessing's betrayals. The words flooded her throat like bile. But instead, she said, "They needed me here. DeeDee put it to me so that I couldn't refuse her. It was a choice I made. You have to choose; I chose. But I don't have to participate in all the rest of it, or pitch in to save the damned farm. My being here is keeping him from having to go to an institution. What more do you want me to say, Sam? What more do you think he wants?"

"More than you've got to give, I guess," Sam Canaday said, stretching bonelessly. "Just don't kid yourself that you made a choice. From what I hear, you've never really made any choices except one . . . to go to Atlanta when you were a teenager and play with the big guys in the sit-ins, and you did that more to get at your father than to make a stand or a statement. Good choice, though, by the way. But after that you ran. And you've been running ever since like a bowling ball down an alley, unless I miss my guess. Not much choice for a bowling ball. And then you came home again . . . because you had no choice. Oh, come on, Mike, I know about your job and your daughter and your apartment; Priss told me, of course. Sorry if it bothers you, but there it is. You ran out of everything, including bucks, and so you came home. I don't blame you; so would I. But you don't know about choices. Not the hard choices that hurt to make and cost you plenty. You haven't made any since 1964."

Before she could reply, her father's frail voice curled out on the air like smoke from his bedroom, calling Sam, and he got up abruptly and left the kitchen. Mike sat where she was, very still, flayed by his last words but at a remove. Like everything else he had said, they had been uttered beyond the anesthetizing walls of the bell jar and the white fatigue. After a while she tried to gather herself up and go upstairs, but succeeded only in shifting positions slightly. She wondered dully if she was going to have to ask Sam Canaday to help her up to bed.

"He wants to take you down and show you the homeplace tomorrow," Sam said, coming quietly back into the room. "Says you haven't been yet. I told him I'd drive you all after work."

Mike simply lifted her head and stared at him. Could either one of them, Sam or her father, be serious? Take a little sentimental family journey together after the smoking, charring words that had been uttered this night?

"It's an apology, Mike. I never heard him make one before. I wish you could find it in you to give him just this one thing. I don't think he'll ask you for anything else."

He looked at her steadily in the clock-ticking silence of the big white kitchen. He looked less substantial than he had at the beginning of the summer, not nearly so squarely *there.* Mike wondered irrelevantly where, if anywhere, he ate his meals. She pulled herself to her feet with great effort.

"All right," she said, feeling the heavy plodding of her blood through her veins, and the weary drag of her heart. "Okay. You win, both of you. Tell him I'd like to see the homeplace. It's been a long time. It's been years."

TWENTY-TWO

It was past eight o'clock when he came to pick them up the next evening, and the light in the west was the bright, pearled gray that comes sometimes to the Deep South with the heat of midsummer. Mike knew that the electricity had been cut off in the old farmhouse, but they would not need lights this evening. The slow, thick dark would not settle until well after nine.

Sam turned John Winship's old Cadillac south onto the highway, idling through Lytton and past the city limits. Mike saw little that she remembered. She had not been this way since she was a teenager, going with her father and DeeDee on some small errand at the homeplace, or to visit her mother's grave in the antebellum cemetery south of town. Most of the old houses and farms that had stood along the highway then were gone now, and there was a Chevrolet dealership, a small shopping center, a Wendy's and a McDonald's, and a treeless new perpetual-care cemetery, engulfing the old one, as gaudy as a Mexican plaza with plastic geraniums. Mike recalled one particular old house, a vast, tumbledown frame structure set in a sunless tangle of honeysuckle, where she and DeeDee had gone to be fitted for silk velvet dresses with smocking and lace-edged collars, identical except for their colors, when they were small. The seamstress had been a tiny, bent gnome of a woman, as gnarled and impossibly old as a terrapin, who had had a frail, fluting voice like miniature crystal and smelled of dusty fabric. Her arthritic child's fingers made stitches so fine that they were nearly invisible, and she wore a length of ribbon around her neck in which glittered hundreds of tiny brass pins. Mike had loved to go there; it reminded her of a story from her illustrated Grimm Brothers fairy tales. All there was hushed, silken, dwarfed, dim, old, child-sized.

"What happened to Miss Tally's house?" she asked her father. "I don't quite remember where it was. She couldn't possibly still be alive, could she?"

"Good God, no," her father said. "She died right after you . . . went. City took her house down for the new cemetery. Godawful plastic thing; you remember I want to be planted in the old one with a real stone that sticks up, beside your mother. Plots there for you girls and your husbands, too. If you ever have another one."

Mike shot him a look, but there was no malice on his face, only a kind of abstraction.

"I came down here and watched 'em knock her old house down," John Winship went on. "Did it with wrecking balls in those days, not bulldozers, like they do now. It was quite a sight. There's some dignity to a wrecking ball, I always thought. Bulldozer looks like an old scrub steer butting down an outhouse."

They stopped at a traffic light that had not been there when Mike went away and a rangy, sandy-haired man in nylon shorts and a sleeveless runner's shirt sprinted up even with the car and put his head in on her father's side.

"Evening, Mr. Winship, Sam," he said affably. He was breathing hard, and sweat shone on his thin, corded arms and legs. His chest and shoulders were prodigiously freckled. "Good to see you out, sir. This must be Mike. I'd hoped to get a chance to meet you, Ms. Winship, but your dad doesn't grace us with his presence anymore, and I can't make an official call because he's threatened to throw me out of the house if I do. I'm Tom Cawthorn."

"It's nice to meet you, Mr. Cawthorn." She smiled at him, briefly and uncertainly. Why would her father have occasion to visit this strange young man, whom she had never seen before? Why would he visit her father? Why would John Winship forbid him the house?

He saw her confusion and laughed. "I'm sorry," he said. "I don't know why I thought you'd know. Sheer ego. I'm the pastor at First Methodist now. I've only been here three years, but I've known who you are longer than that, and I've wanted to tell you how much I've admired your work. It's no good telling your dad. He just snorts. He's one of my notable failures. Just refuses to be reclaimed back into the bosom of the church."

"Goddamn Good News Bible," her father piped peevishly.

"Jazz bands in the sanctuary. Dog collars and robes. Might as well be St. Peter's."

The young preacher and Sam Canaday both laughed.

"I'll get you yet," Tom Cawthorn said.

"Over my dead body, that's how you'll get me. That's *just* how you'll get me," her father snapped.

"I hope not. Well, I've got another couple of miles before I can call it quits. See you tomorrow night, Sam?"

"Right," Sam said. The young man flipped his hand at them and loped off, and Sam slid the car back onto the highway.

"Going to choir practice, Sam?" John Winship said sarcastically.

"Nope. Going to play poker with the preacher and a couple of deacons. You know we've got a game every month, Colonel."

"It's certainly not the church I remember," Mike said, watching the near-naked pastor dwindle into the distance along the heat-shimmering highway.

"Not much in Lytton is, I'll be bound," Sam Canaday said.

They rounded a deep bend in the highway and the bulk of the homeplace rose up on the right, dark in its grove of old pecan trees against the clear evening sky. Something turned in Mike's chest. How many times had she seen it like this, from the window of John Winship's car, approaching in the evening light? Nothing seemed to have changed about the house and the fields around it that swept off on both sides toward stands of woods. But the outbuildings that stood behind the house at a distance of twenty yards or so were huddling and sliding near to the earth, and the grape vines and flower and vegetable gardens that surrounded the house were gone now to lush and surging wild. It looked as it was: derelict and poignant, but beautiful in its loneliness. Dignified, like a widow. The particular cant and sweep of hills, woods, and fields around the homeplace were sweet.

I never realized it was such a pretty piece of land, Mike thought. I guess I never really looked at it.

Instead of turning in at the overgrown driveway, off the dirt road that ran down beside the house, John Winship directed Sam to follow the road for a short distance and turn the car off into a deep, overarching avenue of gnarled old cedars. Mike remembered playing house in the magical, enclosed spaces inside the ground-sweeping branches. She had named the little kingdom, for some unremembered reason, Skunktown.

"Want to sneak up on the house," John Winship said. "You can't see a car parked here from there, and if there are any sons of bitches prowling around there I want to catch 'em redhanded."

"Who do you think would be hanging around an empty house?" Mike asked, curious.

"Didn't used to be empty," her father said. "That's why I'm trying to catch 'em. Sons of bitching niggers have stolen just about every piece of furniture and pot and pan and dish in there over the years, even took the coat hangers. There's nothing left, except a few things I got out early and put in the basement, or up over the garage for J.W. Goddamn it, my folks didn't have much, but I wanted to keep what they did have. Didn't want niggers using it. Never have been able to catch the bastards, though; I tried having tenants here, but they were so sorry they were worse than the niggers. Police say they come by here every night, but they never see anything. How come everything's just disappeared out of here, then, I asked Olin Henderson. It just happens when a house is abandoned, he says. But it didn't used to . . . not in Lytton. I know it's because the police aren't looking. Half of 'em niggers themselves. Half of 'em probably got my mama's furniture in their houses. So I try to catch 'em myself when I can. Don't get down here much anymore, though. Oh, well, not much left to take now, I reckon."

Mike sighed faintly. The desire to fly furiously at her father's bigotry had long since faded under the leavening of Bayard Sewell and the bell jar.

There was no one about, but Mike was startled to see that new scaffolding had been put up around the back door, framing the wheelchair ramp that had been installed sometime past, and spanking new paint gleamed whitely in the dusk. The shutters had been removed, and stood, scraped and bleached, against the fender of the old covered well beside the doorstep, ready for new black paint. Cans and ladders bulged under tarpaulins. Mike's breath caught in her throat; the old well house was literally covered in a hectic pall of red roses, and their perfume was so heavy and evocative on the still air that for a moment she was literally plunged into another country, that of her childhood. It had not seemed so vivid and near in all the weeks she had been home. Pure sensation dove and shrieked at her like bats.

"I remember those roses," she said. "I remember that smell as if it were yesterday. I don't remember them being all over the well like that, though."

"Paul Scarlets," her father said. "My grandmother planted the first ones, I think. Climbers. Mama always used to keep 'em cut back, and I did too, up until a few years ago. Make a real show, don't they?"

"What's with the painting, Colonel?" Sam Canaday said, halting the wheelchair at the foot of the ramp. His voice was neutral, but Mike saw that his mouth was tight.

"Got Amos Butler down here with a crew finally," the old man said. He did not look at Mike or Sam. "Been putting me off for almost a year, but finally got around to it. About time, too. The place was about to rot. Looked like a nigger shack. This ought to last another ten years, though."

In her mind, Mike saw the great mandibles of the bulldozer, blood-rust red against the new white paint. Oh, God, Daddy, she thought in irritation and pain.

"Looks like a good job," Sam Canaday said mildly. He pushed John Winship's chair up the ramp and into the house, and Mike followed.

Mike had been in the homeplace hundreds of times, but it was altogether alien and strange to her now, in the half light, its slanted, warped floors bare of her grandmother's rag rugs, the stained beaverboard walls empty of the massive old mail-order fumed oak furniture she remembered. There had never, in her memory, been anyone living in the house, but before, the artifacts of a hundred-odd years of hardscrabble life had filled the myriad small rooms to bursting. Even then, though, she had never been able to imagine people actually living here; had no sense of her kinsmen moving in their joy and pain and rage and fatigue and laughter through these rooms, of her father as the living and lively small boy he must have been. The homeplace had always seemed as flat and two-dimensional as a stage set.

Now, though, in the blue-dim, empty, and filthy rooms, smaller than they had seemed when furnished, shadows stirred in corners and surged at ceilings; fragile, voiceless voices drifted in stale, hot air; smells curled ever so faintly into her nostrils. Or rather, not smells, but the ghosts of them, phantom scents. The whole house whispered with phantom life.

Silently, she followed her father and Sam Canaday from room to room, the wheelchair leaving stark snail's tracks in the thick felting of dust on the random boards of the floor. In some rooms in the oldest part of the house, the boards were joined and secured not with nails, but with pegs. Her father talked as they went; under his reedy voice, other voices whispered, whispered. Mike did not want to hear them. She fastened her eyes on the knobbed parchment back of her father's skull and focused her whole attention on his voice. Occasionally he had to stop for a long moment to gulp drafts of the thick air, but then he would begin again. He talked and talked, of the time when there was life and living in this dead house.

"Mama always kept a white flour-sack tablecloth over the dinner table," he said, in the vast kitchen. "Did it to keep out chickens and me and the cats. We had two when I was growing up, and Mama called 'em the ashcat and the tray-riding cat, because one of them always slept in the warm ashes from the fireplace in the winter, and the other kept trying to sneak up under the tablecloth and get at the cream and the crackling cornbread and boiled potatoes on the tray she kept under there. I don't remember if they had names or not, but I sure remember them. Old yellow tiger and a big tom as black as the ace of spades. I tied their tails together once and hung 'em over the clothesline, to see 'em fight. Lord God, they nearly killed each other before Mama caught me and made me let them go. She tanned my hide good for that." He cackled aloud. "Used to tie kernels of corn to string on the end of fishing poles and trail 'em around in the chicken yard, too. Old Dominecker hen would swallow the corn and you could lead her around all day. Got a hiding for that, too."

"You must have been a devil," Sam Canaday said, chuckling. Mike did not laugh. He might have been talking about a boy in a Victorian youth's novel. She could no more imagine her father's childhood than she could his vigorous youth. He had, for her, only two personas: remote, glacial middle age and this molting old raptor's dying.

"Worst hiding I ever got, though, was for jumping out of the cottonseed loft down onto the wagon full of cotton, before it went to the gin. Pa had the team hitched up all ready to go, and I was up there with a pitchfork, just a little old thing, pushing it out to him, and all at once I just hollered, 'Look, Pa! Look at me!' and I jumped right out of there and landed on top of a whole bale of cotton. I don't know if it was me or the cotton he was worried about, but he took me out behind the calf shed and made me drop my britches, and just wore me out with his belt. He never did that before or again. Mama always had to do it, and she used a switch from the privet hedge. Made me go out and pick my own, and sent me back if it was too little. Must have done it a hundred times. But it was that one time with the belt that I remember."

In one room there was a small, whitewashed fireplace, blackened on the inside and stained around its perimeter with odd, star-shaped brownish splotches.

John Winship smiled. "Daddy chewed tobacco. Used to sit here every night before they went to bed . . . we all sat in their bedroom in the winter, because it was the only bedroom with a fireplace . . . and I'd eat Yates apples out of a basket by the fireplace, and Mama would tell me stories about the family and all, and Daddy would nod and rock and chew and every now and then he'd let fly . . . and usually miss. I can still hear Mama squalling at him. She whitewashed that fireplace four or five times a year, and it never went a week before he'd get it again. He never drank or smoked or cussed; no other bad habits, but he did love to chew. I can still see him. You're the image of him, Micah."

He did not look around at her, did not seem to realize, even, that there was anyone in the room with him.

He showed them the front parlor, and the pantry, and the little glassed sunroom where his mother had kept her sewing machine and her churn and her quilting frame.

"This is sort of her place; I always remember her here," he said. "When I think of her, it's here that I see her."

He motioned Sam through the room and out to the small veranda off it, and pointed with one thin old claw to the dried bed of an old lily pool. There was a high, curly stone bridge over it, cracked and fallen now, and the collapsed corpses of old white lawn furniture around it. Mike remembered when the pool had been kept full, and there had been great, thick, glossy lily pads in it, and huge, starlike pink and white waterlilies in the summer. She and DeeDee had caught tadpoles there.

"This is his place, Daddy's. This is where I see him. He used to love to sit out here by the lily pond at night, after supper, and listen to the frogs and watch the lightning bugs. There was one big old frog that hung around here several years; a real monster. I saw him once, and you could hear him to College Park when he let go. Daddy called him Gikiwalli. Said somebody told him that was Italian for frog. Doesn't sound right to me, but that's what we called him. He was still here when I went away to law school. I don't know what happened to him; wasn't a cat or a coon alive that could catch him. Pa was out here every night it wasn't just out and out cold." He paused, his eyes traveling over the ruined pond and bridge and furniture.

"It was here that I came when he died and cut my hand and let it bleed into the ground," he said. "Right over there, by that Spanish bayonet. That's where his chair always was. I've still got the scar."

He looked down at the luminous, withered hand in his lap as if he had never seen it before. Neither Sam nor Mike replied. It was not to them that he spoke.

As Sam rolled him through the house and toward the ramp at the back door, he indicated a small, shedlike room off the porch, no more than a closet, really. In Mike's time it had been used to store garden tools. Sam Canaday wheeled him to the mouth of the room. There was no door.

"This was my bedroom," John Winship said. "This was where I slept for eighteen years of my life. It was real snug in here. Ceiling snugged right down over me, and there were no windows, so it was like being in a cave. Way back here at the back of the house, where nobody came unless they had a special reason. Used to feel like I could hide from the world back here and nobody would ever find me; nobody would even know I was in the house. Like Tom Sawyer in that cave. I used to lie here and pretend I was Tom Sawyer. I could hear the train whistles coming up and down the tracks for miles and miles before they got here and I'd pretend it was the Mississippi River out there, and they were riverboats. I'd sleep real good in this little old room, summer and winter, with feather mattresses and

Mama's quilts piled over me. Felt as safe as a bear in a honey tree. Haven't slept like that since I was eighteen years old. Kid nowadays wouldn't be caught dead in a little old closet like this, but I thought it was the finest room in the world."

He gestured at Sam to take him out of the room and down the ramp to the path to the car, but then signaled him to stop.

"What's that over there, in the corner?" he said. "Looks like some kind of china, vase or something."

Mike reached over and picked the object up. It was a shard of a pottery pitcher, with the curved handle still attached, glazed blue and white in a pattern of stripes and whorls. It was incredibly filthy. She picked it up with one finger through the handle and brought it over and laid it in his lap.

"Why," John Winship said, "it's the Yankee pitcher. I haven't seen it since I was a boy. I didn't even know it was still in the house. Looked all over for it. Look here, Sam and Mike, this pitcher is way over a hundred years old, and some son of a bitch has found it and broke it and just thrown it in a corner. By God, if I had a gun . . ."

"Why is it called the Yankee pitcher, Colonel?" Sam broke in hastily.

Her father was diverted. "When my great-grandfather Worthy . . . your great-great-grandfather, Mike . . . was off fighting in Virginia, there was only my great-grandmother and a couple of nigger tenants left on the place. She was just a little thing, not shoulder-high to a man, with dark red hair down to her waist, about nineteen, I think. One summer day a troop of Sherman's boys came through on the way down to Lovejoy and the lieutenant rode up and saw her on the porch and asked her if she had anything to drink, and she brought him out this pitcher full of cold buttermilk. It was the last she had, but I guess she figured she'd better be nice to him since she sure couldn't fight him. She had a cow and a couple of calves and a mule down in the swamp bottom; used to go down there at night and tie up their muzzles with strips off her petticoat to keep 'em from making any noise when there was Yankees in the neighborhood, or so my mama always told me. Anyway, he took the pitcher off without thanking her, and she just figured she'd never see it again, but at least he didn't burn the place. The next day one of the niggers found it resting under that big pine that leans out over the dirt road, on a nest of moss, all washed out. We always called it the Yankee pitcher after that."

He looked at the broken china in his hand, and then out the door of the house and off across the field to the woods, where night was settling down like a cast net.

"He walked home from Appomattox," he said. "Took him four months. She never knew when to look for him or even if he was coming home. One day, at twilight, she was sitting out on this porch and he just came walking up that cedar avenue and sat down on the porch and leaned against the house and said, 'What we got left?' God knows, they didn't have much, but they had enough to start over again."

He tossed the scrap of pottery back into the corner, where it rolled crookedly and came to rest against the baseboard.

"They don't leave you much," he said.

The muttering army of ghosts suddenly leaped into life as if touched by the very finger of God. A sallow, filthy young soldier walked up an avenue of cedars and she could smell the sweat and dust of his journey; a worn old-young girl lifted callused, broken, sunburnt hands to him and she could taste the salt of her tears. Mike heard living laughter and weeping and the cries of children and animals and the phlegm of deaths; she smelled sweat, dirt, manure, tobacco, roses, pine fires, earth after rain, hay drying sweet in fields, frying meat, strong lye soap, the melony smell of pig slops and souring buttermilk in the cool morning pantry. The tiny cubicle was alive with people, and they were as densely fleshed and clothed with particularity as the three who had come tonight into this house. At their forefront, a small boy with thistledown hair and light-spilling gray eyes leaped forever from a barn loft into empty, sunshot air, shouting, "Look at me!"

Mike stumbled blindly down the steps of the homeplace and into the cooling air outside. Her head swam; her ears rang with the cacophony of her kinsmen. She barely heard Sam and John Winship come down the ramp behind her. When her head cleared slightly, she turned to her father. She cleared her throat.

"I'd like to help you stuff some envelopes and lick some stamps, if you'll still have me," she said.

"Well, I reckon I can find something for you to do," he said, looking past her to the curve of the distant wooded hill. "Mout's well earn your keep."

"Mout's well," Mike said.

He still did not look at her, and he did not look at her during the long, slow, lurching progress back to the avenue of cedars in the wheelchair, but when Sam helped him from the chair and opened the door of the Cadillac, he laid his hand, as light and scratchy and dry as the talon of a long-dead hawk, on his daughter's arm, and Mike handed him into the car and closed the door.

They were home before dark.

TWENTY-THREE

"What was it that did the trick?" Sam Canaday asked, looking at Mike through the wire-rimmed glasses that made his face seem somehow vulnerable and oddly old-fashioned, an earnest, unworldly Victorian assistant master in a barely standard British public school. "I thought we'd get you on our side sooner or later, but I figured you'd put up a bigger fuss than you did. You fell without a shot being fired."

He had insisted on coming by before work the morning after their visit to the homeplace to tell her about the action against the Department of Transportation. She had tried to dissuade him; she still had no interest in the court action and was still reluctant to hear about it. But he had been adamant.

"If you're going to get involved in it at all, I insist that you know what you're fighting," he said. "I won't butt in after this, but it's important to me and your dad both that you know."

So she had agreed. They sat now, drinking coffee and waiting for the sweet rolls he had brought from the all-night Kroger to warm. Outside, early sun was touching the tops of the tallest trees. In his room at the back of the house, John Winship slept deeply. Mike had not heard him stirring in the night, as she usually did.

"I think it was the old pitcher," she said, in answer to his question. "That and when he said, 'They don't leave you much.' Somehow I only just then realized how very little he was going to have left if that old horror of a house comes down. And then, it just seemed all of a sudden that . . . everybody who had lived in that house was real; alive somehow, not just names I'd heard in old family stories. And I could almost see him as a little boy . . . Oh, I don't know. I can't explain it . . ."

"You don't have to," Sam said, grinning faintly. "St. Paul did it for you. Happened to him once, too, on the way to Damascus."

"I'm really weary of all this biblical crap of yours," Mike said peevishly. She had not slept well; had fought dreams and shadows all night, and was tired. "I know what an epiphany is. Let's get on with the Department of Transportation business if we're going to."

"Right," he said, straightening up and pulling a small sheaf of papers toward him. "Well, it started about six months ago. Usually you hear rumors about new roads and things like this, but this time there just weren't any that anyone around here heard. The Colonel got a letter from one Leonard Tinsley, a DOT Relocation Officer— great term, isn't it?—saying that the department had acquired property that the homeplace is on the day before, and that all personal property had to be moved out within sixty days. As soon as it was moved, said our Mr. Tinsley, he'd come inspect the property and have your dad sign a claim form and then he'd send it in for payment of $441.84."

"*$441.84!*" Mike was appalled. Surely, the lumber alone was worth that much.

"Of course, it was a ridiculous price," Sam Canaday said, "and they probably knew it was. You'd be surprised how often that first offer gets accepted, though. Officialese scares a lot of folks. Well, anyway, he called the number this Tinsley gave him, and Tinsley told him that the state planned to put in an access highway from Carrollton, over at the river in the west, to I-85 over east yonder. When John said there was already an access not five miles down toward Newnan, Tinsley said all he knew was that now there was going to be another one. So the Colonel came to see me, and I contacted Tinsley and objected on the grounds that the offer was not acceptable. And I filed for a writ of injunction and for consequent damages in Superior Court because, of course, without that strip of highway frontage that the house sits on, John couldn't sell the land for ten cents, or even develop it, if he ever wanted to, or his heirs did. It was all I could do, Mike. There wasn't anything I could do about the house; there never has been. That was gone the minute he got the letter from Tinsley. But I knew we could delay for quite a while negotiating the price and filing for consequential damages. Of course, the DOT maintained that the so-called improvements—the demolition of the house—would offset any consequential damages that might exist.

"So what I've done so far is simply refuse any offer they make on the house, and refuse to name a firm price. I can't string it out forever, but I figure I can delay it a while yet. Sooner or later, though, they're going to get tired of it all and move on it."

"And then what?"

"Then they'll file condemnation proceedings and get it condemned, file a declaration of taking, get a court decree and take title, and the rest, as they say, is history."

"You mean . . ."

"I mean they'll let out bids to subcontractors and the dozers will come on in. They surveyed and took test borings and drove the stakes back in the winter. It's all in place."

"My God, Sam! This what-you-macallit . . . this declaration of taking . . . they can just do it whenever they want to, whether or not you're even satisfied with their price? That's *wrong,* that's *criminal . . .*"

"No, that's legal. And they sure can do it, and they do, and will, in this case. Up until World War II they couldn't take title or take a hoe to dirt or anything until there was a final property settlement, which of course could take years. But in wartime you just can't wait, sometimes, for roads and munitions plants and such. You can sort of see their side, Mike . . . without a tool like the declaration of taking, there probably wouldn't be any freeway system, for instance. But now that they can do it anytime and anyplace they want to, of course it's often misused, like every other law. I frankly don't know why they've let me drag this on as long as I have, except that I've pleaded illness and family distress, which, God knows, is true enough. But it rarely stops the DOT."

"Maybe Bay has been able to influence them," Mike said. "I know he's trying."

"Oh, yes," Sam Canaday said. "I'm sure he's had considerable influence. Well, that's it, essentially and in a nutshell. I wanted you to know what you were getting into. I wanted to be sure you understand that we're not going to win it. Only delay it."

"Does he . . . does Daddy understand that? He doesn't seem to; that painting he's having done, and the way he talks about it . . ."

"The Colonel understands it," Sam said. "He's a lawyer, after all. Whether or not he acknowledges it is another matter. But I'm sure he understands it."

"Sam . . . is it right, after all? This delay; it can only put off something that will hurt him badly in the end. And he's not going to get stronger, you know, only weaker . . ."

"It's right," Sam Canaday said, taking off the glasses and rubbing his eyes. There were dark smears of fatigue under them, and the strong tan of his face had faded until, in the dawn-lit kitchen, he looked almost as mustardy as J.W. "You know why I'm delaying; we talked about it. It's keeping him going. And it's buying him time to try and get you back."

"He's got me now; I'm in the fire right along with the rest of you," Mike said. "I told him we'd start with the letters this morning. I'm going over and get Priss's typewriter . . ."

"No," Sam Canaday said. "He's got your participation. He hasn't got your love."

"Ah, *God* . . ." Mike cried, pushing back her chair and whirling around to stare sightlessly out the windows over the sink at the brightening day. "You ask too much! Both of you, all of you . . . you just plain ask too damned much!"

"You're right," he said, gathering up the papers and stuffing them back into his shabby old briefcase. "We ask everything."

Mike was not prepared for the reaction her participation in John Winship's media-blitzing campaign engendered in her sister and Bayard Sewell. She had not expected DeeDee to be pleased, since she was more or less forsworn to try and discourage her father in his fight against the Department of Transportation. But she had not expected rage and fear.

She and John Winship were just finishing the last of the morning's letters—these to the editors of the small dailies and weeklies in the surrounding communities—and Mike was stamping them while Lavinia Lester prepared lunch and her father settled into his chair to watch *Tic-Tac-Dough* when DeeDee came into the kitchen of the Pomeroy Street house. She was hot and flushed in a pink-striped cotton tent of astounding proportions, and she carried a foil-covered pie pan in one hand.

"Peach pie from the first of our peaches," she said, kissing her father and peering around the cool, bright kitchen. "What on earth are you all doing? Planning a party?"

"I'm helping Daddy with his correspondence," Mike said brightly, hoping to divert her sister. But DeeDee would not be distracted.

"What kind of correspondence?" she said. "Who on earth does Daddy know that he has to send so many letters . . ." She picked up a couple of envelopes from the pile Mike had stamped and stacked neatly at the edge of the kitchen table, and actually turned pale under her habitual high flush.

"You're helping him with these crazy, awful, horrible letters," she squealed. "Mike, you *promised,* you said you thought this DOT stuff was as crazy as we did . . ." Her breath gave out and she stood glaring at Mike, great shelf of chest heaving, breath bubbling in her small pink piglet's nose.

"Well, I changed my mind," Mike said equably. What was that strange, shrill note in DeeDee's voice? Why on earth was she so agitated? If DeeDee considered the letters foolish and futile, what did it matter to her who typed them and sent them out?

"What's your problem, Daisy?" John Winship said, his voice strong and sharp as DeeDee's own. He had been animated and almost ebullient all morning, dictating clearly and decisively, cackling appreciatively at his own prose occasionally, seeming almost to shimmer with a faint, strange light of his own that Mike had seen only once or twice in her life and barely remembered. She had caught the mood herself, and had found her fingers flying over the keys of Priss's old manual typewriter and her veins humming with more energy than she had felt since the first slumberous coupling with Bayard Sewell. She turned now to her father, and saw that his cheeks were so flushed they were almost vermilion, and his eyes had sunk back into the flesh around them and acquired a feverish glitter.

Apparently DeeDee saw, too, because she wrenched her little pink mouth into a smile and said, "No problem, Daddy. I just don't want you to get overtired. Mike means well, but she hasn't been here since the beginning, and I'm afraid she doesn't know yet what's good for you and what isn't."

"Micah knows what's good for me better than anybody else in this house except Sam Canaday," her father rasped. Mike saw his frail chest beginning to labor, and so she said, "Daddy, you promised you'd take a nap before lunch when we finished," and the old man looked from one of his daughters to the other, flashed them his swift, grotesque half-grin, and said, "So I did." DeeDee did not speak again until Lavinia Lester had wheeled him into his room, and then she turned on Mike.

"You're going to kill him. Do you know that? What you're doing is going to kill my daddy, and I hope you're happy when he's lying dead! It's cruel, what you're doing, and it's dangerous, and it's awful . . ."

"DeeDee, I am *not* hurting him!" Mike said. "Look at him! His color is good, and he's lively, and he's eating well and sleeping, and he hasn't had one of those attacks of pain in several days . . . he's come out of that awful lethargy he was in; you just haven't seen it, you haven't been around lately. He's *much* better, much stronger . . ."

"It's the last of his strength! He'll have another stroke; he'll collapse . . ." DeeDee's eyes were unfocused with what could only be terror, and tears tracked her cheeks and chins.

Mike's heart turned over. Her sister was obviously in anguish. No matter how nattering and unfounded her concern, it was still causing her pain. She did not look well, either; the thin, stretched skin around her blue eyes was violet and crosshatched with tiny fatigue lines, and her blue-black hair straggled, lusterless, on her neck and down her back. It looked heavy and flat and rusty, like the wings of a dead and rain-soaked crow, and Mike saw for the first time that DeeDee had been dyeing it. She thought of the terrible little ersatz bunkhouse on the edge of the mobile home park, and the cawing, slavering old woman so irrevocable and eternally there in it, and of Duck Wingo.

She put her hand on DeeDee's shoulder. "I won't let anything happen to him," she said gently. "We'll stop the minute he looks the slightest bit tired. I guess I did get a little carried away this morning, and let things go on too long. We won't do that again."

"But Mike, *why?*" Dee's voice actually trembled. "You thought it was all as silly and unnecessary as we did . . ."

"What can it hurt?" Mike said. She wasn't about to go into the evening at the homeplace that still burned in her mind. In DeeDee's present mood, she would probably think Mike was trying to secure the farm for herself, and nothing could have been further from the truth. Mike did not want the old house. She simply wanted it, and her father, to be left alone.

"I'm only doing it to keep him company and to keep an eye on him," she said. "He was doing it anyway, you know, on that old tape recorder of Sam's, and half the time he couldn't make it work, and he'd lose his temper and wind up twice as tired and upset as he is now. At least this way I can monitor him. Really, Dee. It isn't going to change anything, but if it makes him happier, why not?"

Her sister peered at her out of tear-sheened eyes, and then let her massive shoulders slump. "I guess you're right. It's just that I love him, Mikie, and I don't want anything to happen to him."

"Oh, Dee . . ." Mike's own eyes prickled, and she covered DeeDee's fat, ringed little hand with her own. "Something is going to happen to him, and we can't change that. But not because of this."

Seeing the tears start again in the beautiful, myopic blue eyes, she said hastily, "Tell you what. Next week, let's take off and do something together, just the two of us. Something silly and fun. I'll send Lavinia over to stay with Duck's mother and J.W. can sit with Daddy, and we'll make a day of it. What would you like to do? Go to Atlanta and have lunch and go shopping, or see a movie? My treat."

"You know what I'd really like to do?" DeeDee said, her voice rising. "Bay's a member of the country club, of course, and he says that anytime we want to go and swim or sun or just have lunch and lounge around the pool, he'll leave a guest pass for us. We haven't been yet, and I . . . well, I'd like it if you'd go with me. I think that would be fun. We might even join, Duck and me, if we like it . . ."

Mike's heart sank, but she said, "Of course. You name the day and we'll do it." Could she really bear it, DeeDee in a swim suit, sipping fruit-laden drinks around the Lytton, Georgia, country club, clothed in her maddening, heartbreaking airs? She supposed she could. What difference did it make, after all?

"We can go any time at all," DeeDee said, her face brighter. "Bay's already left instructions with the staff. He was president for several years before Sally got so bad." She paused, and then said, "Do you have something that isn't . . . well, you know, Mikie . . . so bare?"

"I won't embarrass you, DeeDee," Mike said, suppressing the impulse to smack her sister. Just when you were feeling better about DeeDee, kinder, she would invariably put her elephantine foot into your goodwill.

"I didn't mean that," DeeDee said, turning to leave, impervious to her effect on Mike. "It's just that you're so thin. You'll be meeting a lot of the new people, and you'll want to put your best foot forward."

"Oh, well, of course," Mike said sarcastically. She could think of nothing about which she cared so little as impressing the new people of Lytton. Did DeeDee think, then, that she had changed her mind and would be staying on indefinitely? And if it came to that, would she? She did not know, had not thought about it after assuring everyone that she would be here only temporarily, until something could be decided about her father. But that was before Bayard Sewell . . .

He called that afternoon, scarcely an hour before she was to have met him in her bedroom upstairs.

"Worse luck, Mike. I've got to go out of town. I'm at the airport now, and I've only got a minute."

"Oh, Bay . . . *why?* It's been almost a week . . ." Her heart contracted physically and painfully in her chest. She was hollow and electric with wanting him, and had already bathed and shaved her legs and smoothed her body with bath lotion.

"I know, love. I know. It just can't be helped. Partly it's Sally; she's getting sicker and sicker, and Dr. Gaddis says there's liver involvement now, and she'll have to be sent somewhere they can give her specialized attention. So I'm going up and check out Silver Hill, in Connecticut. It's supposed to be tops. If they'll take her, I'll have Shep Watson, our lawyer, put her on a plane and I'll meet her and admit her. Tough for poor Sal, darling, but better for us. And then, there are some people in Boston I need to see about some business. It can't wait."

"How long? I don't think I can do without you very long, Bay . . ."

"Me either, or I'll end up with one of those inflatable ladies from Japan in my hotel room. I'm sorry, Mike. A few days. No more than a week. Can you find something to do with yourself?"

"Well, it just so happens that I have something to do with myself," she said. She told him about the letter campaign, and about helping her father. "I know you probably think it's silly, darling, but it keeps his mind occupied and it keeps me off the streets. Without it, I'd probably be hanging around the Red Rose Motel lounge with the good old boys, yowling around the piano bar and trying to get this itch scratched that you leave me with."

She expected his deep, easy laughter, but it did not come. Instead there was silence, and then he said, "I don't like it at all that you're egging him on, Mike. As I've told you, I don't think he's got a prayer, and this is just going to make it harder on him when he loses."

There was ice in his voice, and small whips.

"You're always telling him you're doing the best you can to head it off in the legislature," she said defensively. His voice cut her badly.

"I've also told him that I don't think I can do much. I really don't have much influence in committee, and he realizes that. I'm pretty junior. I just want him to know I'm on his side, mainly. I don't actually encourage him, and I don't like it that you're doing it. You're stringing him along. It's worse than cruel. It could be dangerous for him."

A curl of something alien, a faint, unborn rebelliousness, moved inside Mike, underneath the shock and pain. "I'm not going to hurt him, Bay," she said crisply. "But I'm not stringing him along. I've changed my mind, I guess. I really do think he's right. The state should not take a man's property against his will. You know that's wrong as well as I do. And it's just as wrong not to try to fight it. Even if you lose. If he gets too agitated, I'll try to get him to slack off. But I'm going to help him try."

There was another silence. Then he said, in the same tight, frozen voice, "I take it you know what the plan of action is, then."

"As a matter of fact, I don't," Mike retorted, close to tears. She wasn't going to tell this cold-voiced stranger what Sam Canaday had told her. Not yet, anyway. He could damn well wait. She might tell him when she chose, and then again, she might not. What possible difference could it make in the outcome of the decision, anyway?

"Well, I want you to find out right away. And I want you to call me at the Ritz Carlton when you do. Maybe I can undo some of the damage you're doing, if I know what's going on. Mike, if you go on with this, you are doing it without my sanction. With my extreme disapproval, in fact."

"How very unfortunate," Mike said, around a lump of agony and coldness in her throat that threatened to choke off her breath.

He hung up.

By dinnertime she was prowling and miserable, and could not eat the excellent fresh vegetable soup and cornbread that Lavinia had left. She felt a terrible black, lightless weight, a sadness as deep as if certain catastrophe or death waited ahead for someone she loved very much. Nothing in the entire world seemed to fit in its pattern or orbit. This is how I should be feeling about Daddy, she thought. Bad luck for both of us that I don't. She remembered the summer of her fifteenth year, when she had discovered the poetry of Dorothy Parker and had memorized great chunks of the brittle, brilliant doggerel. "The sun's gone dim and the moon's turned black / For I loved him and he didn't love back." She had especially loved that one, and had yearned to be the kind of sophisticated, mocking, life-used woman who could say those words out of experience. What a fool I was, Mike thought. They aren't funny. She wasn't a funny woman. She meant that, and this is how it feels.

Her father seemed to catch her thoughts and lifted his head from his soup like a starved old hound.

"Bay not coming tonight?" he asked querulously. "Hasn't been here in quite a spell, has he?"

"He called while you were asleep. He's had to go to Boston to see about a clinic for Sally. I . . . he says she's sick again."

Her father's eyes lost their avian glitter and his voice was gentler. "Poor Miss Sally," he said. "She hasn't had much luck. Hasn't had much luck. Sometimes I think I should've stayed out of it. Might have had an altogether different life."

"Well, it's been my experience that an alcoholic is going to drink wherever he or she winds up," Mike said, for some reason stung by his solicitude for Sally Sewell. Then she remembered that Bay had said her father did not know about Sally's drinking, and her hand flew involuntarily to her mouth.

"You think I didn't know she was a drinker?" he said, looking at her out of the corner of one filmed raven's eye. "Knew before anybody else around her, practically. Not much I don't know, Micah. I know why she does it, too."

"Well," Mike said again. "It was awfully sad about the little boy, but it's been . . . what? twelve years? . . . and you'd think she might start pulling herself together. You don't see Bay soaked in gin because his son drowned."

"No. That's one thing you'd never see," her father said. "Got too much at stake, he has. Got too much going for him. But Miss Sally . . . not got much at all, seems to me."

"Oh, Pa, don't be so damned sentimental," Mike snapped in exasperation. "She's got a beautiful home, and two terrific sons, and a wonderful husband. Bay couldn't do any more for her than he has."

"You can say that again," her father said. Soon he lapsed into a nodding doze in his chair in front of the television set, and Mike cleared the dishes and started the dishwasher. By the time she had wiped off the counters and hung up the cloth, it was only eight o'clock and still bright outside. The evening chorus of birds had not yet begun to chirp down toward sleep. Mike roamed from room to room, straightening an ashtray here and wiping off a film of dust there with the tail of her shirt. Her misery roamed with her, and howled and sang in her ears. If he would only call, if he would just call . . . she would apologize for being willful and childish. She would tell him that she would stop her part in the letter-writing project. She would beg him not to be angry with her. She knew she could make it right. She could find the words. If he would just call.

The phone rang and she caught it up in the front hall before it could ring again. "Hello?" she said. Her breath was so faint that she could hardly get the words out.

"Hi, it's me," Rachel said from California.

Disappointment so profound that it buckled her knees flooded Mike, and she sat down on the edge of the old Jacobean table that had dominated the hall since she could remember. And then the thought registered: This is Rachel. My daughter. My first and best love. To whom I have not talked since that awful day at LaGuardia, six weeks ago.

"Hi, darling." She forced gladness into her voice. She heard her voice in her own ears, taking on the slightly forced and affected tone she had always used when talking to other children. But never to Rachel. Rachel was not children. Rachel was her daughter. Daughter? Mike Winship had not been, for many days now, a woman to whom children were a reality.

"How wonderful to hear from you," she said.

"You, too. Hope things there are great. Is . . . everybody okay? You know, your father . . ."

"He's doing very well," Mike said. Why should Rachel call him "grandfather"? She herself had choked on "father" until just recently. "How are things with you?"

"Oh, just *wonderful,*" Rachel caroled across two thousand humming miles. Her voice sounded different, older, harder, brighter. "I've just come in from a late lunch at Spago . . . you know, Wolfgang Puck's place . . . and we saw Warren Beatty and actually talked to Emilio Estevez . . . he said I was a fox; said he'd be glad to hang around a year or two until I grew up . . . and we had lunch with this man; he's an independent producer and he's reading a script by a client of Daddy's and we think he's going to take it and do the film in Puerto Vallarta, and actually, that's why I called . . ."

Rachel's voice lilted on, the voice and words of a changeling without innocence, a spoiled and chiming Venus. Mike listened in simple amazement. Who was this knowing little piece who called herself Rachel Singer?

". . . so Dad said I could if I asked you first, and you've just got to let me, or I'll die. I'll kill myself."

"Let you do what?" Mike said stupidly. "I'm sorry, Rachel, I'm not tracking very well tonight. Slow down a little."

"Oh, *God,* Mother, don't be obtuse! Let me go with them to Puerto Vallarta and do a part in the movie. It's just a little part; just a teensy cameo, but it's a starmaker, Paul says . . . that's the producer. A kind of now Lolita, very young, very sensuous. He wants the contrast of the innocence in all the depravity and excess of the rich, jaded resort crowd." Rachel might have been reading aloud from a bad paperback. "He says I have just the right quality, a kind of mocking prepubescent angel. There wouldn't be any sex or violence in my sequence, and no real nudity . . ."

"Absolutely not," Mike said, her blood seeming to thicken and run cold.

"Oh, *God,* I told him and Daddy you'd be stupid about it," her daughter shrilled. "I told them you wouldn't have the slightest inkling on *earth* what it meant to me, and what they were trying to accomplish with the film . . ."

"Rachel, I am not going to give you my blessing to go traipsing off to Mexico with some cokehead arty-farty producer and make a soft-porn movie, not at age twelve and not at any age. You must be out of your mind, and your father must be simply and irrevocably

213

insane. Put it right out of your mind, and put him on, please."

"He isn't here. He's out . . . with Lacey Schiller. The one who just finished *Lush Life* and is probably the hottest property in the country right now. He's been sleeping with her for months, and he'll probably marry her. And then she'll be my mother, because if you don't say I can go I'm going to stay out here forever, and I'll never come home, and you can bet your ass she'll let me make films if I want to. She'd never stand in the way of an opportunity like this."

"Rachel, listen. Listen to me. I'm not going to forbid you to do this idiotic, awful, tasteless, sleazy thing, because I've always let you make your own decisions, and you know that. But I want you to remember who you are and what wonderful potential you have; remember all the advantages you've been given. Do you want to just throw all that away?" Mike felt as if she were in a movie herself, one in which the speed and sound had been slowed down.

"Oh, God, that's really good," spat Rachel. "That's just really too super-wonderful for words. What potential? What advantages? A stupid roach house in Greenwich Village and a mother who can't even keep a job or a man or a roof over our heads? Who isn't ever, ever, *ever* home, even? Some potential. Some advantages. And you're right, you're not going to forbid me to do it, because I'm going to do it anyway. And the bloody *hell* with you!"

Rachel slammed down the telephone, but not before Mike could tell that she was crying hard. Where was Richard? Had he even the faintest notion of what he was doing to his daughter? Was he past caring? Was there anyone there who could put strong, sure arms around Rachel and comfort her? Like Mike herself, Rachel almost never wept, and when she did, the loss of control upset and frightened her badly and for a long time. Those were the only times that she permitted Mike to hold her and rock her and croon to her. She could still feel the wildly trembling little shoulders, and the frail bird's bones. Mike felt, instead of pain and anger, an abrupt onset of the great white emptiness and fatigue that had nearly drowned her on her first evening in this house. She put her head down on her arms and closed her eyes.

Sam Canaday, coming into the hall from the front porch with a fresh stack of stationery and new tapes for the recorder, found her there. She did not know how long he had stood looking at her in the failing twilight of the hall, for she had not heard his step on the porch.

"Want to talk about it?" he said, switching on the old brass library lamp on the table and settling himself on its other end.

Oddly, she did, and she repeated the conversation word for word, in a voice that held neither pain nor grief nor anger nor even regret. Mike might have been reading him a shopping list. He listened without changing his expression, and when she was finished, he was silent for a long moment, and then he said, "And so what are you going to do?"

"What can I do?" Mike said faintly. "She says she'll never come home if I try to stop her. He could get her for good, Sam. I've always known that he could. He just never wanted to. I don't think she really interested him before. Now apparently she does, since she's fitting so neatly into his world. He's got all the money and all the contacts and all the big guns, and she can legally decide who she wants to live with when she's fourteen, anyway. What options do I have? I'm not her jailer. I've always tried to be a sort of mentor to her, a sister, or a friend. I've always wanted her to be her own person."

"Good Christ, in Puerto Vallarta with a cocaine dealer in a skin flick? She's twelve years old! You really want her to be next year's Princess Stephanie?"

"Of course not . . ."

"Then go get her! Scream at her, smack her, kidnap her, if you have to!" The intensity of his febrile green eyes in the lamplight was almost frightening. The light threw slanted shadows over his sharp face and under his cheekbones, so that he looked wild and Mongol, lit from beneath. She said nothing.

"You know, Mike," he went on presently in a more even voice, "I've been waiting to see the whole woman in you, but you've never let me, and I'm beginning to think there isn't one. Why aren't you so angry you could walk to L.A. and carry her home on your shoulders? I've seen your admirable forbearance, and God knows I've seen your fabled journalistic detachment, and I've seen you so jazzed up with terror you were about to jump out of your skin, when you first came. And I've seen you softer, lately, a kind of amiable sleepwalker, which is admittedly an improvement. But I've never seen you really laugh, or get blazing mad, and I've never seen you grieve, and I've never, never seen you even start to cry. What are you, lady? And as for loving . . ."

"Oh, what the hell do you know about loving?" Mike said tiredly. "Do you think I don't love my own daughter; do you think I don't love . . . if you're such an expert on loving, where's *your* family? Where's your wife and your children, or your woman? Who do *you* love, Sam? Let me be. Get off my case. You've been preaching at me ever since I set foot in this house. I don't want to hear any more of it. I'm so tired I think I could die right here."

Sam Canaday was silent, and then he raised his shoulders high and dropped them, and rubbed the back of his neck.

"You're right," he said. "About all of it. I have been on your case, and I'll get off it as of right now. A pot as black as I am has no right calling the kettle anything at all. Listen. I've got to go take a deposition in Atlanta tomorrow afternoon. Why don't you come with me and we'll get some dinner and have a few drinks and hoot and holler a little, or whatever else you'd like to do. J.W. can come sit with the Colonel. He used to do it all the time. You need to get out of this house."

In her mind's eye, Mike saw a dim, anonymous, cool restaurant, saw the little shaded lamps rose-lit and the waiter handing the wine bottle to him to inspect, smelled good food and wine and the night smells of the summer city, felt chill, urban air on her cheek and the silky sheen of stockings on her legs and the slim embrace of narrow high-heeled shoes on her feet. Her fingers seemed to touch heavy silverware and cold crystal.

"I'd like that," she said, raising her head in the lamplight and looking at him. He smiled. There was nothing in the smile of question or portent. He looked, simply, like a young man who had tasted the moment and found it exceedingly good.

TWENTY-FOUR

Sam's appointment was for a deposition from the first of the surveyors the county had sent to the homeplace, and the firm's office was in a shabby transitional area of Atlanta to the west of Peachtree Street, near the Greyhound and Trailways bus stations. Once it had been a respectable, if unimposing, area of small wholesale and manufacturing operations and family-owned businesses. In her childhood and teens Mike had walked these banal streets often, when she had come to and from the city on the bus with DeeDee or with Priss, who refused to drive her old Hudson Hornet in urban traffic. Then, the area had contained all Atlanta had and knew of ethnicity: a few yellow and black and coffee-colored faces peppered the sea of working-class white ones. Now, the streets were largely bare except for prowling bands of young blacks and the sheeplike flocks of passengers departing the bus stations and scurrying east toward Peachtree Street and safety. Even automobile traffic was sparse, and ran to creeping old junkers or astonishing vehicles Mike thought of as pimpmobiles. The freeway system, completed since she left the South, channeled traffic away from the area, and the few weedy and littered parking lots were only half full. Sam nosed the Toyota into a space in a lot half a block away from the dun-colored, four-story brick building that housed the surveying firm, and helped her out. The late sun was fierce and the air was thick and wet and unmoving. It felt like New York in August.

"Want to come with me?" he said. "There's probably a chair or something for visitors, and I don't like leaving you around here. These are mean streets."

"Are you kidding?" Mike said, lifting her head and sniffing the city like a stallion. "I've spent twenty years in Manhattan. And I've been in some of the meanest streets in America in my time. I'm not afraid of these."

"My streets are meaner than your streets, huh?" Sam said. "Well, please yourself. I don't feel like worrying about you. I should be about an hour and a half. Why don't you meet me at the Parasol on top of the Sunbelt Plaza on Peachtree? Food's not all that hot, but the view is spectacular, and there's really not any place downtown that doesn't cater to tourists. All the good stuff's out in Buckhead, and that gives me a pain in the ass. Get us a table by the window and order me a Canadian Club and water and I'll see you at six. What are you going to do, shop?"

"Walk," Mike said. "I don't even remember what it feels like to walk in a city."

She did. She walked for miles, up and down and across the main thoroughfares of Atlanta, looking in windows and up at massive, beetling towers and down mirror-glass canyons. It wasn't Manhattan; nothing was, but it was unmistakably and viscerally a city. As a child, being in downtown Atlanta in the late afternoon had had an eerie and alien quality to her; an emptiness, an aloneness that had nothing to do with the number of people on the streets, but everything to do with the stark, merciless dead light on the barren brick facades. Edward Hopper light, she had come to think of it. It came near to frightening her. Sometimes that doomed city light still figured in her nightmares. Now, though, the skyscrapers rose so thick and tall that the downtown was washed in the permanent half-twilight of really large cities, and at the sunless street level the shadows lay thick and blue. Mike slipped into it like a sea creature sliding back into its element after long, gasping imprisonment on land. Her stride lengthened into the easy city lope that was so familiar to her that her muscles seemed to cry out for it, and her arms and shoulders felt almost nakedly light without the accustomed tape recorder case and the big Gucci bag. Feeling free and young and somehow released from a somnambulistic spell, Mike walked and walked and walked. Her sense of herself grew with every step. What have I been doing with myself all these weeks? she thought. This is me here, not that languid, tentative woman back there in Lytton. Bay needs to know about this woman; I have to show him this. And then she remembered the estrangement and the cold, stinging words, and shrugged impatiently. That could and must be fixed. She would call him in Boston when they got home and fix it. Enough of this silliness. Meanwhile, the whole city lay ahead, and the night.

They had drinks and an overpriced, underheated dinner at the big restaurant that might have been any panoramic restaurant atop any premier tourist hotel in any city in America, and Mike enjoyed it immensely. She talked and talked, as she had never talked to Sam or anyone else in Lytton; not about herself, but about her work and the places it had taken her and the things she had seen and the people she had met. She talked about books and writers and theater and artists and their hangers-on; she talked about Manhattan and its excesses and absurdities and enchantments. She giggled and gossiped. She laughed and gestured and threw back her head so that the silvery hair flew free around it, loving the weight of it and its silken swish against her cheek, loving the feeling of the slender Italian shoes on her feet and the soft silk of her shirt against her breasts and shoulders, loving the good smell of smoke and stale-chill air and the Casaque that she had splashed on before leaving home; loving the jeweled net of the city winking at their feet, liking his amused and approving green eyes on her as he listened. Off to the west a great purple thunderhead grew and spread like an anvil, and lightning forked silently to earth, and a faint mutter of thunder permeated even the thick gray-tinted glass of the great windows, and the primal energy of the storm seemed to slide somehow into her blood. Mike had had only two glasses of white wine, but she felt wonderfully, powerfully high.

"We'd better get back to the car before that thing breaks," he said finally, signaling for the waiter and pulling out a bent American Express card. "I hate to interrupt you; I'd like to sit here and listen to you all night. But I don't want to drown you, either. We'll make some coffee when we get home and continue the conversation."

Mike felt deflated and crestfallen. She had, she realized, completely dominated the conversation. He had scarcely said two words all evening. She did not want the evening to end; she did not want to go home . . . but of course he was right. The storm looked bad. And she could not remember if she had told J.W. about her father's ten o'clock medicine. I've probably bored him silly, she thought, and felt the hated flush start up her neck.

"That's more than enough about me," she said ruefully.

"There's nothing now that you don't know about me, and nothing I do about you. I'm sorry, Sam; it was rude. I guess I'm just high on being in a city again, and I needed to get away more than I thought I did. I usually don't run on like this."

"I know it," he said. "That's why I've enjoyed it so much. It's been like getting a present, listening to you talk about the things that matter to you. I've wondered what did. I might well have missed it if I hadn't drug you into town and plied you with liquor."

Night had fallen, and they hurried out into the thick, heavy darkness, feeling the wet breath of the storm approaching. By the time they reached the Trailways station the first great swollen drops were spattering on the hot pavements, and the neon-blinking streets were nearly deserted. A wind prowled high above their heads, and in the lightning flashes low clouds flew. The parking lot lay two blocks away. It was obvious they were not going to make it.

"Come on in here," Sam said, pulling her toward a tiny, horrendously filthy bar and lounge whose pink and blue neon gleamed evilly and wetly, like entrails in the rain. It was sandwiched between an abandoned theater supply company and an industrial laundry. Its windows were so thickly encrusted with decades of hopeless urban grime that she could not tell if there was anyone inside or not, but a smaller neon bar below the main sign said OPEN!

"I don't mind getting a little wet," Mike began uncertainly; mean streets were one thing, but this kind of place looked like sure and certain trouble.

"Well, I do," he said. "Come *on!*"

The rain hit in earnest, frying straight down on the pavement and bouncing back nearly waist high, and a great fork of lightning split the sky, followed by a gigantic bellow of thunder, and they jerked open the torn screen door and tumbled inside.

The inside of the little bar was so dark that it was fully five minutes after they had groped their way to a torn and scarred leatherette booth and sunk wetly into it that Mike could see that it was empty except for themselves and a mountainously fat, pale man behind the bar at the other end of the room. She breathed a sigh of unconscious relief. Her shirt was plastered so tightly to her breasts that she might as well not have it on, and the air-conditioning in the room was glacial. She crossed her arms over her breasts, and Sam got up and put his coat around her, and she drew it gratefully close.

"I'm not even going to argue," she said.

"Canadian Club and two glasses of ice, please, and leave the bottle," Sam said efficiently to the sluglike man who had oozed over to the booth as phlegmatically as if the likes of them came into the bar every day, instead of what must have been a steady clientele of winos and derelicts with welfare checks.

The man lapped and surged away and Mike said, "I'd really just rather have a glass of wine," and Sam Canaday laughed.

"A, you need the whiskey, as wet as you are, and B, the only wine they're likely to have in the house is Rolling Thunder Fortified. Knock you clear into Tennessee," he said. The fat man reappeared with the whiskey and glasses and thumped the bottle down onto the table, and Sam poured them each a generous tot. "Drink up," he said. "Here's looking at you, kid."

The whiskey went down smoothly, burning in a pleasant, sinuous way, and he poured them another. He lifted his glass and peered into it.

"Somewhat austere, but a unique perfume," he said judiciously. "Presumptuous but amusing, what? Well. Of all the gin joints in all the cities in the world, we have to walk into his. Can you hack it until the rain quits?"

"I like it," Mike said, the whiskey a little secret well of mirth and well-being in her stomach. She felt warm and sequestered and tucked away, safe. The filthy little bar had, all of a sudden, the feel of a haven.

"It's romantic, when you think about it," she said. "In a Claude Raines kind of way. Or Jack Nicholson. Don't you think it has a certain go-to-hell air of romance about it?"

"I think it's about as romantic as pigeon shit," he said. "I hate to leave you alone, but I've got to go to the john, and I'd better do it while there's nobody in here to hassle you. Wish me well. I'll probably come back with herpes, or worse."

He tossed down another ample slug of the whiskey, and poured Mike another, and rose from the booth. Mike thought there was just the faintest list to his walk. She herself had the feeling of being in a fun-house booth, hilarious and protected by a pane of glass. It was distinctly different from the bell jar.

We're both sitting here in this lowlife joint getting drunk, she thought, sipping and giggling to herself. What on earth would

DeeDee say? I can't wait to tell her about it, our big night in the . . . what's the name of this place, anyway? She leaned out of the booth so that she could see the flickering sign on the door, and turned her head as far around as she could so that she could read it backward. Cameo. The Cameo Lounge. Oh, my God, giggled Mike, clapping her hand over her mouth and shaking with silent glee. When Sam got back to the table she could hardly contain the bubbling laughter.

"What's up?" he said, smiling at her.

"Sam, I know this place," Mike chortled. "The Cameo Lounge. My God, it might as well be Sodom or Gomorrah. I used to think it was only slightly better than the gateway to hell; I was always told it was the first stop on the high road to perdition."

He laughed aloud at her laughter and poured another drink from the diminished bottle. There were spots of color on his high cheekbones, and one lock of the pale hair looped down over his eye like a yellow comma. He had loosened his collar and removed his tie, and looked young and raffish and slightly dangerous.

"Who told you that?" he said.

"Miss Ora Campion. My Sunday school teacher when I was about ten and she was about one hundred and forty. Great, tall, rawboned old maid with a huge face like a cliff hanging up there, and a perpetual black cloud over her head. Eyes like an egg-sucking dog. She was forever going on about liquor and places that served it, and how the first sip was the first step on the road to the gutter and beyond. She always used the Cameo Lounge as her example . . . it must be thirty years old, at least . . . and somebody asked her once how she knew about it and she said she'd seen the young soldiers and sailors coming in here from the bus station and coming out again dead drunk and falling in the gutter. We always wondered what she was doing hanging around the bus station. Oh, I love it. I wish that old trout could see me now. She always knew I'd come to a bad end. I wish the whole Lytton United Methodist Church could see me. They thought so too, even if they didn't say it as often as Miss Ora Campion."

"Did you hate the church so much, Mike?" he said.

She looked at him. He was not smiling anymore, and there was something preternaturally focused in his light eyes that was not gaiety or liquor.

"No," she said, the laughter seeping out of her as abruptly as it had risen. "Not then. Not when I was very small. Sometimes it was wonderful. Christmas, the hush and the sheer tender holiness of it, the waiting, and Easter . . . that first hymn at the sunrise service, when it was still dark and cold . . . *'Up* from the grave he *arose* (he arose) / With a *mighty* triumph o'er his *foes* (o'er his foes)' . . . you could just taste the triumph. Almost shout with it. We did, in fact. But I always hated the Peace. All that hugging and squeezing and cheek kissing, when you knew nobody meant it. I guess it was my first brush with hypocrisy. That's what I hate. The awful hypocrisy of it. Love God, but hate the niggers. Well, you know, after that thing with old man Tait. I hope I haven't offended you, by the way. I forgot what a big churchgoer you are. Somehow I just can't reconcile you with religion, Sam."

"I'm not really religious anymore," Sam Canaday said, gesturing with one finger for another bottle of whiskey. "Not like I used to be. What about you, Mike? Are you religious? It's not the same thing as being a believer, you know."

"I don't know," she said slowly. "No, no more for me. I can't quite talk now. I think all writers are a little bit religious, at bottom. There's too much that goes on that you can't explain; like your best work always coming from outside of you somehow. Your mind leaping to connections where none exist. If I am, it's for a kind of mystery, or mysticism. I've always thought I might have been drawn to the Roman Church, or some very high one . . . for the sheer mystery. That seems to me to be at the very heart of it. But Lytton had to explain it all, tidy it up, simplify it down to doggerel with the 'thou-shalt-nots.' Run your entire life with it."

He was drinking steadily, but he did not seem any longer to be tipsy.

"But it is at the heart of life," he said. "It *is* life, in Lytton, the church is. Kind, compassionate, helping, always there in trouble. The church in Lytton and little towns like it is far more than just thou-shalt-nots, Mike. Or bigotry, though it undoubtedly has its share of both. It's the machinery by which the necessary human things get done. It's better than the sum of all its members. It only makes mischief when things are too uneventful or its members come to depend on it for virtually everything in their lives. Then, like a bored child, it sometimes stirs up stuff it really doesn't need to. But you mustn't forget the real use and goodness. Throw out the baby with the bath water."

"But the narrowness, the *censure,*" Mike protested. "I don't know how you can take it Sunday after Sunday. All in the name of religion. I don't know why it just doesn't kill something in you."

He was silent so long that she leaned closer across the table and peered into his face. In the guttering light from the candle stub jammed into the grimy Chianti bottle, it seemed to shift and change, as though different muscles than any she had ever seen were coming into play. He looked up, and a stranger looked out of the green eyes: unformed, austere, painfully young.

"It did," he said. "It did indeed. Want to hear about what of mine religion killed, Mike?"

She realized that he was not a little drunk.

"Yes," she said. "I want to hear."

"Well," he said, settling back into the booth and propping a foot up on it, "I was a preacher once. Still am, I guess; I haven't been un-ordained yet. A bona fide, Bible-toting, ordained minister of the Southern Baptist Church, graduate of Marian Breathitt Bible College in West Tennessee, shepherd to the good flock of the Mount Moriah Baptist Church in Ottley, Mississippi, population nine hundred eighty-eight after I got there, twenty miles west of Greenville in the Mississippi Delta. Good preacher, too. Baptized eleven people at my first revival. Started the country's first Christian preschool program. In demand all over Washington County for weddings and baptisms and funerals. Does any of this surprise you?"

Mike stared at him across the burn-scarred Formica, slowly shaking her head. A part of her was speechless with surprise, but an older, deeper part was not. She could imagine his stocky figure in a stark country pulpit; see the coiled power in his arms as he gestured, the fervor in the narrow green eyes, the light on the slant-planed, sunburnt face.

"Well, it didn't anybody else, either," he went on, tossing down a swallow of Canadian Club and grimacing. "Least of all my mother. My mother was a saint, Mike. You don't want to mess with one of those. Loretta Jasper Canaday, born, lived, and died a saint in Birmingham, Alabama, without ever leaving home to go anywhere but the company store and church. Married my dad to reform him, had my older brother and sisters and me, much later, and then threw him out when I turned six and he wouldn't give up the booze. I guess you couldn't blame her . . . he used to beat up on her some. I remember the bruises and the Band-Aids. She'd never complain about them, but we'd all get down on our knees and pray for Daddy an extra hour after one of those sessions. I don't remember much about him. I heard later from my aunt Doreen that he died in Texas after my mother did. Anyway, my brother was old enough to go into the mill when Daddy left, and so there was a little bit of money, and the girls helped out some, and Mother made cakes and pies and things for neighborhood affairs. All so little Samuel could be a preacher. I don't know how it got into her mind that that's what I should be, or why I went along with it, but I was so accustomed to praying and being prayed over that it seemed to me the natural thing to do. I got used to thinking of myself as special and sanctified. Besides, I had no desire to go into the mill like Daddy and Frank, my brother. Godalmighty, but Tennessee Coal and Iron cast a long and dirty shadow over my childhood. I remember the stink and the burns and the filthy clothes when they came in. Uh-uh. No way. Not for little saint Sammy. I took a job as assistant to the sexton in our church when she decided I was old enough to do a little seemly labor, and that's what I did until I got out of high school. The Lion's Club sent me to Marian Breathitt on a scholarship, and since Mama died right after I graduated, I didn't go back to Birmingham. Not for a long time.

"But before she departed, Mama picked my wife out for me. Oh, yeah, Mike, I was married; it was almost a scandal for a young Southern Baptist minister to take his first church without a wife. People might get to wondering if he was spilling his seed upon the ground like Onan, or worse. And God knows I had the seed. I met Jackie at Marian Breathitt when I was a junior and she was a freshman, and Mama approved, and we got married the day I graduated. Jackie was a pretty thing then, little and round and red-haired with a little turned-up nose and crinkly blue eyes and almost as many prayer calluses on her knees as Mama. It was a marriage made in heaven. Me, Jackie, and Mama. I guess she felt like she could go on and die after she got our knot tied, and that's just what she did. We went to Memphis to the Peabody Hotel for a weekend on our honeymoon, and of course little Jackie got pregnant the first time she took off her panties, and so by the time I was settled in Ottley and knew my way around town, Frannie, our little girl, was born, and we were the perfect little preacher family. Looked like we ought to be on the top of a wedding cake, all of us. Cute little cusses. It was 1961 and I was twenty-one years old and she was nineteen. We had a tiny little asbestos-siding house right by the church, not much more than a shack, really, but it was ours, and neither of us had ever even had a room of our own before, and we thought we were in grown-up heaven. She planted flowers and tomatoes and beans and a row or two of corn, and I built a little fence and got a barbecue grill from the A&P and a push lawn mower, and Frannie grew a head of curls that the Gerber people would have killed for, and her first word was Dee-sus. For Jesus. Really. They could have hung a Pray-TV series around us."

He fell silent, lost in some 1960s idyll that Mike had not known actually existed; it was so alien from her own first days of marriage. It was hard for her not to stare at him. His air of stolid aloneness was almost complete, had been since she had first met him. She could not imagine him kissing a small, round wife or fondling a little curly-haired daughter. She thought he was not going to continue, but finally he did, looking up and smiling at her. It was not a pleasant smile.

"I don't guess I have to tell you what happened," he said. "The same thing happened to you, and in Mississippi, too. Except I didn't go looking for the Civil Rights Movement. Lord God, no. Outside agitators down here stirring up God's order of things? What would the Southern Baptists say? What would Mama say? So the movement came to me. There wasn't anything on the order of Freedom Summer in Mississippi in 1961, but there were advance people down there starting a voter registration program, college kids from the North and East, and some young blacks from King's organization in Atlanta. You might even have been in jail with some of them a couple of years later. Well, they were just my age, and it was inevitable that they'd seek me out and try to enlist me. A young, white southern preacher in their ranks? I would have been a perfect agent in place. I was morally outraged, but I decided that the only Christian thing to do was hear them out; guess I thought I could convert *them.* Hell, I thought I could have converted Genghis Khan in those days. So I met with a few of them at the parsonage.

"Jackie carried on like they were devils out of hell. Took Frannie and went in the bedroom and locked the door. Prayed the whole time they were there. At least they had the good sense not to bring a Negro with them. Not then, anyway. The first time they came, I had the Bible out, all ready to match them Word for word. Only it never came to that. They didn't even need to fire a shot across my bow. I was in the ranks after two hours."

He looked at her intently. "Do you remember what it was like, Mike? Those early days in the movement? You must. It got you too. The camaraderie, the sense of yourself as part of a small, elite band of idealistic revolutionaries; the exhilaration of danger; the . . . sensuality of it, somehow; the sheer charisma and force? Do you remember?"

She nodded wordlessly. She remembered.

"Well, I'd never been a part of anything attractive in my life. Never been a self-activator, but only a follower. Followed my mother, Jackie, my teachers, the Lord. And here came this bunch of self-assured, immensely attractive, Ivy League kids who brought with them a world of books and ideas and cities and easy manners and smart talk and good clothes; who came down there following a cause so noble and selfless that you'd have to be made of iron not to want to fall in behind it. Like your Richard. I'd have probably followed that dude clear back to Cambridge. And there was the sheer physical glamour of the danger. The electricity in your gut. It didn't take long for them to show me a Sam Canaday I never knew was in there. Fearless, reckless, committed, passionate, dashing . . . me. Dashing. I learned to smoke cigarettes and drink, Mike, and not the way an Elyton Village mill hand smoked and drank, either. I learned to really read; I read constantly, night after night, till dawn, and got up without being the least bit tired. I learned to say shit and fuck and squint through cigarette smoke. Pretty soon I was marching and working for the poor, shit-scared blacks in Washington County, who only wished I'd shut up and the Yankees and city niggers would go home, and then I started putting up the visiting blacks who came over to Mississippi in the parsonage. I worked with SNCC and CORE, and I traveled around Mississippi with one of the advance teams for a week one summer, setting things up and saying shit and fuck and squinting through smoke. Jackie was terrified and furious. She was at the point of leaving me and taking Frannie back to her folks in Tennessee, but by that time she was pregnant again, and had gained almost fifty pounds, and she just couldn't get around very well. Of course, the church was ready to throw me out, but I was oblivious to all of it. I was doing God's work; I had found me a new God, one the country Baptists didn't know existed, one who said it was all right to say shit and fuck, one who said it was meet and right that Sam Canaday from Elyton should be a charismatic and fearless freedom fighter. Looking back, I really believe I thought I was immortal in those days."

"We all did," Mike said. "It was pretty heady stuff. Stronger and older heads than yours got turned in those years. And after all, Sam, if a pastor can't be in the vanguard of a fight that's so obviously for the right, who can?"

"I wasn't a pastor by that time, Mike. I didn't give a shit about the welfare of my congregation. I hardly even spent any time in the church. And I'm not sure the movement itself mattered all that much to me. I spent all my time sitting around in curtained rooms late at night, with the lights turned off so the Klan wouldn't get suspicious. Drinking and smoking and saying shit. What I was was a world-class, monumental, pain-in-the-ass romantic. The movement itself was romantic in the extreme. All revolutions are. Christ, we were like the RAF, such little elitists . . . but what we really were was killers."

"Come *on,* Sam . . ." Mike broke in.

"Yes." His voice overrode hers. "Killers. Romantics are the ultimate killers. I read something in *Esquire* just last week; a guy from Harvard being quoted as saying, 'Romanticism can lead to Dachau.' It's true. A romantic refuses to look at things as they are, and that's the most dangerous thing in the world. I know. I was one, and I killed my wife and child."

"Sam!" Mike's breath hissed out in cold, pure shock.

"Oh, I didn't beat 'em or shoot 'em or anything like that, Mike. I just preached one too many sermons about the blacks in a white county in the Mississippi Delta in the early 1960s, or took in one houseful too many of blacks and Yankee agitators. I'll never know which it was. Jackie kept telling me it was dangerous. God, she was scared; she was terrified, cried all the time, wouldn't go out of the house. I remember that I felt nothing for her but a kind of holy contempt, for her blubbering, and anger for making a coward out of my daughter. Frannie was cringing at her shadow by that time. I should have listened to her. One night a carful of night riders came easing by the parsonage, vroom-vroom-vroom, and pitched a little old homemade bomb into the house, and blew fat little Jackie Jefferson and her curly-headed kid into very small pieces. Hardly even found a chunk of either one big enough to bury. They never got the guys."

"Oh, Sam," she whispered. "Oh, my God. I had no idea . . ."

She remembered only the night before, her own voice saying, "If you're such an expert on loving, where's *your* family?" She closed her eyes in pain. Salt burned behind them.

"How could you know?" he said, in a normal, even cheerful voice. "No reason you should or could have known. Listen, Mike, I'm not telling you this to make you feel sorry for me, so save the tears. It was a very long time ago, and I've done what atoning I can for it. There's no grieving left for me to do. Come on, now. Don't you want to hear how I overcame my sorrow and became a world-famous legal advocate?"

"Sure," she said, looking at him through a swim of faintly tipsy tears. "I guess so. Sam . . . those scars on your hands. Were they . . . were you . . .?"

"Naw. I wasn't even home. I was off in the next town in a black juke joint down by the river saying shit and fuck. The fire was almost out by the time I got home. No, I got these working in the mill. The good old Tennessee Coal and Iron, back in Birmingham, where I started out. It got me after all."

"You went back and worked in the mill?"

"Yep. I couldn't have stayed in Mississippi after that. If the Klan hadn't gotten me, my own congregation would have. And I couldn't preach anymore; I was still too much a romantic for that, if a failed one. God is not a romantic. And I wasn't fit to do anything else. So I went back home and moved in with my sister and her family, and spent the next ten years puddling steel and drinking everything wet in north Alabama and fighting and whoring, and when I was sober and not working, I'd hole up in my room and read. I never lost the itch to read that those rich, liberal white kids lit in me that year. And I never forgot that other world that they showed me. I think, even if Jackie hadn't—died—I would have soon outgrown her, Mike. God help me, I was already on that road. I don't know what I'd have ever done about it. Eventually I just got tired of sulking in a tenement room in Birmingham, and I came over to Atlanta and went to Georgia State at night and on to Oglethorpe Law, and . . . here I am."

"Is it better for you?" Mike said. "Is it different, the law? Are you different?"

"I don't know." He frowned into his glass. "I thought it would be. I thought I was. But maybe not. I'm still carrying on like a romantic, and I really do know better than that."

"The law is hardly romantic," Mike said.

"This case is. It's Don Quixote and Sancho Panza. Or maybe not. He can't win it, but maybe we can help him win something else."

"What? After he loses his house he's going to die. What's there left to win?"

"Haven't we been over this already?" Sam Canaday said. "Come on, Mike, use your imagination, like a good and true romantic."

"That's one thing you can't accuse me of," Mike said. "There's no such thing as a romantic journalist."

"Are you kidding?" Sam Canaday jeered at her, holding his half-full glass of Canadian Club aloft in a toast and squinting at her through it. The past half hour might never have happened; the searing, intimate words might never have been said. "You're as hopeless as Walt Disney and Norman Rockwell put together. Take your daughter, Rachel, the would-be nymphet, she of the prepubescent sensuousness. I quote: 'I've always tried to be a mentor to her, a sister or a friend.' Romantic bullshit, Mike. It's dangerous, remember that. You're her mother. Stop being her friend and *be* her mother. And be a mad mother."

He laughed, and some of the whiskey slopped over the glass onto the tabletop. "Be one mad muthuh, sister. God, this is disgraceful. I think I'm drunk. I haven't been drunk since I left Birmingham. We'd better get out of here, before I revert completely and put the move on you. Do you think you can drive the Toyota?"

"Of course I can," she said stiffly. His remark about Rachel stung.

Outside on the wet pavement, he put his arm heavily around her shoulder and peered into her face.

"I'm sorry about tonight," he said, and his voice was clearer.

"I didn't mean to dump on you *or* jump on you. I'm not a good drinker, and it was a great night until I got started. Don't let this ruin it."

"I won't," she said. "It didn't. I . . . like knowing about you. It changes things."

"Not too much, I hope," he said.

"No. Not too much."

He walked quite steadily beside her through the cool dampness of the deserted streets to the parking lot and fished the Toyota's keys out of his pocket and paid the somnolent attendant, but when his head touched the back of the front seat his eyes closed, and he leaned against the door on his side and slept. Mike did not know how to get home on the freeway, so she pointed the car home the old way, straight down the old Roosevelt Highway beside the Atlanta and West Point Rail Road track. It was like driving through the demilitarized zone in West Berlin: the wet, oil-slicked, barren streets and the row after row of deserted and padlocked warehouses. It occurred to Mike that they might be in real danger if she were forced to stop the car, but somehow the thought did not bother her. An occasional unbroken streetlight cast a halo of sodium orange over broken railroad tracks and weed-buried cement blocks, but she saw no living thing, not even a cat or a rat. The green glow from the dashboard showed the time to be past midnight.

After half an hour she was out of the city and on the road home, passing through one after another of the shabby, quiet little industrial towns that lined the highway toward Lytton. Traffic thinned, and soon only an occasional set of headlights swept through the Toyota, and then none at all. She switched on the radio, and Nat King Cole's voice swam out of the green-lit darkness: " 'She wore blue velvet, and bluer than velvet were her eyes . . .' "

Sam Canaday muttered something in his sleep and shifted his weight so that he slumped over toward her. His head rolled against her shoulder, his cheek loose and vulnerable against her upper arm. She flinched and started to shrug away, and then, feeling suddenly shy, did not. He murmured again, louder, and she put her head closer to hear him, and her lips brushed his hair. It felt cool and silken, and looked very pale in the dashboard light. She did flinch away this time.

"What?" she said.

"Said you looked awfully pretty tonight," he mumbled, not opening his eyes. "I've never seen you look so pretty."

"Thank you," Mike said.

"Welcome."

He was silent again for the rest of the ride, breathing deeply and regularly. He did not move his head from her shoulder. Mike drove steadily and quietly through the late-summer dark. Once she looked over at him.

"Who are you?" she whispered.

When she turned into the driveway of the Pomeroy Street house, he was still fast asleep. She started to wake him, and then, looking at him stretched across the front seat in heavy sleep, went into the house and got the sofa afghan and covered him and shut the Toyota's door quietly.

The car was still there, a lighter bulk in the dark pool of shadow under the water oak, when she looked out before going to bed, but when she got up in the morning it was gone.

TWENTY-FIVE

She did not, after all, call Bay Sewell in Boston. When she came into the Pomeroy Street house, walking softly in her stocking feet and carrying her shoes in one hand, she found her father in his wheelchair in the kitchen, drinking bourbon and watching David Letterman with J.W. Cromie. His face was pallid and pinched in the fluorescent overhead light, but his eyes were bright with their accustomed malice.

"Well, Micah, have you taken to sneaking in my house after midnight again? Thought we got done with that a long time ago."

A sharp reply died on Mike's lips as she looked more closely at his face. It looked as if the flesh had shrunk and fallen in against the brittle old bone, so drawn and desiccated was it. His nose stood out more beaklike than ever, and she saw that the pallor was not white, but the dreaded pale yellow of advancing cancer. She had not seen that promissory jaundice before. The faint flush that had crept back during the past few days was gone.

"You two are a fine pair yourselves," she said mildly, searching J.W.'s face. "Drinking in the kitchen in the middle of the night while I'm gone, like a couple of teenagers. Is something the matter?"

"Nothing's the goddamned matter," her father said pettishly. There seemed to be no breath behind his words.

"Mr. John been havin' some pain," J.W. said laconically, setting his glass down on the kitchen table and rising to go. "Them pills didn't do no good, so we thought we'd try us some whiskey. Worked fine."

Mike looked at her father. He stared back at her with a sick old hawk's belligerence. His brow was smooth and dry, though, without the terrible great oily drops of sweat that the worst pain brought. She turned to J.W.

"You should have called Dr. Gaddis," she said. "He said to call him if the pain came back. He could have given him a shot or something. Really, J.W., whiskey in the middle of the night . . ."

"It worked, Mike," J.W. said curtly, dropping the slow, thick speech and accent. "He don't like the doctor and the doctor's medicine don't help him. He likes the whiskey and it does. What difference does it make?"

She stared at him for a moment and then shrugged. She was very tired. She wanted only to be in bed in the heavy, total darkness of her room, drowned in the glottal underwater song of the air conditioner. What difference did it make, indeed? She'd call the doctor herself in the morning. Meanwhile, sleep.

"If you don't mind putting him to bed, then, I think I'll go on up," she said. "Thanks for staying. And by the way, Mr. Canaday's asleep in his car out in the driveway, so be quiet going out. Though I doubt if you'll wake him."

J.W. grinned at her and her father gave a startling eldritch cackle of laughter.

"You and Sam really did get into it tonight, didn't you?" he said gleefully. "What'd you do, drink him under the table and then drive him home and leave him to sleep it off in the car?"

"Something like that," Mike said, smiling back at them tiredly. She wondered fleetingly if her father and J.W. Cromie knew about Sam, about the time in Mississippi and his wife and daughter.

"Wait'll I see him tomorrow," her father crowed as J.W. wheeled him out of the kitchen and toward his room. Despite the ravages of the pain, Mike had seldom seen him as cheerful. By the time she had peeled out of her clothes and turned back the bed, it was nearly 2:00 A.M., and she wanted to sleep more than she wanted to call Bayard Sewell or anything else in the world. Bay and his cold anger had waited this long. They would wait a while longer.

Her father was cheerful and energetic the next morning, waiting impatiently with a cassette of correspondence for her to transcribe and joking clumsily with Lavinia Lester, who was putting a pot roast into the oven. He must really be better, she thought. He usually treated Lavinia as if she were not in the room, although when he was forced to address her he always did so, elaborately, as Mrs. Lester. Lavinia treated him with the same remote and gracious courtesy that she did everyone else in the household, and Mike knew that her father's heavy-booted sarcasm bothered Lavinia not at all. They seemed, in fact, to rather enjoy each other's company; or, at least, to tolerate it well.

"You look better," Mike said to her father. "Have you had any more pain?"

"Not since J.W. poured me that shot of whiskey," he said. "And I had another one just now. Lavinia gave it to me herself. I'm through with Gaddis's damned medicine. Doesn't do a bit of good. Whiskey's the only thing that helps. Stops the son of a bitch cold."

Mike was surprised. He usually denied any pain at all, no matter how evident it was that he was hurting. She looked at Lavinia Lester, who gave her back a composed, small smile. If a nurse sanctioned whiskey, it must be harmless at least. She sighed.

"It must have been pretty bad, then," she said.

"Right bad," he said. "Right bad. Okay, Micah, let's start the TV stations today. What do you think, those fellows on the six o'clock news, or the noon ones? Or are you too hung over to do any work today?"

"The station managers, I think, or the news directors," she said. "And I'm not hung over at all, thank you very much. Though I can't say the same for your friend Sam Canaday."

And surprised and annoyed herself profoundly by blushing to the roots of her hair when she said his name.

Her father saw the flush and cackled his old eggshell cackle. "Look at you, Micah, redder'n a beet," he chortled. "What else did you all get up to besides drinkin' in some Atlanta juke joint? Not neckin' in the car, I hope. Or worse. I'm gon' have to get on him, I can see that much right now. Can't have him messin' around with my daughter and her a big-shot city journalist. Not fittin' for an ol' country boy like Sam."

"Oh, God, Daddy, lay off it, will you?" Mike snapped, aflame with embarrassment and something else . . . What? Guilt? Bayard Sewell's dark, carved face swam before her, and she wanted to grab for it as a drowning man might a ring buoy in an empty sea. But over it drifted the image of Sam Canaday's sleep-loosened face in the green light of the dashboard radio the night before, soft against her shoulder. She could feel again his cheek against the flesh of her upper arm, his breath warm through the thin stuff of her shirt, and smell the fleeting, musty silk of his hair. The heat in her face and chest deepened. Bayard Sewell's face faded and was gone.

For the rest of the afternoon they worked in near silence, John Winship sipping occasionally at the glass of whiskey beside him. Mike did not look often at her father, but from time to time she felt rather than saw his gaze on her, felt the full weight of it, probing. But he said nothing further about Sam Canaday or the night before. Mike fled upstairs to her room when Sam came by that evening after dinner, and then sat on her bed stiff with annoyance at herself. You'd think we'd gotten drunk and had an orgy or something, she thought disgustedly. I'm acting like a sixteen-year-old the morning after losing her virginity, and he didn't even touch me. Not that he meant to, anyway. God, I don't even *like* this man very much, and he probably wouldn't have me on a platter with a kiwi in my mouth. Enough of this shit. I'm going back downstairs where it's cool and have my coffee like I always do.

But she did not. Instead, she called Bayard Sewell at the Ritz Carlton in Boston, and was disappointed out of all proportion when the hotel operator said that he was out and had left no messages. After all, it was eight o'clock, and the middle of the dinner hour.

"No, no message," she said to the hotel operator. "I'll try again later."

But she didn't do that, either. She got into bed with a tattered volume of Albert Payson Terhune's dog stories, and lay propped against the thin old pillows alternately scanning the pages and listening to Sam Canaday's deep voice and laughter downstairs, counterpointing her father's frail piping. She could not make out their words. He must have stayed a long time. Her watch was on the bureau, but it felt very late when she heard his step moving toward the front door and heard it open.

"Night, Mike," he called up the stairs, as if he had known all along she had been lying there awake, listening to the sound of his voice. Her face burned again.

"Night, Sam," she yelled back.

For the next few days, he was elaborately offhand with her, as heartily casual as she was with him, and she would turn her head and find his eyes on her, and he would look away quickly. She in turn jumped like a pony bitten by a horsefly when he spoke to her, and took great pains to keep someone . . . Lavinia or J.W. or her father . . . in the room with the two of them at all times. John

Winship looked from one to the other, obviously enjoying the prickling discomfort in the house, but said nothing. Finally Sam Canaday
followed Mike into the kitchen and cornered her there, and said,
"Look. I didn't ravish you and I didn't proposition you, and you
didn't compromise an iota of your honor and dignity. Your panties
and your virtue are safe with me, I promise. I'd like to go out and
get drunk with you again sometime, but I can't if you're going to act
like a newly fallen teenager around me. Okay?"

"Okay," Mike said in relief. "I was getting awfully tired of
being Veronica to your Archie."

He laughed, and everything was suddenly normal again, as it
had been. But a new easiness and a loose, stretched kind of comfort
spun out warmly between them. He did not hector her sarcastically
anymore, and she did not cast her thin, remote webs of ice over him.
He teased her frequently, in a way he had not before, and she found
herself laughing often at his nonsense. Even her father seemed to
enjoy the running evening banter. The querulousness left his voice,
and a frail, high tension in him seemed to ease. It was a small,
humming, suspended time of well-being, except for the ever-present
leaden ache of the words Bay Sewell had left her with, and the hurt
of Rachel's call. She had tried a couple more times to reach Bay in
Boston, but he had not answered, and she did not want to call his
office to ask when they expected him back. After a day or two she
did not call again. She made no attempt to telephone Rachel. There
was between them too much to say, and nothing.

A few days into the peaceful hiatus, on a Saturday, DeeDee
called before breakfast.

"I talked to Bay last night, and he said for us to use those guest
passes at the country club before they expire," she said. "Come on,
Mikie. You've had your nose to the grindstone with Daddy for days
now, and we're not going to get a prettier day for the rest of the
summer. August is just around the corner, and then it's going to be
too hot to sit in the sun. Duck's sister is taking Mama Wingo into
Atlanta to the doctor, so I've got almost the whole day, and Duck
wants to go, too. Everybody needs a break."

"How is Bay?" Mike said, keeping her voice carefully neutral.
But her throat filled and tightened with pain. He found time to call
her troublesome sister, but not her. He must be angry indeed.

"Oh, okay. Having some problems with a business deal, I

think, but nothing he can't work out. He said he'd be home soon, and really insisted about the club. He said he was going to call you later, and for me to make you go with us and not let Daddy monopolize you."

Mike's heart zoomed and sang, and the sharp lump of submerged anguish that the estrangement from him had left in her chest melted away as if it had never been. It was, she knew, his roundabout way of apologizing. She felt giddy, light, exuberant. Even the prospect of Duck Wingo and DeeDee around a steaming suburban country club swimming pool was bearable; seemed, suddenly, rich with comic possibilities. She could tell Bay about the day, safe in the curtained gloom of the bedroom and the welter of the sheets when he got home, making a wry and funny story of it. Apparently his business in Boston was not going well, and on top of the new trouble with Sally, it would be good to see him laugh. She knew she could make him. She had always been able to.

"You promised we'd do something together soon," DeeDee cajoled, mistaking her silence for hesitation.

"So I did." Mike smiled at the telephone. "I'd love to, Dee. What time will you be by?"

"I thought about eleven. We can have lunch there. Bay wants us to. Everybody goes for lunch. Listen, Mike . . . could we take Daddy's car, do you think? Duck wants to go over earlier in the good car, and my old junker just looks so awful. Most of the people who belong to the club have nice cars."

"Of course," Mike said, her heart contracting with pity for her sister, who was at the mercy of so many hungers. "I'll tell J.W. to spit-polish it."

"See you then," DeeDee caroled. Her voice sounded young and very happy.

Mike's heart fell when DeeDee parked in the driveway and struggled out of the Volkswagen. She was wearing a vast striped beach caftan with a thrown-back hood that made her look, with her black, opaque sunglasses and feverish scarlet mouth, like the obese emir of some impossibly rich and savage oil-producing state. She wore giant white plastic hoops in her ears, and one great arm had multicolored plastic bangles on it nearly up to her elbow. On her feet were the gold mules she had worn the night of her dinner party, and she wore a gigantic straw sun hat in a shade of fuchsia that had never bloomed in any earthly garden. It was impossible not to stare at her. Mike knew that the outfit must have been put together with infinite care from the pages of the current *Vogue* or *Elle;* women from Bar Harbor to Boca Raton would wear the same costume this summer. But chic women, rich women, *thin* women. DeeDee must have spent a small fortune assembling it. It couldn't look worse if she'd tried, Mike thought in pity and annoyance. I wonder if I could talk her out of this awful expedition somehow? Everybody's going to laugh at her. But from the flush of pure pleasure on her sister's face and the lilt in her voice as she sang out, "Morning," she knew she could not. At least I can keep Daddy from sniping at her, she thought, and hastily gathered up her beach bag and towel and ran down the front steps.

"Don't you have anything a little gayer than that?" DeeDee said, taking in Mike's oversized white shirt and the soft old fisherman's hat she wore in the sun. "These are all new people, and first impressions are everything in this town."

"Nope," Mike said equably, getting into the driver's seat of the old Cadillac, which gleamed with wax and J.W.'s sweat. "What you see is what you get. Relax, Dee. I didn't wear my teeny-weeny polka dot bikini. Perfectly maidenly tank suit. Nothing shows."

"What's to show?" DeeDee said, but there was no malice in her words. She was too excited. She wiggled around on the car seat and drew a mirror from her enormous tote and slicked another coat of the scarlet lipstick on her mouth. Some of it remained on her teeth, making her look as if she had been feasting on the fresh corpse of something small. The caftan slid up her arms and Mike saw, in all the dimpled, shifting whiteness, a peppering of fading old bruises and startling purple new ones, looking suspiciously like fingerprints. She said nothing, but disgust at Duck rose in her throat like gorge, and she did not know, suddenly, if she could even be civil to him. Whether the bruises were the stigmata of his passion or his anger did not matter. They nauseated her.

"Is Duck already there?" she said.

"He left about an hour ago," DeeDee said. "He has a poker game in the men's grill on Saturday mornings. Bay usually plays too. Duck never wins anything, but he doesn't lose, either, and it's a wonderful opportunity for him. The best new people in town go to the club, and most of them sit in on the game. He's gotten to know several of them real well."

They pulled up in front of the Lytton Country Club, a meager, flat-roofed jumble of vaguely Spanish architecture on a road that had been largely pine woods and farmhouses when Mike had left, and a sullen young black boy ambled forward from the portico to park the car. Looking around, Mike saw other black teenagers piling golf bags into carts, carrying laden trays toward the out-of-sight pool, and scratching at the sparsely planted, sun-blasted flower beds with rakes and hoes.

"Ah," she said. "Lytton's solution to blacks at the country club. I wondered."

"Don't start on that, Mike," DeeDee said. "The club has put lots of local Negroes to work. They offered J.W. a good job on the maintenance crew; he'd have made a lot more than Daddy pays him, for doing the same thing. But he didn't take it."

"Maybe J.W.'s particular about who he maintains," Mike said.

"*Mikie . . .*" Dee's voice was a wail.

"Sorry," Mike said. She was. She did not want to spoil DeeDee's day in the sun. She handed the keys to the boy and they followed the path around the side of the clubhouse to the pool terrace.

It was already crowded at eleven thirty. Children and teenagers jeered and splashed in the pool, shouting something incomprehensible over and over that sounded to Mike like "Marco Polo" and seemed to have to do with a noisy water game. Young women in knots lay on chaises or sat on the edge of the pool, halfheartedly watching the children while they talked and laughed and oiled their reddening hides with lotions. All wore bright, brief, shiny scraps of suits and sun hats, and a few lay back with white cups over their eyes, stunned under the punishing fist of the sun. On an upper terrace, tables of older women in flowered and skirted suits or cover-up sunsuits played bridge and sipped at virulent pastel drinks brought by the bored young blacks. A haughty young woman in a wet T-shirt that said "Go Dawgs" and white zinc nose ointment was apparently the lifeguard; she sat staring into space atop a tall chair, ignoring the preening, jostling pack of preadolescent boys milling about the base of the platform. It was an indolent, completely banal little suburbanscape, with nothing in it that Mike could see to so charm and succor her sister. The younger women had slack bodies and snub, vacuous little faces; one or two wore pink plastic curlers under scarves. The older women all seemed to have the same swim- suit and freshly teased hairdo. The pool apron was cracked and sprouted valiant tufts of weeds here and there, and the cars in the lot beyond the pool did not run to Mercedes and Jaguars, but to compact wagons and TransAms. There were no men in sight over the age of sixteen or so. It was a little aquatic kingdom of women and children.

"Isn't this something for Lytton?" DeeDee said proudly, surg- ing down the steps to the pool terrace like a billowing, deflated circus tent. "I hope we can work it out so we can join by next summer. It's too late to get anybody to stay with Mama Wingo this year, but Bay's going to put us up sometime this winter."

Behind her dark glasses, Mike looked around. At their en- trance, the heads around the pool and the bridge tables lifted and myriad sunglass-shielded eyes were fastened on them. As had been the case all summer, she saw no face she recognized from her time here before. Maybe old Lytton, as DeeDee persisted in calling it, did not exist; had never existed except as a context for her childhood. Or perhaps it surfaced only once a century, like Brigadoon. In any event, the focused eyes had in them no ken for Mike Winship.

She could see that all conversation had stopped. DeeDee sailed down the steps and across the apron like the QE2 coming into Southampton, nodding to a group here and giving a little offhand wave and a trilled hello to one there. Her eyes played back and forth over the pool area, assessing and cataloging the crowd. Her smile included one and all. It was definitely in the nature of a royal prog- ress. Mike, trailing in her sister's wake, saw what DeeDee did not: the rolled eyes, the hands clapped to mouths to stifle laughter, the heads coming together again to follow her elephantine promenade. Mike's face burned with embarrassment and fury. She wanted to crack the teased and sprayed heads together; she wanted to shake her sister for her preening complacency. She decided, feeling the virulent bite of the sun through the nylon of the fishing hat, that she would plead a headache and escape immediately after lunch. DeeDee could ride home with Duck.

DeeDee settled herself at an umbrella table at the far end of the upper terrace, and pulled off her sun hat. Her hair was loose again, down her back, spread like a cape over the sausagelike bulk of her shoulders. Mike could see the precise line near her scalp where the ebony dye ended and the rusted black of Dee's own color began. She prayed that her sister would not remove the caftan. She could not imagine what she would look like in a bathing suit. DeeDee didn't.

"Let's have lunch first," she said. "Then we can swim. Or you can. I'm thinking of playing a little bridge with Helen Apperson and her crowd over there, and I know you hate cards."

She waved gaily at a thin, dun-colored woman at a nearby table, who gave her back a stiff little salute and a perfunctory baring of huge Chiclet teeth. The other three women at the table smiled, cutting their eyes at Helen Apperson and then staring again at DeeDee and Mike. Mike knew that they would talk about them both, the grotesque Wingo woman and her strange northern writer sister whom nobody ever saw around town. She could feel their eyes on her back, almost feel the smoking pits left by the avidity of the sensation-starved eyes.

"Come on over and I'll introduce you," DeeDee said. "I'll take you around to all the others after lunch."

"Oh, let's eat first," Mike said. "I'm starved, and they're in the middle of a game."

"Well, then, maybe you'd like to ask somebody to join us," DeeDee chirped, favoring the assemblage with a sweeping smile. "Oh, there's Lolly Bridges. She's darling. Her husband's a pilot and she does catering, really cute things. She's real creative. Everybody's using her now for weddings and anniversaries. Hey, Lolly," she called to a leathery red-haired woman in a golf skirt and sleeveless shirt who had just come onto the terrace and was obviously looking in vain for an empty table. "Come join us and meet my little Yankee sister. She doesn't know anybody anymore, and I was just telling her about you."

The woman started, and then gave DeeDee a brilliant, totally false smile. "Oh, I'm so sorry, Mrs. . . . . Wingo, isn't it? I'd love to, but I can't stay; I was just looking for my son, but I don't see him so I guess he's gone on . . . another time, though."

"Oh, sure," DeeDee sang out, smiling happily. "We'll probably be joining this winter, so we'll see plenty of you then."

"How nice," Lolly Bridges said, and fled the terrace. Heads

turned to follow her, and one or two women put out hands and touched her arm as she passed and said something to her, laughing, and she shook her head rapidly and went around the side of the clubhouse.

"Save the whales," Mike heard one of the women say, and everyone around the woman laughed again. Mike's face and chest burned as if she were being martyred at a medieval stake. She shot an oblique look at her sister, but DeeDee had apparently not heard, for her face lost none of it self-satisfied well-being.

"This is the life, isn't it?" she said. "It's a pity none of old Lytton will join. Not that there's much old Lytton left. But I doubt if these people would have anything to do with them, anyway. This is the in crowd now. Of course, Bay and his crowd would be welcome anywhere, but they're the exceptions out of the old families."

"Is Sam Canaday a member?" Mike asked.

"Oh, Mike, of course not. Who on earth would put him up for membership, much less vote for him? You may not think so, but it really is an exclusive club."

"It looks it," Mike said, taking in the snickering women on the pool apron. "I doubt very much if I'd make the grade."

"Of course you would," her sister said. "A Winship? How can you say such a thing? Besides that, anybody Bay nominated would be a member in a minute."

Their waiter came then, and they placed their drink orders. DeeDee had a towering pink frozen daiquiri, and Mike ordered, perversely, a beer. When it came, she waved away the glass and drank it straight from the can. She did not like beer, but the first frosty gulps on a boiling-hot day like this one were always good. After that, it began to taste like soap. But she ordered another, simply because she knew DeeDee thought it unseemly, and then regretted the trifling spite. She swirled the tepid liquid around in the can and wondered if she could get a forkful of tuna salad down in this heat, and how quickly she could convincingly develop the headache. The air smelt powerfully of suntan oil, perfume, and chlorine.

A shadow fell over the table, and Mike looked up to see a small, round man with very pink cheeks and the only leisure suit she had seen in years standing beside them. He was not smiling, and his eyes, black and shiny like currants in a pastry, flicked from her to DeeDee. He looked, Mike thought, like the Pillsbury Doughboy.

"Mrs. Wingo?" he said.

"I'm Mrs. Wingo," DeeDee said, smiling her ferocious social smile.

"I'm Sonny Sampson, the club manager," the little pastry man said, and DeeDee held out her hand graciously. He took it limply, as if he had been offered a dead sea creature to hold, and dropped it quickly.

"This is my sister, Micah Winship." DeeDee dimpled. "You'll know all about her if you read the newsmagazines."

Sonny Sampson looked at Mike in vague alarm, and nodded.

"Miz Winship," he said.

He obviously thinks I'm a hot ticket in the news, Mike thought, suppressing an unseemly bubble of glee. Somebody in Washington's mistress who has just Told All.

"Mr. Sampson," she said, and nodded.

"How nice of you to come over and say hello," DeeDee warbled. "We're guests of Bay Sewell's. Bayard Everett Sewell. I'm sure you know him. He's a very dear friend of my husband's and mine. Won't you join us?"

"No ma'am, thank you, I can't stay. Ah . . . Mrs. Wingo, I hate to mention an unpleasant subject to one of our guests, but . . . uh . . . Mr. Wingo seems to have passed out in the men's grill and I think we ought to get him home. Mr. Collingwood called me down just a minute ago; they can't get him up . . ."

"Oh, my God," DeeDee squealed, putting a hand to her throat in a gesture Mike had last seen Bette Davis make in *Dark Victory*. "What's the matter with him? Is it his heart? Have you called a doctor?" She half rose from her seat.

"No, ma'am," Sonny Sampson said, not moving to help her. "He's not sick, Mrs. Wingo. He's drunk. He was pretty abusive before he passed out, and he's going to have to leave the premises. If you'll have the boy bring your car to the front, I'll have a couple of the grill stewards get him around to it. I'm sorry, Mrs. Wingo. Mr. Sewell would be the first to tell you that the club can't tolerate disorderliness."

DeeDee's face flushed a deep, dangerous crimson, and her chest rose and fell like a neap tide.

"My husband does not get . . . intoxicated," she hissed. "And he certainly does not get disorderly. You'd better watch who you're talking to, Mr. Sampson. Bay Sewell is not going to like this, not one little bit."

"Your husband is drunk as a pig, Mrs. Wingo, and this is not the first time," the little man drawled, an edge of wire-grass southern Georgia circling into his voice. "Last time he broke the pinball machine and scattered peanuts all over the floor arm wrestling. He's run up a bar tab of seventy-seven dollars, too, setting up the house. Of course, Mr. Sewell always picks up his tabs, since he's a guest, so I'm not going to push that. But this time he can't cover his bets, Mrs. Wingo, and we don't put up with that at this club. We think the world of Mr. Sewell, but we don't put up with that at all."

"You snotty little pipsqueak," DeeDee began shrilly. "Don't you call my husband a cheat! I'm going straight home and call Bay Sewell in Boston . . ."

Heads turned toward them, and conversation stopped again. Mike laid a hand on DeeDee's arm. Her sister was quivering. Her breath was audible, hissing in her nostrils.

"Shh, Dee. Let's just go. You don't want to hang around here," she said.

"I'll have the boys bring Mr. Wingo around," Sonny Sampson said. "But I'm afraid I'm going to have to ask you how he intends to cover his debt. The other men insist that he do so. They don't want to have to go to Mr. Sewell with this."

"They can go and be damned to them," DeeDee said furiously. "I'm going to Bay myself, the minute he gets home. I'll pay the debt myself. How much does he owe?" She reached for the gargantuan beach bag.

"It's eight hundred and sixteen dollars," Sonny Sampson said impassively.

"*Eight hundred and sixteen dollars . . .*" DeeDee's voice sizzled out in a whisper, like air escaping from a balloon. "I . . . my checkbook is at home . . ."

"I've got mine, Dee," Mike said, not looking at either one of them. There was a resinous stillness, in which all sound seemed to go out of the day, even the splashing of the children. All motion stopped. She slid her checkbook out of her tote and wrote out the check to the Lytton Country Club, and folded it and gave it to Sonny Sampson, who pocketed it.

"Thank you, Miz Winship. Sorry about this, ladies. I hate to do it, but I'm going to have to ask that Mr. Wingo not come back to the club."

"You little stuck-up son of a bitch," DeeDee shrieked. "You can take your two-bit club and you know what you can do with it! Bay Sewell will have your job so fast you won't know what hit you! I wouldn't come back to this crummy little place if my life depended on it, and neither would my husband! We can do better than this any day of our lives . . ."

"Hush, Dee!" Mike said, and DeeDee did.

Sonny Sampson gestured and two of the impassive black boys emerged from the men's grill, half-dragging, half-carrying Duck Wingo between them. His head lolled down onto his chest, and he had obviously spilled a good bit of liquor on his plaid double-knit pants, because they were stained from crotch to knee. From the smell of him he had thrown up on himself, too. His white loafers dragged on the concrete apron as the two boys bore him around the club-house toward the front. He was semiconscious and mumbling. In the dead silence Mike could hear small gasps and stifled laughter from the bridge and pool women, and the pounding of her own heart. Sonny Sampson vanished abruptly back inside the clubhouse, and Mike steered DeeDee along behind the cumbersome procession. She could not see her sister's face, but she could still hear her breathing. DeeDee said nothing. The walk until they gained the waiting Cadillac was interminable. Mike had never run such a gauntlet, not in Watts, not in Chicago, not at Kent State. She tried her old crisis trick, going far back into the core of her mind, completely and totally disassociating herself from her surroundings, but it did not work this time. The bell jar was gone. She was conscious with every fiber of her being of the eyes on them, and the following arrows of laughter.

The black boys wrestled Duck into the backseat of the Cadillac, and Mike hastily rummaged in her tote and pressed bills into their hands. She did not know how much she gave them. They muttered thanks and loped away. Mike pushed DeeDee gently into the front passenger's seat and went around to the driver's side. They drove away in silence. From the rear, amid the powerful fumes of vomit and liquor, Duck Wingo mumbled and cursed. "Motherfuckers don' know their asses from a hole in the wall. Buy and sell those mother-fuckers and their fuckin' club this time next year; they'll be shittin' their pants to get me in the game next year . . ."

"I suggest that you shut up, Duck," Mike said over her shoulder. "You'll be lucky if Bay ever even looks at you again."

"Ol' Bay?" He laughed, a slurring, snorting laugh. "Ol' Bay, he ain't gon' say a goddamn word to his good friend Duck. He gon' treat his good friend Duck real good, he is . . ."

"Shut your stupid mouth or I'll shut it for you," DeeDee screamed. Duck fell silent.

Mike looked sideways at her sister. DeeDee's great red face was splotched with white, and tears ran silently down her cheeks and into her mouth. Mike had not seen her cry since they were small. DeeDee had been a happy child, airy and pattering, but her fears thunderstorms, the dark, large animals, and above all, abandonment —had been matters of desperation to her, and the occasion for bitter, frantic tears. Rusky's or their father's soothing ministrations could finally quiet them, but DeeDee sobbed just as despairingly and unfeignedly the next time she was frightened. Only much hugging and the magic incantation, "Everything will be all right," could succor her. Now, everything was not all right, and had not been for many years; and in all those years there had been no one to comfort her. Mike's heart turned like a gaffed fish in her chest.

"DeeDee, honey, please don't cry," she said. She put her hand over DeeDee's clenched fists in her lap, and Dee gripped it with astonishing force.

"I hate him," she whispered. "I started hating him not long after I married him, and I've never stopped. I've been so afraid, so afraid . . . I wish he was dead. I wish he would die. He's never given me anything but work and worry and shame; I've never had anything, *anything!* And what I did get, what little I did scrounge, he's lost for me. I can't go back to that club now; how could I ever face any of those people? Mike, those are the people who matter in Lytton now. And now we don't matter to them, and we never will, all because of that sorry, no-account son of a bitch I married. Showing off, getting drunk, bragging, cheating . . . ah, God, Mikie, I'm a Winship. A *Winship!* I could have had anybody! I could have married anybody in this town, and I wish to God I had. I could have been safe. I wish to God I'd stayed single, even; Daddy would have taken care of me. But I had to marry *that* and I'll never have any kind of life as long as I'm stuck with him. Never!" She strangled on the tears.

Mike took a deep breath.

"Dee . . . why don't you leave him?" she said. "Daddy would still take care of you; and you know you'll have the house and the homeplace property. You could do that. There's nothing to stop you. Bay would help you. I'd help . . ."

DeeDee laughed, an ugly, watery little sound. "Thanks, Mike, but I'll be able to take care of myself pretty soon. Pretty soon I won't need Daddy or Bay, or you, and I'll get rid of him so fast he'll think a tornado hit him. You just wait. Just a little longer, and that bastard and his horrible old mother and that horrible little dump of a house will be *gone!*" There was something so abstracted and dreamlike in her voice that Mike stared across at her. DeeDee did not seem to see her, or the inside of the car, or the bright day that had brought her so much pain and shame. Her blue eyes were fixed on middle distance, and they looked a little mad.

"What are you waiting for?" Mike said. "What's going to happen that's going to make it all right? It won't get any better, Dee!"

"Oh . . . I just mean that it will take me a while to get myself together and figure out what to do," DeeDee said. "I can't just up and leave him, Mike. I don't have any money and any skills. I haven't taught in years. I don't even remember how. I don't know what I would do. I can't just walk out . . ."

"Will you promise me you'll talk to Bay about it when he gets back?" Mike said. "He can help. I know he can. Will you promise me that, Dee?"

"I promise I'll talk to him," her sister said. "Sure, I'll talk to him. Mikie, thanks for paying . . . you know, for writing the check. I don't know when we can pay you back. We don't have that kind of money . . ."

"What do I need with money in Lytton?" Mike smiled. "Forget it, Dee."

In the backseat, Duck Wingo vomited again. DeeDee put her face into her hands and sobbed. She cried all the way home, and when Mike stopped the Cadillac in front of the dreadful, stark little ranch house beside the mobile home park, she was still crying.

TWENTY-SIX

The telephone was ringing as she came up the driveway, and Lavinia Lester came into the front hall to meet her when she walked into the house.

"Mr. Sewell is on the phone from Boston," she said. "He's been talking to Mr. Winship and now he wants to talk to you."

"Thanks, I'll get it upstairs," Mike said. She flew up the stairs and snatched the telephone from its cradle in the old-fashioned niche in the wall of the upstairs hall.

"Bay?"

"Hello, Mike," he said in his soft, deep voice. "Can you talk?"

Mike heard the telephone downstairs being replaced.

"Yes," she said.

"I've missed you so much I've been doing unspeakable things to my pillow these past few nights," he said. "I want to come home and do them to you now."

"Well, come on home," she said, her voice vibrant with joy. "I'll show your goddamned pillow a few tricks."

"Oh, God, Mike, I want you."

"Me, too. Oh, Bay, me too. When are you coming home?"

"Tonight, late. It will probably be Monday afternoon before I can see you, but I'll be there then. Don't let anything get in the way, Mike."

"Oh, no. Oh, no. Has it been a good trip? Is it going to work out for Sally at Silver Hill?"

"No. I can't leave her up there, Mike. It's too . . . sharp-edged, too northern, or something. She'd shrivel and die there. And they don't have the long-term medical facilities for her, either. Her liver is in really bad shape, according to Gaddis. She's been getting booze from somewhere right along; Opal found all the empties in the crawl space just before I left. I'm going to have to have her watched more carefully. She'll die if she doesn't stop drinking."

"Where is she getting liquor?" Mike said.

"God knows. If I didn't know better, I'd say Opal was bringing it to her; how else could she possibly get it? But that's crazy . . . well, anyway. I need to say this, Mike, so don't try to stop me. I'm sorry for being such a horse's ass when I left. You're right. You help your dad with his campaign till doomsday, if you want to. It's worth it just to see you two getting close again."

"Oh, Bay, it's all right . . ."

"No, it isn't. I was miserable, and I made you miserable, and it's not all right. It's just that I worry so about John. But DeeDee says it's doing him good. How is he really, Mike? Is he talking much to you? Anything new about the DOT I ought to know?"

"Just the same old stuff. But oh, Bay, the most awful thing happened at the club today, and they're going to tell you, so I want to myself, before you talk to anybody else. Poor DeeDee, my heart just broke in two for her . . ."

She told him about the dreadful scene around the country club pool, and about DeeDee's terror and tears.

He sighed loudly over the phone. "Good Christ, what a mess," he said. "My fault for going off and leaving him to that goddamned poker game. I've been covering for him all spring, but I guess I knew something was going to have to be done about him, and I should have done it before it blew up in DeeDee's face. The damned fool! She'd be better off without him; she's absolutely right, but I don't know what on earth she'd live on. There's not a cent between them, and she can't go back to teaching. Not in the shape she's in. Mike, listen. She's fixed all right when John . . . goes, isn't she? I mean, she's said she's getting the homeplace land and your dad's house. Is that still true?"

"Why . . . sure, I guess it is," Mike said. "She told me that, too, when I first came, and I don't imagine anything's changed. Daddy knows what Duck is."

"He wouldn't have . . . changed his will or anything? He's getting very close to you, Mike, and you just don't know what old, sick people are apt to do . . ."

"Oh, I'm sure not," Mike said. "He knows I'm not staying. I'm sure he knows I don't want the land."

"Are you certain of that? I need to be sure she's taken care of, Mike. I can help her, I think, but I need to know that she's going to get the land before I know what to tell her. That land is her security."

"I'm as sure as she is," Mike said.

"Who would know for certain? Canaday?"

"I guess so, if you don't."

"I want you to ask him, Mike. Today, if possible."

"I don't want to ask about Daddy's will, Bay," Mike said unhappily. "It sounds as if I'm hoping to get something, and I'm not."

She could hear his sigh again over the wire. "Mike, please. I don't have the time or energy to fight you on this, too. I've got problems up here, and Sally is worrying me to death, and I just can't worry about DeeDee on top of it all."

"I'm sorry. I'll find out and tell you when you get home," Mike said contritely. That heaviness in his voice had never been there before. She could almost see it pressing down on his lean shoulders.

She approached Sam Canaday with it that evening after they had put John Winship to bed. The pain had been kept at bay under the anodyne of the liquor, but her father stayed very slightly drunk most of the time, and slept a great deal. By tacit consent neither she nor Sam had told Dr. Gaddis about the drinking. As J.W. had said, what difference did it make now?

Sam narrowed his eyes at her through the curling steam from his coffee when she asked him about DeeDee's inheritance.

"You getting interested in the homeplace now?" he said.

"No. That was just such an awful scene at the club, I wanted to make absolutely certain she was taken care of."

"Yeah, it was a bad scene, all right," Sam said. "Son of a bitch ought to be shot; she'd be a lot better off. What made you think I'd know about John's will, Mike?"

"Well, I just thought since you're his lawyer, and Bay didn't know . . ."

"Ah," he said. "I thought so. Sewell. Bayard the Good. Well, you tell Sewell he can stop worrying. DeeDee's going to be taken care of."

"I'm glad," Mike said. She refused to take offense at his tone. Bay's imminent homecoming sang too loudly and joyfully in her blood.

Sam finished his coffee in silence and left without saying good night. Mike started to call him back, and then didn't. She really couldn't help it if he had a fixation about Bay. It was not her problem. At that moment, with Bayard Sewell in the air somewhere over Atlanta, Mike had no problems that amounted to more than wisps of high white clouds on a summer day.

"I have to apologize again," Bayard Sewell said, when he could say anything at all. His breath was ragged, and Mike could see the thunderous pounding of his heart in the pulse in the hollow of his throat. His entire chest, sweat-slick and pale in the dim light of the bedroom, shook and surged with it. When he had first rolled off her onto his back in the bed, the breath had literally sobbed in his throat, and he had gasped and choked, and she had been afraid that he was having a heart attack. Her own heart was hammering down toward a manageable level, but her temples and wrists still felt turgid and stiff with rushing blood, and she could not have moved her slack, tumbled limbs if someone had lit a fire in the bed. This time her reaction was not that of slaked passion and fulfilled yearning, she realized. For a moment, at the very height of his climax, she had felt something akin to fear. She did not wish to realize, but did, nevertheless, that their intercourse had very nearly been rape.

She had been waiting for him in the cool, dark bedroom, the air conditioner booming as it always did, her father sleeping in his fog of liquor and illness below, the house quiet, and she had been feeling a delicate languor, a slow and delicious voluptuousness, that had turned her wrists and eyelids heavy and her breath soft and short. They would undress each other very slowly, she thought, savoring the feeling of their hands on each other's starved flesh, letting the tumbling, frantic little spate of words wash over them, tasting and touching and smelling until they could stand it no longer, and would fall into the cool, fresh bed and begin the longest, deepest, and slowest act of love they had ever shared. She had not even undressed, in anticipation of the formal and prurient little ritual of harlotry that he loved, and was not at the door of the room to meet him, as she usually was, but sitting on the bed, arms and legs demurely crossed, when he came into the room. The blouse and skirt that she had worn lay on the floor beside the bed where he had torn them from her, and her lace bikini panties were still at her ankles. He himself still wore his shirt. He had thrown her down and torn her legs apart and been on and in her before she had gotten a word out, and had stopped her cries with his hand, and had bitten her mouth until she tasted coppery blood, and had bruised her arms and legs and reamed the tender, secret parts of her brutally. He had finished quickly, but not without hurting her rather badly. Mike did not feel anger, but she did feel humbled and vulnerable, as if she wanted to curl herself into a ball, so that her nakedness would be hidden from him. And she felt ragged and edgy. She had not achieved her own climax.

Bay rolled over on one elbow and looked down at her. His face was slack and pale, and there were darker circles and deeper etches around his eyes. His black wings of hair were wild.

"I feel like a hun," he said. "There was no excuse for that. It was just that it's been such a hideous week, and I'd been wanting you so bad for so long, and there you were, and you just looked so beautiful. Can you forgive me? Want me to go back and make it good for you? Christ, what a bull elephant you must think I am."

She shook her head. At the sound of his beautiful, familiar voice, all the strangeness and pain and the small shards of fear evaporated, and she felt the old peace and love and spreading sense of home.

"It ain't rape if she's willing," she said. "Glad I could be of service. I'm sorry you've been having such a bad time. What's going on with this business deal of yours? Is it a real problem?"

"No," he said. "Not yet. Just a matter of timing. They're pushing me hard, though, and I don't need that on top of the mess with Sally. I just don't know what to do about her, Mike. It's as if she's determined to kill herself no matter how hard we watch her, and she's getting so *sly* about it. It's just so constant. And then there's the business about DeeDee . . . sometimes I wish I could just dump everything overboard and leave. Cut out and go somewhere on the other side of the world and be totally free, some city where nobody on earth even knew my name."

"I know the feeling," she said. "It's the best thing about a city; it's what I miss most. You don't have to worry about Dee, by the way; Sam says she's taken care of."

"Ah," he said. "What else did he say?"

"Just that. She gets the property, just like we thought. It should keep her going if she does decide to leave Duck."

"Good," he said. "That'll make things a lot easier."

They lay in silence for a little while, and then she said, "Did you ever think about really leaving? Taking Sally and going somewhere else and starting over from scratch? Who knows what a change like that might do for her . . ."

"No," he said. "I can't. Oh, of course I've thought of it. But I don't think Sal could live away from Lytton, and I'm not sure I could either, now."

"Is it that important to you?" Mike said. "I can remember when you were on fire to leave it."

"It was never Lytton I hated, particularly," he said slowly. "Just small towns in general. I don't guess I ever told you, really, but before Mother and I came to Lytton, we lived in three or four different small towns around Georgia, and in every damned one of them we were the official municipal charity. Every holiday, here would come the committees and the preachers with the baskets and the barrels of canned peas and carrots. And the hand-me-downs. I couldn't have told you what size clothes I wore until I got to college. Christ, I remember one town that always had a church Christmas tree, and everybody drew names and exchanged gifts, and old Santa Claus called out your name and you ran down and got your gift, and you held it up and thanked whoever had drawn your name. Mother and I always got at least fifty gifts, when everybody else only got one, and ours were always useful gifts, and they always came from 'A friend.' I'd trot down there and hold mine up time after time grinning like a possum in the middle of a cow plop, and sing out, 'Thank you, friend,' and everybody would grin back and applaud and say what a good boy I was, and how I was going to amount to something one day. And Mother would beam. I found out later that we were that town's Needy Family of the Year. Thank God we moved the next year. I think I might have gone down to the altar and pissed on the Christmas tree. After that, it got to be a real obsession with me, not to be beholden to anybody ever again, not to be chained by gratitude."

Mike's eyes filled with tears. "I never knew all that," she said. "Oh, God, I hope you never felt that way about Daddy, or me, or Lytton. You honestly don't feel tied here? Not by Sally, or your home, or any of it?"

"No," he said. "Not here. And never by your dad. He was all

the father I ever knew. I owe him everything, literally. Lytton's been good to me. There's a lot here for me. There'll be a lot more. I can't leave Lytton. I don't want to."

He was silent for a while, and then he said, "Mike . . . would you stay? Do you think you could stay in Lytton? I honestly do not know before God how I can let you go again."

Here it is, thought Mike. I guess I always knew this would come.

"How can I stay, Bay?" she said. "Nothing of my life is here. Rachel, my work—and Daddy . . . he can't last too much longer. I can't just stay here after he's gone and be your mistress."

"Could you go to Atlanta, then? Could you make that your base, if you need to be in a city? It's a good city, it's growing fast. We could get you an apartment; I could handle that, till you get on your feet. Hell, I could handle that indefinitely. You could have your daughter come there; the city schools are as good as any in the country, and there are fine private schools. I'm in Atlanta almost every day when the legislature's in session; nobody would think a thing if I started staying over, instead of driving back and forth. Most of the guys do that anyway . . ."

"No, Bay, that just wouldn't work; I can't just sit back and let you keep me," Mike said, feeling as though all the corners of her life were rushing in toward her. Oh, why had he had to bring this up now? Why couldn't he have just been content to live in the pure, timeless, mindless bubble of sensation that had surrounded them so far?

"We'll find a way," he said. "It's not as farfetched or impossible as you think. Not by a long shot. I can work this out."

"Please!" Mike cried aloud. "Don't! Can't you see what hoping for that would do to me? Please just let it go, Bay. For now, anyway."

"All right," he said. "I'm sorry. For now I'll let it go. Just for now, though, Mike."

He got out of bed and washed and dressed in the green dimness of the bathroom. Mike listened to the splash of water and drifted slowly and deeply down toward sleep. He came back into the room as fresh and cool in his seersucker suit as if he had just dressed that morning. Mike thought again how impossibly, almost laughably handsome he was.

"You're too beautiful to be a guy," she said drowsily.

"You'd be in deep shit trouble if I was anything else," he said. "Should I go knock on your dad's door, do you think? He wasn't tracking too well when I talked to him Saturday. I don't want him to think I've abandoned him, but if he's sleeping well these days, I want to let him do it."

"Oh, he's sleeping well," Mike said. "Booze is the answer, apparently. Let it go until tomorrow, why don't you? He's seemed tireder than usual lately. I really ought to try and cut him down on this letter-writing business. I'm not so sure this delaying stuff is such a good idea anymore . . ."

"What delaying stuff, Mike?"

His face was still, and his voice was different, somehow. Sharper, lighter, dryer.

"Well," Mike said, reluctant without knowing why, "that's what Sam's doing with the price negotiations on the homeplace. That's about all he thinks he can do, really . . ."

"Tell me, Mike."

Mike told him.

She watched as his face paled underneath its tan and then darkened again, as if he had been slapped. His teeth clenched so hard that the muscles around his mouth stood out in hard white ridges. His hands, jammed into his jacket pockets, clenched, too.

"I ought to have that bloody goddamned fool put in jail for what he's doing to your father," he whispered, and the sound frightened her in its reptilian sibilance. "It's worse than criminal, and by God, he's not going to do it anymore."

He was across the room and at the door before Mike could gather her wits. She bounded off the bed and dashed after him. Why on earth was he so angry? As Sam had said before, her father seemed to be thriving on the course he had charted with the Department of Transportation.

"Bay, wait a minute," she cried. "It isn't hurting anything! Sam wouldn't hurt Daddy . . ."

"You're goddamned right he won't," he said, almost exultantly, and jerked the door open and slammed it behind him, and was gone down the stairs before she even reached it. She heard the front door slam, and then silence.

She trotted out onto the landing in bewilderment, looking down from the head of the stairs toward the empty downstairs hall and the closed front door. The noise of its slamming seemed to vibrate endlessly in the still, hot air. Outside her bedroom, the stored heat of the day was fierce. Mike wore nothing but her pants and bra, but her body was already wet with perspiration.

There was a small movement in the darkness below, at the back of the house, and she started and looked down. In the hot gloom Sam Canaday stood looking up at her, his face a white blur in the twilight of the back hall. Mike froze in simple shock.

"Well," Sam said slowly. "So. I wondered, of course. You've been giving off your own light lately."

"What are you doing here?" Mike's voice was thick and foolish in her throat.

"Your dad had a bad attack," Sam Canaday said. "He couldn't raise you by yelling, so he crawled to the phone and called me. Dr. Gaddis is on his way. You'd better go put some clothes on."

"I . . . have you . . . how long have you been standing there?"

"Long enough, Miz Winship-Singer," he said. "Long enough. Don't worry, Mike. Your secret is safe with me. I'd rather watch *Dynasty.*"

He turned and went back down the hall and into John Winship's room, and Mike went back into her bedroom and shut the door. She sat for a long time on the edge of her bed, listening to the hum of the air conditioner and thinking nothing at all. Then she dressed and went downstairs to meet the doctor. J.W. Cromie was coming out of her father's room with a glass and a washcloth in his hand, but Sam Canaday was gone. She could hear the tinny, diminishing burr of the Toyota as it turned out of the driveway and disappeared down Pomeroy Street toward town.

TWENTY-SEVEN

Mike was at Priss's when the call came.

She had waked slowly and luxuriously at eleven that morning, after the longest and deepest sleep she had had since she had come home, and had dressed in a peaceful and perfect envelope of nowness. There was, for the time being, no past that contained an agonizing scene in the dim hall of the Pomeroy Street house, no closed white face looking up at her near-nakedness, no toneless voice saying, "You'd better go put on some clothes," no battered and vanishing old car. And neither was there a future in which such a scene would have to be dealt with. It was not the bell jar, and it was not Mike's usual crisis management tool. She did not know what it was, but she was peacefully and abstractly grateful for it.

Downstairs, Lavinia Lester was knitting and watching something old and English and flickering on the A&E channel. John Winship was not in the kitchen. Dr. Gaddis had given him a powerful sedative by injection the evening before and had phoned in a much stronger painkiller, which had come immediately from the pharmacy, and her father had slept through the night. From past experience, she knew that he would sleep most of the day, as he always did following a bad bout of pain.

"Let him have the pills whenever he needs them," the doctor had said. "Let him have the liquor, too. I hope this is the worst it will get before it's over, but it may not be. It could be ferocious next time. It isn't going to be long, though, Mike. Let him have and do whatever he wants."

Mike had nodded and the doctor had gone away. It was J.W. who had insisted on sitting up beside John Winship as he slept his still and deathlike sleep.

"I'm off tomorrow, Mike," he said. "You and Mr. Sam save up for when you need your strength."

"Thank you, J.W.," she had said. "You're a better friend than we deserve."

She had not told Bayard Sewell that Sam Canaday had seen him leaving the upstairs bedroom and she knew somehow that Sam would not. Sam had not called; she knew that he would not do that, either. Mike floated on the moment and waited for what would come.

In the afternoon she drifted over to Priss's.

She was drinking iced coffee and admiring Priss's new bird feeder when the telephone rang. Priss displaced a dreadfully snoring Walker Pussy and heaved herself up to answer it.

"Sam, for you," she said, coming back into the room.

Mike picked up the telephone.

"Sam?" she said.

"We've lost," he said briefly. His voice was level. "It's over. They've filed a declaration of taking and they'll be taking title about now. Don't tell him. I'm coming by tonight and we'll do it then."

"Yes," she said. "Thank you."

"What is it?" Priss said, searching Mike's face. "Is it John?"

"No," Mike said. "It's the homeplace. It's gone, Priss. Sam can't do anything more."

Priss was silent for so long that Mike swiveled her head around to look at her. The big, smooth, Buddha-like face was, astoundingly, crumpled in anguish. Mike had never seen such an expression on Priss's face, not even on that long-ago evening in her father's house. Tears slid down her cheeks in the creases bracketing her small, Etruscan mouth.

"Oh, poor Win," she whispered. "Oh, poor Scamp."

"Scamp?" Mike parroted, whispering also, though she could not have said why. She did not know which was more unbelievable, Priss's tears or the roguish, old-fashioned epithet. It fit neither the remote dream-father of her childhood nor the present wreckage of that man.

"I called him Scamp when he was a boy. We all did, all through high school." A small, tremulous smile played around Priss's mouth, and her eyes were far away in memory. "He was a real devil, a kind of perpetual cheeky bad boy, always into something, always laughing. And handsome! You wouldn't believe how handsome he was. I'll never forget how he looked the night of our senior party, in his first real suit, that he worked after school all year for, with one of Miss Daisy's sweetheart roses in his buttonhole . . ."

She drew a long, shuddering breath and took off her glasses and wiped her eyes.

"I'll come on by tomorrow after Sam's told him and he's slept on it," she said matter-of-factly, as if she were in and out of the Pomeroy Street house several times a day. "Maybe I can take his mind off it a little. I always used to be able to make Scamp laugh."

Mike stared at her. Fragments flew into place.

"You were in love with him, weren't you?" Mike said.

Priss did not reply.

"You still are, aren't you, Priss? After all these years? After what he did, what he turned into?"

"Love is a policy, Mike," Priss Comfort said heavily. "It's not a feeling. Time you learned that."

The words had a strange resonance, as if they were an echo of something far away.

"J.W. said something like that a while ago," she said.

"I'm not surprised," Priss said. "J.W. formed his policies a long time back."

Mike left the little stone house and drove, not to the sanctuary of her room to telephone Bay Sewell, as she had planned, but, seemingly by remote control, to Sam Canaday's office. Lytton's main street was all but deserted as she parked the car in front of the peeling old building and got out. Only a town police car was moving, idling lazily through town like a planing hawk. Mike's skirt stuck to the back of her bare legs. It was very still and hot, and no time at all.

She went up the dusty wooden steps to the second floor, her soft espadrilles soundless on the dust-felted tread. The stairs and corridor smelt not unpleasantly of old linseed oil and time. She walked down the long, dim corridor. On either side, dark oak doors with square, white-frosted panes stood closed. The black-painted letters on most of them were flaking off, half gone. Mike supposed most businesses had moved to one of the new shopping and professional centers on the outskirts of town. The last door on the right, though closed like its neighbors, had newly painted black lettering: SAMUEL F. CANADAY, ATTORNEY AT LAW. The brass doorknob was brightly polished.

Mike put her hand up to rap on the glass, hesitated, and then pushed the door softly, and it swung open. The room was in darkness; the only light source was the bright tiger stripes that escaped from between the old-fashioned wooden venetian blinds and lay over the huge, empty mahogany desk in front of the arched double windows. The only sound was the familiar laboring of the air conditioner. At first Mike could see nothing in the old-smelling gloom, but then she saw that Sam Canaday was sitting at the desk with his head in his hands. His hair was bright in the dark room. On his face, through the laced, scarred fingers, she could see the gleam of wetness, but she did not know if it was tears or perspiration. The room, despite the air conditioner, was powerfully and thickly hot.

Mike stood in the doorway for what seemed a long moment, and then walked across the room and around his chair and put her arms around him from behind. He did not move, and then he covered her hands with one of his. She could feel the ridges of the scars against her fingers. She rested her chin briefly on the top of his head. His hair smelled of the sun's lingering dry heat.

"I'm sorry," Mike said presently.

"I'm sorry, too," Sam Canaday said.

He came by that evening, after her father finally woke from his long sleep, feeling better, though obviously weakened by the pain and the drugs. Sam pushed him in his chair out onto the porch and around to the wisteria bower and made them all a whiskey and water, and Mike stretched herself bonelessly on the canvas glider where she and Bay Sewell had first made love, all those weeks ago. It seemed, dimly, like years.

Leaning forward with his burnt hands on his knees, Sam told the old man that they had lost their fight. It was not a long account, and he told it clearly and sparely.

"Well," John Winship said. "What do you know? It was a good fight, though, Sam. Wasn't it a good fight, Mike?"

"The best, Daddy," Mike said. There was a huge, swollen lump in her throat. Her chest ached.

"It doesn't have to be over quite yet, Colonel," Sam said. "I can always appeal . . ."

John Winship waved his transparent hand. "No. Doesn't matter. The fight mattered, and I'm not ashamed of that, not one bit. No, sir. Let it go. Let it go. One thing, though . . . you aren't going to stop coming by here in the evening, are you? Got so I'm used to you. Used to her, too." He jerked his chin at Mike, but did not look at her.

"I'll come as long as you'll have me," Sam Canaday said.

"Mike'll be leaving us pretty soon, I guess," her father said, still not quite looking at her. "Go on back up north and write some more bleeding heart stuff . . ."

"I don't have any firm plans yet, Daddy," Mike said, surprising herself. She was grateful that the news about the homeplace did not seem to have devastated him as she had feared. It was a moment she had dreaded. She heard herself going on:

"I thought I might get serious about . . . you know, this book thing. I guess I could do that here as well as anywhere."

What am I *doing?* she thought.

"Oh, yeah," he said. "The book. Well, now. That would be something. I'd kind of like to see 'Winship' on a book. A book'll last longer than any of us. You gon' put me in that book?"

Sam shot Mike a look. She gave it back to him.

"Why not?" she said, turning to her father. "Shakespeare had Iago. Peck had a bad boy."

John Winship smiled, but he hid it behind his hand.

"Well, how long before they tear the son of a bitch down, Sam?" he said.

"Not any time soon, I don't think," Sam said. "They'll let me know, but I suspect it'll be a right long time yet."

"Long enough?"

"I'd say so, Colonel."

"Well, good," John Winship said.

TWENTY-EIGHT

After that, nothing was changed, and everything. All through August it seemed as though no conclusion had been reached on the homeplace, no struggle lost, no hearts broken, no great rent in the tapestry of days that Mike and John Winship and Sam Canaday had constructed. By tacit agreement, no one spoke of the declaration of taking and the ponderous legal machinery that must be grinding along its appointed path in the Fulton County Courthouse, twenty miles to the north. Mike had asked her father if he wanted to go on with the letters that were their morning routine; he had said he did not.

"Not for now, Micah. Maybe after a while. Think I'll take a little vacation and let you get on with that book thing. Don't want to be wearing the famous author out beating a dead horse."

"It's no trouble," she said. "And it wouldn't hurt to let everybody know what happened about the house. Maybe we can't change anything, but we might be able to help somebody else stop it happening to them. At least show the DOT up for what they are. I hate to see you giving up."

"Not giving up," he said. "Just taking a breather. I'll show the sons of bitches up when the time comes. Don't nag at me, Micah. Pour me some of that whiskey and get on out of here and let me watch my goddamn game shows. I know you hate 'em."

She poured out the whiskey and put the glass and the bottle on the table next to his wheelchair. He drank steadily all day and into the evenings now, and no one made a move to prevent it. Even DeeDee had stopped her railing after Dr. Gaddis had told her to let her father have his liquor in peace.

"It stops the pain better than anything we've found so far, Daisy," he had said when DeeDee called him in a blind rage after she had found Mike giving John Winship whiskey in the middle of the morning. "And that's keeping him alive. It's not the cancer that's going to kill him; his heart is going to go before that. It's pretty weak. Anything . . . bad pain, any kind of shock . . . could do it. Keep him calm and let him drink." And so DeeDee did, reluctantly. And for the moment, John Winship seemed better than he had all summer.

Priss was as good as her word. The day after Sam Canaday called with the news about the declaration of taking, she appeared in the kitchen of the Pomeroy Street house bearing a lemon cheese cake going plushy in the heat, and pulled a kitchen chair up to the table at which John Winship sat, and sat down herself, heavily.

"Well, Scamp, you look like you've been whupped through hell with a buzzard gut," she said, and he stared at her, loose-wattled like an old turkey, and then laughed aloud. It was by far the most robust sound Mike had heard him make in all the weeks she had been home. He laughed until the pallid tears ran on his shocking-white skull's face, and when he finally stopped, there was color in his cheeks. Priss grinned at him evilly. Her green eyes swam with unshed tears.

"Some kind of talk for a schoolteacher," John Winship said. "Always did have the meanest mouth in Fulton County on you. Look at you, old woman. You look like the hind axle of bad management yourself." His own eyes shone wetly and he blinked several times, turtlelike. He reached out slowly and covered Priss's hand with his splotched mummy's claw.

Sam Canaday, coming into the kitchen hours later in the hot twilight, found them still laughing together and talking as if twenty-odd years of bitter silence had never lain between them. John Winship was down near the bottom of the whiskey bottle and Priss and Mike had eaten more than half of the cake, and the kitchen of the Pomeroy Street house was, at that moment, a better place to be than it had ever been before Mike had gone away.

"About damn time, Colonel," Sam said matter-of-factly, and dropped a kiss on Priss's red head. He said nothing else about the reunion, but poured himself a drink and cut a slice of cake and settled down at the table with them.

"Mike," he said, nodding affably at her.

"Sam," she said.

She knew that he would say no more. The old distance and

formality was back between them, without the undercurrent of faintly admiring mockery that had been there at the first, and she knew that he would not stay long. Bay Sewell had said that he would drop by that evening, to try and cheer her father up, and Mike knew without knowing how she did that Sam Canaday would not be in this house again while there was a chance that he would meet Bayard Sewell here. Priss and John Winship looked keenly at the two of them and then at each other, but said nothing, and soon the rough, foolish talk spun on again like a river eddying around a rock. Sam did indeed leave before Bay arrived, but for a time the sunset kitchen was easy and comfortable and full of laughter, and Mike thought that forever after, when she heard the word "home," this was what she would think of.

After that, for a bright and seemingly endless span of days, Priss Comfort came every afternoon to the house, and Sam came in the evenings, and between the two of them, they seemed almost physically to hold John Winship's illness at bay. He sipped and nodded through the mornings in the kitchen, while Lavinia Lester pottered tidily about and Mike dozed and daydreamed and read in her room upstairs, but when the screened door banged in the afternoons and Priss came into the room, his palsied head came up and the color flooded back into his dead face, and life and vigor thrummed in the house like the beating of a great heart. The well-being lasted until Sam came and went, and then her father was often ready to be slipped into his bed by Mike and Priss like a drying feather, and was usually asleep before they turned off his lights. In those long, timeless days, he took very few pain pills and no sleeping tablets. Defeat and the ruin of old dreams seemed never to have happened. Nothing much at all seemed to have happened.

Nevertheless, things were different. Because Priss was there in the afternoons now, Mike could not meet Bayard Sewell in the upstairs bedroom, and both of them grew edged and sharpened and famished for each other. He came by once or twice to see her father after Sam and Priss had left, but John Winship was drifting far out on his whiskey sea and could not or did not respond to him, and Bay could not stay until the old man fell asleep so that he could take Mike up the dark stairs and slake himself at her body. Sally and the old nurse waited at home; Sally eddied now in a poisoned sea of her own. There were frantic, starved kisses in the darkening foyer, and frenzied hands on each other's body, and gasps and hot, wild words torn out of laboring chests, but there was for them no surcease and no release. Once, when John Winship slept through a morning of darkness and thunder and Lavinia Lester was at the dentist, he came hurriedly into the house and up the stairs and they took each other standing up in the upstairs hall, braced against the wall, silently and savagely and so quickly that they did not even remove their clothes, their ears straining even through their sobbing breath for any sound from the old man below. It was wrenching and emptying and awful, and he was gone in less than ten minutes, and they did not attempt it again. He became grim-faced and so tense that even a small noise would make him start, and Mike was consumed with a prickling restlessness that was more than sexual, and prowled the house through the empty hours. A relentless and ungovernable motor seemed to have started up within her, throbbing sturdily and steadily through the heat-jellied nights and days, and it neither roused her to any action nor left her any peace. It was not a return of the early summer's terror, but more a kind of pulsing waiting, a sense of slow and inexorable gathering. Something was growing, something was deepening, something was coming.

And yet, nothing did. Priss came and went, Sam came and was gone again, DeeDee trundled in and out, paler and damper and more distracted than Mike had ever seen her. She did not mention the terrible morning at the club; seemed, in fact, to have forgotten it in her concern for her father. For she was obsessed in those long, heavy days with John Winship. She came nearly every day, leaving a presumably chastened and biddable Duck to stay with his mother, and fussed and whimpered and fidgeted until Priss and Mike and sometimes John himself shooed her home again. She had reacted with tears and wails when Mike had told her about the Department of Transportation's ponderous victory over their father and had insisted on coming directly over to flutter at his side until he had exploded at her, and she had gone home in fresh tears. After that, she was on to Mike about him several times a day, either by telephone or in person, dropping in in the mornings before he was up or in the evenings after he had been put to bed.

"But how is he *really?*" she would say, and her voice would tremble on the edge of hysterics. "I know he's putting up a brave front, but how is he really, when he's by himself with just you?

266

Didn't it just about kill him? What does he say? Did he ever cry, or anything? Oh, God, poor Daddy, poor Daddy . . ."

"It's not a front," Mike would try to reassure her. "He's really fine. He took it wonderfully; we're surprised at how well. Of course he didn't cry. When did Daddy ever cry? He's accepted it better than the rest of us. He doesn't say anything at all about it; he seems to have almost forgotten it. Really, Dee, what on earth is *wrong* with you? You wanted this over. You'd think you'd done the black deed yourself, the way you're carrying on. You're upsetting him far more than the DOT with all this crying and hovering."

And DeeDee would take herself off, tear-stained and distraught, but she would call again, or come by again, and again she would say, fearfully, the tears standing in her blue eyes, "How is he, really?"

Mike had never seen her sister so agitated and finally she asked Bay Sewell if he could reassure her, as he seemed to have done after the debacle at the country club with Duck. He must have done so, because after that DeeDee did not come so often to the Pomeroy Street house, and she did not call, and the airless stasis of the suspended time between the end of the fight and the death of the homeplace dropped down again. August was totally stopped and still, an underwater place.

In the last week of the month, Sam Canaday learned that the Department of Transportation would move onto the homeplace the Tuesday after Labor Day with a bulldozer and crew. He told Mike and Priss and J.W. that evening, on the shadowy porch, before he came in to see John Winship, and he cautioned them to keep the news from him.

"Treat it as a normal day," he said. "Don't do anything different. Try not to think about it. Don't go down there yourselves. You don't want to see that. I'm not going. We'll tell him when it's over and cleaned up."

They agreed.

"But I really think he's made his peace with it," Mike said.

"Oh, sure," Sam said. "Like a death he can't prevent. But that doesn't mean he has to watch the execution."

Mike's heart lay heavy and stonelike within her for the rest of the days in that week. The heaviness damped, for a time, the prowling, prickling unease.

"It's like waiting for another death, a second one," she told Bayard Sewell on the phone that evening, after her father was in bed and everyone had gone. "In a way it's worse, because I know the date of this death. Bay, you mustn't let on to him. You know what Dr. Gaddis said about his heart, and a shock . . ."

"Jesus, Mike, what do you think I am?" he said. "God, poor John. It'll be better when it's all over. It really will. We can all . . . get on with things, see where we are, sort of. Make some plans. Mike . . . if I don't see you soon I think I'll go out of my mind."

"Me, too," she said miserably. "Oh, me too."

Three days later her father waked her in the night screaming hoarsely and terribly with the pain, and he screamed over and over again, monotonously and rhythmically, thrashing from side to side in the sweat-soaked bed, the cords of his gaunt old neck standing out, the bursting veins crawling like worms under the dead-white skin of his forehead, his eyes vacant and focused far away; screamed and screamed and clawed with his corpse's fingers at the agony-reddened air until the running feet and plunging needle of Dr. Gaddis hurled him fathoms deep into unconsciousness. Mike, dripping wet and shaking so that she could scarcely stand, cleaned his wasted, motionless old body of the excrement that it had ground itself in, and J.W. helped her put clean pajamas onto him and strip the fouled sheets. There was blood and mucus on the bedclothes as well as feces, and a ghastly, fetid, green-black stain that was like nothing she had ever seen before. Sam Canaday arrived after the doctor had come out of her father's room, and they all sat drinking the coffee that J.W. had made, not speaking. It was nearly four in the morning, but no one, not even the bonelessly slumped doctor, made a move to leave. No one broke the silence. There was, Mike knew, nothing now to say. They had come to an ending. Whatever it was she had felt coming was here.

"What now?" Sam Canaday said, finally. His voice was rusty and hoarse, as if it had not been used for a long time. "The hospital?"

"If you want to, Mike," Dr. Gaddis said, looking at her. "I can admit him in the morning. Maybe save you a good bit of work and grief. But they'll just give him more of what I've been giving him, and I can up the dosage as high as he can stand without killing him as well as they can. He might as well stay here, if you can take it. He'll need lots of nursing."

"I can take it," Mike said. "I don't want him to go to the hospital. I can look after him, Lavinia and I. But he can't stand anything like tonight again, and I can't either."

"He won't have that again," the doctor said. "That's one thing I can make sure of. I guess I should have upped that dosage before now. He was doing so well, though, and it seemed like he was enjoying those visits with Priss, so I wanted to let him stay lucid as long as he could. I can stop most of the pain, but he isn't going to know much from here on out."

"Do it," Mike said. "I'm not going to have him hurt like that. I don't want him aware that he's . . . not in control. Priss and I will be here when he *does* wake up and Sam, too . . ." She looked at him, and he nodded. His face was as still and white as that recent afternoon in the back hall, looking up at her . . .

"We'll all be here," he said. He turned to the doctor. "Is it . . . now? Is this going to take him out, like in the next few days?" Mike knew he was thinking of the bulldozers crawling insectlike onto the swept white yard around the homeplace, of the terrible mandrake scream of splintering wood. Better, maybe, if it were now . . .

"I don't have any idea," the doctor said. "Probably not. His heart's still hanging in there. It's amazing."

"Way to go, Colonel," Sam Canaday said softly.

John Winship did not wake up until the following afternoon. Mike and Sam had been sitting in silence for almost two hours, in kitchen chairs drawn up beside the old bed in the dark, monkish bedroom. The air conditioner pumped steadily, almost in rhythm with the pulse that beat shallowly in the parchment-yellow throat. Mike had slid almost into sleep, and she jerked awake when she heard her father's voice, sharp and birdlike and clear in the thrumming room, say, "Are you still working on your book, Micah? I don't want you to let that slide, whatever you do."

She looked up. He was staring at her, his eyes brilliant with something . . . fever, or some sort of importuning. It was a look she could not read.

"Yeah," Sam Canaday said, and the old jeering, sardonic note was back in his voice, under something that sounded like an anger born of grief. "You still holed up these hot afternoons with that book, Mike?"

Mike looked at him and felt the traitorous heat flood into her chest and neck and up into her face.

"Yes," she said. "I'm working on the book."

That night, aching with fatigue and stiff with a kind of promissory dread, she reached into the bottom of the suitcase she had stowed at the back of her closet on the morning after she had come home, and took out a fresh yellow legal pad. She pulled a felt-tip pen out of her desk drawer and uncapped it. She stared at the slick, lined yellow surface of the paper for a long moment, and then she wrote at the top of the first sheet, *Going Back*. After a moment, she added, *by Micah Winship*. Then, in a little rush, she wrote on the paper, "Two months ago, in the summer of my fortieth year, I came back for the first time in a quarter of a century to my father's house."

She stared at the words, flung in a strong, slanted backhand across the paper, for a little space of time, and then she dropped her face into her hands.

"Oh, God," Mike whispered to herself. "Oh, God."

And then she raised her head and began to write again, and she wrote and wrote, for a long time, far into the night.

TWENTY-NINE

"Don't go yet," Bayard Sewell said, reaching out and taking Mike's arm just above the elbow. His hand was cold, almost shockingly so, in the hot, dim room. His fingers were surprisingly hard on her flesh, biting deep. Mike lay back against the piled pillows and looked at him. She had thought he was asleep.

"I ought to look in on Daddy," she said. "We've been up here for nearly three hours. It's been four since he got his last pills."

"I looked in on him when I came in," he said. "He was cutting Z's like there was no tomorrow. Relax, Mike. You're strung as tight as a bow. He's not going to wake up. You gave him a double dose, didn't you?"

She nodded, feeling somehow guilty, though the doctor had told her that two pills, or even three, would not be amiss if her father needed them. They would, he had said, only make him sleep more deeply and longer. Bay Sewell had asked her to do it when he had told her that he wanted to come to her that afternoon, and she had agreed with no hesitation. It had been almost a month since they had made love, or even been alone together. And on this of all days, she needed him with a pain that was deeply and pungently physical.

"I just cannot wait any longer," he had said earlier in the Labor Day weekend just past. "And I want to be with you on the day that they . . . take the house. I want to be in the house with John, just in case. Can't you persuade Priss and Canaday to back off just that one day? And can't you give your dad a little something extra to make sure he sleeps through? It would be better if he just slept the day away, Mike. That way there'd be no chance at all he'd find out. We can tell him when it's over."

"Sam was going to do that anyway," Mike said.

Bay scowled, but said only, "Well, then. Can you fix it?"

"Oh, yes," she had breathed in relief and anticipation. "I'll do it right away. Bay, I'm so glad. I didn't know how I was going to get through that day."

"Do you all mind if it's just Daddy and me next Tuesday?" Mike asked Sam and Priss on the Sunday before the bulldozers were scheduled to destroy the homeplace. "I'm going to give him an extra pill and let him sleep through it all, and I'd just as soon be by myself. We can meet for supper and decide then if he's up to hearing about it."

"If that's what you want to do," Priss said, frowning a little. "I don't like the idea of doping Scamp to the eyebrows, though. It's as if we were giving belladonna to a fussy baby."

It was so like that that Mike flushed and averted her eyes. "I just don't think I can sit in that room by his bed in some ghastly deathwatch for the homeplace," she said, and it was true. "I used to think he could read my thoughts, and I'm still not sure he can't."

"You *are* a pretty bad liar," Priss said. "All right, if you'll promise you won't sit around moping, and you'll call me if you get broody."

"Sam?" Mike said. "Is it okay with you not to be here?" She thought of the tumbled bed that waited for her upstairs and could not meet his eyes, but she had to make sure he would not come to the house.

He nodded, but said nothing. He did not look at her either. Mike thought that he looked almost ill; gray-faced under the tan, and much older. Soon after that he went in and said good night to John Winship, and left, and Priss followed him. She did not go in to see John.

"I'll be here whenever he's awake, if he wants me," she had told Mike after the terrible attack of pain, when the doctor increased the sedatives and painkillers so drastically. "But I'm not going in there and stare at him while he's knocked out. Scamp sets great store by his dignity. He'd never forgive me."

"He has to have the medicine," Mike said pleadingly. The implied criticism stung, and she herself hated keeping her father in the eerie twilight sleep in which he had lived for the past few days. "You didn't hear him screaming; you didn't see him. He can't go through that again."

"I know he can't," Priss said, and tears stood again in her clear green eyes. "And I can't look at him drugged up. I'll see him when he surfaces."

And he did surface, once or twice a day, usually in the early morning and again toward evening. When he did, he was peaceful and lucid and actually smiled at them, a very different smile from the fierce rictus that Mike had seen since she had returned home. It was almost a gentle smile, if skewed, and a totally knowing and full-dimensioned one. There was no question but that he was fully with them at those times, and free, now at the last, from the rage and tension that had ridden him, furylike, for so long. He was, in those moments, a man Mike did not know; had never known, and she was not sure how to deal with him.

He had been awake when she took in his two o'clock medicine earlier, and had been lying peacefully, listening to his television set but not looking at it, regarding the ceiling of the curtained room with interest. Mike had sent Lavinia Lester home early and brought a glass of chocolate milk with the pills. It was one of the few things John Winship could still tolerate. He was growing thinner and more transparent daily; it seemed impossible that life could pulse so stubbornly in his wasted body. But his voice was strong and his color distinctly visible, if faint.

"Two pills?" he said.

"Can you manage two?" Mike said, turning down the volume on the television set. "Lavinia's gone for the day, and Sam and Priss aren't coming until after supper. I thought you might like a chance to get some extra sleep."

"Fine, if you'll get some, too," he said. "You look tired. I'm afraid it's been hard on you, baby-sitting me."

"Not a bit of it," Mike said. For some reason a great knot of aching, unshed tears had gathered in her chest, just at the base of her throat, and it was difficult to speak. He seemed, there in the monastic white bed, hardly even to make a rise in the covers. He was very still. She could actually see the light through his old, curled hands. She remembered that when she was a small child, his forearms had seemed to her as strong and knotted as the limbs of a tree. She adjusted the curtains, closed the venetian blinds, and stopped to raise his head so that he could swallow the pills.

"Just leave 'em," he said. "I'll take 'em directly. I sort of want to hear the end of *Perry Mason*. If Sam Canaday was that good a lawyer he'd be rich."

Mike smiled around the salty knot and walked to the door of the room.

"You take them after the program is over, though," she said.

"I will," he said. And then, "Micah?"

"Yes?"

"You've turned out to be a real pretty girl. Real pretty girl. Ought to have told you before," he said.

"Thank you, Daddy," Mike said, and fled up the stairs to her bedroom before the tears could spill over her bottom lashes. But once there she did not cry; could not.

Bayard Sewell had come an hour later, at three, rapping softly at her door and coming quietly into the room on the soft soles of his Topsiders when she called out, "Come in." She wore a simple white column of charmeuse night dress that he especially liked, and had brushed her hair to drifting gilt, and sprayed on a gust of the Giorgio that he had brought her from Boston. She did not like the musky, insinuating perfume, but he claimed that it was a powerful aphrodisiac, and it had become a sort of joking symbol between them. Whenever Mike wore it, she meant to be taken hard and with roughness.

He had smiled today when he smelled it and had laid her back with haste and hard hands and had gone quickly into her, without the teasing, indolent ritual of foreplay that they sometimes prolonged almost past endurance, and she had arched her back and set her hips in preparation for him, but almost immediately she had known it was going to be no good. She was tight and dry, and after the first great swollen thrust or two he went suddenly flaccid and spilled out of her. They tried it again, intent and sweating, but he could not stay erect. Finally, flushed and disheveled from laboring under him, she rolled aside and hugged him to her and buried her face in his damp neck.

"Truce, darling," she said. "It's just not the day for it."

His face was dark with blood; he looked almost angry.

"That's never happened to me before," he said tightly.

"Well, it certainly doesn't matter to me," she said. "And it's no wonder, both of us lying here and knowing what's going on down at the homeplace. Do you think that it's . . . you know, down yet?"

"I don't know," he said. "If it's not, it will be soon."

"What will they do with the . . ." She had been going to say "remains," and changed the word to "wreckage."

"Burn it, probably," he said. "Those old places go up like tinder. It's the cleanest and fastest thing. Don't want to leave debris lying around indefinitely."

"No," Mike said, shivering involuntarily. "That would be awful."

She thought he would leave after his accustomed hour, but he did not.

"I've cleared the deck for the rest of the afternoon," he said "I meant it when I said I wanted to be with you and John." But he did not seem glad to be with her in the humming, time-stopped room. He was abrupt, edgy, harrowed-looking, and yet there was a kind of wildfire exhilaration to him, too, that reminded her of the first night they had made love on the old glider in the wisteria arbor, a kind of interior humming. He could not seem to keep still.

"Would you like something to eat?" she said inanely, finally, after he had gotten up off the bed and prowled to the window and lifted the blind for the third time, looking out at the hot, still afternoon. He grinned sheepishly and boyishly, and came back to the bed.

"I just can't get it out of my mind," he said. "I almost wish I'd gone down there and watched."

"I know. It's sort of like letting a relative die alone, isn't it?" Mike said. "I've been in a terrible state all day."

He looked at her keenly, his blue eyes almost white in the semidark.

"You went over to the other side there at the end, didn't you?" he said.

"Not really," Mike said. "I could always see the wisdom in just letting the damned old thing go. But it's been so awful to watch him go through it . . ."

"I know. I wish it could have been prevented. But it's going to be better now, Mike, for everybody. You just don't know. And with the house gone, the land will be the saving of DeeDee. You want that for her, don't you? That edge?"

"But after he's gone, Bay! Not now! He's not dead yet!" Her voice rose shrilly, and she dropped it. "Don't bury him yet."

"I didn't mean that," he said. "You know I didn't mean that."

After a time he slept. Mike lay on her back, listening to the drone of the air conditioner, which after a time began to sound like a long and gentle rain. She looked over at him. Even in sleep, he was not relaxed; a small tic jumped, rodentlike, in his eyelid, and his mouth twitched occasionally. He looked, as ever, almost ludicrously handsome in the gloom, but, like Sam Canaday, older on this day, tired. She wondered if Sam sat silently at the empty desk in the darkened office, or if he had made business for himself in the city and gone away for the space of the day. She wondered if DeeDee and Duck had somehow found out about the demolition of the homeplace and gone to watch it. She hoped not; she knew that Sam had not told them, and she had not. She did not, somehow, like to think of them there in the hot afternoon, watching the old house come to its knees. She wriggled restlessly in the bed and then lay still so as not to wake Bay Sewell. The sweat had dried on her body, and she felt sheeted with cold stickiness. She moved again, the heaviness in her chest almost stopping her breath. She wished for night, an end to this endless day. This day divided time. After it, she felt that a great gear would creak rustily and ponderously into place and grind forward, and some huge business, some large thing, would be set into implacable motion. She did not know what. Whatever, the lovely, iridescent, motionless bubble of the summer would be gone and another sort of life would resume itself. She did not feel ready to move with it.

Mike got up and padded into the bathroom and looked at herself in the greenish, underwater light of the mirror. She remembered Priss's words at the beginning of the summer: "You look about fourteen. An Ethiopian fourteen." She did not look fourteen now; was a child no longer, but inalterably a woman, with a woman's lined face and used eyes.

"Hello," Mike whispered to the green, underwater woman.

She got back onto the bed and drew the sheet up over her and, finally, drifted into a fugue of half-sleep. Rachel's face swam before her, Rachel when she was younger, about six or seven, laughing in her dark delight. In half-sleep, Mike smiled too.

The knocking ripped her awake so suddenly she was on her feet in the middle of the room before she even came to herself. It seemed to have been going on forever, insistent, frantic. Mike went suddenly and mindlessly cold with fear.

"Who is it?" she called, through stiff, prickling lips.

"It's J.W., Mike." His voice came as distinctly through the heavy, locked door as if he stood in the room. "Open up. I got to talk to you."

"Jesus Christ," Bayard Sewell hissed from behind her, leaping out of the bed. "Keep him out of here! Don't open that door!"

He scrambled for his clothes, swept them up from the floor beside his bed, and bolted into the bathroom, shutting the door behind him. Mike heard the scrape of the big, ornate iron key in the lock.

"What's the matter, J.W.?" she called, wanting with all her heart not to hear.

"It's Mr. John," he called back. "He not in the house. He gone!"

"Gone," Mike repeated mindlessly. "Gone? Where could he go?"

J.W. knocked again, furiously.

"Mike, befo' God, you come out of there or I'm gon' knock this do' down! I think you daddy's foun' out about the house, and got hisse'f down there somehow. The car gone from the garage, and his wheelchair layin' beside it."

"Oh, dear Jesus in heaven," Mike breathed, leaden and motionless with the cold fear. "Oh, dearest God! I'll be right there, J.W.!"

She skinned into her crumpled blue jeans and a T-shirt and jerked the door open so hard that it banged back against the wall. She was halfway down the stairs, J.W. sprinting before her, before she realized that she had put on no shoes, and that Bayard Sewell was calling to her from behind the locked bathroom door, over and over: "Mike! Mike! Come back here! Mike!" Disregarding both, she plunged down into the foyer. From the look of the sun, it must be around six; nothing stirred either inside the house or outside it. Mike ran first, stupidly, to her father's room. It was as J.W. Cromie had said. The bed was empty, the sheets and thin summer blanket drawn neatly up. The two pills lay on the bedside table, alongside the untouched chocolate milk. Mike moaned in her throat without knowing that she did. Whirling, she ran back into the hall, and J.W. came to meet her, gasping for breath. He was actually ashen.

"Sam," Mike said, her voice queer and small and whistling. "Get Sam, J.W. Call Sam." She did not think of Bay Sewell, still upstairs in his locked fastness, though his nimble little BMW stood just around the corner on the next street. Sam, if she could just reach Sam . . .

"He on his way," J.W. said. "I called him first thing. Did you hear anything, Mike? Mr. John stirrin' aroun', or anything?"

"No," she whispered. "I've . . . I was asleep. I left pills for him; I thought he'd be dead to the world . . ."

"He ain't take the pills," J.W. said.

"I know," she said. Her breath still would not come. "Oh, God, Sam, where *are* you!"

He wheeled into the driveway of the Pomeroy Street house then, brakes squealing, and was out of the car almost before it stopped rolling. The motor still ran.

"Get in," he said, and his face and voice were very calm and even, but his words were bitten off short. "Why in God's name weren't you with him, Mike? I thought you said you were going to give him an extra dose of medication . . ."

"I left it for him," she breathed. "He didn't take it. He said he would, but he didn't. I . . . I went to sleep . . ."

"I hope you had a good nap," he said. "J.W., you've got no idea how long he's been gone?"

"Naw," J.W. said. "I seen the wheelchair turned over in the garage and the car gone when I come in 'bout ten minutes ago. I called you right off." He got into the backseat of the Toyota. Mike sagged bonelessly against the fender. She could not seem to move her arms and legs.

"Get in the car, Mike!" Sam Canaday shouted, and she did, stumbling. He slammed it into gear and spun it out into the street and headed it south, toward the highway.

"I guess you didn't hear anything while you were . . . napping," he said, his eyes slits against the westering sun. "He must have made quite a racket, getting that wheelchair out of the house. Not to mention crawling into the car and starting it. It must have taken him hours."

"No," she said. "The air conditioner was on high. I had no idea he could . . . how could he possibly *do* that? For that matter, how could he have known it was today? I don't see how . . ."

"Don't you?" Sam said. "I see how. God knows what it must have cost him to get to that car, but he did it. He did it."

"You're sure that's where he is . . ."

"Oh, God, Mike, where in hell else would he be? Of course that's where he is! God damn us all!"

Time was playing tricks on her. One moment it telescoped upon itself and rushed backward, so that it seemed only a breath's time since she had held out her arms to Bayard Sewell in the bedroom, clad in white silk charmeuse. The next, it spun itself out into infinity, so that the distance between Lytton's two stoplights, in the center of town, seemed frozen and enormous. The light was strange, too; the town seemed to lie in a flood of impossibly bright, shadowless radiance. And sound had stopped: the normal 6:00 P.M. street life of a small town went on as if on a movie screen with the sound off; Mike felt that no one could see the car, or her and Sam and J.W. inside it. The interior of the car was very hot. A fly buzzed and bumbled frantically at the windows, seeking escape. Mike watched it.

"Did you know that a fly flying around inside an airplane going six hundred miles an hour is a perfect example of Einstein's theory of relativity?" she said.

Sam shot a look at her, and then reached over and laid a scar-webbed hand over hers, clenched and icy in her lap.

"I want you to stay in the car when we get there," he said.

"You go to hell," she said back, and he did not speak again.

They saw the wreckage from the road. Where the familiar bulk of the house had stood against sunsets for the entirety of Mike's life and long before, now a maimed and alien silhouette crouched. It was almost exactly half a house; the front two rooms and roof still stood as they had, under the great pecan and walnut trees, and the central chimney still clawed skyward, but the back half of the house, the back porch and kitchen and bedrooms and the well house, were gone. The empty air seemed to shimmer where they had stood. A mound of forlorn and perfunctory rubble lay where the back rooms had been; brick and plaster and mortar and wood and shingles spilled out like entrails into the swept yard that had been Daisy Winship's day-to-day task and pride. White dust and denser, rusted red effluvia lay in the still air in planes, like geological strata. A small knot of men in overalls and billed caps stood watching as another man maneuvered a great bucking, orange-jawed backhoe into position alongside the remaining walls and chimney. It seemed to paw and butt and nose at the mass of whitened rubble like a great, mutated beast from a terrible, younger age, crouching over the corpse of its prey. There was no sound except the strangely trivial buzzing and snarling of the backhoe. The old Cadillac was nowhere in sight.

"Oh, Christ, maybe he's *not* here . . ." Sam's voice, like hers, had no force behind it.

"Go down to where the cedars start," Mike said. The dread in her chest was so cold and heavy that she could not even feel her heart beating under it. She knew with a crystalline prescience that the car would be there, hidden from the sight of the men with the backhoe and passersby on the highway beyond.

It was. The door on the driver's side sagged open, and a dreadful snail's track scored the dust in the alleyway between the cedars, running like an open wound all the way from the car to the house. There were no footprints, just the track in the pink dust. He must have dragged himself with his hands and forearms. No one who did not know about the cedar alley would have seen him or known that he was there.

Mike was out of the car before Sam stopped it, running in her bare feet toward the wreckage of the house. She seemed to be running in slow motion and silence, as in a nightmare. She heard a man's voice crying, "Lady, you can't go in there; it ain't safe!" and Sam Canaday's voice shouting, "Stop that goddamned thing! Mike, come back here! Back it up, you motherfuckers, there's a man in there!"

"The shit you say!" shouted the man on the backhoe, but the noise of its great jaws stopped, and utter silence fell. In it, Mike could hear the slide and scuffle of her bare feet in the rubble, but she felt nothing. Everything was white and thick with plaster dust, and the nearest edge of rubble, where the well house had stood, was overspread with a tangle of mutilated red roses, like blood, or a pall on a coffin. Mike ripped them aside, not feeling the thorns tearing her hands and legs and feet, and waded into the body of the rubble. She could not see for the planes of dust, but she seemed to know what she sought. Her hands and feet took her of themselves.

She found him lying under a great fallen beam, the central ridge beam of the homeplace, where his boyhood bedroom cubicle had been. He could not have been seen from the road or from where the men and their machine had positioned themselves. A partially collapsed wall shielded him, and she knelt beside him, behind it. He was totally white with dust, and still, and lay as formally posed as an effigy on a crusader's tomb, on his back, his hands folded almost primly over the beam that had crushed his chest. Mike thought that he was dead, but then she saw the faint rise and fall of his chest, and he opened his eyes. They were clear and free of pain, the lucent gray of rain, fully focused and spilling a kind of opalescent light. Incredibly, he smiled. A thin red line of blood crept from the down-drawn corner of his mouth, cutting like a scarlet thread through the thick whiteness. His white lips moved almost imperceptibly. Mike leaned down over him to hear. The air around her face vibrated with shock and stillness; plaster dust gritted in her eyes and mouth, and choked in her throat.

"Lift . . . up," John Winship whispered. His voice was barely audible and high, like that of a very sleepy young child. Mike plunged her hands into the rubble under his head to lift it, and felt a stinging in her palm. A murderously bright strip of sheared tin had bitten deep into it; she looked incuriously at the blood that flowed over her wrist onto her father's face and down onto the rubble under it, to soak finally into the earth beneath. She felt, after the first sting, no pain. But her blood on her father's cheek, making a dark red paste of the dust there, bothered her, and she tried to wipe it off with the edge of her other hand.

"Cut . . . yourself," he wheezed. "Sorry." The blood bubbled in the corner of his mouth.

"It's okay, Daddy," Mike said. "It's nothing."

"You . . . wrong," he said, very faintly. "It's everything."

She looked down at her blood, soaking through the plaster and into the earth of the homeplace, and she felt again the great salt swelling of the tears that had lodged in her chest earlier in this interminable day. But still they did not fall. Mike felt a kind of remoteness, as if she were watching herself through the wrong end of a telescope, and the peace of distance. She watched his chest rise and fall, rise and fall. She was aware of someone standing behind her, and she heard, dimly, running feet and a voice calling for an ambulance, but they did not seem to penetrate the stillness that enclosed her and John Winship. He was quiet for a time, and she did not move, kneeling there beside him. Then he spoke again, his voice a little stronger.

"Who does she look like? Your dau . . . this Rachel of yours?"

"Your granddaughter, you mean?" Mike said. "She looks like me. And like you, Daddy. She looks just like you."

He closed his eyes, and then they opened again, and lifted to the sky where the roof of the homeplace had stood for 135 years, and then moved to Mike's face. Then they closed once more. Mike was motionless, scarcely breathing.

"I feel sorry for her, then," John Winship said, and the breath went out of his throat in a long sigh, and his chest did not rise again.

Behind her, Mike heard the shrunken, painful man's sobs of J.W. Cromie, and felt hands on her shoulders, and knew they were Sam Canaday's. He knelt beside her in the white rubble, saying nothing, only kneeling there with his hands touching her. Mike crouched in what was left of John Winship's homeplace and finally she cried. She dropped her head into her bloody hands and cried for all the lost things in the world, and for that first and last long love.

THIRTY

Later in her life, when Mike dealt with other deaths in other places, she would reflect on the sheer effortlessness of her father's. Not his dying, but all that came after. In small towns such as Lytton, especially in the South, the machinery of death goes into operation silently and swiftly, as if oiled. It is like an intricate insect ballet, in a way; some ancient and immutable ritual of ants or beetles. From the moment that John Winship's life rode out on his last breath, Lytton swung into action. Not a foot was put wrong; not a beat missed. Mike was awed and grateful for the clockwork pageantry, for it could, and did, operate totally without her. For the first six hours that her father was gone from the world, she could not stop crying.

Downstairs, the telephone rang and was answered, the screened door twanged open and shut again, soft, grave footsteps came and went, florists' vans and cars and bicycles appeared in the driveway and idled quietly out again, the death certificate and coffin were dealt with, preachers and undertakers and casseroles and cakes flowed into the house on Pomeroy Street.

All the while, in her darkened bedroom upstairs, Mike cried.

Sam Canaday had brought her home in the Toyota, leaving J.W. to wait for the ambulance and the police, driving away from the silent knot of workmen and the foreman, who was even then explaining his blamelessness to his chief. She had sobbed quietly and steadily all the way home, and he had not attempted to comfort her or stop her tears, except to keep one hand on her shoulder as he drove. He led her through the dim, still house and upstairs into the bathroom, where he sat her down on the edge of the old clawfooted tub and washed the white plaster dust from her hands and feet and face. Some of the scratches and cuts went deep, and the cut in her palm gaped with white lips, but she did not flinch at the hot water, or when he poured peroxide into her hand and bound it with brittle yellow gauze that he found in the medicine cabinet. She said nothing, only sobbed monotonously, and he did not speak, either. He walked her back into her bedroom and sat her down on the bed and brushed the plaster dust from her tangled hair as best he could, with the brush he found on her dresser. Then he said, "Hold up your arms, Mike," and she did, obediently, and he pulled the filthy T-shirt over her head, and gently and slowly drew the blue jeans down over her hips. Mike wore no underwear. The tepid breath of the still-laboring air conditioner washed over her naked body, and she looked up at Sam Canaday, as if seeing him for the first time that afternoon. She stared at him for a long time, seeing the white dust in his light hair and eyebrows, and the streaks on his cheeks, where his own tears had coursed and dried. There were no tears now in the light green eyes. He stared back at her.

"You have a beautiful body," he said softly. "Like a greyhound, or a willow tree. Get into bed now, and let me cover you. I'll stay with you until Priss comes."

As if motorized, Mike lifted her arms and put them around his neck. She pressed her body hard against his, feeling the triphammer of his heart and the tensing of the muscles of his arms and neck. She buried her face in the hollow where his neck and shoulder met, smelling the heat of the sun and the plaster dust and the drying sweat of him, and let her tears run hot against his skin. She pulled at him, tugged, pulling him down over her in the bed.

"Get in bed with me, Sam," she sobbed. "Get in with me."

He held her for a moment, very lightly, and then he removed her arms, one by one, and stood up.

"Not yet, Mike," he whispered. "And not in this room, ever."

He picked up the white night dress from the floor where she had dropped it three hours and an eternity before, and she let him slip it over her arms and head, weeping quietly as he did.

Priss came then, grim-faced and dry-eyed, and sat down on the side of the bed. She had a glass of water in her hand and two small red and gray capsules.

"Dalmane," she said. "I want you to take them both. Knock you right out, and you won't have a hangover when you wake up. Go on and do your crying, Mike; you need to cry, and you can cry between naps. But when you do get up, you're going to have to get on with it. I've just been over to tell DeeDee, and we had to call the doctor for her. She went completely to pieces; I thought she was going to shriek that godawful little shack down. Gaddis gave her a hypodermic that should put her out until tomorrow, and I want us to have some decisions made by then. You'll have to make them. This'll give you about five hours' edge. I'll be downstairs when you need me."

Mike sat up and pushed her hair out of her eyes and looked at Priss, still crying.

"He crawled all the way down that goddamned horrible cedar alley and just lay down in the little room where his bed had been, Priss," she hiccuped. "He just lay there and waited to die. And I didn't stop him. I didn't even hear him!"

"Shhh," Priss Comfort said. "He did just what he wanted to do. Scamp always did. He went out of this world in the exact same place he came into it, and it was the place he loved best on this earth. I'm glad you didn't stop him, Mike. After that last pain, there wasn't anything but more of the same waiting for him. He knew that. Be glad he could choose his own death. Most of us can't."

"But how did he *know!* I need to understand how he *knew!*"

"Scamp would know," said Priss.

Mike turned her face into the pillow and sobbed harder. She wondered dimly where all the tears were coming from. It seemed impossible for her thin body to hold so many tears. Presently, not knowing when she did, she drifted into sleep. Priss Comfort looked at Sam Canaday and nodded as if in satisfaction, and they left the bedroom, closing the door behind them.

Downstairs, Priss set up her command post in John Winship's kitchen. She did not weep, then or ever. She dispatched J.W. Cromie, his yellow face streaked with silver grief tracks through the scrim of dust, to fetch Lavinia Lester and take her over to DeeDee Wingo's house, so that she would not sleep her despairing sleep alone. The mad old woman in the tiny back bedroom could not help her, and Duck Wingo had appeared in the Winship kitchen, obsequious and bursting-faced with important grief, and no hints could budge him home. Finally, glaring at him over her shoulder, Priss went into John Winship's bedroom and stayed for a while and came out with the clothes she had selected for him to be buried in. Her old hawk's face was serene as she went about the business of death, but her hands lingered over the clothes. Then she handed them briskly to Duck and waved him off to the funeral home.

"And then go on back home and stay with your wife," she said. "There's nothing for you to do here. Save that long face for the living."

Duck went without an argument. He had always been in awe of Priss.

At ten that evening, Bayard Sewell came in, white-faced and stricken. "May I go see Mike for a minute?" he said deferentially to Priss, who nodded. He gave J.W.'s shoulder a little punch and went lightly up the stairs to Mike's bedroom. J.W., eating a late supper of chicken and congealed salad from the Methodist Church Altar Guild with Priss, looked impassively after him. Priss did not lift her eyes from her plate.

Mike was drifting half-awake when Bay came into the room. She smiled groggily at him, but did not speak and did not sit up. He sat down on the side of the bed and took her hand. Presently he said, "I'd have been here sooner, but I just heard. Oh, Christ, if I'd only gone with you . . ."

"You couldn't have done anything," Mike whispered. Her voice was scratched and husky in her swollen throat.

"I could have looked harder at him when I came in this afternoon," he said. "I thought he was sleeping, but he had his back to me, and I didn't go around to make sure." He rubbed his eyes hard with his thumb and middle finger. "I must have been a charming sight, bolting for safety like a skinned rabbit when J.W. knocked. I wish you had never seen that. I wish you could put it right out of your mind, somehow."

She shook her head wearily; she had forgotten entirely that he had fled naked into the bathroom when he had heard J.W. Cromie at the door. It did not matter; it seemed to have happened years ago, to two other people entirely.

"It doesn't make any difference, Bay," she said.

"What can I say to you that will help?"

"Nothing," she said, feeling the tears pushing again at her nose and eyelids. "Just maybe leave me by myself for a little while longer. I thought I was cried out, but I guess I'm not. I don't like to have people around me when I cry."

"You never used to cry," he said, smiling slightly. He touched the skin of her forehead very lightly, under the tangle of ashen hair. "Are you sure you don't want me to stay? I have a great shoulder for crying."

She considered, and found that she did not.

"I can't do it right with you watching," she said, trying to smile at him around the tears that were already spilling down her cheeks and into the corners of her mouth. "I'll see you in the morning, okay? Will you be here in the morning?"

"You bet I will," he said, rising from the bed. "In the morning and a lot of other mornings."

And he left her in the darkness, weeping again, feeling acutely and hopelessly the void in the world where John Winship was not.

Two hours later, just after midnight, Mike stopped crying and sat up and turned on the bedside lamp. She knew, somehow, that she was done for now with tears. She felt hollowed and light-headed; her scratched and cut bare feet felt as though they skimmed inches above the carpet when she walked. She opened the closet door and reached in for something to put on. She saw the neat, spare ranks of her clothes there like hanged women: strange women whose crimes she did not know. They looked, in this musted childhood room, precious and overstylized and sybaritically fragile. The shoes in tidy rows on the floor looked too narrow, too fine-drawn, too expensive. The enormous Gucci tote sat on the closet shelf. Even ten years ago it had been expensive; today it would cost a fortune. The labels in the clothes read New York, Milan, London, Paris. Mike made an involuntary mouth of distaste. She did not remember the thin, crisp, smart New York woman who had bought those clothes, worn those shoes, carried that bag. She walked over to the bureau and studied the small silver-framed photo of Rachel that went with her wherever she went, taken three years before on an afternoon when they had been out sailing with Derek Blessing off Montauk. Rachel wore enormous black sunglasses and a terry sweatband around her dark, flying hair, and her braces dazzled in the sun. She looked, in the photograph, almost as old as Mike, and nothing at all like her. I lied to you, Daddy, Mike thought. She doesn't look a thing in the world like you, or me, either. She wondered, suddenly and oddly, if Rachel would one day weep for Richard's death as her mother had done for John Winship's. I suppose she will, thought Mike, but I can't imagine it.

Downstairs, the kitchen light was on, but there was no sign of Priss. Mike thought that perhaps she had gone home after all, and rummaged in the refrigerator for something to eat. She did not feel hungry, but she knew that the light-headedness meant physical emptiness, and that she would need what strength she could muster during the next few days. She felt a great, dead fatigue at the thought of them.

"Mike? Is that you?" Priss came out of John Winship's bedroom in a nightgown and old cotton flannel robe. She wore improbable pink satin mules on her feet. She held a paperback book in her hand.

"Were you asleep? I'm sorry I waked you," Mike said. "I guess I'm hungry."

"I hope you are. There's already enough here for an army; I hate to think what that refrigerator's going to look like tomorrow. Scamp knew a lot of people, and they all think they're cooks. No, I wasn't asleep. I was just sitting there thinking and reading some."

"In Daddy's room? It's an awful room. There are much better bedrooms upstairs. Let me fix one for you . . ."

"No. I don't want another room," Priss said. "Somehow that hidey-hole feels like the only place I want to be." She smiled. "Do you know what your dad was reading?"

"No. What?"

Priss held out the paperback. "Mary Roberts Rinehart. *The Circular Staircase.* Can you imagine?"

"No," Mike said, starting to laugh, and then feeling the laughter skewing over into the hated, monotonous tears once more. "Oh, Priss. Oh, shit."

"I know," Priss Comfort said.

Finally, after Mike had eaten a ham sandwich and they had both had coffee, they settled down on the porch under the wisteria arbor, and there they stayed the night. Mike slept, when she did, on the old glider. Whenever she opened her eyes, she saw Priss's bulk in the old wicker rocking chair, rocking, rocking. Once or twice she saw the light-struck gleam of Priss's green eyes. When the dawn crept in all gray and began to pinken in the east, and the first of the sleepy birds began to stir and call faintly in the still-dark trees, Mike sat up. She saw that Priss was watching her peacefully, still rocking.

"I haven't done this since I was about eight," Mike said, stretching. "I remember that I begged and teased and pleaded to be allowed to sleep out on the porch, and finally one night Daddy got tired of it and let me. But he made me promise that I'd stay out here all night, and not come running back in the house scared. He even locked the door so I couldn't."

"Was it as much fun as you thought it would be?" Priss said.

"No," Mike said. "It wasn't fun at all. He was right. I was scared to death."

DeeDee and Duck did not appear until midafternoon. DeeDee came into the living room, where Priss and Mike had been receiving visitors all day, but which was for the moment, mercifully, empty, leaning on Duck's arm and shuffling as though she were a very old woman. Even though she knew from Priss that DeeDee had taken their father's death badly, Mike was profoundly shocked at her sister's appearance. Her face was the white of old tallow, and she wore no lipstick or eye makeup or blusher, so that all of her flesh and skin that was not covered by her clothing was the same spoiled, ailing white. Her blue eyes were puffed almost shut, and her little tilted nose was red and raw at its roots, giving her more than ever the look of a dolorous piglet. Her black hair straggled out of its ponytail and over her massive shoulders, and when she stopped in the middle of the faded Bokhara rug, she swayed on her little fat feet like a squat tree in a gale. Duck attended her solemnly, a deferential consort to a great, grieving queen.

"We just went and saw Daddy," she said, in a bruised little voice, to no one in particular. "He looks wonderful. So natural, like he had just dropped off asleep. I kissed him good-bye, and he didn't feel a bit cold. They said you hadn't been yet, Mikie, so I signed your name until you can get on down there. You ought to go on as soon as you change. There are just *hundreds* of people coming by to see him, and none of the family is in there with him. It doesn't look right."

"I'm not going down there and sit beside my father's coffin and grin at people who come to stare at him." Mike was honestly outraged. "People who want to see if they can tell where the beam mashed him. It's bad enough that we had to leave the coffin open . . ."

"Those people are my friends and my father's friends," DeeDee squealed. "Those people are old Lytton! And if you want them all talking about you because you won't even go and sit beside your own father *in his coffin,* when he is lying there *dead . . .*"

"Dee," Duck said warningly. He pressed her hand and patted her great, hamlike upper arm, and she jerked away from him. "Don't pretend you care, Duck Wingo!" she shrilled. Tears ran from her eyes and mucus bubbled in her little nose. She was clearly on the very ragged edge, and Mike felt the old, grudging contrition. DeeDee, the favored one, the pretty, adored little womanchild of the dead father . . .

"I'll go in a little while, Dee," she said, and her sister nodded, wordless in her tears.

It was a long afternoon. People came in quiet, steady streams, talking in low voices, shaking hands solemnly with Duck, hovering over DeeDee, who wept afresh at each greeting and embrace. They all spoke to Mike, who sat opposite DeeDee on her mother's little loveseat with Priss, and a few hugged her perfunctorily, but they were all brief and formal, and soon moved away again. To them all, Mike nodded politely, dry-eyed, and murmured her thanks. The hams and casseroles and plates of potato salad and fried chicken, the congealed salads and cakes and cookies, overflowed the refrigerator and mounted up on the kitchen table and counters. Lavinia Lester kept the coffee freshly brewed, and passed plates and platters and napkins, and collected empties on trays and bore them back to the kitchen. The dishwasher stormed endlessly. Toward the end of the day, Bay Sewell, crisp and immaculate in a blue seersucker suit, slipped unobtrusively into the foyer and displaced Duck at the door, where he seemed to know everyone who entered and left, and shook all hands and kissed many cheeks as if he were the blood son of this house and not just its appointed heir. He kissed DeeDee, who clutched him and wailed, and hugged Mike briefly and formally, but his fingers pressed hard into her back, and his breath was warm in her ear as he whispered, "Later, darling. Hang on."

The people who came were all kind, and Mike recalled a few of them, but no one seemed to want to tell her they remembered her when she was knee-high to a duck, or remark that she looked just like her father. A handful complimented her on her writing and asked when she was going back to New York. Mike smiled and said, over and over, "Thank you for coming. It would have pleased Daddy a lot to have you here." They all seemed glad to escape to the more vocal and accessible DeeDee. New York hung, dense and impenetrable, in the room between Mike and them.

More than once, Mike found herself looking around the room, and she realized finally that she was looking for Sam Canaday. But he did not appear. She knew that he would not, that he felt that this day was for family and old friends, but there was a void where his stocky figure should be. Under the dullness and fatigue, Mike felt uneasy.

They gathered in the kitchen in the dusk, after the last caller had left. DeeDee, restored and proprietary, tackled a plate of ham and potato salad, and Duck tucked into chicken pie. Bay Sewell drank coffee, watching them, his eyes holding Mike's now and then. "Soon," the blue eyes said. "Soon."

She went upstairs to change into a dress that DeeDee would deem suitable for sitting up with the dead, and when she came back into the room they were discussing her father's funeral. Priss had set it for the following afternoon, and had phoned the announcement in to the local and Atlanta papers and alerted the young jogging minister Mike had met with Sam and her father . . . was it only a month ago? But they had settled on no details up to now.

Brushing aside her unaccustomed linen skirts, Mike sank into a kitchen chair and listened, astounded, as DeeDee outlined a mountebank's funeral, ticking off one rococo horror after another: open casket at the foot of the altar, banks of flowers, a full choir, honorary pallbearers by the dozen, the full pantheon of Methodist hymns, texts, and eulogies. A policeman on duty at both the funeral home and church to handle traffic, and a motorcycle escort to the old Lytton cemetery, where John Winship would rest, finally, beside his beloved Claudia and his parents. And then another graveside service. Duck grinned and nodded his approval as she talked. Priss and Bayard Sewell, like Mike, simply watched her. J.W. Cromie, coming in with another armful of floral arrangements, leaned against the kitchen counter and listened too, his opaque eyes stonelike and unreadable.

DeeDee stopped for breath, and Mike took a deep breath. Where ice had packed her heart before, now molten lava flowed.

"You forgot the photo opportunities," she said. "Or, how about a funeral pyre? Fireworks, maybe?"

DeeDee whirled on her.

"If you don't like it, go on back to New York with your sophisticated bohemian gang of . . . trash," she hissed furiously. "Where do you get off prissing down here and telling me how to bury my daddy? You couldn't even look after him; you couldn't even keep him from getting *killed;* you haven't lifted a finger for him since you broke his heart wallowing around with the niggers twenty-five years ago! Go on back up there and squirm around in some more beds . . ."

"Shut up, DeeDee," Bayard Sewell said in a soft, dangerous voice. DeeDee looked sidewise at him, red-faced with rage, but she dropped her eyes and snapped her mouth shut.

"Don't you talk to my wife like that!" Duck Wingo said truculently.

"Shut up, all of you, for God's sake," Priss Comfort growled in her beautiful bronze voice. "DeeDee, hold your flapping tongue. You ought to thank your lucky stars your sister came down here; you'd have been in a fine fix if she hadn't. Mike, I know how you feel, but DeeDee is right about the funeral. God knows it's not your way or mine or even Scamp's, but it's Lytton's way, and that's what we ought to give him. He's earned a little pomp and circumstance. Duck, sit down and shut *up.* "

Duck sat.

"All right," Mike said reluctantly. She was very tired. The night ahead of her, and the day after that, loomed enormously; she could not see beyond them. "But I want you to okay every step and every detail, Priss."

"That's fine with me." DeeDee shrugged. She gazed sullenly at the kitchen floor for a moment longer, and then she looked up at Mike and smiled, a wavering, propitiatory smile.

"But now Mikie, really," she said. "I know you've got to get on with your life. You've given up a whole summer already; your work must be just piling up. And Rachel will be coming home to start school. You've been just wonderful help; we truly couldn't have managed without you, but it would be selfish to keep you any longer, even though we'd all love it if you'd stay forever, of course

. . . but you really must feel free to go on back as soon as the funeral's over. J.W. and Priss will help us out, and Bay will . . ."

She looked earnestly around the room at one and then another of them. Bayard Sewell nodded, but his eyes were on Mike. Later, they promised. We'll talk later.

J.W. did not look at DeeDee. He stared steadily at Mike.

"Maybe Mike would like to stay on just a little while in her home," Priss said dryly. "Until she can get herself together. Or were you planning on moving right in, DeeDee?"

"Why . . . no. Of course not. Not right yet," DeeDee said.

Mike was surprised at the feeling of loss that flooded her. Of course DeeDee had inherited their father's house, she had known that from the start of the summer. Of course she would want to live in it, rather than that flimsy shotgun horror she had lived in with Duck for so many years. And she herself had never planned to stay on in Lytton. Had she? Mike shut out the image of Duck Wingo in her father's chair at the dining table, in the big double bed that had once been John and Claudia Winship's.

"I guess I do need to get on with it, Dee," she said. "And you're right. There's really no reason to stay now, is there?"

She did not look at Bayard Sewell as she left the room to go out to her father's Cadillac in the driveway and drive to the funeral home. He did not speak. Well, of course, she thought, shutting the door behind her. He can't. Not in front of everybody.

Much later that night, when she came wearily into her bedroom after saying good night to Priss Comfort, she turned back her freshly made bed and found a note on the pillow beneath the bedspread.

"Roses are red and violets are blue," it said.

"All naked ladies should look like you."

It was not signed, but the nauseatingly ubiquitous little smiling circle had been penciled in at the bottom, with a salacious leer on its face, and she recognized Sam Canaday's spiky, sprawling handwriting.

Mike crawled into her bed and turned out the light and clutched the note to her breast, and once again, she cried.

THIRTY-ONE

At five fifteen the next morning, on the day of John Winship's funeral, J.W. Cromie knocked once more at Mike's bedroom door.

Mike came instantly awake out of skeins and webs of sweating dreams, her heart knocking with fatigue and alarm, her hair in wet strings at the back of her neck. She was at the door in a moment, clutching her robe around her.

"Priss?" she called out softly.

"J.W., Mike. Can I come in?"

She opened the door and he came silently into the bedroom and walked over to the window and raised the venetian blinds as if he had been in the room many times before. Soft gray light filtered in. Somehow, even in the chill of the air conditioner, the budding morning looked hot.

J.W. stood with his back to Mike and looked for long moments over the emerging front lawn of John Winship's house. It was neat and trimmed and raked and mowed; he had done all that the day before, in preparation for the people who would stream through the house this afternoon, after her father's funeral. Mike wondered if he had ever before been able to see his own handiwork from the vantage point that those who lived in the house did.

"I need to tell you something, Mike," he said. He did not go on, and she sat down on the edge of the bed, dread beginning in the pit of her stomach. She sensed that this was going to be bad. But what could there be left? The worst had already happened; was over.

"You'd better go ahead and tell me, then," she said.

"I didn't want to tell you this," he said. "But I think you got to know. And there ain't no more time. DeeDee and Duck been planning to get that house tore down an' a road put in there for more than a year. Maybe even longer. I do yard work for DeeDee some, and that's when I first heard 'em talkin' about it, when they didn't know I was there. After that I listened whenever I could. They ain't been too careful about talkin'. Don't reckon they think I got sense enough to know what they're sayin'. They stopped askin' me to do work for 'em about the time you come home, so I ain't heard any more than that, but I'm sure of what I did hear."

Mike could not think of anything to say. Nothing seemed to track. She stared at this black man whom she had known all her life, totally strange to her now, in silhouette against the lightening sky.

"How could they do that?" she said numbly, conversationally. "They don't have any . . . power, any clout. Who would listen to them? And why? Why? What earthly good could it do them, a road to nowhere?"

"I ain't sure," J.W. said, not turning from the window. "Soun' like there's gon' be some kind of big sale of that land when DeeDee gets it . . . now, I guess, with Mr. John gone. They standin' to make a lot of money. Heard 'em talkin' about what they gon' do with it. It gon' be one big chunk of change if they sell off yo' daddy's land to some big developer wantin' to put up houses or a factory or somethin'. I don't know who in it with 'em. I listened all I could, but they never did say. Got to be somebody big, though, could get that road in and the house tore down."

"But . . . how could they? They didn't own that land. DeeDee didn't own it. Not till Daddy . . . but he *did* die, didn't he? How could they possibly know all that long ago that the land would . . . be theirs?"

"It don't take magic to figure a sick old man ain't gon' live long. Specially if he frettin' and grievin' over somethin' like he done that house."

"Did . . . did you tell Daddy? Who else did you tell? Why didn't you tell me about it?"

Her voice in her ears sounded querulous and whining. He turned to face her, and she saw that his face was drawn to bone and his black eyes swollen.

"I didn't tell your daddy. No. I knew it would kill him to find out DeeDee would do that. I only told one other person, Sam Canaday. I didn't tell nobody else because he made me promise I wouldn't. Especially not you, Mike, when we knowed you was coming. He didn't know you back then, he didn't know whose side you'd be on. And later, I think he didn't want to hurt you. He knew DeeDee raised you, practically. I think he wanted you to have some family left."

"I never would have known," she said in simple wonder. "I never would have, if you hadn't told me. Why did you break your promise to Sam, J.W.?"

"You never did see us plain, Mike," J.W. Cromie said. "Not any of us. I didn't want you to leave here again without seein' them two plain, like they really are. Even though they got what they were after, and we can't do nothin' about that, I just wanted you to *know* 'em. Your daddy deserved better than that. You do, too. I thought for a while that maybe you'd stay on here; he'd have loved that. To have his girl at home after he was gone . . . the girl he never did stop mournin'. I saw him every day of his life after you left. I know how he felt. I wouldn't have told you about this if you'd have been goin' to stay, but then you said you were goin' back . . . and so I did."

He leaned against the thrumming air conditioner as though he were so tired that his two legs could not support him any longer, and put his hands into the pockets of his work pants.

"Might be I should have waited until after this afternoon," he said. "But I didn't want you feelin' sorry for them when they get to cryin' an' carryin' on over him in that church I figure you ain't gon' break down now."

"No," Mike whispered. "Not now."

Neither moved for a long time, and then Mike went to him across the soured, thin old carpet and simply laid her head on his chest. He was still, and then he put his arms around her and held her lightly.

"Thank you, J.W.," Mike said.

"You're welcome, Mike."

Presently he went across to the door as softly as he had come, and slipped out and closed it. Mike dressed in the hot dawn silence and went quietly down the stairs so as not to waken Priss Comfort, asleep in John Winship's back bedroom, and out to the car and drove to the mean little house on the edge of the mobile home park to confront her older sister.

Mike knew that soon she was going to be very angry, worse than angry: furious, red and murderous with rage, maddened with it. But for the moment, rage was frozen under the ice of disbelief. As she drove, she hoped simply and fervently, as a child will hope for something, that the rage would not break through until she had seen her sister and the dreadful, trivial, blustering man she had married and was home again. She did not know what she was going to say to DeeDee and Duck, but it was the most important thing in the world at this moment that she say it, that it be said, and then be over. Then, Mike thought, I can leave; I can go away from here. When she had been very small and had had to be taken to old Dr. Gaddis for one of the childhood shots, of which she was terrified, Mike had comforted herself by sobbing to herself, over and over, "And then and then and then, it will all be over. And then and then and then." She was doing that now, as she drove the silent old Cadillac: "And then and then and then."

DeeDee and Duck were sitting at the round, varnished yellow pine table in what DeeDee called the breakfast nook. DeeDee wore a vast, knee-length no-color duster and rubber flipflops. Her hair had not been combed, and her great face was swollen almost unrecognizably from hours and hours of crying; her lovely blue eyes had vanished almost completely, and the skin of her face was streaked and mottled with angry red. She was drinking coffee from a mug with Kermit the Frog on it, and breathing wetly through her mouth. Her small, inflamed nose seemed to be completely blocked with the dregs of grief. Duck wore nothing but his undershorts. If Mike had been able to focus her eyes clearly, she would have been repelled by his sagging fatness, the gross ruin of him. But she could see nothing but her sister's face. She walked stiffly into the breakfast nook, her hands clenched at her sides, the car keys biting deeply and unheeded into her bandaged palm.

They looked up at her, dully surprised, as if she were a spectral materialization. She had not been back in the little house since the night she had met Bayard Sewell here. She supposed she might look like a madwoman; she had not combed her own flyaway hair, and the clothes she had put on were the same ones she had thrown down beside the bed the night before. She realized dimly that she was barefoot.

"Mikie?" DeeDee said tentatively.

"It killed him, you know," Mike said. Her voice surprised her; she might have been talking of the weather. "I don't know if that's what you planned or not, but it killed him as surely as if you'd put a gun to his head and pulled the trigger. Congratulations, DeeDee. It couldn't have worked out any neater for you. The timing was perfect. You got the house down and the old man out of the way in the same afternoon. When does the road come through?"

They did not protest or pretend that they did not know what she was talking about. Duck said nothing, but put his coffee cup down on the varnished tabletop, to which a dismal collection of breakfast effluvia was stuck in the morning heat. He clasped his hands together on the table and watched her, his hooded eyes drooping almost closed. DeeDee's mouth sagged into a great rictus, like a child's heartbroken wailing, and fresh tears spurted down her vast cheeks, and the breath came and went in her throat in great sobs, but for a moment she made no sound. Her enormous shelf of bosom, unbound at this hour, heaved up and down atop her stomach as she struggled to get her breath. Finally she did, and her words poured out on her strangling sobs, a lava of woe: "I didn't mean for him to *be* down there! We didn't know he knew what day it was! I didn't think he could move . . . I thought it would just be over, and then he wouldn't care anymore about the rest of the land! Oh, Mikie, I loved my daddy, and I didn't think he would *care* . . ."

"Well, he cared himself to death, DeeDee." Mike was implacable; her sister's grotesque anguish did not touch her. "God, I can't believe you! I'm not surprised at Duck; I should have known about Duck. But you . . . DeeDee, you were his baby; you were his pet! Didn't you ever know him at all? Even a little bit? How could you think he wouldn't *care?*"

"He'd had the stupid house all his life." DeeDee sobbed through laced fingers. "The famous, wonderful homeplace. He wasn't ever going to use it again; it had just stood there all those years. Just stood there. He hadn't even been down there for months. And he'd *had* his life, and you'd been gone all that time, and you had such a fine, great life, and you weren't ever coming back again, and I . . . I haven't ever had anything! Not ever *anything!* And it was my land anyway . . ."

Mike saw, as if for the first time, though Priss had hinted of it, that DeeDee must have hated her for every by-line, for the imagined life of luxury, privilege, and excitement, for the ersatz glamour of the great cities of the world, for the prosperous husband

and the exemplary daughter and the fancied warm, secure marriage.

She's never once known the truth of me, either, any more than I knew hers, Mike thought. Far down, the rage quivered.

"It wasn't your land yet," she said to her sister. "And it might not have been for a good while." Her voice began to tremble. "Couldn't you have waited? You must have known he couldn't last forever. Couldn't you have *waited?* Did you have to make him *watch* it?"

DeeDee said nothing, but cried harder.

"What's the harm, Mike?" Duck said, smiling winningly at Mike. It was the old smile: slow, insinuating. It crawled over Mike. "The land was just sitting there. The old house was falling in. It wasn't like he was ever going to even see it again, and all along it was going to be ours . . . DeeDee's . . . anyway. We never meant for him to know when the old heap was going down. I don't know how in the hell he found out . . . but the chance came, Mike. It wouldn't have come again. The investors were there, they had the money ready, and they wanted to move. You have to move when you see the chance. We'd have lost it if we'd waited. Hell, John would *want* the people he loved to be provided for, his daughter, his grandchildren. He'd have given them anything in the world . . ."

"Maybe there was something else he wanted to give them," Mike said. The rage was beginning to eat through the ice. It frightened her.

"What?" Duck Wingo said. "He didn't have anything else. Christ, it was just an old house . . ."

Mike screamed suddenly. The world around her reddened. "Well, by God, it was *his* house! It's not right! What you two did is *monstrous!* It's *evil,* it's *wrong! It was his house! Nothing justifies it!*"

DeeDee was on her feet in front of Mike, rocking on the tiny, grubby thongs, her teeth clenched and bared, her furious breath bubbling in her clogged little nostrils.

"Don't you dare call us evil, Mike Winship!" she shrieked. "Miz Micah Gotrocks Winship Singer! It wasn't our fault; it wasn't our idea! You want to call names, you call the right one! You talk to your dear, sweet lover baby, Bayard Sewell! Oh, yeah, we know about that; everybody in town knows about that! Who do you think came to us with the proposition; who do you think found the backers all the way up there in Boston, and put the package together, and offered us enough money to fix us up for the rest of our lives? Who's going to put the world's biggest cat food plant and a whole industrial mall right in the middle of that land, once the road goes through? And who's going to be a partner in the whole thing? Who do you think got that road through the legislature in the first place? Bay Sewell has been screwing you more than one way this summer, baby sister!"

"You are a goddamned liar," Mike said. DeeDee sucked in a breath so quick and deep that her chins quivered, and slapped Mike across the face. Then she began to laugh.

"DeeDee, sugar . . ." Duck Wingo said. He heaved himself to his feet and put his hand on DeeDee's arm. She whirled and slapped him, too.

"Don't you ever touch me again, you sorry son of a bitch." She choked on the bubbling laughter, and he stepped back, his hand going to his cheek. DeeDee's laughter slid swiftly over into tears.

Mike stood still, her ears ringing with the slap. As soon as DeeDee's words were out, she realized she had known the truth ever since J.W. had awakened her, and perhaps long before that. Like misted breath over a glass, love vanished in that instant as if it had never been. There was not, then, any pain, only the ice of rage. She turned and walked out of the terrible little house and got into the car. DeeDee's spiraling wails followed her. Mike shut the door of the Cadillac and the wails stopped abruptly. She drove home to Pomeroy Street. Somewhere along the way the rage sank back, but the ice remained. She wanted, simply, to take a bath and go upstairs and crawl back into her bed and go to sleep.

When she walked into the kitchen, Bayard Sewell was standing at the counter, immaculate and beautiful in a dark gray suit and white shirt and yellow tie, pouring himself a cup of coffee.

"The screen door was open, so I came on in," he said, smiling his wonderful white smile at her. "Priss made coffee and went home to feed her cat. I was worried to death when she said you weren't upstairs in bed. Where've you been this early?"

She swallowed in remembered pain at the sheer beauty and treachery of him.

"I've been to DeeDee's."

He set his cup down and came over and put his hand gently beneath her chin, and lifted it until she looked directly into his eyes.

"Couldn't you sleep?" he said. "Neither could I. I thought all night about you up there in that bed alone, what you must have been going through. God, I wanted so badly to come to you . . ."

Mike turned away and sat down in one of the kitchen chairs and put her head down on the table on her folded arms.

"DeeDee told me all about your little real estate venture," she said.

There was a long silence, in which Mike watched the blackness behind her eyelids turn to dark red and pinwheel with parabolas of white light. Then he said, in a voice that was Bay's familiar deep voice, and yet different, "Well, I wish she hadn't done that. I hoped you wouldn't have to know about that for a while, Mike, and maybe not ever. Maybe it would have been better all the way around if you could have gotten away to New York and let things down here just . . . be. Though I was serious when I said I wish you could have stayed, too. I think, if DeeDee had kept her mouth shut, we could have really worked something out. Now, of course, it's all spoiled."

Mike's heart, which she had thought frozen, dropped, cold and leaden, as if through fathomless black water. She had, she realized, hoped that he would deny it.

She lifted her head and swiveled around to look at him. He looked back, his handsome face grave but very faintly amused, hands in his jacket pocket. He looked like a sketch in *Gentleman's Quarterly.*

"Why have you been fucking me all summer?" she asked. Her voice in her ears did not sound like her own. "DeeDee was going to get the land all along, not me. *Has* got it, now. Why not just bang her? She'd have loved that. And Duck would have sold tickets, if you'd wanted him to."

He chuckled. It was a merry, companionable, incredible sound.

"Can you imagine anybody humping DeeDee? You're light-years out of that class, Mike. No, you were my information pipeline. And I wanted you on our side. It was you he wanted to come down here when he had the stroke; you he kept asking for. Not DeeDee. We were going to get you to persuade him to deed the rest of the property over to her, once it was all over and he'd lost the appeal. We thought he might be glad just to get it off his mind. And then he was getting fond of you; we all saw that. And cold to DeeDee. I had to warn her off coming over here. That worried us. Who's to say what you two might have cooked up, between you? You'd already gone over. And he was a crazy old man, there at the end."

"Yes, he was," Mike said. "He really was a crazy old man. Well, Bay, he saved you all a lot of trouble by checking out, didn't he? Too bad he didn't die right off when he had the stroke. He could have spared you a lot of sack time."

The old smile flashed at her, crazily, in all its gay charm.

"Oh, I didn't mind that part," Bay Sewell said. "You're a fantastic piece of ass. Must be all that foreign travel. I've never had anything like that."

She screamed at him, the same words she had screamed at DeeDee and Duck Wingo: *"Couldn't you have waited?"*

"No," he said earnestly. "The syndicate was ready to move. You almost queered it all when you started in with him on that crazy letter-writing campaign; I had to fly to Boston and try to put that fire out, and for a while there I thought we'd blown it all. Or you had. I practically signed my life away. But it's done now. I've already got a big chunk of the money. They wired it last night. The rest comes when we break ground. Winship Farms Industrial Park we're calling it, just like he was going to. You know he'd like that, Mike. Look, you have to move when the time is right. I've known that all my life. I've lived by it. It's going to take me all the way. You have to take your chances when they come. You took yours, Mike, when you left me . . ."

The rage burst. "When I left you! Goddamn you, Bay Sewell, you stood right here in this house and cast your lot with him! With him and his money! I watched you do it! And you—you just can't keep your hands off what's his, can you? Whether it's his money, or his land, or his daughter . . .

"You've hated me for a long time, haven't you, Bay? You and DeeDee and Duck. All this time . . ."

He looked down at the linoleum. "I certainly never hated you, but you shouldn't have put me in that spot," he said. "Everything was all set up. You had no business doing that to me." Suddenly his dark face contorted. "You were my ticket out of here, Mike," he said softly, but with such venom that she stepped instinctively backwards, out of his range. "My air fare. Don't you know what a town like this does to winners? Do you think I didn't know what I was, what I had, what I still have? I could have made the world shake

. . . out there. You could have helped me. His money was going to kick us off. But you ran out, and I've been stuck all these years with a drunk and a crazy old bigot and two fools. And it's been *your* name in all those magazines and all those newspapers. And all the time I was the smart one; I was always the best one . . ."

"You could have left anytime," Mike whispered.

"No. His money had me tied here like Gulliver. His money put me through school. His fucking land started my business. Jesus Christ, he even picked out my wife!"

"He *helped* you, Bay!" Mike cried.

"No. He bought me. The real estate business and the wife were how I paid him back for going to school. Those, and a life lived here in nowheresville in his shadow. But that debt's cleared now. It's off the books."

She looked up at him for a long time, at his chiseled face, his good hands, his beautiful eyes, not, perhaps, quite fully sane.

"Did you ever love me?" she said.

"Of course," he said, surprised. "You were the first thing I had ever owned. And I still do love you. If you'd inherited that land . . . or if you'd gone along with us . . . I'd have been married to you in a year."

"I see. And how were you going to manage that? Was Sally going the way Daddy did?"

"God, Mike, I won't have to kill her, no more than I did your father. Can't you see she's doing it herself? She'll be dead before Christmas."

His mouth continued to move; he was saying something more, but Mike did not hear him. She turned and went upstairs and got into the bathtub, filling it as full as possible with scalding hot water, and stayed there a long time. She closed her eyes and thought of nothing at all.

When she came back downstairs, Bayard Sewell was gone and Sam Canaday was sitting in his accustomed place at the kitchen table, finishing up the coffee and eating doughnuts from a greasy white sack in front of him.

"Don't you ever lock your door?" he said. He was dressed in the blue blazer and gray slacks, and his tie today was dark blue with a thin red stripe. His fair hair shone almost white in the overhead light, and his sallow-tanned face was not as grayed with weariness as when she had last seen him, though the yellow-green wolf's eyes were ringed with darker saffron. He smelled of soap and some kind of piny aftershave.

Mike sat down at the table and fished a doughnut out of the sack. She was, she realized suddenly, ravenous. She bolted the doughnut and then began to talk. She talked for nearly an hour. When she had finished, she looked at him, waiting for some reaction: anger, pity, regret . . . something. Nothing crossed his face except a kind of deepening of the weariness. Her own anger began to mount again.

"Well, so you know about it," he said. "At least you heard it straight from the horses' mouths. Or asses, as the case may be. I can't say I'm sorry you know. But I can say I'm glad I don't have to tell you. I was going to, once the funeral was over. Sewell is something else, isn't he? He would have made a great Borgia. Cat food, huh? Well. Something new in Lytton, some honest-to-God Yankee cat food. They can call it Lytton Liver and Lights, Limited. Boy's real presidential material."

Mike stared at him.

"Is that all you have to say about it?"

"I'd say your pretty friend Bayard Everett Sewell had said it all, for the time being," he said.

"And you're not going to do anything about it?"

"What do you want me to do, Mike? They haven't broken any law."

"They killed my father! There are laws against that!"

"No, really, they didn't. You just can't say they did, not publicly, anyway. You'd be in the funny farm in three weeks."

"By God, I *will* say it," Mike cried. The fury ran through her like heat lightning; stormed through her like a great wind. "I'll tell everybody in this town what they did! Everybody in this state! Better than that, I'll write it and send it to every paper in fucking Georgia. They know my by-line; they'll take my stuff. And if you won't help me do it, I'll do it by myself!"

She had risen from her chair and was standing, supporting herself against the edge of the kitchen table. She shook all over, profoundly. He popped the last bite of doughnut into his mouth and rose himself, and pushed her gently back into the chair.

"No," he said. "You're not going to do that, or anything else.

You're going to say nothing to DeeDee or Duck or Sewell, or Priss, or J.W., or anybody else. You're going to help them give the Colonel the numero uno funeral the Lytton Methodist Church can throw, and you're going to go to it, and thank every little old blue-haired lady and chicken-necked geezer for coming, and smile and smile, and serve coffee and cake to ten thousand people afterward if you have to, and then you're going to thank them all again."

"Sam, I *can't!* I can't watch those three wail and carry on over his grave; I can't watch people go up to them and *comfort* them— especially not him! Everybody thinks he loved Daddy like his own father, and they'll be all over him, and he'll just lap it up . . . they all three will. You're telling me to just . . . to just . . . let them get away with it!"

"That's right. I am."

"*Why?*" It was a great, despairing howl of anguish and incomprehension.

"Because there isn't anything else you can do about it, Mike. Not now. They have not, repeat *not,* done anything illegal. DeeDee hasn't, and Duck hasn't, and Bayard Everett Sewell hasn't, and the Georgia Department of Transportation hasn't."

"Sam, there is goddamned well something on this earth that I can do about it, and I will find out what, and I will do it."

"All right, Mike. Fine. I'm not going to tell you that the day will come when you won't feel like this. But it will, and sooner than you think. Meanwhile, though, I want you to leave it alone. Just for now. Let's just give him a real Viking funeral. Can you do that? For him? For me?"

"Just don't, please, give me any pious shit about time the great healer," Mike said, her voice shaking low in her throat.

"Okay," Sam Canaday said. "No shit. Now you'd better go up and get dressed. We need to be at the church a little early."

"Sam," she said, rising again. "Will you say something at the church? For Daddy? Like a . . . you know, like a eulogy?"

"I can't do that, Mike."

"Why not? Aren't you a good friend of what's-his-name, that young preacher?"

"I . . . can't. I don't talk in churches anymore, Mike. I haven't done that in . . . a long time. And Lytton would have a fit. You know I'm not exactly everybody's favorite son . . ."

"Please, Sam. You were his. You really were like a son to him. Sam, listen." Mike felt the hated tears start again and shook her head impatiently, but they rolled down her cheeks unchecked, warm. "I don't have anything to . . . give him. To send off with him. This funeral stuff, all this to-do . . . this isn't from me, it's from DeeDee. It's from Priss. It's from Lytton. I want something at his funeral to be from me."

He walked around the table and brushed the tears from her face with his thumb, gently.

"All right, Mike," he said. "I'll ask Tom Cawthorn if he minds. And I'll try to come up with something."

"Don't try, Sam," she said, stopping in the kitchen door. "Do it. Please. For me and Daddy."

He put his thumb up, in the manner of fighter pilots and race car drivers.

"You got it," he said.

THIRTY-TWO

The Lytton United Methodist Church had stood on the corner of Trinity and Elder streets, just west of the main business district, for more than one hundred years. It had been refurbished since Mike had left, and the sanctuary was comfortable and modern now, with light, plain oak pews and deep red altar and kneeling cushions and carpet. There was a new organ with a cathedral-like tent of gleaming pipes, and a high, spacious choir loft, and a suspended pulpit that would elevate its occupant fittingly above the congregation. Not much remained of the dim, time-stained stucco sanctuary that Mike remembered, but the smell was the same: filtered sunlight and ecclesiastical dust, and somehow, minty white paste from the primary Sunday school classrooms, and the ghostly breath of the old, long-vanished coal furnace.

The light was the same, too. Mike had hated the interminable Sunday morning services; had fidgeted restlessly through the droning messages of a succession of earnest, seemingly ancient ministers, and had been badly frightened by the frequent and apocalyptic revivals. But she had always loved the light that came in through the old church's stained-glass windows. There were eight of them, four down each side of the sanctuary, and they depicted vignettes of Jesus with his disciples. They were as old as the church, made in Germany, and beautiful. When they were small, DeeDee had piously professed to love the window in which a Teutonic-looking Christ calmed the tossing waters of the Sea of Galilee while his faithless followers quailed in the bottom of a large flat boat. But Mike had liked the one where an abject Peter bowed his head in shame as a cock as large as he was crowed lustily, and a betrayed Jesus looked suitably long-suffering in the background.

The light that streamed in through the windows had made of

the ordinary Lytton congregation something magical to Mike, rows of enchanted, roseate people, and even on this day the lambent, deep-glowing light was the first thing she noticed when she walked into the church. The second was the enormous bronze casket standing, half-buried in flowers, at the foot of the altar. Mike's stomach tightened. DeeDee had, she knew, gone to the funeral home and canceled the simple mahogany coffin that Priss and Sam had chosen and substituted this bronze monster, that looked for all the world like a 1956 Buick. DeeDee had ordered the casket pall, too, a great blanket of red and pink and white carnations. It looks like something they'd drape over Seattle Slew, Mike thought. Her own flowers, old-fashioned red climbing roses as near to the Paul Scarlets at the homeplace as the florist could find, spilled out of a tall white wicker basket at the casket's head. Priss had sent massed, glowing Gerbera daisies from her own garden, and Sam had sent nothing at all. "I hate funeral flowers," he said. "Somehow they all smell like embalming fluid. I'm not going to dump any more on the Colonel." An urn of slender, opalescent pink spider lilies, out of season and as perfect as Chinese jade, bore a card that read, "Bayard Everett Sewell and family."

She sat in the front row of pews where the family of the bereaved habitually sat in this and other southern churches. DeeDee was on her left with Duck beyond her, and J.W. Cromie sat, rigid and reluctant, on her right. Mike had grabbed J.W. by his alien navy blue arm on the way into the church and marched him down the aisle to the family pew where Duck and DeeDee were already seated, and plumped him down beside her. DeeDee had glared tear-scrimmed daggers at her, but Mike had only looked straight ahead. To J.W. she whispered, "If you get up and leave I'm right behind you, and I won't come back." He stayed put, looking impassive and grand in the unaccustomed suit, and utterly miserable. Mike could feel the eyes of Lytton on their backs and hear the soft tide of whispers that broke against them, but she did not turn. Behind her, Priss Comfort and Sam Canaday sat on the second family pew, alone. Behind them, on the rest of the pews, the church was packed to bursting. Old Lytton, that Mike had not seen since she had been home, had come at last to send off one of their own.

The choir loft was full of men and women and teenagers in robes of a soft red that matched the seat cushions, and white surplices. Mike had never seen a full choir at a funeral before, and wondered how DeeDee . . . or, more likely, Priss . . . had managed to amass such a formidable army on short notice, and a weekday to boot. The choir sat silent and properly solemn in the rays of colored light that slanted through the stained-glass windows . . . Mike had called them holy miracle rays when she was small . . . but they had not yet sung. Instead, the organ, manned by a small, stout, energetic woman in robe and surplice and carved blue hair, had noodled a soft medley of solemn, old-fashioned hymns as the sanctuary filled, segueing from "Rock of Ages" into "The Old Rugged Cross" to "I Come to the Garden Alone" to "Softly and Tenderly." As the organist reached the refrain of the latter, the choir rose as one and sang, softly: "Come home, come ho-oo-me, Ye who are weary come home," and DeeDee gave a great sob. Mike's mouth twitched. She would love to have smacked DeeDee's pale, tear-wrecked face. The choir remained standing and slid into the hymn that always brought a lump to Mike's throat, no matter where she heard it, and she heard it often, for it seemed, of late, to have become somewhat in vogue for ecumenically elegiac purposes: "Amazing grace, how sweet the sound . . ." Mike swallowed hard, past an aching lump. She was determined not to cry. The lump dissolved as Bayard Sewell walked past her down the aisle with Sally Sewell on his arm, and seated himself in the front pew across the aisle from the Winship family.

He did not look at Mike as he walked. But all eyes were on his tall figure, slightly bowed with this newest of the sorrows he carried, the beautiful, burdensome wife clinging hard to his arm, her face ravaged with real grief as well as alcohol. Mike heard the soft catches of breath and the murmurs of sympathy as Lytton watched this most lustrous of its native sons bear his burdens gallantly to the foot of the coffin of the only father he had ever known. Behind them, Priss Comfort snorted.

Mike looked steadily at him. She seemed to see him, suddenly, in a kind of pentimento, in some vast, paneled office with crossed flags behind his fine head. She thought, inanely, that he looked like one of those photos that you find in drugstore wallets when you first open them, and remembered with absolute and instant clarity the photographs in the terrible flamingo-pink plastic wallet she had bought when she first ran away from Lytton to Atlanta and had kept there in place of her family's photos, and his. She looked at vulnerable, dwindling little Sally Sewell. She isn't going to be a burden to him at all, not a bit of an obstacle, Mike thought. She can drink herself to death, and probably will, and people are only going to say what a saint he is, and how brave and good he's been. It's going to help him. His poor, drunk, doomed wife is going to be a political asset. It's amazing. Nothing can stop him. She let her mind play fully and unswervingly over all the afternoons in the urgent upstairs bed, all the things they had done and said to each other, all the heat and writhings and frog-leaping excesses of their two bodies. Nothing in her, mind or body, flinched away from the memories. That flesh had been the flesh of another woman entirely. All Mike felt, looking at the face of the man who had been her love and her lover, was a faint and clinical distaste.

The choir sat down and the organist began to play again, not a hymn this time, but the achingly sweet and delicate Largo from Dvořák's *New World Symphony*. "Goin' home, goin' home, I'm just goin' home . . ."

Oh, Daddy, Mike said soundlessly, and turned to Priss Comfort behind her. Priss gave her a small nod and a smile. Mike knew the music, including the homely, dignified old hymns, had been her choice. "Thank you," she mouthed. Priss nodded again and blew a brief kiss.

There was a silence, filled with rustlings and soft coughings and a few more whispers, and DeeDee made as if to rise, and Mike thought, suddenly and frantically, that her sister was going to get up and go to the foot of the altar beside the coffin and sing. She remembered the awful days of Yma Sumac. It ain't over till the fat lady sings, she thought, idiotically, and for a moment laughter so flooded her chest and throat that she was afraid it was going to burst free and spew over the congregation. But DeeDee only straightened her skirt and subsided massively onto the pew again. She looked surprisingly handsome today, in a simple dark shirtwaist that Mike had never seen before, and obviously new black patent pumps. In her little pink ears were small pearl buttons, and her dark hair was pulled back into a French knot. Her face was scored and swollen with her grief, but DeeDee today wore a dignity that Mike had never seen, and that sat upon her well. Priss again, Mike thought. She must have taken DeeDee into Atlanta or to one of the nearby malls and bought her the dress and shoes. It must have been earlier this morning, after the terrible business at DeeDee's house. She wondered if Priss knew, somehow. She thought not. DeeDee would wear the scars of Priss's wrath in some visible way if the truth had come out.

The young minister Mike had met earlier in the summer came out of a door beside the choir loft and mounted the steps up to the pulpit. Mike almost did not recognize him without his jogging clothes. He wore a dark robe and white vestments, and his face was calm and open and thoughtful. The rose light glinted off round, metal-rimmed spectacles. He looked very young. He paused a moment and looked out over the congregation, and then at Mike and DeeDee, and smiled faintly, and then picked up a leather-bound prayer book. In a soft, slow voice dense with the melodic drawl of one of the old Creole coastal towns, Mike thought perhaps Savannah or Charleston, he began to read: "I am the resurrection and the life, saith the Lord; he that believeth in me, though he were dead, yet shall he live; and whosoever liveth and believeth in me, shall never die . . ."

The words were music, the music of the old King James version of the Bible, the music of childhood. Mike felt herself borne up and out on the music of the young minister's words, back into the world of her own childhood and into whatever of safety and sweetness she had known in it: Rusky, Priss, sometimes DeeDee, once or twice, in moments of great stress and childish anguish, the brief haven of her father's hard arms. It was warm in the church, and the warmth seemed to curl around and through her and wrap itself around her heart, shrunken cold and small and stonelike, somewhere deep within her, so that it swelled just a little, made as if to bud. Something in her chest, which might have been that child's fiercely guarded heart, seemed to loosen and expand. Her muscles let go of themselves, and her hands relaxed in her lap. Around her, the grief of these people who had long known her father reached out to her and gathered her in, and though it was not fresh grief, nor deep, nevertheless it was real. Mike closed her eyes, hearing the beautiful Creole voice going on and on: "Hear my prayer, O Lord, and with thine ears consider my calling; hold not thy peace at my tears; for I am a stranger with thee, and a sojourner, as all my fathers were . . ."

Mike felt washed, lapped, bathed, if not in mystery, then in a kind of peace and the beginnings of a small hope. This is what Sam meant, she thought, and Priss. This, right now, for just this minute, is goodness.

"O spare me a little," said Tom Cawthorn from the pulpit, "that I may recover my strength, before I go hence, and be no more seen."

Presently he was finished, and the congregation shifted and murmured, getting ready to rise for the final prayer. But instead, Tom Cawthorn said, "John Winship's family has asked someone who loved him as much as they did to say a few words for him. Sam?"

And Sam Canaday rose from the pew beside Priss and walked down the aisle and up into the pulpit.

DeeDee drew in her breath sharply and turned to glare fiercely at Mike, and the congregation frankly buzzed among themselves. Duck turned a reddened face to Mike that seemed to swell and grow in girth as she looked at it. Bayard Sewell did not turn around, but Mike felt, rather than saw, his shoulder and neck muscles harden. She gave DeeDee and Duck back a long, level look. She was not sure what she would have done if they had made any sound or gesture of protest, but she knew she would have done something irrevocable and shocking, and apparently they read it in the look, for both subsided, looking away. They did not turn to her again.

"Good girl," Priss whispered from behind her.

"Way to go," J.W. said under his breath.

Sam Canaday clasped his hands loosely and laid his forearms on the pulpit. He looked slowly over the church, up one row and down the other, letting his green eyes drift over and past everyone in the light-flooded sanctuary. He saw, fully, Mike sitting there beside J.W., but he did not acknowledge her. He continued his slow sweep of the church, and then took a deep breath and straightened himself slightly. In a voice that was like and yet totally unlike Sam's voice, soft and resonant and clear and carrying, he began the great, joyous words of John Donne:

> "Death be not proud, though some have called thee
> Mighty and dreadful, for thou art not so;
> For those whom thou think'st thou dost overthrow
> Die not, poor death; nor yet canst thou kill me.
> From rest and sleep, which but thy pictures be,
> Much pleasure; then from thee much more must flow,

And soonest our best men with thee do go,
Rest of their bones and souls' delivery.
Thou art slave to fate, chance, kings, and desperate men,
And dost with poison, war, and sickness dwell;
And poppy or charms can make us sleep as well,
And better than thy stroke; why swell'st thou then?
One short sleep past, we wake eternally,
And death shall be no more; death, thou shalt die."

He did not read the words, but recited them as from long and easy familiarity, and in the absolute silence and stillness that followed them, the power of him thrummed in the air almost audibly, almost palpably. Something that belied and exceeded the quiet, measured words leapt and flickered around the old church like captured lightning. What a preacher he must have made, Mike thought, shivering. From somewhere outside himself he has pulled about him this complete and incandescent new persona. No wonder he stopped preaching. No one could live with that kind of responsibility.

Sam leaned on the pulpit again. "We come today to say goodbye to our friend John Winship," he said. "And before we see him off, there is something I want to say to you. There will inevitably be some question as to whether he knew what he was doing. Whether he was clear in himself when he went into the wreckage of his family home and lay down there to die. Some of you might wonder if this death was what the world calls a suicide.

"Well, let me tell you that he knew. He absolutely and truly and totally knew what he was doing. Oh, yes, he knew; there was not a thing he didn't know. He knew about love and betrayal in equal doses, at the end of his life, and he also knew that the greatest of these is love, and he proved that with his death."

Sam paused and took another deep breath. He let it out slowly. The congregation seemed to breathe with him.

"It was a magnificent death," he said. "It was a hero's death. Don't let anybody tell you that there are no heroes anymore. A hero died last Tuesday for what he loved best, and we lay a hero to rest today."

He looked at Mike and J.W. and DeeDee and Duck, and then over at Bayard and Sally Sewell. DeeDee sobbed aloud and dropped her face into her hands, and Duck looked down at his lap. Bayard Sewell did not move his dark, narrow head. Sam Canaday raised his

313

voice suddenly, and his words rang out as if being struck from sparking stone: "Deliver me from mine enemies, O my God; defend me from them that rise up against me. Deliver me from the workers of iniquity, and save me from bloody men."

He fell silent and looked at them all again, and then said, in an ordinary, conversational voice, "John Winship was not a suicide, and he was not a victim. He was a victor. He lived as his kind of man should, and he died as any man would be proud to die. And what he won was immense." He looked directly at Mike and smiled, and she smiled back, holding the tears at bay with all the concentrated force of her will. DeeDee caught a great, ragged breath and sobbed on.

"This was a man," Sam Canaday said. "We shall not look upon his like again."

He stood there for a moment, and then walked back to his seat and sat down. The church was silent. Then the young minister said a benediction, and the funeral of John Winship was over.

Mike said nothing to Sam on the short drive to the old Lytton cemetery, except, briefly, "Thank you."

"You're welcome," he said.

The midafternoon sun beat down mercilessly in the old cemetery, glancing knifelike off the dingy, pitted old tombstones, hurling itself in arrows from the few large statues of angels and saints and cherubim, and the two or three modest family mausoleums. The old cemetery was not well cared for; Mike had heard her father say that the town could not keep a sexton, and all the work that was done around the graves and plots was done now by the families of the dead. Weeds and vines straggled up out of the hard red earth, and plastic pots of geraniums leaned drunkenly against some of the graves, bleached and bled to blotched pink by the suns and rains of many seasons. There were few newer graves here, and no fresh ones except John Winship's. People in Lytton laid their dead to rest now in the new perpetual-care cemetery down the highway to the south. Mike got out of the shining old Cadillac and walked with Sam Canaday to the hole that yawned in the dry earth toward the back of the old cemetery, covered with the undertaker's canopy and banked with florists' wreaths and sprays.

The Winship plot was edged with granite coping, and its scant grass was neatly mown. J.W., Mike knew. Beside the new grave there was a neatened stone that read CLAUDIA SEARCY WINSHIP. BELOVED WIFE AND MOTHER. 1918–1946. There was space behind the two graves for four more. Folding chairs had been set out around the new grave, and DeeDee and Duck were already seated in the front row, under the canopy. Duck's arm was around DeeDee's shoulders, and she was still crying monotonously into a sodden handkerchief. She did not look up as Mike slipped into the chair beside her. Neither did Duck. J.W. and Sam and Priss stood behind Mike, and the small knot of people who had come to the newly dug grave filled in the chairs around and stood in serried ranks behind them. The young minister, still in his vestments, stepped up to the head of the coffin, which had come there in the hearse, and began the brief graveside service: "All that the Father giveth me shall come to me, and him that cometh to me I will in no wise cast out . . ."

Mike sat with her head bowed under the fist of the sun, eyes closed, resolutely thinking of nothing in particular, only half listening to Tom Cawthorn's voice. Her father had nothing to do with this place and these people; nothing to do with this raw new hole in the earth and the mound of pink dirt piled beside it; nothing to do with the grave and beautiful words that he had abjured in his later life. She wondered, suddenly, what he looked like, lying inside the great, Buick-like coffin, and was grateful that Priss had talked DeeDee into having it closed at the funeral. She did not want to look upon her dead father, and she did not want anyone else to look at him, either.

"Unto Almighty God we commend the soul of our brother John Winship, and we commit his body to the ground; earth to earth, ashes to ashes, dust to dust; in sure and certain hope of Resurrection unto eternal life . . ." Tom Cawthorn intoned. Presently, his voice stopped, and Mike looked up to see a stumbling, weeping DeeDee, supported by Duck, dropping a handful of earth onto her father's coffin. It made a flat, splatting sound. Mike looked around to see if anyone was going to give her some earth to drop upon her father, but no one made a move to do so, and she supposed that DeeDee, as the oldest, automatically had the honor of casting clods at him. And then she felt something being pressed into her hand from behind her, and she looked down at the finger-printed ball of red clay that rested there, and the single drooping vine of fiery scarlet roses that J.W. Cromie held out to her.

"From the homeplace," he said in a low voice. "Go on an' throw 'em in there, Mike."

Mike closed her eyes and tossed, and the earth and flowers hit the casket with the same dull and final sound, and the electric winch began to whine, and John Winship rode into the earth of Lytton, the earth and fire of the homeplace riding with him.

At seven o'clock that evening a great storm broke, driving the thick, still heat before it and lashing the trees outside the Pomeroy Street house with muscular silver skeins of rain. The air darkened until the twilight became full night, and Priss and Lavinia Lester dashed onto the porch and pulled the wicker furniture to safety. The last of the guests who had come to nibble at the buffet Lavinia had produced and hug the Winship girls had fled as the first great spatters of rain bounced and sizzled on the hot pavement outside, and only the core group remained.

Mike sat, silent and dull with fatigue, on the loveseat in the living room, sipping cooling coffee. DeeDee and Duck and Bayard Sewell sat on the long white damask couch against the opposite wall. Under the ministrations of the mourners, who had hugged and petted and made much of her, DeeDee had at last stopped crying and looked, now, stunned and uncomprehending. Duck made rambling, jocose conversation about the funeral and the turnout and the sermon and the food Lavinia had provided . . . a sort of free-lance funeral review, Mike thought dimly. He was obviously uncomfortable in this room, with Mike, and did not look at her. Bayard Sewell lounged, grave and composed, balancing a coffee cup, his long legs stretched out elegantly before him. He looked often at Mike, and his gaze was mild and clear. But he said little, only listened to Duck. He had taken a wasted Sally home much earlier, and had come back, and remained as the crowd thinned and then was gone. He and DeeDee and Duck had been on the verge of leaving when the rain started. Now they were unwilling prisoners together in this room that had loomed large in all their lives, trapped by the teeming bars of the rain. Mike did not want to be in the room with them, or even the house, but she was too tired to get up and leave, too tired to speak, too tired to think. And so she sat still.

Sam Canaday came into the room just as a great bolt of lightning struck somewhere nearby and the lights flickered. He and Priss

316

had been in the kitchen most of the afternoon, out of sight but standing by. Mike felt rather than saw their presence, and was dumbly glad of it.

"Yow," said Sam. "The big guns are out. Listen, everybody, I wonder if you'd mind coming into the Colonel's study for a minute before you go. There's something I need to go over with you. It won't take long."

DeeDee's head came up, like a cow swinging at a fly.

"What?" she said suspiciously.

"I want to talk a little about your dad's will, DeeDee," Sam said. "I know it's probably not the time for it, and we'll do a formal reading later if you like, but he specifically wanted this covered directly after his funeral. I know you'll want to abide by his wishes."

"What do you know about my daddy's will?" DeeDee said crossly. Her swollen blue eyes were hostile.

"I'm his attorney of record," Sam said mildly. "Have been for some time now. I thought you knew that."

"Well, I certainly didn't. I thought he handled his own affairs."

"It's customary among attorneys to get a colleague to handle your will," Sam said. "I won't keep you. It's been a hard day for all of us."

She sniffed, but rose with an effort and followed him down the little hall and into her father's study. Duck and Bayard Sewell came behind her, Duck peering truculently at Sam, Bay looking levelly and consideringly after his square figure.

Sam stopped and turned.

"Coming, Mike?"

"I'd rather not, please," she said, with an effort. She wanted no part of the division of her father's spoils.

"We can't do this without you," Sam said. So she rose and followed them into the dim, austere room that had been off-limits and thus mysterious to her throughout her childhood.

J.W. Cromie was sitting in the half-lit room, stiff and uncomfortable. He did not rise or look at them. Priss Comfort sat in another straight chair beside him. She smiled at Mike and nodded at the others as if she were accustomed to receiving visitors in this Holy of Holies every day of her life.

"Take seats, please," Sam said politely. They did, still staring suspiciously at him. He seated himself behind John Winship's vast, polished rolltop, where pretty, silver-framed Claudia Searcy smiled forever into the long gloom, and switched on the green-shaded brass lamp that John Winship had salvaged from the old Fulton County Courthouse, and laid his hands on the desk top.

"As I said, this is not a formal reading of the Colonel's will. Maybe we won't need to do that, but we surely can, if any of you still feels we need to later. I have copies for all of you, of course, and I'll pass them around in a while. John asked me to ask Priss Comfort if she would serve as his executor"—he nodded at Priss, who nodded back, Buddha-like and unsurprised—"and she has accepted. It is Priss who will actually see to the transfer of properties. See that the torch is properly passed, so to speak.

"Well. It's a very simple will. Skipping the legalese, I'll tell you that the garage and garage apartment of this house, and the Cadillac, and a cash sum of fifteen thousand dollars, go to J.W. Cromie."

Sam nodded to J.W., who ducked his head. His eyes glistened, and he shut them.

"The Colonel's gold studs and collar pins and pocket watch, and the collection of Rose Medallion porcelain that is presently in this house, go to Priss Comfort."

He nodded at Priss, and she smiled, an involuntary and very sweet smile.

Sam cleared his throat and said, "The rest of the estate, including this house and its contents, cash and assets amounting to fifty thousand dollars, and the proceeds of the sale of the old Winship house to the Department of Transportation, goes to DeeDee." He smiled at DeeDee and she smiled back, a wavering, unwilling smile, her eyes filling again with tears.

". . . except for the remaining eighty acres of land comprising the Winship family homeplace, which go to his younger daughter, Micah Winship Singer."

He looked around the room affably. "Are there any questions?" he said.

For a long moment there was absolute silence. Mike, sunk in her fatigue and unwillingness to be in this room, did not, at first, comprehend Sam Canaday's words. It was the thick totality of the silence following them that made her raise her head, not the sense of them. By the time their import had sunk in, DeeDee had begun to scream.

Mike had once seen a television program on African lions, narrated by Marlin Perkins, in which a small gazelle had been caught and dragged down and killed by a hunting pair. The gazelle's screams had haunted her sleep for weeks afterward. They were hoarse and minor and not very loud, and went on and on, and the absolute despair in them was terrible to hear.

DeeDee sounded like that.

She did not stop screaming until Dr. Gaddis had been summoned once more and given her yet another shot, and when she did stop, it was only because she was sagging into a semitorpor and had to be supported out to the car by Sam and Duck. In a perfect, ringing shell of shock, Mike thought, Dr. Gaddis has made a fortune off the Winships this past year. We could build him a hospital. No one else spoke while DeeDee was being ministered to and taken away; Priss and J.W. sat calmly in the kitchen, simply waiting, and Bayard Sewell had, at some point, come to stand quietly beside Mike, in the living room of her father's house.

Sam came back into the house, and Duck came raging in behind him, wet with rain, his face a congested magenta, the hooded eyes wild and ringed with white. He was inarticulate with rage; it was some moments before they could tell what he was shouting.

He put a scrabbling hand on Sam's shoulder and spun him around.

"I ought to kill you, you lying son of a bitch," he screamed, and Sam shrugged his hand away, green eyes narrow.

Duck turned on Mike.

"You sneaking, scheming, rotten New York *bitch* . . ."

Sam started for him, but Bayard Sewell's voice sliced through the ringing air, and Duck Wingo stopped.

"Shut your mouth, Duck, and get on out of here," Bay Sewell said. His voice was like a frozen whiplash. He did not move from his position beside Mike. "Get DeeDee home and don't come around here anymore. Mike's been through enough without this sorriness."

Duck Wingo swung his big head from Bay Sewell to Mike and Sam and back again, like a vicious and cowardly dog whose master has suddenly turned on him. He stank of violence and stupidity. Bay stared straight into his eyes, his face still. In a moment, Duck turned and shambled heavily out the front door and through the diminishing rain to the car, where DeeDee slumped in her drugged peace against the door. Mike did not hear the engine start.

Bay Sewell edged himself closer to Mike across the Oriental rug. She had seen him do that once before, in this same living room, across this same rug. Only then he had been edging away from her, not toward her. Edging toward her father, and his deliverance. He put his hand lightly on her shoulder and looked down at her. His eyes were soft and clear and very, very blue.

"You need to rest, now, Mike," he murmured. "Get some sleep, and I'll come by in the morning. We need to talk, but we have all the time in the world."

She looked at him.

"Get your hand off me, Bay, or I'll cut your balls off and make cat food of them," Mike said.

He stepped jerkily back as if she had slapped him, and the muscles around his mouth leapt out in white ridges. He looked at Sam Canaday.

"We'll break the will, of course," he said. His voice did not sound quite right; was higher, thicker. "It should take about fifteen minutes. I have access to some of the best lawyers in the United States."

"Had, you mean," Sam drawled. "You'll be lucky if your business associates stop at cat food. But by all means, have at it."

"I'll have you disbarred! If you're even a member of the bar . . ."

"Oh, I'm a member," Sam said, walking to the door and opening it. "But you might as well have at that, too. Give you something to do; keep you off the streets. Meanwhile, you were just leaving."

"Mike," Bayard Sewell hissed, "before God, if I ever find out you knew about this and didn't tell me . . ." The blue eyes were, she thought, very slightly mad.

Sam stepped in front of her and pushed Bayard Sewell lightly between his shoulder blades.

"Say good night, Bay," he said.

Bayard Sewell whirled and strode across the porch and out into the last of the rain. He splashed unheedingly through the water that always stood at the bottom of the front steps. Sam shut the door and leaned against it. Mike sat down abruptly on the bottom step of the stairs to the second floor.

"Cat food, huh?" Sam Canaday said, beginning to laugh.

"Well, it's better than what I had in mind. Madame Tussaud's, I thought, or maybe the Smithsonian."

"Sam, I'm just so very tired," Mike said, her voice dying in her throat.

He pulled her to her feet.

"Go on upstairs and go to bed. I'll bunk down here for tonight. Don't come down for at least twelve hours."

"Will you be here in the morning?" Mike asked.

"I'll be here," Sam Canaday said. "Now go."

Mike went.

THIRTY-THREE

When she came downstairs the next morning, Sam was just heaving himself up off the old couch in her father's study. The sofa afghan trailed onto the floor, and he sat up, knuckling his face. His pale hair drooped dispiritedly over his paler eyes, and the smudges underneath them were deeper than ever. Silvery bristles glistened on his jaw. He smiled at her. Mike smiled back. He's not ever going to be able to avoid looking like a wolf who just ate a lamb, she thought.

The world outside the Pomeroy Street house was washed and crystalline. Spider webs were frosted with the faintly chill breath of September. The long heat had broken in the night, and autumn had come ghosting in behind it. It would be hot again, Mike knew; noons would burn, and long afternoons simmer, but the big heat, the monstrous great heat of summer, was gone. Sounds had a new clarity. She could hear a dog barking a street away, and J.W.'s power mower seemed to purr with pleasure.

"The squire is tending his acres," Sam said, seeing her head tilted toward the sound. "He's been working around that garage since dawn."

"Bless Daddy for that," Mike said.

"Bless him indeed," said Sam Canaday.

Sam put the coffeepot on, and Mike found leftover doughnuts in the refrigerator, and put them into the oven. They ate in silence, and then she said, as if they had just been talking of it, "What I don't understand is why the DOT would accommodate Bay with a road, if he's so junior in the legislature. I mean, he's persuasive, but no-body's *that* persuasive . . ."

"Oh, Christ, Mike, he's obviously going to be governor one day. Or was. They could have seen to that. They were grooming him.

You need to have a governor in your pocket. It's the classic way of southern legislatures. He got wind of this developer, whoever this great cat-food mogul is, in Boston; he knew where there was a nice piece of land he could maybe get his hands on, and the rest, as they say, is history. The only problem was, the developers insisted on highway access. So he went to the Highway Committee, or whoever rattles the DOT's cage up there, and . . . voilà. A little roady-poo. In exchange, of course, for untold future favors. He had to move fast, or the Boston crowd would have gone somewhere else. He couldn't wait for the Colonel to die and leave it to DeeDee, and he didn't know then about the cancer. And he had to form a partnership with Duck and DeeDee in order to get at the land. God knows what he promised them. I'd guess that his cut was a considerable joint venture partnership, plus a hefty finder's fee, already in hand. It's not really very complicated. Just neat."

"You know," Mike said, "nothing is really ever fair, is it? Even when you win, you don't win. Bay and DeeDee and Duck may have lost their big shot at whatever, but Daddy lost his war."

"No," Sam said. "He lost his battle, but he won his war. And what a legacy he left. He showed us the power of total passion, of love. How it can work. Look at you. Christ, when you came down here, you were nothing but a child. All we saw of you for the longest kind of time was children. The 'good' child, the rebellious child, the little nymphet, playing with sex . . . oh, yeah, that was plain as the nose on your face . . . but you were nowhere near being a whole woman. But then somehow you managed to find him again, that father you'd been looking for all those years, and when you did, even at the very moment he died, you turned into one of the realest and wholest women I've ever seen. That skinny, iced-up New York child-woman lit out for good, and you were a woman who could cry, and scream, and hate, and love . . . you were something to see. Are something to see. That's the power of love, Mike. That's what it can do. It can make you whole. If he left you nothing else, he showed you how to let the unimportant go and put your passion where it counts."

"Where did his count?" Mike asked, genuinely curious.

"Well . . . 'the earth abides.' And so does the daughter. And that woman she turned into."

Mike smiled.

"You *are* a romantic," she said. "I don't care what you say. What about that wonderful, beautiful eulogy? What do you call that but sheer romanticism?"

"No," Sam said. "That wasn't romance. That was part of the package, part of the Viking funeral we promised him. It was okay; it was even fun, but I don't want to do any more of it. It misleads people. The law is better."

They sat silently for a time, drinking the coffee. Outside the power mower stopped and the cicadas began. They sounded like somnolence and heat, but, this time, the dry, dreaming heat of autumn.

"Poor Daddy," Mike said. "I'm so glad he didn't know about them."

Sam drained his tepid coffee and looked at her.

"He knew," he said.

Pain poured again through Mike like lava. "Ah, *God!*" she cried. "Oh, my God! It must have nearly killed him! Oh, Sam, how ever did he find out?"

"It did nearly kill him," Sam Canaday said. "That's when he had the stroke, when he first found out. I told him, Mike. J.W. came to me with it, and I swore him to secrecy, and then I told your father."

Her voice would not come out of her throat. "How could you?" she whispered, finally. "Look what it *did* to him!"

"I know. How do you think I've felt all these months, every time I looked at him in that goddamned wheelchair? I really loved your dad. And yet how could I not tell him? He was a man, Mike. He was not a child. Two people he loved were lying to him. I wasn't going to be the third. I couldn't just let them turn him into an old baby, an old *fool,* not on top of everything else they were doing to him."

"Why didn't you tell me, then? Didn't I deserve to know? Was it okay for me to be a fool?" Angry tears were smarting behind Mike's eyes.

"I didn't want to have to tell you about your sister, in the first place. I guess I kept hoping that some miracle or other would happen. That they'd call off their road. And then, we didn't really know you at first. You might have thought it was a great idea. You made

324

no secret of the fact that you barely tolerated him at first, you know. And as for Sewell—I'm not a fool, Mike. I've been in love, too. Would you have believed me?"

Mike's face flamed. She knew that she would not have.

"After a while I did want to tell you, after you'd swung over to his side," Sam went on. "But he made me promise not to. On that old Bible of his father's. Really. He said you'd had enough of family treachery. But I'm awfully glad J.W. had the sense and guts to break his promise to me. I was going through hell; I couldn't bear the thought that Sewell might get his hands on that land through you when he couldn't get it his own way."

And of course, he would have, Mike thought. He was headed that way. I was the queen of all the fools, not Daddy. She grimaced. Aloud, she said, "When did he change his will?"

"As soon as he could talk some, after the stroke. And then he asked for you to come home. He really did, Mike. He wanted a Winship to have the land. The right Winship."

"So he found a way to save his land."

"That's not why he asked for you to come. He knew you were pretty apt to refuse it. He knew you might sell it or give it to DeeDee, whatever he did. It wasn't for that he called you home."

He looked up at Mike. She poured herself a fresh cup of coffee and wrapped her hands around it. She felt, somehow, cold and diminished.

"He wanted to make things up to you," Sam said. "He never could find the words; he never could have said, 'I'm sorry. I was wrong. I love you.' But he tried to do it another way. He gave you what he loved best in this world, besides your mother. He spent the last three months of his life, in his own way, saying 'I love you.'"

"All that time," Mike whispered. "All that time, and I never even heard what he was saying. I thought he was just barely suffering me. I never said it to him, either . . . 'I love you,' I mean."

"Yes, you did. You did, that day down at the homeplace when you asked if you could help him lick stamps. You couldn't have said it any clearer. Didn't you see his face?"

Mike began to cry again. Once again, she covered her face and wept for the father unknown, the father new-given. Under the weeping was impatience. She had thought that she was done with tears.

"I'm awfully tired of crying," she said at last to Sam Canaday, through her wet fingers.

"Me, too," he said. "I wish you'd stop."

Mike splashed her face at the sink and sat blearily back down at the table.

"There's something else," Sam said. "I'm telling you because J.W. says he's going to if I don't, and he shouldn't have to. He's pretty sure Sewell told your dad they were wrecking the house that afternoon. He believes he woke your dad up and told him before . . . he went on upstairs, hoping for just what he got, or something like it." His face was grim.

"Before he came upstairs to my room!" Mike said, incandescent with fury. "Goddamn his murdering soul, I *will* write that story! I'll run him clear out of Lytton! I'll ruin him in the legislature; the closest he'll ever get to the governor's office is on public tour day . . ."

"And all you'll get is a libel suit," Sam said. "The papers would never print an unsubstantiated charge, and the legislature would never rat on one of its own. This is small potatoes to the Georgia legislature, Mike. And J.W. can't prove it, of course, and Sewell could make things pretty hot for him in Lytton, if it got out that J.W. told me that. He still needs to work, even if he is landed gentry now. Let it alone. Bayard Sewell has lost his main chance, and he ain't got a prayer of paying back that chunk of change the big boys have already given him. All he's accomplished is to cost the state a road to nowhere. That's enough to cook him in the so-called political arena. He'll be lucky if he doesn't wind up with his knee caps blown off in some dirt-road gravel pit in Coweta County. He's had Sally Sewell on his back for twenty years, and now he'll have Duck and DeeDee on his neck for the rest of his life. It's enough. I wouldn't be surprised if he packed up his toys and his poor wife and left Lytton before long, anyway. From what you say, he's hated the place all his life, and there's sure nothing to hold him here now."

"They'll appeal the will, you know," Mike said. It seemed impossible, on this jeweled morning, that they could be having this conversation.

"Let 'em. It's as airtight as the law can make it. I worked on it for a long time. I knew I couldn't help him much against the DOT, but I *can* draw a right nice will. I even took the little precaution of hunting up two good shrinks and getting him to go see them so they could testify to his mental state, if they want to claim unsound mind. Getting him there was worth a year's fee, believe me."

"Sam. You know I can't pay you for what you've done for him. I don't know when I can. I can't even think of a way to thank you."

"It was, as they say, my pleasure." He was silent for a moment, and then said, softly, "Do you mind so much, Mike? About Sewell?"

"No," she said unhesitatingly. She held his eyes with hers. "It happened to somebody else. And that's not shock talking, or bravado. There's not even going to be any delayed reaction. I'm sure of that. That simply happened to somebody who does not exist anymore."

"Thank God for small favors," he said. "That was a good-looking broad, but she was a real pain in the ass."

Mike laughed. "Was she not," she said.

"So then, what now?" Sam Canaday said. "You said the other night you were going to go back and get on with it; did you mean that?"

"I . . . don't know," Mike said. "I need some money. I'm almost out. I *could* go on back and round up some assignments . . ."

"But?"

"But . . . I think I really might have a book, Sam. Or rather, the beginning of one. It's . . . I don't know; it's not like any kind of writing I've ever done, and it's terribly hard to do, and coming slow, and it would need an iron lung . . . but I think I really like it. I think I'd like to finish it. Whether anybody would want to print it, I have no idea. I could take it to the editor who was interested in the other book, and see if they'd give me another advance. At least, that way, I could pay back the first one."

"Where would you write it?"

"I don't know that either. I can't raise the cost of a co-op in New York, but I might swing a little place, a sublet of some kind."

"You might try writing it here," he said, elaborately casual. "If it's about Lytton, you might as well write it in Lytton."

"Where on earth would I live? DeeDee's going to want this house as soon as she can pack," Mike said.

"She can't legally take possession of it until the will is probated, and if they're going to contest it, that'll tie it up until kingdom come. And I can probably string it out even longer. You'd have plenty of time, time enough to write two books," he said.

"No. I don't want to stay in this house." Mike surprised herself, but knew it was true. "This house never did feel like home to me, really, and with him gone, it's going to feel even less so. Let Dee have it."

He looked at her sharply. "You're not having second thoughts about your inheritance, are you? No bright ideas about nobly turning it over to her after all?"

"Oh, no. Not that, not ever. Maybe I'm being hard and selfish, but I don't think Dee . . . *deserves* that land. Not after what they did. Not that I've got any idea in the world what to do with it; what am I going to do with eighty acres of Georgia farmland? But I just couldn't . . . but, Sam, that doesn't mean she doesn't deserve better than she's got. She never meant to hurt Daddy. I'm sure of that. She might be greedy, but she adored him. She's going to be just— stricken about this, for the rest of her life."

"She'll be okay, if she's careful," Sam said. "She has this house, and the money the Colonel left her. She has a teaching certificate. I could help her."

Mike laughed. "I doubt if she'd welcome your help," she said. "But I can help her a little now by letting her move on in here. And maybe later I could help her some more. I think she just might turn herself into something, if she could dump Duck . . ."

"Well, now's her chance. But don't count on DeeDee changing much," he said. "She's been poor and unhappy a long time. It does permanent damage. It might be she's just been too poor too long."

"I don't count on anything," Mike said.

Sam Canaday said, "You know you can always stay with Priss for as long as you want. I'd offer you haven myself, but as you know, I live over the store. Or you could sell off your land, or some of it, and buy yourself a house. He really wouldn't care." He looked, not at her, but out the kitchen window, where J.W. was trailing the lawn mower back and forth, back and forth. They could not hear him over the mower's noise, but they could see his mouth moving hugely, and knew that he was singing.

"No," Mike said, with a swift, unbidden certainty that had the weight of a long-held belief. "I'm not going to sell the land. I don't know where I'll live, or even if I'll come back here, but I'll never sell that land. I need a place to be *from,* Sam. A homeplace of my own. And Rachel needs one, even if she never sees it. You can't be *from* some sublet in the East Eighties, which is what I'll have to settle for if I go back. I guess what I mean is—you're free to wander only as long as you have a taproot. Without one, you can just—fly off the face of the earth, if you're not careful. That's what I've been trying to control all my life, I think . . . that awful feeling of free flight. It can turn right into free fall. I know. I was in it. It was . . . terrible."

"Well, you have a taproot now," he said. "Okay, so you're going to go back and see if you can get a book advance. And then?"

"I'm going out to the coast and get Rachel." It was all falling into place now. Mike felt very clear in herself. "She's got no business in that damned sex boutique out there. He's no more a fit father than Roman Polanski. I'm going to go get her by her smartass little pierced ear and yank her home where she belongs."

"And where's that?" His voice was slow and soft.

"Someplace where she can go to public school and wear flip-flops and cutoffs without somebody's name on her ass," Mike said. "Someplace with privacy and space and real trees and real people who aren't in any danger of being chic. Someplace where I can write that isn't my bedroom and where I can go to the grocery store without locking twelve locks. Someplace I can have a big dog and a big car. Do you know that I've never had a car of my own? I want a big Chevrolet station wagon."

"I know a place like that," Sam Canaday said. "About two miles down the road. Pretty land. No neighbors breathing down your neck. Trees. Creek. Woods. School bus goes right by there. Brand-new road, too. It wouldn't take a lot to put up a nice house on it. It wouldn't take more than—oh, what you'd make on a middling good book. How long do you figure it takes to write a book?"

"I don't know," Mike said. "I never wrote one. Maybe a year."

"Hmmm," he said. "A year. Long time, a year." And then, "Oh, wait, I almost forgot. I've got something for you."

"Something for me?"

"Yeah," he said. "Just a minute." And he was gone out of the kitchen. She heard his footsteps receding down the hall toward her father's bedroom, heard the door open and shut, heard the steps coming back down the hall, and then he was back in the kitchen once more, carrying a large cardboard box that said J&B SCOTCH on the side. He brought the box over to the kitchen table and set it down in front of Mike. She peered into it. Inside, a tiny, quivering, silky brown rabbit crouched, its miniature nose trembling tinily, in the palm of a new tan catcher's mitt. The mitt was large and smelled wonderfully of leather and was stenciled with the name Rawlings.

Mike reached in very slowly and picked up the tiny creature and held it close under her chin, feeling the minuscule vibration of its terror and the incredible, small softness of it. It nestled close to her throat. A great, silly, trembling smile bloomed inside her; the corners of her mouth twitched with it. Sam reached into the box and plucked out the catcher's mitt and put his hand into it.

"Good fit," he said. "Nice leather."

Still cradling the rabbit, she walked slowly around behind him, lifted her free hand, and put one finger lightly on the cowlick that whorled on the top of his blond head. Outside the September day seemed to shimmer.

"Will you be here a year from now?" Mike asked.

Sam Canaday tossed a cold doughnut into the air and caught it neatly behind him in the catcher's mitt. He grinned his white wolf's grin.

"Oh, yeah," he said. "I expect I will."